I0766945

Court

of

Beasts

USA TODAY BESTSELLING AUTHOR

K.A KNIGHT

Court of Beasts (Court and Kings).

This is a work of fiction. Any resemblance to places, events or real people are entirely coincidental.

Copyright © 2024 K.A. Knight, all rights reserved.

No part of this book may be reproduced in any form or by any electronic or mechanical means, including information storage and retrieval systems, without written permission from the author, except for the use of brief quotations in a book review.

Written by K.A. Knight.
Edited By Jess from Elemental Editing and Proofreading.
Proofreading by Norma's Nook.
Formatted by The Nutty Formatter.
Illustrated cover by Dily Iola Designs
Art by Dily Iola Designs
Naked hardcover by Moonstruck Cover Design & Photography

Please note, this is a dark romance and as such, there may be scenes that you find triggering. This book includes scenes with sexual violence, graphic violent scenes, explicit scenes, consensual play, rutting, mating, torture, and much more.

Step into the wilderness and find the darkness within . . .

PROLOGUE

"Look at me," I order, using the blade's edge to tilt the man's tear-stained face up. Disgust fills me as I meet his watery eyes. He's weak, so very fucking weak. "Do you know why we were sent to hunt you?"

"Because you found out we helped the vampyrs," he blubbers.

"Very good," I say. "You fool. You betrayed us all. You betrayed the cause, and worst of all, you worked with the monsters. How could you?"

"She offered us immortality, power, and money—"

I slash across his face, the wound opening as he screams. The wooden dock creaks with approaching footsteps, and I don't need to turn to know who it is—my brethren, my family, my fellow hunters.

The moon hangs high, and somewhere far off in the distance, I swear I hear a howl over the tethered boats and crashing waves. It's empty at this time, just like we wanted.

"You betrayed everything we stand for. You broke your oath as a hunter." I tower over the coward. "I hope it was worth it." I kick the centre of his chest and watch as he screams in terror and falls backwards, hitting the cold, churning water with a splash. With a wicked grin, I watch the ropes tethered to him slip into the water until it tugs the cinder blocks in, dragging him down to the bottom.

If he wants to play with monsters, then he'll die like one, alone, afraid, and drowning in his own regrets.

Turning away, I meet the eyes of the men who have hunted at my side since we were children. "Pack up, we have a meeting to attend."

They fall into step beside me, our footsteps quiet.

"Do you know what it's about?" The voice is soft, dangerous.

"We've been assigned a new hunt," I respond, a sardonic smile curling my lips. "It's time for us to take our place at the top. We're hunting wolves, boys. We are hunting the beasts themselves."

CHAPTER ONE

Quinn

Six months later . . .

Blood sprays across me as I grin, my claws covered in gore as the wolf howls and falls away. Another takes its place. They surround me, fighting each other to get what they want—me.

It's another claiming ceremony. I have survived six so far, five more than any other female in wolf history, and this will be my seventh. I will not be claimed this day or any. When I want to mate, I will chase who I want, when I want, but not until then. I have far too much to do before then—like becoming the Red Mountain Pack's alpha, the strongest pack in all of history.

I will be the first and only female alpha.

Fuck those who stand in my way. It's what I was destined for since birth, and that won't change as long as I can defeat these pesky male wolves, otherwise they will share my power and take my throne via matehood.

I manage to push them back, and risking the seconds it takes me to turn, I throw myself backwards and land on my paws as I set off into the woods. I only have to survive unclaimed until sunup. I cannot kill. It's gotten dicey in the past, but I've managed to survive on my wits and power. I take a familiar path, but a huge black wolf jumps out, waiting for me.

Tertrim, fuck, he's hunted me since I was able to be mated, and it seems each time I'm thrust into this ceremony, he gets smarter. He watches and waits, learning my moves.

He plans to mate me this ceremony.

Over my dead body.

Spinning, I dive into the forest, my paws hitting fallen trunks and squashing grass and bushes. Prey squeals and hides as I tumble through the trees that make up the pack's hunting grounds. I hear him howl and give chase, so I drop my muzzle and put on a burst of speed.

No one can catch me. I'm the fastest wolf in the pack for a reason.

He should have known better than to try to hunt me. After all, I'm the ultimate survivor.

As I skirt through our lands, my ears twitch, hearing him panting, but it seems far off. I splash through the stream, heading away from where he is, and it's only when I reach the craggy cliff edge that I realise he has herded me here. I am trapped and cut off from every other route, so I won't have anywhere to run since he knows he cannot catch me otherwise.

Smart wolf. I turn to face him as he slinks from the shadows, a victorious grin tugging at his wolf lips.

You know what they say about trapping a wild animal?

They fight twice as hard.

I leap at him, using the element of surprise. We end up rolling, my teeth digging into his shoulder as he yips in pain, his claws raking my side. I dig my teeth in deeper, unwilling to let go despite the agony.

The wounds will heal, but my pride won't if I lose.

I will not spend my life mated to this brute.

He ends up beneath me, belly up, and I claw at it as he howls, but like me, he has power and strength. He tosses me off with his bucking body, and I skid across the cliff, scrambling to stop myself from falling over the edge. I spare the plummeting drop a brief glance before turning back to him, watching as his black fur recedes into skin. There's a wicked wound on his shoulder from me, but as he crouches there, naked and human, he seems more determined than ever.

He's a big, hairy bastard, with long, shaggy black hair. He's not bad looking, but it's the cruel look in his eyes that has my canines flashing.

"Just stop fighting. Give up and give in. You know we are made for each other. We would be unstoppable together," he says, trying to reason with me.

I take a page from his book, unwilling to face him as a wolf while he's human. It's cowardly. I quickly change back to human form, uncaring about my nudity as I stride closer to him. His eyes drop to my body—rude, wolves know better. Nudity is part of our lives, but by looking at my form like that, he is insulting me.

"Haven't you learned that about me yet? I never give up." Grabbing a branch, I sweep his legs out, sending him tumbling on his back as I leap over him, my hands tingling as I change them to my claws. As one of the only wolves in the pack who can partially transform, it comes in handy. Most hated me when they realised I could do it, and they called me a freak. I believed them until I understood it was a strength, not a weakness.

I lift my claws, letting him see them gleam. His eyes turn shrewd as he stills beneath me, knowing better than most what these claws can do. After all, he wears their scars along his side from his last attempt at the mating ceremony.

When will he give up?

I don't want to kill him. Despite everything, he's one of us, one of our pack. He is family, and we protect family even when they are fools, but I need him to stop. I need him to understand I will never belong to anyone but myself.

"Surrender," I command, infusing my power into it.

Most others would have no choice but to obey.

"Never," he responds. "I will never give up. I will enter every ceremony until we are one."

Snarling, I slam my claws into the ground by his head and rip them out. "Stop this."

He lies beneath me as a human, as naked as the day he was born, with a wicked grin on his face. If it wasn't for the fact that he's power hungry, he would have made a great mate for someone. He's attractive enough and clearly a strong wolf, but he's not for me.

I raise my claws as I snarl down at him.

"Sun's up." He grins, and I turn, gaping to find it rising, saving his life.

Pushing him away, I retract my claws, unwilling to break pack rules.

"Next time, Quinn, you are mine," he warns as he transforms and slinks back into the woods.

Well, fuck.

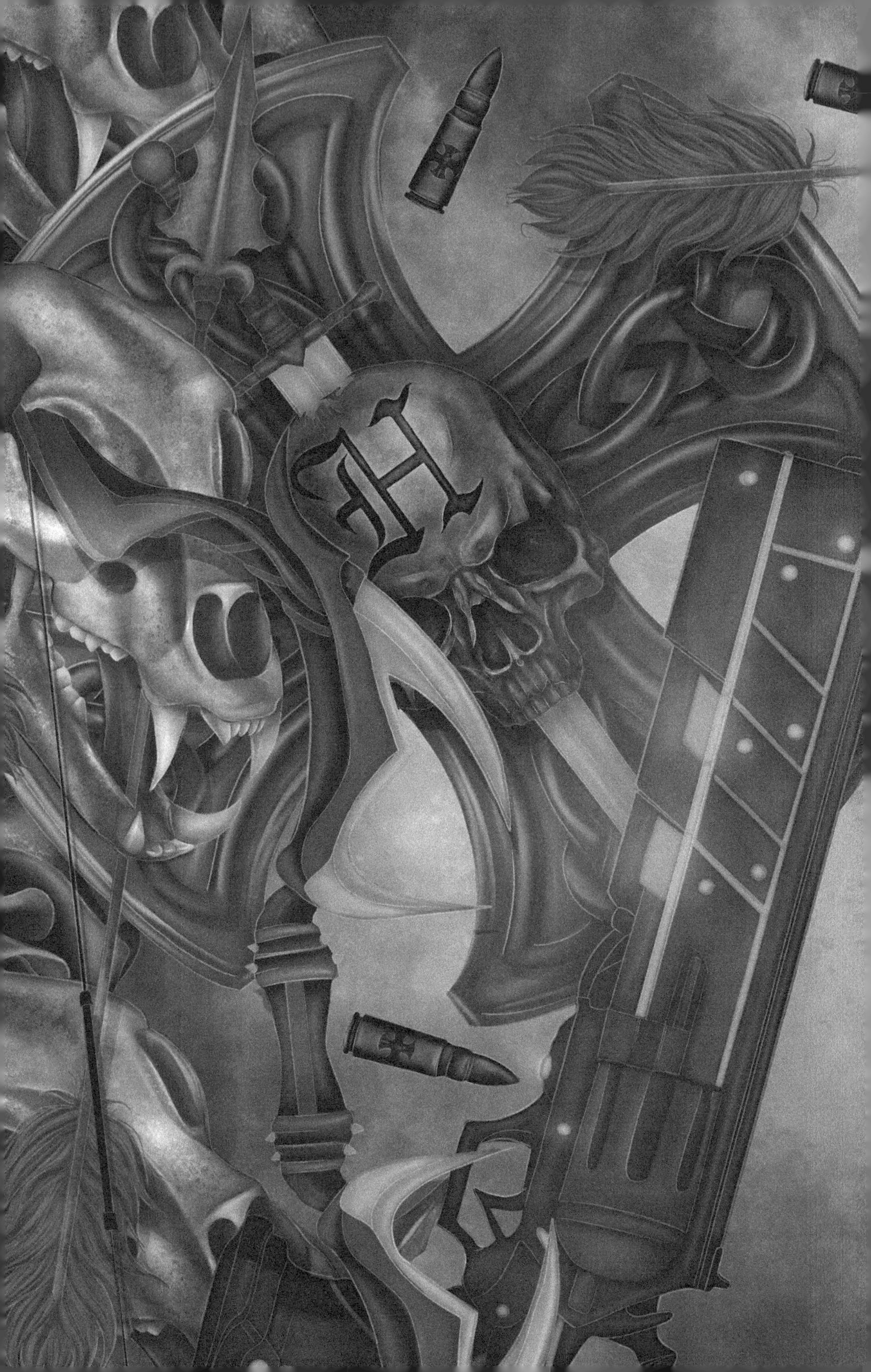

CHAPTER TWO

"They must be somewhere," our commander barks, pacing before the smart board where the map is laid out. "Find them, find the pack, and kill them. How hard is it? They are abominations! Just this week, there have been eight kills!"

Eight innocent humans dead at the hands of wolves.

There are many monsters that lurk within the darkness and shadows of our world, but wolves are one of the worst. Their ability to shift into animals makes them lethal, and their ability to blend in with humans makes them hard to hunt.

They are fierce fighters, hunters, and killers.

They are the best of the best in our world, which also means the highest reward and the best trophy kills.

They are just what I need to boost my reputation.

When we were allowed to visit the head of our organisation, we were so hopeful. A promotion to hunt wolves here is the highest form of respect and strength. We were so sure, but it has been months, and we have found nothing but some ferals for our trouble. If this carries on, we'll be demoted. As it is, there are already whispers spreading about us being subpar.

We cannot afford another failure, not after the vampyr mess.

"We should trap a feral," Jai says, and we all turn to face him. His shaggy black hair hangs over his ears, and some falls into his eyes, but it doesn't disguise the jagged scar crossing through one and continuing down to his chin. His mismatched eyes, one black and one blue, glance to Lucien and me, an unspoken conversation going on before he turns back to our commander. "We can either use them as bait or torture the information we need out of them to hunt down the local packs. Despite being feral, they will know basic information that we would struggle to find since we are unwelcome and untrusted." His voice is dark and low, measured.

Despite being smaller than both Lucien and me, Jai makes up for his lack of size in attitude and speed. He's a brutal bastard and one of the best hunters I've ever seen. He also hates monsters, wolves especially, more than any of us. His thirst for blood may scare us at times, but it does come in useful.

"Vale?" the command callers, waiting for my response.

I lead our little team, so the choice is mine. He knows full well he can't make my men do anything they don't want to. They are loyal to me until the end. If he wants the pack he suspects is hiding in our area, then he needs my help.

"It is a good plan." I incline my head. "We'll get to work on it right away and report back."

"Good, do that and come up with something or you'll be back to trapping pixies," he snaps, adding the threat to make it seem like he's in charge when we all know he's a washed-up hunter. Too many hunts, too many injuries, and age's made him slow. He couldn't survive hunting anymore, so now he leads and leaves it all to us.

One day, one of us will replace him as the head of the southeast hunters. Jai and Lucien want it to be me, but I prefer being out on the road, hunting. I suppose, though, when I get older, I might have to take the role just like he did. It's the cycle. If you live long enough as a hunter, you become a liability when you're old, which means working behind a desk.

It's like being a soldier—our minds stay in the fight but our bodies betray us.

While the meeting disbands, I nod at familiar faces. Hunters stick to our own teams, since we're highly competitive, but there's one easy way to spot a veteran—the scars. We are all covered in them. If you are lucky enough to win your hunt against a monster, the odds are you'll come out with a few more, but it's the price for hunting the evil that lurks in the darkness and kills innocent humans.

This is the humans' world, not theirs. We simply remind them of that.

Jai and Lucien fall into step at my side, and I tug my phone from the pocket of my cargo pants. "Are we trapping a feral?" Lucien asks, his voice deep and dark.

"Yes, tonight," I respond without sparing them a glance. "He's right. We need information, and we need it now. Jai, set the trap. Lucien, you're the lookout." I lift my head and grin. "And I'll be the bait."

Lucien spares me a narrow-eyed glare, and I raise an eyebrow in challenge. He knows better than to argue, and I would never order them to be bait. If I wasn't willing to play that role, then I shouldn't be leading them. When we first passed our training, I often argued that Lucien should lead since he's the oldest and my brother, but he said he didn't have the necessary people skills. It means he has to put up with my reckless ways, even if he hates it, because we all know he will always have my back.

"Tonight." Jai nods, a cruel grin tugging at his lips.

"You know, man, if we weren't friends, I'd be scared of you," I say, putting my phone away. The crowd in the hallway parts as we walk, but we don't spare them a glance. Everyone knows who we are. Our hunts are things of legend. As one of the highest-ranking teams with the most monster kills under our belts, they know better than to get in our way.

"Who said you shouldn't be anyway?" Jai retorts before wandering off.

Lucien and I share a look. "He's on you. I told you he was a psychopath when we met him in basic. You called him inventive."

Jai might be crazy, but only the monsters have to fear his fury.

"He gets the job done and doesn't mind getting his hands bloody. It's better to be crazy than a coward," I remind him. "Besides, he's just passionate about his work." I sling my arm around him, or try since the bastard is huge. Lucien shrugs me off with a wince, hating to be touched, and for a moment, sadness fills me before I push it away. "Now, let's remind them who we are."

Crossing my arms, I present them to him in an X. Sighing, he presses his own against mine. "Hunters," we say.

Hunters forever.

CHAPTER THREE

My pride is wounded. I hate losing, and I was so close to making him surrender.

I slink back in wolf form, my shoulders bunched in exhaustion and dejection. I foiled another mating ceremony, but it's only a matter of time before they succeed. The only thing that can save me is becoming alpha.

Or the alpha's word.

Sighing, I transform at the tree line, pulling on one of the loose shirts we stash around the perimeter for unexpected shifts. On bare feet, I pad across the grass as the pack comes back to life, those with children waking for the day. Little pups stuck in wolf form howl as their parents chase them. Shaking my head, I wave at those who greet me, ready for their day at work.

Most work here within the pack to keep our land and people going. We are sustainable here with our own food and water sources. We have hunters and trackers, defenders and feeders. There are also some who go out into the world to make us money and keep us connected. I am a mixture of both due to my beta position. I help keep the pack running and work at the alpha's side, which often means leaving the safety of our land for meetings with other packs or to control the businesses we own outside of here that enable us to stay off-grid and protected.

Spread across our lands is housing for the pack. We do have one big pack house that the alpha and his mate live in, as well as any unmated females and betas if they choose, but most decide to build their own house somewhere on the land. I stayed inside the pack house until I turned eighteen, and then with the help of the pack, I built my own slice of heaven here.

It's where I head now, needing the solace of my quiet place before the rest of the pack pry into what happened. I already feel expectation lingering in the air. They want to see if I've been mated despite my scent not changing. Wolves mate for life, and as a beta and the one vying for alpha, whom I choose is important.

That isn't to say I don't have fun and fool around. Wolves are inherently sexual creatures, and sex is as normal for us as hunting, like scratching a primal itch. Mating, however, under a full moon where you bind your souls, is something I've firmly been against. I want to stand on my own as alpha before I consider anything like that. Logically, I know one day, I will have to mate, but right now, I have bigger dreams than being tied down and forced to have pups.

All my thoughts distract me enough that I reach my house quickly, my feet carrying me down the familiar pathways without even being told to do so. The dirt path cuts through the trees in a natural curve so as not to disturb nature. Wildflowers grow on either side, and bunnies scurry away at the sight and smell of me. I pause for a moment, taking in my cabin with a soft smile.

It's built by the lake. Most wolves stay farther inland, but I chose this specially. The waves lap at the pebbled beach before my little cabin. The pointed roof reaches up into the sky, the panels there catching the sun and using it for energy. The blue water calls to me as the sky turns red and orange.

The wooden cottage smell invades my nose as I head closer. The wraparound porch has swings and a massive egg chair to relax in when I need to escape the manic side of pack life. It screams comfort and home.

Solar lights hang down, off now that the sun is up, yet the chimney pumps smoke, letting me know one of the pack, probably an omega, has been here to ensure it's ready for me. The door stands open like most of the cabins here. We are good at respecting privacy, and no one will disturb a beta in their nest unless it is necessary.

However, the alpha has no such qualms, and I see his bent back as he tends to the fire as I walk inside. The kitchen is open plan, connecting to the dining room and living room. Although it's on the smallish side, it's cosy and warm, done in a farmhouse style with blues and yellows, deep sofas and a huge TV, and bookcases on either side. The soft yellow curtains flutter in the wind. Upstairs to the right is the loft with my bedroom and bathroom. It has everything I could ever need. The alpha ensured it.

"I didn't know you did an omega's job. I feel honoured." I smirk, padding inside on dirty feet. There is more than one claw mark within these walls, and dirt never bothered me anyway. This is my house, my home, my sanctuary, and he's the only one to ever dare enter without permission.

It's his pack and his land, and I'm his beta . . .

And his daughter.

"You know, even as a beta, you should show your alpha respect," he mutters as he straightens and lumbers over to the wooden chair positioned by the fire.

I throw myself down in the matching one opposite his and grin at him. His face is wide and square, handsome even in his older age. Wrinkles now line his eyes and mouth, ones that weren't there a few years ago. There's a rough scar across his forehead from a feral challenger who once tried to scalp him. His hair is now greying, but it has streaks of the burnt amber brown that I stared at for way too long as a kid. His brown eyes are kind and familiar, yet his huge body screams of power, as does his alpha stare—the alpha's power. Once, I couldn't withstand it, along with everyone else, but as I grew and came into my powers, so did my ability to meet his eyes. However, I lower mine slightly out of respect, and he huffs out a wolfish sound.

Alpha Jang is a good, kind man who fights for his pack in every way. He's also the most feared and powerful alpha in this world, but at two hundred years old, he's nearing his retirement age.

There are only two ways an alpha retires—either he stands down, nominating an alpha, or he is killed. I know which one I want to happen.

I don't think I could survive losing him, even if it meant I never got the position I crave, knowing I could lead just as well as him and wanting to make him proud.

I grin. "Most fear you, I don't."

"You never did." He snorts. "It got you into more trouble than anything else."

Laughing, I stare at the flames, a comfortable blanket of silence stretching between us. It's always been this way with us. He's a man of few words, and when he speaks, everyone listens, so he's here for a reason. I just need to wait it out. I learned at a young age not to rush him and that getting impatient would only prolong the wait. Instead, I now enjoy our companionship, one that has changed through the years.

"Quinny." He sighs. "You must mate."

"Don't start this again." I groan as I clamber to my feet. Ignoring his searching look, I move to the kitchen and quickly pour us two coffees before heading back. I hand him the mug I keep here for him. It looks tiny in his meaty hand, but he holds it delicately with a nod as I sit down and warm my hands on the porcelain, my eyes on the flames. I don't want to meet his gaze. No matter how old I get, I still worry about disappointing him, and that is one thing I couldn't live with.

Not after everything he and Marie have done for me.

"Quinn," he murmurs, and that's when I know he's serious. It's always been kiddo or Quinny with him. I only ever get Quinn when

I'm in trouble, something I strive never to be, not wanting to hurt him. I'm lucky to be here. I know that.

"David," I respond, and his eyebrows rise, his lips curving before his stern expression returns.

"I'm not getting any younger. I want to know you will be taken care of when I'm gone."

"Stop talking like that. You'll live forever." I wink.

"I don't want you to be alone in the end, Quinny," he says, and I swallow hard, meeting his kind eyes. "That's my biggest fear for you, that you will be alone in the end. Being in the middle of the pack, or even being alpha won't stop that from happening. All I want is for you to be happy, to be complete."

"That doesn't mean I need a mate to be complete."

"As a wolf, it does. Without a mate, your wolf will always wander. Please, Quinny, I know you are annoyingly independent and think you have something to prove to everyone, but do not hinder your own happiness just to make a point. You owe no one, least of all me, anything. Now, that's all I will say on the matter as your father. As your alpha, I applaud your escape in the mating ceremony. It demonstrated good hunting and tracking skills."

I smile, but it's sad. Does he really worry about me being alone?

"Alpha Jang." I lower my eyes out of respect. "I do not fear being alone. I fear never being able to live up to your name. I have dreams, and I have drive. You understand."

"I do." He stands, taking my hands as he crouches before me. "When you were a little girl, you were always so independent, always doing everything your own way. It scared me as much as it made me proud. I always knew you would take your own path. I just wish you didn't walk it alone. Do you remember what you told me on your fourteenth birthday?"

I groan. "I was a kid!"

"Do you?" he questions.

Swallowing hard, I search his gaze. "I told you about my nightmares. I was all alone in the darkness, and I begged you to never leave me because I was scared of being alone." His lips turn down as I sigh. "I'm not that kid anymore, and being alone doesn't scare me now. What does is tethering myself to someone who would make me unhappy or never help me with my dreams for the rest of my life."

"One day, you will find someone who will support you in every way. You will find your equal, I'm sure of it, and I hope I'm around to see it," is all he says.

"Why morbid talk about you not being here all of a sudden?" I ask, leaning forward, my heart squeezing in panic. "You don't have wolf sickness, do you?"

He stands, draining his mug. "I'm perfectly healthy, you cheeky pup. Now get some rest and come to the meeting in a few hours."

"Yes, Alpha." I incline my head as he tousles my hair.

"Sleep well, kiddo." He pauses at the door. "I'm proud of you, no matter the path you take, Quinn. You have nothing to prove to us. We will always love you."

He departs, heading back to the pack to complete his day-to-day duties, which I know better than my own thanks to following him since I was young. "Night, Dad," I whisper, knowing the wind takes it to him.

Setting my mug down, I climb the ladder and collapse into my bed, staring at the wooden ceiling. Sighing, I roll over, my hand sneaking under my pillow to tug out the worn and slightly torn picture. I stand in front, young and smiling. David is on my left with his hand on my shoulder, grinning widely at the camera, and to the right is a man with a kind smile. Curving my hand around the picture, I close my eyes and succumb to my exhaustion.

He's wrong. I do have something to prove.

CHAPTER FOUR

T he trap was too easy to assemble. Hunting used to be exciting and fun, but now it's almost too simple and boring. Wolves are the hardest challenge, and this is personal, so I focus on the metal hidden in the brush.

Lucien is in the trees, keeping watch, his scent and body obscured by stolen pixie magic, and Vale is on the opposite side of the trap. We are all waiting. We know there are ferals in this area. They must be outside of the pack's reach, and they are desperate to hunt and run in peace. The woods here are perfect for that, which makes it a perfect place for us to capture one.

Now all we have to do is wait.

Luckily for us, we don't have to wait long. Although I enjoy hunting, I don't enjoy downtime. Unless my hands are covered in blood and my heart is pumping, it just isn't worth it. I need to move and outrun this... this thing inside me that's baying for blood and death. The others say I'm crazy and that it makes me a good hunter. If only they knew the truth.

I hunt because I have no choice. It's the only thing that stops me from becoming a monster and preying on innocents.

The wolf appears in the shadows of the trees, no doubt scenting Lucien's blood in the trap. It's skinny and big, but all bones and fangs. The shaggy hair and unkempt appearance indicate it is indeed a feral, and the intelligence in its eyes as it ambles across the clearing to the trap tells us it's a shifter and not a wild animal. Its natural instinct to survive is overtaken by its hunger, and within seconds, it leaps at the trap, expecting an injured animal—the idiot.

The huge claws snap up, piercing its legs, and the trap closes around it as it howls in pain. Sprinting from our hiding spots, we descend on the animal. I quickly check the locks and secure them, ignoring the snapping jaws aiming for me. Once I'm finished, I step back as Lucien walks the length of the cage, while Vale eyes the beast.

"This one is nearly dead anyway," he grumbles in annoyance. "I hate ferals even more than pack wolves."

Ferals are the worst of the wolves, but I don't argue about who I hate more. Most of what we know is from knowledge that's been passed down, but I have my own experiences with wolves, and ferals are definitely the worst. Unlike pack wolves who have laws, family, and expectations, ferals are rejected wolves who break the rules and are kicked out. They live like wild animals, uncaring about being exposed or killing innocents. They have no laws, and they are nothing but beasts.

They feel no loyalty or guilt. They feel nothing but hunger.

Even now, this one foams at the mouth, trying to get to us, unbothered by the danger it's in. Snarling, he laps at the blood on the ground, making my lips curl in disgust. While it turns, I capture its tail and close the teeth around it. It spins, only tightening the trap on its tail, causing it to whimper and lunge as we watch it.

"It might be too far gone," I comment as I kick the cage. "Turn back."

It lunges at me again despite the agony that movement sends through its body. Sighing, Lucien reaches into his pocket for the vial and syringe, drawing the dose as we watch the wolf.

"Change back or we will force you," I command. I don't tell it that the drug that forces the change can also kill them if they aren't strong enough. It will give us the time we need to question it, though, and that's all we need.

I give it a moment, but when it just howls, I dive at the cage and stab the needle in hard to pierce the skin, depressing the plunger. I step back to avoid its claws, grinning as it spins, trying to dislodge the needle, but it's too late. The drug is already in its system, working through its blood, and within moments, the fur melts away to reveal a naked, filthy man.

Long, greasy hair hangs unkempt across the scarred, dirty face of the wolf. He's middle-aged, skinny, and starving, and when he lunges at the bar, snarling, I realise he's truly feral, more monster than man. Can he even speak?

"Ask." I nod at Vale.

He frowns at me but turns to the beast. "Answer our questions and we will end your suffering. If you don't, we will make this hurt. Jai craves your pain, so if I were you, I would play nice." Vale clears his throat. "We know there is a pack around here. Where is it?"

The man sinks back onto his haunches. He's covered in scars and dried blood, and who knows when he was last in human form. It's easier for ferals to stay as a wolf to keep themselves alive. Grinning, I grab my metal cattle prod and shove it through the bars, watching as he writhes and howls as electricity courses through him. I don't stop, not even when he pisses himself. Lucien drags me back before I finally release the beast.

Snarling, I kick Lucien away. I wanted to watch him thrash and see him beg for his pathetic life and then watch his life drain from his eyes.

"Answer us and we will spare you." Vale steps before me, blocking my view.

My hands fist at my sides, and anger surges through me. How dare he take my prey away? Pacing, I force myself to relax, focusing on my breathing. My eyes lock on the wolf, hoping he doesn't answer. When he ignores us, Vale sighs and steps away, giving me access.

Grinning evilly, I drop the prod and grab the man's leg, dragging it through the bars as he kicks, but he's weak. Pulling out my knife, I start to carve his skin as he howls and kicks. His screams fill the air, my cock hardening at the scent of his blood, until Vale's barking voice brings me back.

"Enough."

I hesitate but drop the leg, knowing if I don't respect his command, he will send me away, and no one else will work with me. I need this job, and I need them, so I bow my head in respect as the man writhes in the cage, bleeding and gasping.

The dark part of me likes that and wants more.

"Will you answer now, or shall I allow him to continue?" Vale asks conversationally, used to my ways.

"Fine," the wolf hisses, his voice more of a growl, and Vale leans closer to hear. "There is a pack, but you will never get to them."

"Where?" Vale demands, hitting the bars.

The wolf jumps but laughs. "The Red Rock Pack. They are close, but you don't stand a chance. Nothing can defeat them." He lifts his head, his eyes fading to the black of his wolf as he fights the drug.

"Watch us," Vale says as he stands. "Put this feral dog out of its misery."

The feral snarls, leaping at the bars as I step before him. "Gladly," I say as I take out my knife once more. "This might hurt a little . . . or a lot."

His screams fill the air within minutes, echoing across the land.

It's a warning to the other wolves.

I'm coming for them.

CHAPTER FIVE

Quinn

I manage to get a few hours of sleep before I roll out of bed and dress. Most spend their time naked, but I always dress when I'm attending an important pack meeting. It seems wrong to plant my bare ass on leather and discuss strategy, plus I know Tetrim will be there as a beta, and I don't want to give him any more opportunity to ogle me.

I slip on some cut-off jean shorts and a white tank top before stuffing my hair into a bun and jogging over to the pack house. Unlike the rest of the cabins and houses here, the pack house is three stories and huge. The top story is for the alpha and his family, and I still have a room there. The second floor has guest bedrooms, and the bottom floor has the kitchen and communal dining and living areas, which are always filled with pack members.

I slip through their masses, ignoring the calls from those eating or watching films, and head down the stone steps at the back that lead to two double doors—the only room in the house that's soundproof. I don't bother knocking. I just let myself in, closing the doors behind me and instantly relaxing at the familiar, homey scent of Jang's office.

Jang is already behind his desk, a cup of coffee before him, with his hands steepled under his chin. The chairs to the right have been taken up by the other betas, so I drop onto the brown leather settee. I've slept in here more times than I can count, wanting to be near Jang while he worked when I was younger and falling asleep, only to wake to him carrying me to bed.

The walls are the same dark wood as it was when I was a kid, decorated with paintings from one of our artist pack members. There are glass-fronted bookcases on either side, and behind Jang is a window with the deep green curtains partially pulled shut.

It's cosy, and I love it.

The door opens, emitting Tetrim and Dom, the final betas.

I widen my eyes at Dom, pleading silently, as Tetrim spots me and grins, heading my way to sit way too close, but Dom shoves him out of the way with a good-natured grin and flops next to me, lifting my legs and laying them across his lap. I snuggle closer, throwing a dirty glare at Tetrim, who snarls and slams the door, sitting stiffly in the final seat.

Dom's fingers stroke my leg. It's a comforting gesture since us wolves are all about touch, and I blow him a thank you kiss. I've had Dom before. He's strong and capable. As one of the betas whose duty is to protect the pack, he never oversteps his mark or gets ideas about us. Plus, it helps that he's so pretty. He has dark auburn hair, bright green eyes, and muscles to die for. He's so beautiful, sometimes I get jealous.

Leaning into me, he rubs his lips across my ear. "Tonight?" he asks.

Another thing I like about him is that he asks and never assumes. He knows I will never be his, never be tied down, and he's happy with what we have.

"Tonight," I confirm as Jang clears his throat, throwing us a narrow-eyed look.

Dom chuckles and sits back as I wave at him. "You should show respect for your alpha," Tetrim snarls.

I ignore him, yawning and patting my mouth.

"Let's begin," Jang says before a war can break out.

Another thing that's common with wolves is fighting. We run hot, both physically and emotionally. It leads to a lot of brawls, and there is more than one claw mark along these floors where Jang has had to drag us out. Betas are better about keeping it outside, but it happens a lot.

Sparring is a way to work out arguments, and it's natural.

When Jang glances down at his list, I put my thumb into my mouth and blow into it, pumping my middle finger up like a balloon before I shoot it at Tetrim. He snarls but quiets when Jang throws him a glare filled with alpha power, making him shrink back.

No matter how much Tetrim wants it, he will never be alpha. He isn't strong enough nor able to control his wolf sufficiently. That's why he needs me, and he knows it.

"So there is some worry about crops for the harvest festival," Jang begins, ignoring our antics. He only gets involved if he has to, and he can't show favourites.

"The corn is good, but they are right about the latest tomato crop. It isn't great," Filmia, the only other female beta, replies. "I have suggested that they dig up the old plants, leave that area of soil to heal, and replant on the southside. It means we will have less this harvest but more next year, and in the meantime, Dom has contacted a supplier to deliver what we are missing."

"Good, very good." Jang nods, marking it off, and Filmia sits up taller under the praise. She's a middle-aged lady with bright blonde hair, brown eyes, and a kind face, but she can kick some serious ass. I know since she kicked mine often when I was a bratty teenager. Despite that, she's never been anything but lovely and welcoming to me, even when some were not. I throw her a thumbs-up now, and she grins.

"Next issue. We need three new mate houses after the recent joinings. I suggest we start structures on the left side of the mountain where there are fewer. Leave the details up to them, but we will need extra supplies and help while they nest. Get their positions covered for now."

"Got it," White, the oldest wolf here other than Jang, responds. With a shock of white hair and eyes, it's no wonder the nickname stuck. He's a big bastard but a gentle giant. Jang told me that when I was younger, I never feared White. Instead, I always ran right towards him with kindness, and White has never forgotten that I didn't show fear. He avoids pups even now so as not to scare them, which always saddens me. He is a great caretaker and has a way with stories. We all hoped he would have his own one day, but he has never mated, much to Jang's shock.

He meets my lingering eyes and smiles softly, and I smile back. When the time comes, he will support me, but I wish he would find his own happiness. He's always been focused on taking care of this pack and looking after my father—his best friend.

Jang once told me he could have been alpha. He could have bested him in a challenge, but instead, he conceded, and when Jang asked why, since they were so young, White admitted that he was a good fighter but not a good leader. Despite his strength over Jang, he knew Jang would be a better alpha. That's White, always doing what's best for others. It makes an idea form in my mind—get White mated.

It will have to wait, though, since Jang is still talking.

"Our final issue is the hunters. I'm worried about the rumours I'm hearing from other packs. They are moving closer. Ideas?" Jang says.

I sit up taller. We all have our own areas, and mine is pack protection as well as overall education. It is my responsibility to keep the pack safe. Tetrim starts to speak, but I beat him to it. "I'm going to lean on some ferals I can trust or buy out and have them scout the new hunters' HQ. They are within fifty miles, which is worrying, but I've heard there are only one or two teams around here. They could be searching for local packs like ours, but more likely, they are hunting trolls or something else in the area. Even so, I will handle it.

I suggest we double patrols over our territory, but for now, let's not scare our people," I rationalise. "We don't know if they are here for us, and creating unnecessary panic would only cause loss of earnings, fear within the younglings, and eventually rebellion. Until we know the truth, we'll continue moving forward with the fact that we have been safe for this long and just take extra precautions."

"Very well said. Fine, I will leave it to you. Keep me updated, but take one of the betas with you," Jang orders. "Just in case."

"Of course, Alpha." I bow my head and lower my eyes out of respect, but when I lift them, his shine with pride, and Filmea shoots me a thumbs-up.

I'm getting there. Once, I would have rushed into battle and signalled the alarms. They are not the first group of hunters we've had to deal with in our area, but I've learned raising the alarm each time isn't the way to go. Sometimes, you have to ignore your wolf instincts and use your human brain. A good alpha can use the best of both our sides, making us more than wild animals.

It's what's kept this pack alive and safe for generations.

"Are there any issues we need to discuss?" Jang opens the floor.

I elbow Dom, giving him his chance. He takes a deep breath and lifts his hand. Jang nods for him to speak, and Dom clears his throat. "I was hoping to propose a gathering for next Friday. There are some of us who have recently graduated from our masters, and I was hoping to surprise them with a celebration."

"Of course," Jang replies, like I knew he would. "They are our future, so they should celebrate their accomplishments. Outline what you will need, and I will sign off on it."

"Thank you, Alpha," Dom says, grinning widely. He was worried Jang would reject his idea since it's a human university and some of the elders are still stuck on the old ways, thinking we shouldn't have any connection to the humans, but Jang is new school.

Fuck those wrinkly old elders, respectfully.

Humans aren't all bad. Hunters are asses, but they don't make up all humans, just like ferals don't make up all wolves. I even have a few human friends in the local town. We don't hang out a lot, though, since I can't exactly bring them home. I'm pretty sure they all think I live in some local convent, but they don't complain. Our pack brings in business, and we keep to ourselves.

"Anyone else?" Jang asks.

Tetrim speaks without even putting his hand up, the asshole. "I would like to formally request a mating with Quinn."

The room goes silent, and my claws sharpen. Dom covers my hands, reminding me what will happen if I gut the bastard.

"No," is all Jang says, and I blow out a relieved breath.

"Are you rejecting me as an alpha or her father?" Tetrim asks, daring to meet Jang's eyes.

Oh, the boy is dead.

"I wish we had popcorn," I tell Dom, who nods, looking between Jang and Tetrim.

Jang stands, his power washing through the room. "I will let you have that one comment, but any more and I will think you are challenging me. I always answer as alpha. Quinn can choose her own mates like any wolf. I will not force one. I never have, father or not. Do you understand me?" His voice is deadly.

Tetrim whimpers, pressed to his chair, his eyes on the floor. "Yes, Alpha. I apologise. I let my feelings get in the way."

"Do not let it happen again," Jang warns. "Meeting adjourned."

Everyone files out. Dom winks at me as he leaves, and I wait until everybody is gone.

The door shuts, and I meet Jang's eyes. He sighs and rubs his head. "I cannot keep him at bay forever."

"Don't worry, I'll just kill him," I tease.

Jang groans. "I'll pretend I didn't hear that."

"I'd prefer if you pretended like I didn't do it." I widen my eyes, making him chuckle.

"As much as I'd love for you to be able to, you need to deal with this and make it final. He will not stop."

"I know." I thought I could just keep outrunning him, but eventually, I'll tire.

We lapse into silence as I consider my options.

Jang focuses on his paperwork, and my gaze falls onto the photo on his desk. It's of him and me when I was little. I'm grinning widely up at him.

It was taken just a year after he saved me.

Jang isn't my father by blood, but by choice.

"I can never repay you for saving me, Alpha, never mind making me one of your family and protecting me. I will not let you down. I will handle this matter and make you proud."

"Quinny." He waits until I look at him. "I know you will, and you never have to thank me. You saved us, and you were always meant to be with us. You might not have my blood in your veins, but you are my daughter through and through, never forget that."

"I won't," I tell him, my voice choked. I've always felt like I was a part of his family. He healed and loved me as a father would. I'm very lucky he found me. "I better get out there."

"I'll join you tonight. Don't be in a rush to be alpha because there is so much bloody paperwork," he gripes, making me laugh as I head out, leaving him to it.

After checking in with patrols, I head for dinner, slumping into one of the benches as I eat two plates of burgers and fries. Our metabolism runs high, which means we eat a lot. I like my meat raw, but when I'm human, cooked meat is better, and no one's cooking is better than my mum's.

When I'm done, I wave goodbye to my table mates and walk into the kitchen, sneaking up on her. "Boo."

She smacks my side with a yelp. "Quinn!" she scolds before grabbing my plate. "Let me get another—"

"I've had two servings." I hop up on the counter.

"Only two?" she admonishes, her hands on her hips. Marjorie is just as terrifying as Jang in a maternal way, and Jang is downright terrified of his wife. One of her eyes is white, a scar running through it, and my eyes linger on it in pain.

Jang has a way of collecting and loving broken things.

"I'm full," I promise. "You should rest."

"Are you saying I look tired, young lady?" she snaps with a warning in her tone.

I grin widely. "I would never, mainly because I like my metaphorical balls attached to my body."

Huffing, she passes me an apple, and I eat it as she cleans up. "How did the meeting go?" she asks. She's privy to all pack information, but she doesn't always come, saying she's needed here more. Jang is the alpha, but Marjorie is the heart.

"Good, Jang is going to let me deal with the hunter issue."

"Good, no one is more experienced." She eyes me. "Please be careful."

I sigh. "Mum."

"Please, Quinny," she says. "We both know all too well that they are not to be messed with. They might only be human, but they are capable of great destruction." Her hand lingers at her eye.

Hopping down, I cover the distance between us, kissing her eye and wrapping her in my arms. She lost it when she was a child and her pack was attacked. They survived, but she still wears the scars from that day, and before Jang, she believed she would always be seen as unlovable and lacking.

Now, she's mated and leading the strongest pack.

I'm glad she got her happily ever after. She deserves it. They both do. "I will be, but I need to do this. I cannot avoid hunters because of my past. They are part of the pack's life, and it will be my duty to protect everyone here from them. I need to be able to do that. Plus, I'm not scared."

"You never were, and that's what terrifies me so much," she comments, holding me tighter. "You are so brave and fearless, even when you were a kid. I still remember that night we found you like it was yesterday."

They never used to speak of what happened, worried it would fuck me up, but one day, I boldly told them I remembered and they didn't have to tiptoe around it. I know who I am and where I came from.

"Me too," I admit.

"Enough of that," she whispers, wiping her eyes but not before I see her tears. "It all worked out in the end, and if you say you are okay, then I believe you, but I will always worry about my baby."

I kiss her cheek. "I wouldn't want you any other way, plus the hunters would take one look at you, my fierce mother, and run the other way."

"You better remember that," she mutters. "Now get out of here. I'm sure you have things to do." She leans in. "By the way, I put extra garlic in Tetrim's meals."

Laughing, I shake my head. "Terrifying," I tell her as I steal another kiss and apple before I head out.

Yes, I got lucky, but she's right—hunters are not to be taken lightly.

Jang is definitely more worried than he lets on, which means it's time for me to get to work.

CHAPTER SIX

"Let's set them all over the forest's edge. Don't go too deep, they have better ways to escape within the forest. We want to lure them into the clearings where we can see them and ensure they aren't trying to bait us," Vale explains as he points to the map spread on the hood of his truck.

He's hoping to get lucky. The feral's confirmation that there is a pack around here has him excited. He's desperate to re-earn his place and prove he's the best. I have always been more cautious, and the feral's other warning comes back to me—the pack will not fall easily.

A pack of wolves is usually hundreds strong, and if they all come for us, we are dead. We are resourceful and good hunters, but even the best fall before the monsters. They are stronger, faster, and smarter. It's a never-ending battle we have no hopes of ever winning. We just simply have to hold back the tide so they cannot consume this world with their wicked darkness.

Like my brothers, Vale was such a shy, kind kid.

I blame myself. I allowed us to be led into this organisation when our parents died. They sheltered us and took us in since they were hunters, but I should have gotten us out when I was old enough. I knew all it would lead to was death and heartache, but by the time I realised that, Vale had changed into this—a hunter.

All he thinks about is the kill, of ridding this world of monsters, and he's one of the best at it, but no one else sees the toll it takes on his soul but me. I stay to protect my baby brother and shield him as much as I can. I cannot lose anyone else, especially not him.

I don't know what I believe in, but I know that I believe in him.

If he wants to do this, then I will be at his side until the grave swallows us whole. We will make our parents proud. "Agreed." I nod. "The forest is too risky. There are too many things that could go wrong. We also need a fallout plan in case they come in groups."

"Usually, this far out from a pack, it's just the enforcers or scouts, so we should be okay unless they are on a run," Vale muses out loud, remembering everything we have learned from our training, which was hard-won by teachers hunting wolves themselves. Wolves are the hardest, after all.

You start way down at pixies and work your way up. Those annoying fucks were the bane of my existence for a year.

"Still, we should have a fallout plan," I reply.

"Burn it all down with us and them in it," Jai suggests as he climbs onto the hood, grinning maniacally.

"Kill ourselves?" I snort. "I was thinking more along the lines of a bug-out vehicle and deterrent to stop them from following."

"Nah, that's boring." Jai swings his legs. "Where's the fun if you plan to live?"

"Wait, you plan to die?" I ask, confused.

"I'm always planning to die, big guy. The question is, which day?" He grabs a trap and saunters away as both Vale and I watch him.

"I'm glad he's on our side," Vale comments, and isn't that the fucking truth?

Jai is a loose cannon at the best of times. He goes from happy to furious within seconds. He can be cruel and crazy, but he's a good fucking hunter. He has better instincts than anyone I've ever seen—

instincts that have saved our asses more than once. When we first met him, he was just a scarred, angry kid with a partially missing ear and a past so shrouded in darkness, nobody wanted to even train him.

Some still assume he is the enemy, like a sleeper spy, but I say it's been too long.

If he was going to change, he would have done it when he turned eighteen.

No, Jai is as human as they come despite everything that happened to him.

Instead, it just made him hateful, angry, and vengeful towards wolves. He's been waiting for the day he was allowed to hunt them, and God help the ones in our sights now.

"Brother," I start.

Vale groans, folding the map and leaning into the car as he eyes me. "I know that tone. It will be fine."

"I have a bad feeling," I grumble.

"You always say that, and we're fine. We're doing this, Luc. Are you with us or not?" he demands.

"You know I am," I snap, my brow furrowed. "I just want us to be careful. There is a reason so many hunters fall while hunting wolves. It might be the highest we can climb, but it's not worth our lives."

"If you're not willing to die for what you believe in, then what's the point?" Vale snaps. "This is our life, and if this is where we die, then I'm fine with that."

I watch him leave, and for a moment, I see the little boy who walked away from me when I told him what happened to our parents, but in his place now is a man. I cannot stop him, I can only protect him, so I haul up four traps and set out in the other direction to place them.

It's been ten hours since we set the traps and killed the feral, and the crescent moon is high in the sky. The night drags on as I shove some emergency rations in my mouth, needing to stay fuelled even if my eyes are continually scanning the tree line. They could be watching even now.

The night is the wolves' time. That isn't to say they don't come out during the day, but like most animals and predators, they are smart, and they know they are better equipped than we are to hunt at night.

Even with our goggles and sensors, we are basically sitting ducks, and I hate the feeling of eyes on my back even though I know it's probably just my imagination.

"Anything?" Vale asks in my ear, the mic crackling with the sound. The shitty equipment could get us killed, but being a hunter doesn't necessarily pay well, even at our level.

"Not yet. You?" I question as I shove more rations into my mouth.

"Nothing. Nothing on the sensors either," Jai chimes in. "Maybe the feral was wrong or lying to us."

"He wasn't," I comment, wiping my mouth. "At the end, he was too scared to lie. No, there is a pack around here, but they could be lying low or playing it smart. It takes time to hunt."

"Very true. Remember when we waited three whole months to capture and kill that vampyr den? We've got all the time in the world. They will have to come out eventually," Vale comments cruelly.

"I think we should plant some cameras and come back tomorrow night. Our scent could be throwing them off," I murmur, scanning the area. "There is no point in us sitting here day and night without rest. We'll get sloppy—"

"And getting sloppy is what gets you killed," they parrot back, making me glare into the night.

Vale sighs. "Alright, fine. We'll wait another hour, and if nothing happens, we'll come back tomorrow."

The hour passes, and I'm packed up and waiting when Vale and

Jai appear, both looking disgruntled, but they climb in without protest. I quickly reverse us out, leaving the forest behind and heading back down to the town we are staying in.

It takes us over two hours, and once we arrive, I collapse onto the cheap hotel bed. Our room has a door that opens to Jai's adjoining room. Vale is in the shower, his bed perfectly made next to mine. Nobody shared with Jai, since he tends to stab in his sleep.

Closing my eyes, I ignore the pink pastel wallpaper and old TV and settle in to get some rest.

We are going to need it for this hunt.

We go back tomorrow.

And the next night.

And the next.

On the fourth night, we are starting to lose hope and arguing about moving the traps as we get out of the truck, but the distinct sound of a whining trapped animal reaches us, and we stop.

"Is that . . . ?" I reach for my stun gun. Its voltage is enough to kill a human, but it knocks monsters out.

"Three of the cameras are down, so it could be," Jai murmurs. "Let's find out, shall we?"

I yank him back and behind me as we fall into formation, fanning out. Vale watches our backs, and Jai guards our sides as I head to the tree line. The whining increases, and from here, I hear heavy panting. Leaves crunch under my boot as I still at the line, peering into the darkness beyond. It must be one of the deeper traps.

When they tap my shoulder, I advance forward, stopping under the half-broken branches of a tree. Our cameras, shattered like broken toys, are scattered around the clearing, and pieces of them crunch under our feet as we spread out.

In the middle of the destruction, trapped in the metal cage, is a wolf with bright, intelligent eyes. It's small, either a kid or a small female, with all brown fur except for some white markings on its face.

It's not a feral or a wild wolf.

No, this is a werewolf, and a pack one at that.

"Well, boys, looks like we trapped a live one," Jai comments, laughing as he kicks the cage. The wolf swipes out at him, but he dances back with a grin. It hunches down, keeping all of us in its line of sight.

I prowl the perimeter, but I only see one set of prints within the trees. Why would they let a female or a child come out here alone? It's not a trap. I don't sense anyone else around. No, the wolf is alone . . .

Why?

When I come back, Vale is crouched at a safe distance away, his head cocked. "We're not killing it," he commands as Jai pulls his massive machete.

"What? Why?" he whines.

"It's a female, and females are protected. It's a pack wolf, so that means someone will come looking, and we'll be waiting."

"You want to use her as bait," I comment, leaning back into the tree.

"Exactly, big brother." He grins. "We'll take this pack down right here. Just you wait."

The wolf snarls in warning, and it raises the hair on the nape of my neck.

CHAPTER SEVEN

Quinn

"**Q**uinn!" Toby calls as he jogs over to me where I'm filling my plate with wraps. The urgency and worry in his tone instantly put me on edge. Something is wrong.

"What's wrong?" I pass my plate to the nearest wolf and grab Toby's arm. Tears well in his eyes as he looks at me. Toby is skinny, especially for his age. He is only two years younger than me, and he should be a powerhouse, but he's an omega and was born with hardly any power. It makes him weak and vulnerable, but luckily, the rest of the pack takes care of him.

"It's Sarah. She was supposed to meet me last night." He ducks his head, his cheeks flaming. That's news to me. Sarah is a lawyer in town, middle pack. They would make a cute couple though. She's hard, and he's funny and outgoing, so they are just what each other needs. "But she didn't show. I got worried and asked around last night. Turns out she went out into the woods for a run, saying she needed to burn off energy. She was dealing with a nasty divorce case in town, and it was wearing her down," he rambles.

"Toby," I snap, infusing some of my power into my tone. His wolf whines as he practically flattens himself against the floor.

"She hasn't come back." He lifts his eyes for a second. "She always comes back. She even missed work. Something happened, I feel it."

"Go tell Jang, okay? Gather the other enforcers and send them out into the woods." I turn and scan the crowd, but the only one I see is Tetrim. Snarling, I head his way. "Assemble the others. I want every acre of the woods searched inch by inch. Report back to Jang, who will stay here. We are looking for Sarah. She's missing."

"Oh, now you want my help," he sneers.

"Do it!" I order, infusing my power into my tone as I rush outside, jogging towards the trees.

"Where are you going?" Toby yells after me.

"It's already been half a day. I'll run the edge of our territory since I'm the fastest. Tell them I'll be back!" I call as I use a fallen log to throw myself into the air, changing mid-jump. As soon as my paws hit the dirt, I sprint off, using familiar paths through the forest. My nose is in the air, trying to scent her trail or blood.

She could be hurt. A broken leg would force her to change back, and I've warned her and the other runners to stop going out alone, but they don't always listen. Let's hope that's all it is. The trees blur around me. I leave the closest areas to the trackers and other enforcers, since I'm the fastest, but my ears swivel for any sounds of distress or howls.

I stop every so often and drop my nose until I finally find a trail deep in the woods. It's old, at least six or seven hours, and almost faded, but it's hers. Snarling, I sprint through the trees as I follow the trail as quickly as I can, doubling back when she does. It's clear she was just running and hunting for fun.

Something has definitely gone wrong. Toby was right, and a bad feeling starts to well inside me.

My instincts have never steered me wrong, and I slow, careful of my steps. I manoeuvre through the trees as nothing but a shadow. I'm almost at the border that leads to the national park near the local town, deep out of our pack's reach and away from anyone who could help.

I need to be smart. I can't save Sarah if I rush in and get myself hurt as well.

The trail leads back and forth before shooting straight ahead, as if something caught her attention. It's not long before I find a dead rabbit. The kill is left, however, and her tracks continue on. When I sniff the ground, I realise why—fresh blood.

It leads to a trail right at the tree line. As I retreat and pace, I hear whines.

Tilting my head, I move swiftly through the trees as silently as possible. Even the other animals are silent here, and when I stop, I see her.

Sarah cowers within a black steel cage at the base of a tree. It's almost too small for her, her nose sticking out. Her back legs are at an odd angle and bleeding.

Lifting my nose, I scent the air and nearly snarl before I swallow it back.

Hunters.

Despite their clear attempts to conceal themselves, the scent of their sweat fills the air. Sarah shakes her head at me, clearly seeing me even if they don't. It's a warning. They are watching. She whines, glancing to the top lever which clearly dropped the cage door.

Slinking through the trees, I create a circle as I search for the human hunters. There are three distinct scents. I can kill three humans without even trying. The trails are old, only an hour or two, but I can still smell them. Is it from the stuff they left behind, or are they here?

I don't know, but I sit back and watch. Sarah whines again. Her back leg is bleeding badly, soaking the leaves below the cage, and it's clearly broken. She needs to turn to heal it. If she's trapped for too long like that, she will have to live with a deformed, broken leg, which would be the end of a wolf.

I cannot wait for the pack's help, since they are too far away. It could take a day for them to get here, and I cannot leave her to go back and get them. They could kill her while I'm not here.

No, I'm a beta, and it's my job to protect them and Sarah.

I eye the clearing once more, coming to a decision. It's impulsive, but it's all I have. I let out a low call, and she lifts her head, nodding in understanding. When nothing moves after my sound, I slink to the edge of the trees, once more scanning the area before deciding it's now or never.

Leaping onto the top of the cage with a snarl, I bite through the rope. The cage door springs open, and Sarah rushes out, fleeing into the woods, but I need to watch our backs, especially since three humans drop into the clearing from the trees.

Fuck, I didn't look up.

They are big, armed, and clearly experienced.

They used her as bait. They didn't want her; they wanted me, recognising I'm clearly more important. My mind spins with scenarios as I back away, dropping from the cage and heading back to the trees. If I can get in there, then I'm safe. I can outrun them and warn the pack they were right. Hunters are here, right on our doorstep.

"Do you know how long it took us to trap her? That was rude," the one in the middle comments. He stinks of blood and anger.

He's big for a human, with huge muscles that rival even a wolf's, and they are clearly well used. His face is angular, with bright green eyes, and his hair sticks up on the top of his head, his right ear partially missing. Scars litter his exposed skin, but it's his cruel smile that makes me hesitate.

This one wants to make it hurt.

The one to the left is bigger than the other two, with more muscles than I've ever seen on a human. He's dressed in all black and holding a gun in his hand like he knows how to use it. There is ink on his skin, with writing crawling across his neck. Stubble covers his cheeks and chin, dark black just like his short, styled hair. There's a wicked glint in his brown eyes.

The last one watches me carefully. He's smaller than the other two but still big for a human. His hands are empty and out to the sides. His skin is a sun-kissed gold, and he looks vaguely like the big one but with sharper features, no hair on his chin, and a shaved head. A steel cross hangs from his shirt, swaying as he walks.

"Easy there," the shaved one murmurs, clearly in charge. "We aren't going to hurt you."

I snort as I continue to back away, and they track my movements, spreading out to cage me, which tells me they are smart and probably have backup traps. These are not regular hunters.

"Not too badly . . . yet, anyway," the middle one with the scarred face and crazy smile comments.

"Jai," the shaved one snaps. "Lucien, right."

The big guy moves right, and then I'm left with a choice—run or fight.

I could take them, but their weapons pose a problem. I could change, but they would outpower my human form, and with one stab of that sword, I'd be in real trouble.

The scent of Sarah's blood still fills the clearing, and I know two things with certainty.

They'll chase us onto pack land, and I need to protect Sarah.

She's hurt and can't run as fast as I can. That means biding my time.

They want a wolf? Then they'll get one.

Hopefully, they'll leave then, and my pack will be out of danger. If I don't have to worry about them, I can focus on saving myself.

The sacrifice is easy. It's my job.

I'll stay and fight to buy her time.

I lunge at the big bastard, knowing he's the most dangerous. He leaps back and swings his weapon at me. I dodge it and spin to snarl at the bald one, kicking out before jumping over the reaching hands of the one in charge.

I'm fast and strong, but there are three of them.

Something hits my back leg, and pain splinters through me, but I keep fighting. Swiping my claws, I manage to slice up the shoulder of the one in charge. He roars as he falls back.

"Vale!" the big bastard yells, but Vale snarls with one hand pressed against his shoulder, blood seeping through his fingers.

I feel one creeping up behind me and leap to the tree, kicking off and slamming the menacing one, Jai, to the ground, ragging at his side and shoulder, but something hits me again—something that makes my whole body jolt.

The electric gun knocks me to the side.

Spinning with a whine, I raise my head and howl to let my pack know where I am. Fuck this, I need backup.

Another jolt hits me, then another.

Their weapons are too strong, and another current flows through me, knocking me to the ground as I thrash. It gives them the time they need, and when I feel something pierce my neck, I howl in anger, but darkness takes over.

The last thing I see is the menacing grin of the one they called Jai. "Goodnight, wolfy. I can't wait to play."

CHAPTER EIGHT

"You okay?" I look Vale over. He's holding his shoulder, and I pry his fingers away as he grunts. "It's deep. It might scar, but otherwise, it should be fine," I tell him with relief. "We'll disinfect and bandage it."

I turn to Jai, who is holding his side. He rolls his eyes and yanks his ripped, bloody shirt up. There are teeth marks all over him, both deep and shallow, but he'll live—just another lot to add to his collection. My eyes go to the wolf. It's out cold and will be for at least a few hours.

It's a stunning white and brown colour with bright blue eyes, which are currently shut. It's big for a female, but there is no question it's female. She's smart too. She avoided all the cameras and tried to figure us out. So why did she fight and not run?

"Should we stay and wait for the others?" Jai grins, wanting blood as he kicks the downed wolf.

I frown. "No."

"Lucien is right." Vale looks around. "They will have heard that howl and the other wolf. We cannot fight a whole pack, especially on their territory. She seems important. I'm betting she's our key to it. Let's take her out of here and question her before they find us."

"We could take them," Jai whines.

"Not with both of you hurt," I snap as I haul the wolf over my back, ignoring its teeth which are way too close for comfort.

We hurry to the truck, where I toss the wolf in a cage in the back and double-lock it before jumping in the front. Jai sits in the back, and Vale drives despite my protests. We are out of there in minutes, but as we pull onto the road that leads out of the forest, we hear howling.

Turning, I spy wolves racing alongside us in the tree line. There are so many of them, they pour out of it like ants. "Definitely a pack," I comment.

Vale grips the wheel harder. "Good, this means she's important. Hang on." He floors it, knowing not even we could take that many wolves.

One throws himself at the car, a black one, and Vale spins the wheel to hit him. He flies into the woods. Another leaps into the middle of the road, and Vale grunts, gunning it before it rolls out of the way. They quickly realise we will run them over, and when we skid out of the valley, the biggest wolf I've ever seen bounds into the road behind us, letting a mournful howl ring out.

Mate maybe?

Either way, we are out free and clear. Jai whoops as we hurry through the wilderness towards our hideaway just outside of town, which we secured just for this purpose.

"Why did she do that?" I ask, peering back at the wolf knocked out in the cage. She seems smaller like this.

"Luc?" Vale frowns, confused.

"She sacrificed herself to save the other wolf. Why?" I ask.

"Who knows, but don't think about it. They are smart fuckers. It was probably a trap to confuse us. Remember, they might have a human form, but they are nothing but monsters," Jai responds.

I nod, turning back to look out the front window, but something doesn't sit right with me. Animals don't run towards danger, they run away, so then why did this one risk it all to save the other wolf? I shouldn't care because they are monsters and we are hunters. It hurt my brother and friend, but for some reason, the thought sticks with me, even as we pull up at the old mill we rented.

It's secluded and has a fence around it to separate it from the woods. We added new security to the gates and cameras, and we can drive right inside, shutting the huge doors behind us. We didn't do much in here, just added three cots, and our equipment takes up most of the room with our boards of locations.

In the centre of the room is a huge metal cage we constructed, and since I'm the only one unhurt, I haul the wolf from the cage in the truck and toss it none too gently into the bigger one. I slam the door and lock it. It doesn't move, but I have no doubt it's starting to wake.

It's probably trying to feel us out.

I add another lock to the door just in case and step back. It's big enough for the wolf to walk around in and lie down, but not much else. Turning away, I grab the first-aid kit and move to Vale, who is sitting on his cot.

He tugs his shirt up and off without a word, and I quickly treat and bandage the wound as he hisses. "Keep it clean and changed," I remind him.

"I've been injured enough to know," he mutters but then laughs. "Thanks, brother. I'm not going to update the commander yet, not until we have something. I don't want him to send others who will swoop in to steal our hunt."

I nod as I move to Jai, who's watching the wolf as he sharpens his knife. I make sure to slowly approach him from the front. His eyes snap to me, but I see no recognition there for a moment before he blinks.

Jai heals fast, almost inhumanly fast. It was why so many others were wary of him when he was younger, thinking him a monster, but it's just a trait of his. Even so, it will need to be cleaned, so I wait.

Sighing, he rips off his shirt, and I quickly wash the wounds and apply cream. He'll heal in a day or two, but it will take Vale weeks.

Not for the first time, I wonder if they were wrong about Jai, and when I meet his eyes, it's like he knows my thoughts.

"It's awake," he murmurs, making me snap out of it.

I spin to see the wolf silently watching us. I didn't even hear it move. Its eyes are open and sharp, and I see anger in its very human orbs. Its maw is shut, but its huge fangs still flash. As we watch, it tilts its head, watching us right back.

"Good, then it's time to get started," Vale says. "The less time we have this mutt here, the better."

She snaps, making him laugh.

"Make this easier on yourself and turn back. We just want to talk." Vale smirks. "Or make it hard and we will enjoy it either way. One way gets us answers and you will have a swift death, and the other way means you'll get some personal time with Jai here who, as you can see, truly hates wolves, and then you'll die a long, painful death."

The wolf simply bares her teeth in a mocking grin.

"We can make you turn, you know," he says conversationally, walking around the perimeter of the cage. The wolf isn't dumb. It tracks him, knowing he's the biggest threat, but she also stays in the middle, keeping us in her peripheral so we cannot sneak up on her. "It does tend to kill you in the end, but we have heard of some wolves holding out for days, even weeks. You look strong, so I reckon you could survive long enough. Do you?"

The wolf cocks her head, then her gaze clashes with mine and then Jai's. As we watch, the wolf inhales and narrows her eyes on Jai. He bangs on the cage, but the wolf doesn't even flinch. "What are you doing?" he hisses.

Grinning at him, she lies down with her head on her paws and watches us. I turn away to hide my smile. This is one strong wolf, but my smirk soon fades because I know what that means.

The harder they are, the harder they fall.

She should have made it easy on herself, but now we will have to hurt her to get answers.

"Jai," Vale commands, and I hear Jai grumble but step back. When I turn around, Vale is standing before the wolf, staring her down. He is close enough for her to reach through the bars and gut him with one swipe, but he steps closer, pressing his body to the bars.

"Last chance, wolf," he warns.

She inhales, her eyes widening as she stares at Vale.

"Very well." Vale sighs as if he's disappointed and steps back. "We will begin. You are clearly someone important to your pack, considering they chased you to the edge of the forest. That also means your pack land is nearby, isn't that correct?"

The wolf just yawns and starts licking her paws.

"I'm betting so. I'm also betting we are getting closer and closer. They tell me you're called the Red Mountain Pack, and deep in those woods there are mountains made of red rock. Is that where your pack is?" When she keeps grooming, Vale narrows his eyes. "How many wolves are there?"

She lays her head back down, and Vale's phone rings. He grits his teeth. "Don't touch it until I get back." Storming out, he takes his phone with him, leaving the order for me since I'll have to watch Jai, who is glaring at the wolf while sharpening a wooden stake.

The wolf draws my attention again. I find its gaze on Jai, and she looks confused.

Does she know something we don't?

CHAPTER NINE

I watch the hunters who captured me. I can't believe they got the drop on me, and whatever they knocked me out with did the trick. The last thing I remember is the agonised howl of Jang following me into the darkness before waking up in the cage. I tried to be discreet, but they knew I was awake, and now here we are.

Judging by the smells, it's an old mill probably on the southside of the local town. There are no exhaust fumes, metal smells, or other scents, so there definitely aren't many people around.

Above all that are their scents.

I've smelled one before—the one with the bright, cruel eyes.

Vale.

It didn't hit me at first, but now, with nothing else to distract me and him standing before me, I take a deep inhale and he smells familiar.

I don't know why.

Despite what most people think, I can understand everything they are saying, and they know that, which tells me they've been around wolves before or did their research. They can also make me turn back. I've heard of a similar drug before. It's synthetic wolfsbane, and it's toxic, so it sends wolves into shock. Without the wolfs-bane antidote, I will die a very painful death. Either way, though, there is going to be pain, that much is obvious.

I will never betray my pack, no matter how much they torture me.

They picked the wrong wolf for that. I will gladly suffer and die for my pack. Maybe I was always destined to end up here, considering my life has always been a tragedy, not a fairy tale.

My eyes lock on the scarred one, knowing he's the most dangerous. His eyes possess the same look feral wolves have. They crave blood and death. This one is touched by madness, and the way he's looking at me lets me know he wants my blood.

The big guy by his side moves closer to him, keeping watch, and it's clear he knows it too.

Interesting. The big guy almost seems reluctant to get involved, but his eyes harden when Vale comes back in. "We've been called back. Hurry up," he mutters.

"We can't leave this here," Jai snaps.

"You're right." He sighs. "Lucien, watch the wolf."

"Will you two be okay?" Lucien asks, crossing his arms.

"Why him?" Jai snarls at the same time.

"If I leave you, I'll come back to a dead wolf. We need it alive. I'll be fine. We'll hide our wounds and say we are still working on the ferals," Vale snaps. "Let's go. I want to be back before nightfall so we can clean up outside to stop the wolves from tracking it here."

Throwing down the wood he was sharpening, Jai grabs a coat and storms past Vale, who sighs and glances at Lucien. "Watch it carefully. If there are any issues, call us, brother."

Lucien just nods, and Vale leaves. A moment later, I hear a different car starting up, and then it drives away. I can hear up to several miles. My ears twitch as I glance at the big guy who's ignoring me, cleaning up the mess of bloody gauze.

I show my teeth, scenting the hunters' blood. Good.

Now, it's time to gain an advantage. This one seems reluctant to hurt me. Is it because I'm female?

If I change back and use the *oh, I'm so little* female act, can I trick him?

It's worth a shot.

While he has his back turned, I change. I'm not above using what I have to get free and rip these motherfuckers limb from limb. I cross my knees and stand silently, letting my hair fall across my back and chest as I wrap my arms around the bars, naked and human.

"Lucien, wasn't it?" I murmur, my voice husky.

He whirls around and stumbles back, his eyes wide. I blink, trying to look as innocent and sweet as possible. "Erm . . ." He scrambles for a weapon, still staring at me.

"I'm thirsty. I don't suppose I could have some water?" I ask sweetly.

He blinks and moves automatically, handing over a bottle before he seems to realise what he's doing and snatches his hand back, but not before I've stroked the back of it. He curls his fingers in like he feels violated and moves back, watching me carefully.

I drink as I watch him and purposely drip some onto my chest. He gulps as his eyes follow the droplet, finally looking at my body. He stares before bringing his eyes back to mine in shame.

"Thank you," I say, closing the lid and sitting cross-legged, watching him.

He sits on the edge of one of the tables filled with weapons and just stares until his thick voice comes. In human form, his voice does all types of things to me despite us being enemies. "Why did you change back?"

"You asked me to, did you not?" I respond. "Besides, I cannot talk to you when I'm in my wolf form."

"You know what will happen to you," he warns, yet he doesn't seem overly pleased nor angry about it. It's as if he's just in the middle. Interesting. Hunters are usually all up in arms about skinning wolves as trophies and hating our guts.

For a hunter, Lucien doesn't seem to hate monsters.

"Why are you hunting me?" I ask, not mentioning my pack. I need information. How many of them are there? Where are they? I need to protect my people.

He grinds his teeth.

"Are there more of you? Should I be worried?" I ask, kneeling and making sure to flash my cunt.

He averts his gaze. Fine, he's smarter than he looks.

"My name is Quinn," I say, humanising myself to him. "I'm twenty-six. What about you?" He glances back at me but doesn't speak. "Not a talker, huh? No worries, my dad is like that, so I can talk enough for anyone." I grin, and he blinks. "Vale is your brother? Younger, I'm guessing."

His teeth grind, and I hold up my hand.

"I meant nothing by it, just something I heard you say. So why is he in charge and not you?"

"Because I don't like people."

"Or monsters," I add bitterly before grinning. "That Jai, though, he's mad. I see it in his eyes. There's also something there . . ."

He stands taller. Ah, so I hit a nerve. I note that.

"You've never noticed it?" I ask. "That he's more like the monsters he hunts?"

"You don't know what you're talking about." He grunts and starts to walk away.

I'm losing him.

"No? So you're not three nutjobs hunting me and my family for kicks?" He stills. "Does the hunt get you hard? If so, you're not much different than the wolves you hunt."

"I won't tell them you changed or it's both our heads," he hisses. "If you're smart, though, you'll play along and give them what they want."

"I was never good at playing it smart," I tell him, but I change back, done talking to him. I have what I need for now.

Instead, I close my eyes and rest, knowing I will need it. This cage, though crude, will do the trick for now. With only one of them here—the one that seems reluctant to hurt me—I can almost relax as I sleep, caught between dreams and nightmares.

The smell of smoke fills my lungs, choking me. The acidic taste makes me gag, and bile claws at my throat as tears burn behind my eyes. I turn to look, watching the flames eat what's left of my life before spinning around and sprinting towards the forest—the one place I know I will be safe if I can get there.

I pump my legs and arms faster, pushing my body for all I'm worth. If I don't, I'll die here just like everyone else.

Run! *The roar is in my head, the memory echoing inside me making me sob and stumble.*

"Wolf! I found a wolf!"

I jolt awake, my gaze clashing with a bright human pair. Fuck, I must have slept deeper than I meant to. The nightmares always have that effect on me. They shroud me in their smoke and darkness, making me unaware.

Jai sits before me, close enough to touch the bars.

I feel my body tense, and he cocks his head.

"I wonder what wolves have nightmares about. You were whimpering in your sleep." I flash my fangs, and he grins. "Is it us skinning your brothers and sisters and using them as our rugs?"

I don't give him the reaction he wants. He's practically vibrating with the desire to see me leap at him like the feral animal he thinks I am so he has an excuse to attack me. The others want me alive and need me for answers, but this one? He wants my pain and death, and I will not give him an excuse for it.

I relax, watching him as I lay my head down on my paws.

I can hear the other two snoring on the cots in the corner. It's dark in here, but my eyes can see the specks of dust floating in the air between us. My wolf side lets me know the moon is high, the call to it never leaving. It's late into the night, when the world is quiet and darkness takes over.

Darkness most use to cover their evil deeds.

Like this one.

There is madness in his gaze, but something under his skin has my hair standing on end. It's happened before when I met a true monster in human form, but this is something different—this is an awareness.

This man is not completely human, but from his and the others' reactions, I can tell none of them know.

Interesting.

"When they let me kill you, and they will, I think I'll keep your skin as a blanket." He smirks, pulling out a wicked-looking knife. The slight blue sheen lets me know it's infused with wolfsbane to cause the most damage and stop us from healing as they gut us. He keeps talking, obviously realising I have no plans to respond. "The others think you are someone important, someone we can use. Me? I don't give a fuck who you are. You're an animal—an animal I'm going to enjoy putting down."

I glance at one of the cots as someone's breathing picks up, letting me know one of them is awake. They say nothing, though, so I look back to Jai. He's oblivious to his fellow hunters, stroking the blade like one does a cock as he watches me.

I wonder if he enjoys killing and if it gets him off.

There's certainly enough crazy in his gaze to answer that. Hunters enjoy what they do. Most are trained soldiers who cannot do anything but kill and need an outlet, while others are simply in it for the money, but some like Jai do it for this—the pain, the kill. They hate us monsters so much, they crave our deaths. It usually stems from something, and it makes me wonder what happened to Jai to make him hate wolves so much.

We limit our contact with humans and bar ferals, and we don't ever attack humans. Even hurting hunters is forbidden unless agreed on by our alpha. It can lead to declawing and dismissal from a pack. We are not to draw their attention at all, and murder does that, but the hunters are getting bolder, spreading out into the secluded places we live, hunting our full pack.

Everything is changing, and so must we.

When I kill these three, I will not ask for forgiveness. I will bring their heads on pikes for my pack.

"They say that if you cause enough pain to the wolf, you'll turn back. Shall we see?" He leans forward, but I don't move.

"Jai, enough," Vale calls, half asleep.

My eyes do not move from the threat until Jai leans back. Only then do I glance at Vale to see him scratching his head. He's wearing nothing but low-slung grey joggers, showing off impressive muscles for a human, but I almost smirk at the bleeding gauze covering his shoulder. He notices and glares at me, but that momentary distraction is what Jai needs.

I should have known better than to take my eyes off a predator.

The knife slashes through the bars, and only my quick reflexes save me as I roll back to avoid it. Getting to my paws, I snarl at him, my hackles raised.

"Enough!" Vale commands, his voice hard. "Go outside and get some air, now."

Jai stands, going toe to toe with Vale who is only a bit taller than him. Vale doesn't back down, and Jai eventually snarls before stomping past him, slinging the door open, and heading out. I see the trees beyond the door and smell the fresh air, but my eyes go back to Vale. Why did he stop Jai? He must see the question in my eyes.

"If I let him play with you, we won't get answers. We would only hear your screams before he put you out of your misery. Don't think this means anything. I still plan to question and kill you, wolf."

Lightning cracks just then, and for a moment, those blue eyes flash like a memory before he turns away. "I wouldn't sleep if I were you, wolf. I won't always be awake to stop him."

I watch him crawl back into his cot, and within a moment, he's asleep. My eyes go back to the door and the madman standing outside.

Settling down, I focus on keeping calm. If I get too worked up, I will need to burn off energy by shifting. No, it's better to remain like this for now.

Thunder rolls in the distance as rain splashes down, and my eyes go back to Vale.

Why did he seem so familiar for a moment?

Why did it feel like I've looked into those eyes before?

CHAPTER TEN

"Father," I say, reaching for his hand. He pulls away from me, glaring down at me with hard eyes. Lucien once told me he loves us and that he just doesn't know how to show us. Sometimes, I'm not too sure.

"Stay here," he warns and turns to Lucien. "Watch your brother."

"Yes, sir," Lucien responds, taking my hand and tugging me deeper into the shade of the trees.

Father thought it was important for us to come tonight so he could show us the truth, as he called it. I've always known what hides in the dark. When most of my friends were being told not to be scared of it, my father told me everything that hides in it can kill me.

When I used to ask him to check under my bed, he would bring a knife, and more than once, there was something hiding under it, but tonight is different. It's the first night he has ever brought Lucien and me with him while he hunts the monsters.

I don't like it. It's too dark and scary.

In the distance, I hear the howling of wolves, which makes me shiver and move closer to Lucien. "It's okay, Val. I've got you," he tells me. "They won't let anything happen to us."

I follow his gaze, watching my father command his men as they charge towards the sprawling ranch-style house. There's a slide and a swing set to the left. I've been wanting one for years, yet the monsters have one.

A high-pitched scream of pain has my eyes jerking back to the house as the cocktails my father's men have sail through the windows, the glass smashing and flames instantly engulfing the curtains and wall.

The scream comes again, filled with fear, and it sends shivers through me.

My heart races as something within me responds to that scream.

"Don't," Lucien snaps, tugging me back. "We can't get in the way."

My eyes go back to the wooden house and the flames currently engulfing most of it just in time to see something small dart from the wreckage, racing towards the forest.

Lucien turns to see a hunter stumbling from the house and glares at me, looking so much like our dad my heart squeezes. It doesn't matter that he's only a few years older than I am. "Stay here." Grabbing a bucket of water from the well, he hurries to help him while my eyes follow the streak heading towards the trees.

I glance back at Lucien to find him distracted. Taking a deep breath, I hold my knife and hurry through the trees, knowing Father will be angry if one of the monsters gets away.

No one wants him angry.

He was right. It's time to become a man.

Startling awake, I look at the cage to see the she-wolf watching me carefully. Its eyes almost mock me, as if it knows what I was dreaming of. It's bad enough that it can hear my heart racing and smell the sweat covering my body.

Turning away, I sit up on the cot, offering it my back as I scrub at my face and try to grasp onto the tendrils of my dream, but like smoke, they slip through my fingers until I'm left frustrated and angry.

I ignore the others as I get to my feet and storm into the bathroom.

Slamming the door, I quickly strip and crank on the old, rusty shower in the employees' changing room. I step into the off-white stall and under the freezing water, letting it wash away my dreams and worries.

I scrub at my body until I feel clean, and then I grab a towel and dry off as I head to the sinks.

Wiping the condensation from the mirror, I finish towelling off my head and then wrap it around my waist before meeting my own eyes in my reflection. They flare with anger, my jaw is clenched, and the veins in my neck bulge. I blame that wolf. She's too close, so of course I'm going to be on edge with an enemy watching me sleep, but if I hadn't, she would have known I was worried she could get out and kill us. No, I need to show my power and restraint, and luckily, years of forcing myself to sleep in strange places helped, so I was able to nod off.

The wet, off-coloured gauze catches my eye, and I cover it for a moment, remembering the sharp pain of her claws. She wasn't even trying then, so I can only imagine what she is capable of if she is.

Lifting the gauze, I peek at the wound in the mirror, frowning to see it's not healing at all. What did that nasty she-wolf do to me?

Ignoring the slight pain as it tugs at my skin as I remove the bandage, I quickly wash and redress the wound with the kit we keep in here. After enough hunts, you learn to keep them everywhere.

In nothing but the towel, I head back to the cots and tug out my green khaki duffle bag. Ignoring the eyes I feel watching me, I turn my back, drop the towel, and tug on my dark-grey utility trousers and a black shirt. I add my socks and boots before slipping the wire, wolfsbane, and grenades into my pockets, and then I strap on my knife and gun.

When I'm finished, I look up.

The wolf is sitting in the middle of the cage, watching me, as if she knows what will happen when I'm done. For a moment, familiar brown eyes fill my vision before I turn away and finish securing my holster and head over to the tables we set up.

Lucien is munching on toast, and he hands me a mug as he eats.

Sitting down next to him, I lay my legs across the other chair, sipping the weak coffee as I eye the wolf. "Any issues?" He took over watch early this morning from Jai since we can't trust him. I should have known better than to leave him, but we needed sleep, and I thought putting some fear into the wolf would help.

"None. It has not even moved. She's been awake nearly the whole night. Jai is out for a run since you told him to blow off steam."

My head jerks to him. His hand fists his toast so hard, it snaps, and his eyes are downcast. "It's a monster, remember that."

"I do," he retorts, "but he shouldn't play with them like that. We are hunters, not psychopaths."

"We need answers," I remind him.

"But he wasn't looking for answers. He was looking for fun," Lucien retorts as he stands, dusting off his hands. "Come on, let's get this over with now that you're awake. The longer the wolf is here, the longer we are in danger from her pack."

That's exactly what I said to Jai yesterday. I didn't tell our commander we caught a pack wolf, just a few ferals and that we were on the right track. He was so happy, he didn't even question why we had to hurry back. I want this win all on our own, so I'll call them in once I'm sure of the location. We'll need all the hunters to take the pack down. I'm not dumb enough to go after them with just us three, but I want to be sure.

We cannot afford to fail again.

Taking my mug with me, I follow him to the cage, seeing the marks on the floor from Jai's knives. Leaning back into the table, I sip my coffee as I watch the wolf. I could inject her and force her to change, but there is no guarantee she will talk, and she would definitely die.

No, we need a different approach for now. She's the closest lead we have, our best and only lead, and we need her alive.

"If you help us out and tell us what we want to know, we will give you a fair chance," I begin, trying for a friendly approach. "We'll let you go, give you a head start. A fair chance at surviving."

She blinks and just watches me.

"We can do this the easy way or the hard way. Either you die in there like an animal or outside there with us hunting you. Your choice." I sip my coffee as I wait.

Her mouth gapes in an excessive yawn, flashing her long fangs, and then with a grin, she brings her paw up in what I can only describe as a wolf middle finger. "The hard way it is then." I sigh, pushing off the table.

No matter how much I hate monsters and want to rid the world of them so they cannot hurt innocents, I do not enjoy torture. I am not like Jai. I enjoy their deaths, not their pain. Not anymore. I did once, when I was young and new, wanting revenge. Now, I just want to keep what's left of my family safe.

I made a mistake with a monster once, offering them mercy, and it cost me everything. I won't make that mistake again.

Female or not.

Pushing from the table, I place my mug down deliberately before unsheathing my knife and holding it up to the air. "You know what this is, I take it?" I don't bother looking at her or waiting for a response. I simply carry on. "It is a blade blessed by sunlight, and the metal itself is made with a mix of wolfsbane and pixie steel. The wolfsbane will infect each cut like a poison, stopping it from closing and causing agony as it works through your blood. Eventually, you will be unable to turn at all. The pixie steel cuts deeper than any blade." I look at the wolf. "Let's begin, shall we?"

Stepping closer to the cage, I hold the blade. "Where is your pack?"

She simply watches me.

Cracking my neck, I head to the door. "Vale," Lucien snaps, but I ignore him.

Unlocking the chains, I swing the door open, stepping inside the cage with her. She turns to face me, and I ignore Lucien's curse as I step deeper into the cage, backing her into the corner. I make sure to keep my back to the exit to make a quick getaway. I'm not a fucking idiot. She's been calm, but I remember the sharpness of her claws.

She is a monster, an animal, so she will attack.

They all do.

Flicking my knife, I watch her gaze follow the movement as her tail straightens behind her and she snarls in warning. "I told you we could have done it the easy way." I flick the knife again as I move closer, and her snarl gets louder. The vibration makes the hair on my arms stand up. My instincts scream at me to run, sensing the predator, but I ignore them. I keep flicking as I move closer, and then I slice. She darts to the left, just narrowly missing the blade's edge, but she snaps her jaws shut, and I yank my hand away, missing being bitten myself.

She's faster than any wolf I've encountered before, and smarter too. When I feint right, she doesn't take the bait. I step back, twirling the knife as she watches my eyes, not the blade.

Smart little she-wolf.

"You'll eventually slow or sleep, and I'll catch you, little wolf, then you'll be in trouble." Her eyes narrow, and the next time I lunge, she lunges into my attack, ducking under the knife and slashing her claws across my leg.

I stumble back with a shout, feeling my blood drip down my leg. Her claws sliced through my trousers and skin. It's not deep, so it's a warning shot, telling me she can get to me and offering her own threats without words.

I grind my teeth, ignoring the pain and Lucien's worried cursing. I don't look down like she wants me to, knowing she'll go for my throat. Instead, I place my foot firmly down, ignoring the flare of pain that causes.

She's landed far more blows than any other before her. I'll give her that.

Still, I slice out, stopping my blade an inch before her eye, proving I might be human but I'm also a hunter. "Last warning," I tell her before pulling the blade back, then I walk backwards to the cage as the pain takes hold. I feel blood dripping a steady trail on the floor as I escape the cage.

Slamming the door, I pant as Lucien quickly chains it, leaping back as the wolf slams into the gate, and then with a knowing grin, she turns her back on us and paces around the cage.

"Fucking hell, Vale," Lucien snaps, leading me to a chair and pushing me down. He rips my trousers, further exposing the wound. I keep my eyes on the wolf, refusing to give her the pleasure of acknowledging the wound as Lucien cleans it and covers it as best as he can.

Just then, Jai walks in through the doors, covered in sweat, his shaggy hair pushed back.

"Get the prods. I want answers," I tell him.

Glee fills his eyes as he looks at the wolf. He'll get his wish—her pain.

She jerks her head back to me and bares her teeth, as if to tell me to bring it.

Oh, the little she-wolf has no idea what's coming her way.

She should have taken the easy way out.

CHAPTER ELEVEN

I challenged their leader, and from the dirty look he's giving me, he's mad, and now he's unleashed Jai on me. He's covered in sweat, and I inhale the aroma, noting the wild tint to it. Yes, Jai isn't completely human, but I have no idea what he is.

I glance at Vale to see him glaring at me as Lucien dresses and bandages his leg before shooting me a narrow-eyed, almost betrayed look. He's acting like they aren't actively keeping me prisoner and threatening to put my head above their mantle.

I look at Jai as he opens a trunk, the scent of his glee filling the air. Under that all is Vale's blood. It practically rings the dinner bell as it pools on the floor of my cage.

I took first blood, but he came for me, and he should have known better than to threaten an animal. I know there will be pain now, so I prepare by hardening myself to it.

Jai pulls out three long prods, the electric ones. Turning to me, he palms one as a wicked grin tugs at his lips, forcing his scar up. Despite the brutal, raw look of him, something inside me is drawn by the madness I see in that gaze.

Animal to animal.

When he sticks the prod through the bars, there is nowhere for me to escape. It slams into my side, and I jerk with the force, a whine leaving my lips before I force them shut. He pulls back, and I hurry to the other side of the cage to avoid it again. He laughs as he chases me. I hurry around, trying to avoid it, but there is only so far I can run, and the rod eventually slams into me again.

He keeps it pressed against my skin, the three prongs sending electricity through my body, locking me in a vault of pain until he finally releases me, and I stumble to the floor. My body refuses to move or listen to me, still jerking with aftershocks despite the prong being gone.

I glance at him to see him laughing and stroking the prong. "Hurts, doesn't it? It's got enough power to kill a grown human, but just enough juice to hurt monsters. It won't knock them out because that wouldn't do, but it hurts like a son of a bitch. I can lock you in that agony."

Gritting my teeth, I order my body to move, but it won't, and he sticks me again, making me snarl. Pulling back, he cackles maniacally, wandering around the cell. I stumble to my paws, swaying like I'm drunk as I try to escape him, but he stabs again, and I get slower until I writhe on the floor with the current.

My change wants to come, and I use all my strength to keep myself locked in wolf form despite the current tearing through my body.

"Enough," Lucien barks, and Jai steps back reluctantly as I pant.

I feel my body trying to heal the weakness, to combat the electricity still coursing through me. I can feel the stab marks from the prongs and the singed fur around it.

"Feel like talking now?" Vale asks.

Lifting my head, I meet his gaze and very purposely look down at his leg wound, which is bleeding through the bandages. Nostrils flaring, he turns away. "Carry on," he tells Jai.

Jai drags it out, prodding me and letting me recover before doing it again. I withstand it all. I stop trying to get up during the recovery period until Vale calls for him to stop. He watches me with a bitter grin on his lips.

Rolling my eyes, I force myself to stand on shaking paws, and his eyebrows rise as he meets my gaze. "Strong little she-wolf, aren't you?" he says. "No matter, everyone breaks eventually. I will give you time to think about it. You will have one more chance to speak voluntarily tomorrow, otherwise we'll be forced to start cutting parts of you off. Once the wolfsbane poison kicks in from those cuts, you won't have a choice. It will kill you." He sounds put off about that, like my death is an inconvenience in his plans. "But we cannot afford to be picky, can we?" He slams his fist into the bars, but I don't flinch.

"I'll stay. Lucien and Jai, go check the traps. Make sure there are no more ferals or pack. Be extra careful. They are probably staking out the ones we set for her," Vale commands as he heads behind the cage.

I keep them in my vision. Lucien and Jai shoot me looks before heading out. I hear the rumble of the car engine and almost grin gleefully, hoping the pack is waiting to rip them apart.

Turning, I watch Vale.

Despite his wounds, he picks up some knives and idly tosses them in his hands before throwing them in quick succession at the board placed up on one of the beams. I watch as he practices. He hits the bullseye each time. The circle of knives is so close, I'm surprised they don't fall. He never once misses, and it's clear he's letting me watch to scare me, but the idiot is also letting me know his strengths and weaknesses.

He's fast and good with blades, but I see him tiring from his wounds.

I can outlast him, not to mention his brother is his weakness.

He loves him a lot, enough to give in if I get the right leverage.

Settling back, I lick my wounds before drinking the bowl of water in the corner like a dog and watching Vale practice. He turns with some of his throws, and sometimes he watches me and throws it without looking.

I let my body heal as I observe him, and when he finally limps away, I'm the one who is smiling smugly. He stomps outside, and I relax, focusing on sorting through the scents to pinpoint my exact location. I plan on getting out of here, and when I do, I'll need to know the quickest way back to the pack.

Those three will be dead or dying. I'll make it quick for Lucien, but Jai will suffer.

I must nod off at some point because when I wake up with a start, it's to the skidding of tires and panicked shouting. I sit up and cock my head. The sound of doors slamming fills my ears as well as pained, heavy breathing. Inhaling deeply, I smell blood and, under all that, the distinctive, unmistakable scent of a feral.

That's what has me standing. Ferals all smell the same. When they break from the pack, their wolf turns sour. When the doors fly open, Vale and Jai carry a groaning Lucien between them. The sour smell is all over them—mainly Lucien, Jai too, but Lucien reeks of it.

They ignore me completely as Jai hurries over and knocks everything off one of the weapons tables, sending them scattering along the floor. They lay Lucien down.

"What happened?" Vale demands, his hands moving across Lucien's groaning form.

Jai swears, rushing to grab first-aid kits as I watch. I move around in my cage to get a better view, and I almost whistle when I do. Across his left pec is a ragged bite from a feral. It's ripped through most of the skin, and he's losing a lot of blood. He's pale and groaning. The wound smells bitter, so it's going to get infected. Ferals carry a lot of parasites and infections.

"Fucker was waiting outside one of the west side traps. He must have had a friend caught inside it. It masked him, and he leaped out at us. He was on Lucien before I could snap its neck." Jai grunts, ripping open bags and pressing gauze to the wound as Lucien roars, his back bowing in agony.

Vale swears. "Brother, it's okay," he says, trying to assure him, but even I can hear the panic in his voice.

Something in me twinges, and I don't know why.

Lucien gasps as Jai holds it there to staunch the bleeding. He grabs Vale, yanking him down. "Don't let me," he rasps.

"What? It's okay. You're safe," Vale replies.

"No, no, don't you dare let me turn!" he almost shouts. "Kill me. I won't be one of them. I'll die first."

"Luc." Vale pales and steps back, his hands covered in blood.

He looks so vulnerable and heartbroken, even I wince.

"No, give me the fucking gun. I won't turn!" Lucien bellows wildly.

Huh? I look at the bite. Oh, he thinks he'll turn. Some wolves have the ability to make wolves, but most don't because it's against our nature. Wolves are born, and those that are made are never quite right so we don't often do it. However, it would take a lot to turn a human. Most don't survive the change. Sniffing deeply, I confirm my suspicions.

I could let this play out—one of them will end up dead, maybe all—but for some reason, I find myself turning back to human form as Lucien grabs for weapons.

"You won't turn." My voice drops into the room, turning the chaos into silence.

They all turn. Vale kicks the cage, but I ignore him, my eyes on Lucien.

He sits up, pushes Jai away, and staggers to me, falling to his knees before the cage. "Are you lying, Quinn?"

"What?" Vale snaps.

"You know its name?" Jai demands.

I ignore them, meeting Lucien's worried eyes, seeing the panic there. He's afraid. I can taste it, and it's delicious. Another plan comes to mind, so I move closer and smile softly. "May I—"

He jerks back, and Vale points a gun at me.

I roll my eyes at him. "Do you want me to help your brother or not?"

Lucien ignores him, moving closer. "Quinn, please."

Ignoring Vale and the weapon pointed at me, I slide my hand through the bars, slowly so as not to spook them. I don't need a bullet through the head, thank you. Pulling the gauze aside, I slide my fingers into the wound, and as he grunts, I pull back, quickly dodging Vale's arm which snaps down to break mine.

Tugging it back through the bars, I suck the blood from my fingers, sorting through the tastes. Jai gags as Lucien pales, watching me. "You won't turn." I nod. "It takes a certain type of saliva to turn. Something in our blood recognises that in you, and we actively have to pump it out, like a snake and venom. He didn't want to turn you. He wanted to kill you. The bite doesn't have the venom, so you won't turn. You will always be this weak human."

He slumps, resting his head on the bars. "Thank you," he croaks.

"Don't believe it," Jai snarls.

"We can't trust what she says," Vale says slowly, "but let's just see how it goes."

"However, that wound is already infected." Lucien's eyes widen as I sit back, watching him. "Ferals have diseases, a lot of them. He spread whatever infection he carried into that bite. If it isn't healed properly, and it's not going to be by human medicine, then you will die from the infection, not the bite."

Jai and Vale burst into angry speeches, but I ignore them, keeping my eyes on Lucien. "Believe me or not, I have no reason to lie. I gain nothing from it. Lucien offered me kindness, so I offer it back. That wound is infected. You are going to die unless it's healed."

I change back and scurry away. Lucien watches me, even as they lift him back to the table.

"Ignore it. It's trying to get in your head," Vale snaps. "You're fine. You'll be fine."

Jai quickly washes the wound and gets to work, but Lucien keeps his eyes on me, and in his gaze, I see the truth—he knows he's going to die.

CHAPTER TWELVE

Jai and Vale do not leave his side. I almost soften at the show of comradery and friendship. Despite everything, they truly love each other, and it's obvious they are worried. Vale paces a lot, still wearing clothes with Lucien's dried blood. He's been cleaned, and the wound is dressed, but his eyes are moving behind his closed lids, restless even in sleep.

He's clammy and burning up. The infection is already setting in. I can smell it on him.

His sickness is in the air, polluting his blood.

As the night goes on, they begin to realise the same. He won't wake up, won't drink or eat, and even their human noses can smell the infection. "Let's go get some antibiotics." Jai hesitates because both know this isn't a human infection, which means it's not going to be treated by human medicine. It's hunter basics for sure.

There is no way for them to save him, and they know it.

Vale looks at me, clenching his jaw, and I wonder if he will walk right into my plan.

He has no choice but to trust an enemy. "What can heal him?" he finally asks.

"Vale," Jai snaps.

"It's my brother. I cannot let him die. I want to hear what she has to say," Vale roars, and Jai is silent for once. "I can't lose him," he tells Jai quietly, but I hear it.

When he looks back at me, he appears resigned and tired. "How? Tell me."

I shift back, sitting cross-legged in human form. Despite the situation, his eyes drop to my body before he jerks them back to my own. I pull my hair back, using curly brown strands to tie it off.

"A witch could, but the closest coven is two hundred miles away. He would be dead first. You could pray to the gods, but they don't tend to care about humans and they would let you die for fun. There's fey magic, of course, but tracking one would take days, and he would be dead."

"Tell me!" Vale demands. "Please."

"I can save him," I offer. "Healing is my talent. I can save your brother."

"But?" Vale demands. "Hurry up!"

"But I want something in return."

"What?" He breathes heavily, expecting me to demand my freedom.

I could, but I need information more, so that means staying here. "You leave my pack alone for one week—one full week."

His eye twitches. "No."

"Then your brother dies." I shrug, ready to turn back.

"Wait!" he says, looking at Lucien. "Is he truly dying?"

"Look with your own eyes. Your heart knows what your brain will not accept. I can smell the death and decay on him. If we wait much longer, he will be out of even my skill set," I admit truthfully. "I am not lying. I have nothing to gain from his death, but you will take it out on me."

He works through my logic while Jai glares at me the entire time, and when Vale turns around, his shoulders slump. "Deal. I'll let you out, and you'll save my brother. If you try anything, I'll kill you."

"Deal." Standing gracefully, I move to the door and wait.

Jai grabs a gun and points it at me, while Vale holds his knife and aims it towards my chest as he quickly unlocks the cage and swings it open. It's clear from his bunched muscles that he expects me to leap at him. I slowly walk out of the cage, uncaring about my nakedness, and move to Lucien.

"I need room," I tell Jai when he crowds me, getting in my way. I don't stop until my toes meet his, and I have to tilt my head up to meet his gaze. "If you want me to save him . . ."

"Jai, move. That's an order," Vale snaps.

"One move and I'll kill you," Jai threatens, running his gun down my chest.

I flex my hand and lift it, scraping one nail down his chest in the same movement. "I can kill you quicker, human, now move."

Something in his eyes darkens before he steps away, allowing me access. I move to Lucien's side, pressing my hand to his forehead. "He's slipping away," I say softly. "He may be too far gone."

I feel the barrel of a gun press to the back of my head. "Save him or you're dead."

Rolling my eyes, I press my hands to the wound, ignoring their swearing, and close my eyes once more. "Move the gun away, it's messing with my senses."

"Scared, little wolf?" Jai purrs in my ear.

"No, I'm annoyed. It is causing my natural predatory instinct to kick in, and I cannot heal him like that," I mumble.

"I don't think she can anyway. It's a trick," Jai snarls, but he steps back.

Sinking inside myself, I feel my wolf brush across me, and below that is the talent I keep hidden, one born from need and pain. Only Jang knows about it. Even for a wolf, it's unheard of. I slowly coax it out, knowing better than to force it. Years of secret practice taught me that.

I bring that moon magic from my soul, down my arm, and into

Lucien's body. I keep my eyes closed, but I feel him jerk. I know he's glowing a bright, mystic blue right now, and I hear them gasp.

I push it deeper, searching through his body. He has a fractured rib, so I heal that, and he has an out of place knee from an old injury. I right that as well before moving to his shoulder. I pour my magic into it, starting to heal it. My eyes open as I lift my other arm.

I ignore them as I tear my wrist open and smear my blood in the wound. "He needs the strength in my blood to combat it," I explain, which is partially true. He does, but it will also allow me to track him until it's out of his system, giving me the ability to know when they are coming.

My blood soaks into the wound as the poison is spat out. Black and oily, it rolls away from the wound and down his skin, and then his flesh starts to knit together. I heal as much as I can before dropping my arm and stepping back. There's a pink scar, but I cannot change that. He will bear the mark for life.

I turn to Vale. "It is done. The infection is gone, and I also healed his old wounds." I stumble a little then, feeling dizzy. He catches my arm for me, and I nod my head before ignoring them and moving back to the cell. Leaving the door open, I head inside and lie down, my back to them as I breathe through the weakness that always comes with healing.

Everything has a cost, and this one better be worth it.

CHAPTER THIRTEEN

I stare at her back as she breathes deeply, lying on the ground. My eyes rove unwillingly across her face, noting her beauty. In this form, her eyes are a deep brown, like turned soil, with flecks of amber and gold decorating her pupils. Her eyebrows slant over them as she shudders, wrapping herself tighter. Her face is sun-kissed, though paling now, and dusted with freckles. Her lips are plump with a perfect Cupid's bow and an unnatural pink hue that has me looking away. Her hair, though messy, would no doubt fall in curls down to her waist, maybe even lower. It's a deep brown with a million other shades of brown and blonde intertwined through it. Unlike my last girlfriend, I can tell her hair colour is real, not box died. She's beautiful, with an overly innocent face, sharp, high cheekbones, and an adorable nose and chin.

My eyes drop to her body. Some scars litter her limbs, which gives me pause, knowing how serious the wounds must have been to scar since wolves heal so quickly. Her legs are long, and her feet are tiny and covered in dirt and blood from the cage. Her hips are slightly rounded, and her breasts are small and high, tipped with rosy nipples. When she flexes, I see an impressive eight pack. She's both muscular and feminine.

In her wolf form, she was impressive.

In her human form, she is a knockout.

She's also young, probably even a few years younger than I am.

For a moment, guilt fills me. It's easy to hunt monsters when they are monsters, but when they look so human, it becomes harder.

While she healed Lucien, she glowed like the moon was trapped under her skin. Her hair shone with it, and when I peeked at her face, there were crescent and full moons decorating her forehead, though she seemed oblivious.

This is no normal wolf. She is something else, which means we can't kill her.

We need to understand first, but this also means we have time since I made a promise I intend to keep. As long as Lucien survives, so will her pack, at least for another week.

I glance back to her face, wondering why she bargained for that and not her life. She could have, but she chose her people rather than her own safety.

Why?

"Vale?" Lucien groans, interrupting my train of thought.

My eyes jerk back to him as I grab his hand and hold it tight. "Brother?" I murmur.

His eyes flutter open as he flexes his body, no doubt checking every muscle—an old habit to make sure we haven't lost any limbs. "Shit," he mutters.

"How do you feel?" I ask, panic still lacing my voice no matter how calm I want to remain. I nearly lost him. I cannot lose my brother. I might be the leader, but he's my family, my backbone. Without him, there is no reason to go on.

"I feel—" He blinks, swallowing. "Fucking great, better than I have in years, like someone just shot adrenaline into my heart or some shit."

I turn my eyes back to her to see her shaking in the cage, curled into a ball. "Is that so?"

"Vale," he snaps, and I turn back to him, using my hand to haul him up so he can sit. He glances at the cage, and that reminds me to ask him about how he knew her name later. "She saved me."

My nostrils flare, and I ignore Jai's angry snort. "Yes, but why?"

He shrugs, his eyes going back to the cage. We were so distracted, I forgot about the open cell door, but she hasn't moved. If anything, she seems to be ignoring us.

"Quinn," he asks, sliding to his feet, "are you okay?"

I see her arms tighten around her body and frown. Rounding the cage, I crouch and try to peer through the mass of hair to see her face, but she's hidden away. Tremors run through her every limb.

"She's faking. It's a trick to help her escape," Jai snarls.

"I don't think she's faking it," I murmur. "Quinn, when you healed Lucien, did it hurt you?"

Her head lifts slowly, sluggishly, and her deep eyes swallow my soul as they peer through her locks. "Like you would care. You got what you needed. If you don't mind, at least give me a little time to recover before you start the torture."

"Like fuck," Jai snarls. "You bargained for your pack. You're lucky we don't hunt them and use them for ornaments. Now tell us everything or we will make whatever this is worse."

I hold up my hand, stopping him. As I stare into her dark eyes, I realise that since I met this wolf, this is the first time she's looked vulnerable.

"We will let you rest." I should thank her for saving Lucien, but I know she did it for her own reasons. I understand wanting to save your family, and that scares me. I understand this monster when we are sworn enemies.

She drops her eyes again, and something in that action makes me carry on.

"Look at me," I demand, and those haunting eyes rise and clash with mine, making my heart skip a beat. "We might be enemies, but

I will not break my word. You can trust me in that. Rest now, we will speak tomorrow." I stand and lock the cage then move to stand with Jai. He's not going to like this one fucking bit.

His crazed eyes flash, and his nostrils flare as he stares at me. "Are you really letting that beast rest?"

"We have a deal—"

"For the pack. I know you value your integrity, even with monsters, but we made no deals for her. We need the information," he hisses.

"And we'll get it, but not this way. I don't feel right torturing an injured woman—beast," I correct. "After she saved my brother, do you? We can allow her to recover so we'll face a worthy opponent."

"That is a weakness. It is an animal, not a person, no matter what it looks like. They are more deadly when injured. She is playing you. She wouldn't hesitate to rip our jugulars out if we were injured," he snarls, tilting his head to go toe to toe with me.

"And that's what separates us from monsters," I remind him, knowing how he feels about wolves.

"You're weak," he spits. "Maybe you shouldn't be leading us."

I step closer until our noses almost touch. "Are you challenging me, Jai?" I ask, speaking my words very carefully.

His eyes narrow as he debates his next course of action. A challenge amongst hunters is no quiet affair. If he challenges me to lead this team, one of us could very well end up dead, and despite what he thinks, we both know I'm not weak.

"Well?" I demand.

"Guys," Lucien says, always trying to calm us down. He's the most rational of us all, but right now, this doesn't require rational thought. This requires action, so when Jai jerks his hand out, I'm ready. I won't kill Jai, but I can remind him why I'm in charge.

Despite the madness inside him, he is no match for me.

Grabbing his hand, I spin us and kick his leg, wrapping my arm around his neck and squeezing. "Calm down," I order as he snarls and kicks, hitting my side with his fist as I grunt from the impact.

A bitter, feminine laugh makes us all turn to see the wolf sitting at the bars of her cage. Her face is still pale, but some colour is coming back to her cheeks. "And you have the nerve to look down on us and call us monsters. We are not so different, challenging and fighting amongst yourselves for leadership. Does that remind you of anything?" She winks before lying down again as I thrust Jai away.

"You're making a mistake," Jai snarls, "and you know it. You've never hesitated before, and that's the reason I'm here. You do what must be done. You're the best. If that changes, if you start to help the monsters, I won't hesitate to kill you." He storms out of the warehouse.

Sighing, I look at Lucien who nods. "I'll go after him and calm him down." He claps his hand onto my shoulder. "You're doing the right thing." His eyes go to the cage for a moment before he shakes his head and follows Jai outside, leaving the wolf and me.

Grabbing a chair, I swing it around and drape my arms across the wooden back as I meet her curious brown eyes. She's still shaking, but her quick healing is kicking in and fixing whatever the healing broke in her.

I envy wolves in some aspects.

"Your name is Quinn?" I don't know why I'm speaking to her other than the fact that we clearly cannot just ignore her.

She cocks her head but remains silent, and I smile.

"Oh, now you're quiet?" I taunt.

"I thought you said no torture today, Vale." I jerk at my name on her lips. Her soft, silken voice caresses it almost like a lover's touch. Shaking my head at that foolishness, I focus on her words.

"I'm not. We are simply having a conversation."

"Through bars," she retorts, making my lips quirk. She's quick, I'll give her that. Even now, locked behind bars, she is unafraid and watching me casually, like she has all the time in the world and isn't surrounded by hunters willing to skin her alive for what she is.

"They are there for our safety," I say kindly, thinking maybe I can get what I need this way.

"Very true. Human bodies break so easily." She smirks, holding up her hand, and as I watch, wicked, sharp claws take over, and she clicks them together while grinning at me.

"Now, some might take that as a threat, wolf," I warn.

"Then they wouldn't be fools," she replies, changing her hand back as she watches me. I let the silence stretch on.

"Fine, I at least owe you my thanks—"

"That isn't how you thank someone." She grins. "Say the words properly."

Grinding my teeth, I try to breathe through my annoyance and stop myself from pulling my gun and shooting her smirking face. "Thank you for saving my brother."

"Better." She nods.

She watches me as I just stare at her. "Why did you do it?" I ask, needing to know. "Don't just say for your pack. Why did you save him, wolf?"

I expect some flippant response, but she surprises me when she seems to debate her answer, and when it comes, I know it's truthful.

"Someone saved me, an enemy, a very long time ago, and I am simply returning the favour." My eyebrows furrow as I try to figure out her answer as she stands. I force my eyes to her face and not on her naked body.

"If you're not torturing me today, may I use the bathroom and shower? I might be a wolf, but I don't wish to live in my own filth."

"Why would I let you out?" I murmur, still stuck on her words.

She rolls her eyes. "You can watch me with a gun trained on me at all times if it makes you feel better, Vale. Unless you're scared . . ."

Smart, little wolf.

Before I can question myself or let the others find out, I open the cage and pull out my gun, using it to gesture to the bathroom. "Be quick before I change my mind."

She strolls from the cage like she owns the joint and heads to the bathroom. I follow her in—I'm not a total idiot. She moves to the shower, turning it on and stepping inside with a grateful sigh. The sound heads straight to my cock.

The shock of that makes me jerk my eyes away, even as I keep my gun trained on her, but when she hums, I can't help but look back. That madness fades, though, when she lifts her arm and I see something I hadn't before.

Burn marks stretch across it like a diagonal scar. She must feel my gaze because she looks at me and then the scar. "I got this when I was a child. It never healed since I was so young." She turns away to wash.

I stare at her in disbelief.

It can't be, can it?

Old memories flash through my brain, memories I would rather forget. Memories of a weak moment and a scared kid . . . and a girl.

When I blink, it's to find her stepping from the shower. She quickly towels off, wringing her hair and leaving it wet before heading to the toilet. I let her have privacy in there, and when she comes back, I watch as she washes her hands.

Surely it can't be her.

What in the fuck kind of fucked up fate would that be?

Heading my way, she stops before me, her nipples peeking through her hair, begging to be touched.

This wolf has a body made for rough nights and hard, dirty sex, and she knows it.

"See something you like?" she teases, pressing her wet body to mine, letting me feel every soft inch as I peer down at her.

Pressing the gun to her head, I watch her eyes flare as I lean down like I'm going to kiss her. "You wish, wolf. Your body cannot save you from this." I step back, acting unaffected as I gesture for her to go ahead of me.

She saunters from the bathroom and back towards her cage.

My eyes flow down her wet hair to her drying, naked body, unable to resist.

Something stirs inside me, something that cannot be real—desire.

When I lift my eyes, it's to find her watching me over her shoulder with a knowing look in her gaze.

Fuck.

CHAPTER FOURTEEN

Quinn

W hen I get back into the cage, I turn to face Vale.

"Erm, do you want clothes?" Vale asks, sounding embarrassed, and when I sniff, I scent his unwanted desire and shame. It's natural. I am a healthy human woman, and he's a healthy male not used to our nakedness.

"Why?" I ask, making him more uncomfortable.

"Forget it," he grumbles before leering at my body and turning away just in time for the other two to come back in.

Jai glares daggers at me before storming to the weapons table and taking a gun apart. The smell of the oil and gunpowder mixed with wolfsbane fills the air as he cleans it. It's clear he's preparing to take on my pack.

Lucien checks me over, as if making sure I'm okay, before nodding at Vale. The two of them move over to the cots and sit together with their heads bent, whispering. They seem to think that will make it impossible for me to hear, the idiots, but I don't tell them since it will only make them hide what they are discussing and it could be important.

"I got a call while we were out there. It seems the pack she's from is enraged. There have been five hunter deaths since her capture. They have turned up with their throats torn out and warnings written on their skin. They want her returned now, and we were right. She's important. The boss knows someone has this wolf, but he doesn't know who yet. He wants answers, and he wants to deliver the wolf's head to them."

"If the pack is attacking, it means they are exposing themselves, so that's good. We only have seven days before they are fair game," Vale mutters.

My wolf bays in anger, wanting to rip him limb from limb for daring to threaten my people. They are innocents just trying to live their lives.

"What do we do with Quinn—her until then?" Lucien asks.

"We will discuss the name situation later, but for now, we'll let her rest. Tomorrow, we'll begin again. We need all the information we can get if we are to take her pack down."

"She's smarter than we thought. She won't make it easy." Lucien sighs. "And now that she saved me, I feel wrong for torturing her."

"Don't forget who she is, brother. She is the enemy, nothing more."

Keep telling yourself that, boys, I think, but their wavering commitment is good for me and my plans. Jai, however, is a different story.

I watch his back carefully, wondering how I'm going to get what I need and get out of here. I need to warn the pack, but I need everything I can get first. Clearly, the hunters are organised and someone is in charge.

"I know that." Lucien sighs. "Boss is pulling the hunters back to the southern outpost. We, as well as a few others, are the only ones in the field, so this needs to be sorted quickly."

Interesting. How many outposts do they have?

When they finally stop talking and go about their day, my stomach rumbles loudly. A bowl plops through my cage a little while later, filled with ready instant noodles. I glare at the food and then

Vale, who's standing before me with his arms crossed. "What, not good enough, wolf?"

"Us wolves have high metabolisms, so we need red meat and to eat frequently or we weaken," I admit foolishly.

"Good." He walks away.

Asshole. Knowing some food is better than none, I pick up the bowl and demolish the noodles before sliding it back through. Ignoring them, I curl up in the middle and try to relax my body, needing to rest a little. I know I can't stay here forever, and if they are under pressure, they will kill me to protect themselves, with or without the information, which means I need to get what I need and leave soon.

I fall asleep, but anger and pain follow me into my dreams, conjuring up memories I would rather forget.

Agony tears through my arm as the falling wooden beam spears it. Screaming, I yank out the wood as tears flow down my face. Gripping my injured, bleeding arm, I stumble from the back door like they ordered.

My heart is breaking.

Turning with a sob, I peer at the house engulfed in flames, and when the roar comes from within, I stumble back, crying harder. For a moment, I hesitate before their reminder flutters in my mind.

You must live. Run fast.

Knowing I cannot let their sacrifice be for nothing, I turn and flee towards the forest. I pump my arms as fast as I can despite the agony tearing through my injured one, knowing I cannot be caught.

If I do, I will die here tonight along with them.

No, I must survive. I promised them.

I race towards the trees as fast as I can, plunging into the welcoming shadows. Nature welcomes me despite the heat burning my back from the flames of my childhood home.

The smell of smoke fills my lungs, choking me. The acidic taste makes me gag, and bile claws at my throat as tears burn in my eyes. I turn to look, watching the flames eat what's left of my life, before spinning around and sprinting towards the forest.

It's my haven, the one place I know I'll be safe if I can just get there.

I pump my legs and arms faster, pushing my body for all it's worth. If I don't, I'll die here just like everyone else.

Run! The roar is just in my head, the memory echoing inside me. I sob and stumble, the agony and hopelessness of that one howled word slicing through my heart and soul.

"Wolf! I found a wolf!"

I spin, wide-eyed, to stare at the boy who spoke.

He is half covered in shadows, but he's small, only a little older than me, but my nose tells me he's human despite my senses being burned away.

"Please," I whisper as I hear yells behind me.

"Search the woods for any others!"

He swallows hard, and no more words leave his lips as I stumble closer, wincing and covering my bleeding arm as I cry. "Please." I fall to my knees as exhaustion and pain tear through me. My wolf, which has been trapped inside me up until now, bays within me for help.

For revenge.

The human boy takes a step closer, peering at me as I lift my tear-stained face to the full moon and stare right back, knowing I'll die.

I failed them.

Biting his lip, he kneels in the mud before me. "Go, run. I won't tell them."

"Why?" I whisper, staring into his bright eyes as he smiles softly.

"Maybe I don't want to be like them," he tells me as he stands and steps past me. "I found a wolf!" He runs in the opposite direction as they all follow him, and I turn back to the forest, seeing a clear escape.

For a moment, my eyes track the human boy before going to the flames, and then I turn and flee.

"Wake up." Cold water splashes across my face as a bowl slides in next to me. I jerk up and stare into bright blue eyes as he crouches before me, and for a moment, I see the boy from my past, not the hateful man, before it fades.

"Drink," he commands. "We can't have you dying of thirst."

With my eyes on him, I pick up the bowl and drink it before

holding it out to him. "Thank you," I tell him softly, and he startles before grabbing it. His fingers touch mine and for a moment, we freeze like that.

Call it the aftereffect of dreams, but I could swear I know Vale. It disappears, though, as he jerks away and stands. "Sleep. Tomorrow, we begin again."

I watch him storm away before I look at the door to see the moon hanging low. It's late, and tomorrow will be here soon, as will their need for answers.

CHAPTER FIFTEEN

Quinn

Dawn comes, and the hunters wake up. I watch them as they go about their business, showering and dressing before eating together. All signs of aggression and anger from yesterday are gone. Jai even jokes with them, and it's clear they have a strong bond.

If I can break that, I might get a chance to protect my pack.

I will do anything to keep them safe, even destroy these three, and I would even enjoy it. Despite their kindness yesterday, we are still enemies, and if it came to it, I would rip them to pieces to keep the people who gave me a home safe.

I am a wolf and they are hunters, so there is only one way this will end—with death.

It will not be me.

After they eat, they clean up, and their attention turns to me.

"Are you ready to talk now, wolf?" Vale asks as Jai heads over to the table and hums as he picks out his torture equipment for the day. I watch as he selects a large, three-pronged knife, which he dips into a mixture.

I sniff. Wolfsbane and . . . pixie cum?

That creates a hallucinatory effect and enhances pain.

How lovely.

"Wait, who drained the pixie's cock?" I ask.

"I'll take that as a no." Vale sighs as if he's disappointed, and Jai heads my way.

Just as they are about to start, Vale's phone rings.

The sharp sound splits the air. Vale frowns and plucks his phone from his pocket, lifting it to his ear and wandering far enough away so I cannot hear what's happening on the other side.

Asshole.

When he comes back, his face is shut down and cold as he glares at me then swings his gaze to Jai and Lucien.

"We need to go. There was an attack. They need backup," Vale snaps.

"Who stays?" Jai snarls.

"Not you." Vale sighs before looking at Lucien. "Luc, you stay."

"He can't be trusted with her," Jai argues.

"He'll stay. Come on, I'm sure you can get your bloodlust out." They storm outside, and I watch them go, praying whoever or whatever they are hunting isn't my pack.

An attack, they said. Please, moons, don't let it be my people.

Lucien sighs and sits heavily, propping his elbows on his knees as he watches them go. "It wasn't wolves or they would have said that." I whirl around to face him. "So don't worry. There have been some weird attacks on humans recently. Something dead is eating them. It's probably that."

"Why tell me?" I ask.

"Because I'd want to know if it was my family as well, and we don't break our word."

Pursing my lips, I sit and watch him. With nothing else to do, I find myself talking to him. "Something dead? A vamp?"

"No, it wasn't drained. Parts of it were eaten."

"So a ghoul," I murmur. "They cut it away and eat it, usually cooked. Zombie? But the voodoo queen is down south for the summer, and I don't know anyone else who raises them around here."

"We thought zombie," he replies. "Why wouldn't it be zombies? Can anyone raise them?"

"No, not really. The voodoo queen is of old magic, so she can. Necromancers could for sure, but there aren't any left. They were hunted into extinction by your kind and even their own—witches," I tell him.

"Witches couldn't do it then?" He frowns.

"No, it requires a certain type of magic to reanimate a corpse" I tilt my head. "Look for a human sacrifice site at local graves—blood and organs, that type of thing." I shrug.

"Why?" he asks, leaning forward.

"Because if there has been a summoning, it will be there, and it's for dark magic." I watch him, not smiling anymore. I don't know why I told him that. I might not like dark magic or witches, but I shouldn't betray them to hunters.

We aren't the same kind, but we are on the same side.

"Thank you," he tells me. "We'll do that."

Nodding, I lapse into silence, staring at him like he's staring at me—two enemies, locked together through our actions, unsure what to do. I saved him, but he owes me nothing, so he can still kill me.

"You know, you look at my brother like you know him," he comments quietly, surprising me.

I say nothing, waiting to see where he is going with this.

"But you are a wolf, so it's not like you would just meet. You know him, though, I see it. You weren't sure at first, but today, something changed in your gaze." Fuck, he's good, really good. "How do you know him?"

I say nothing, and he leans forward.

"Was it you?" I blink, unsure what he's getting at. "Years ago in the forest, the wolf he saved."

I blink hard, unsure what to say, my whole body going cold.

How does he know?

The eyes were the same. Is it really the same boy who saved me?

Vale . . . No, it can't be. He was so kind, and he saved me that night from the hunters. He said he didn't want to be like them. Did he mean the hunters? Yet here he is. How could that kind boy who saved a strange wolf girl turn into such a hateful man?

"I saw it all, you know. I saw my little brother save a little girl who was a wolf." I swallow. He could be bluffing. "It was the thirteenth of the month. There was a swing set and slide outside. I know because I was jealous. The house was wooden and large, with a mat that read 'ignore the guard dog' with a picture of a wolf. The girl was wearing a pale pink nightie with wolves on it."

My heart stutters as he speaks. Every detail is right.

He was there. Lucien was there, which means he's not lying.

Vale was the boy who saved my life. Does he remember? Does he care?

He carries on since I don't reply. "If the others knew, they would kill him for what he did that night. He betrayed not only our people, but our father for you. Even Jai would kill him. Please don't be the reason my brother dies. He saved you that night, so you owe him. Please, Quinn, I am begging you. I don't know how this will end, but I beg of you. Do not kill my brother, repay the debt you owe."

Breathing in deeply, I meet his raw eyes and see his worry. How long has Lucien held onto this secret to protect his brother?

Probably as long as I've kept it from everyone, including Jang and Marie.

I never told them who saved me that night. I simply told them I managed to escape while the hunters' focus was on everyone else. They believed me, never questioning it, more bothered with their own anger and grief.

"I have no reason to spill that secret. It does nothing for me either," I admit slowly. "But you and I are enemies. Vale and I are enemies. He will try to kill me. You all will. That's the only way this ends. I won't tell anyone that secret out of honour for what he did that night, but I will kill him when the time comes. No matter what he did. He made a choice that night, and I am making one now. If it comes down to me or him, I will choose myself."

"I can understand that. We are enemies after all," he murmurs. "That night . . . there were others in the house. Who were they to you?"

My breath freezes in my chest as I stare into his eyes. "Your father . . . he was the hunter?"

He frowns. "He led them."

I swallow again before smiling bitterly. "Then I owe you nothing. Your father killed my parents." He jerks, his eyes widening. "He killed my pregnant mother, my alpha father, and he murdered my little sister who was barely a year old."

Anger, an old fury I cannot contain, flows through me as I get to my knees. I wrap my hands around the bars and squeeze until they bend. He watches it happen, his mouth open. "I hope he's dead. I hope he suffered."

His eyes harden. Despite what his father did, if he agreed or not, it's his father.

"You are a monster." He gets to his feet.

I laugh, the sound cold and cruel. "Me? What does that make you? I have never killed a man, but how many have you killed, Lucien? How many has your brother killed? How many did your father kill? I know he slaughtered innocent families and children, so tell me, hunter, who is the real monster here? The one who looks the part or the one who acts it?" I laugh bitterly. "You think you are the hero of this story, but the truth is, human, you are the villain."

I turn away, changing back to my wolf form.

I'm furious, but the reminder was good. These men are monsters. They are evil. Their father killed my family.

He killed the people I loved the most in this world, and whether or not Vale saved me that night, they are evil and deserve everything that is coming to them.

I ignore Lucien all day as he smashes his fist into punching bags as I sleep, my body tired from the lack of exercise and meat. As if conjured by Lucien's words, the memories of that night overwhelm me, dragging me into their horrifying depths I have tried to escape ever since that night.

"Mum?" I whisper.

She turns to me, her soft, familiar brown eyes searching my face, glassy with tears. "I'm scared," I admit.

"Shh, it's going to be okay," she tells me as she drops to her knees before me, gripping my face. Her belly presses to mine, my little brother kicking me. I swear it's going to be a boy, and she believes me. I can't wait. I love my sister, but she won't play with me, so I want a boy to play with in the mud. A tear drips down her cheek as she shivers and a bang sounds from the front of the house. "I need you to listen to me carefully, Quinn, okay?"

I nod, looking over her shoulder as my father hurries into the room, barring the door as he throws his phone with a snarl. "They are too far away," he growls, looking at us. My sister is sleeping peacefully on the sofa in the office we hid in when those bad men pulled up outside. "Willa." For the first time ever, my father looks weak.

"I know," she tells him, crying harder, and he comes over, holding her and reaching for me too. "Listen, Quinny. When I tell you to, you run, and you run as fast as you can."

"I can run really fast." I grin.

"I know you can, baby. Today, I need you to push harder than you ever have, okay? You run, and you don't stop until you find Jang. Do you remember him?"

I nod. "Daddy's friend."

"That's right." My dad grins. "Good job, baby. You run, and you don't stop until you meet him, okay?"

"But what about you and Filly?" I look at my sister. Her thumb is in her mouth as she sleeps soundly. She only just turned back into her human

form. Mummy says I wasn't stuck in it like she was when she was younger. She calls me special, but sometimes I would like to be a wolf like she was.

"Don't worry about us, okay? We'll be right behind you," my mum promises, even as she cries and another bang comes. Something nasty smelling makes my nose wrinkle.

"Jase," she murmurs, and he wraps us in his arms, holding us tight.

"I'm so sorry, Willa," he says. "I'll buy as much time as I can. Take the girls—"

"No, we need to give them the best opening to get away." Mummy pulls away, kissing him. "I promised you forever, mate. I promised to be with you through both good and bad. I will be at your side, and that is where I'll stay."

"Will, I cannot . . ." He shakes his head. "I cannot win against this many. I cannot lose you. Go, take the girls out back."

"They will find us. I am too slow this late in the pregnancy. I'll stay. We'll fight together, giving the girls a shot." Mum's eyes go to Filly, and she sobs. "She won't be fast enough."

"Mummy, what's wrong? What's that smell?"

It smells like that time we had a bonfire under the full moon. The air starts to heat like it did then, as I hear laughter and a crash.

"They are coming in," Daddy says, looking at me and Filly. "She won't be able to carry her." Picking Filly up, he wraps her in a blanket and passes her to Mummy. "When I say so, run."

"Not without you," Mum snarls, her eyes flashing with her wolf.

Daddy says she can't change while she's pregnant or it will hurt my brother, so I tug her hand, trying to calm her down. It usually works when Daddy annoys her. She squeezes my hand harder. "We have no time, change." Putting Filly before me, my mum turns and pulls a fire poker from the side, standing before me with one hand on her belly.

"When I tell you, you run, okay? Don't you look back, no matter what you hear. You run as fast as you can. Don't you dare stop, baby." She sobs, her hand shaking on the poker. "Mummy loves you so much, Quinny, know that."

"Daddy loves you." He leans forward and kisses me. "Run, my Quinny.

Run like the wind, okay?" His eyes turn bright amber. "I will see you again, in this life or the next." He turns, changing into the big brown wolf I love to cuddle with, making me grin as a feeling of safety wafts over me.

His tail isn't wagging today, though, and when the wolf leaps at the door with a mighty roar, I start to cry. "Mummy."

"Shh, Quinn, stay quiet," she begs, holding the poker out.

Filly wakes as the door smashes in, the sound loud and scary. I cover my ears, even as Filly crawls into my arms and I hold her tight. "It's okay, sissy. I've got you," I tell her.

Men in black pour through the door, and my dad lunges at them, snarling and biting as they flow in. My mum runs at them, brandishing the poker.

The sound makes me whimper, and I curl around Filly.

"Filly." I look down, seeing her eyes open wide as they turn bright. "Filly, no!" I scream as Filly turns in my lap, changing into a small brown wolf. With a snarl, she leaps at the men attacking Mummy and Daddy and bites a man's leg.

I watch in horror as one of them grabs her and throws her into the wall, a sickening thud reaching me. "Filly!" I race to her, crying, when something hits my back. Holding her little wolf body, I pull my hands away and see the blood there. "Mummy, something is wrong. Filly won't wake up." I turn when there's a scream and see my mum fall.

There is a sword through her chest, pinning her to the floor, her stomach arched up and moving with my brother inside. She turns her head to me, tears falling down her face. Blood flows from her mouth as she makes her lips work. "Run, Quinn."

There's an agonised roar as my father shakes off the men on him and barrels through them to me. He grabs me then tosses me. I fly through the air with a scream, smashing through the wall in the office to the hallway beyond. Climbing to my feet, I peer into the hole to see the wolf backing up, protecting it, and when he turns to me, I see his silent words.

"Run, Quinny!"

I glance at my mummy, who isn't moving, then to Filly, who also isn't moving, as my dad roars and the men move closer. Sobbing, I turn and run.

I snap awake with a scream, my hand going to my heart and then drifting up to my face to feel the tears there. I don't know when I changed back, but I did.

I'm as human as I was then. I never understood why I wasn't able to change until after that night. Maybe if I had been able to earlier, I could have saved them—

"Bad dream?" Lucien asks kindly, but I cannot take it.

I change back into my wolf, unable to look at him without seeing my mum, dad, and Filly, not to mention my brother who was never born.

Filly never got to grow up, run with the pack, fall in love and mate, and find her happiness. Mum and Dad never got the peace they wanted and a house overflowing with pups and people. All that devastation was because of men like the one I saved.

The one who saved me.

We are equal now. He saved me, and I saved his brother.

Now, nothing stands in the way of me killing them all.

CHAPTER SIXTEEN

Quinn

When they come back, Vale eyes me with a frown, noting my snarl. His eyes cut to Lucien, and I see a question in his gaze.

"How did it go?" Lucien asks instead.

"It was a massacre. Ten dead. Half of the bodies were eaten so we couldn't even identify who they were. We tried to help them track whatever did it, but it was long gone. Boss has assigned half the unit to track and kill it since so many humans are in danger, but he was suspicious about what was happening with us and where you were. We don't have much time."

"So let's kill her now," Jai snarls.

Lucien looks at me, as does Vale. "Not yet, we still need—"

"What? We can draw the pack out with her dead body. They'll smell her. Stop making excuses just because you want to stick your dick in that monster—"

"Enough!" Vale roars, and Jai's mouth snaps shut. "I am sick of you questioning me. If you have a problem, submit a request to transfer, otherwise be quiet."

Jai stares at him in shock, as if he has never heard him lose his temper before. "Fine, I will after this mission. You are not the man I thought you were."

With one last glare at me, Jai heads out again, no doubt to kill innocent animals or some psycho shit.

Vale glares at me and storms past Lucien, who sighs, and then his head swings to me. There is blame in his eyes.

Snorting, I lie back down, exhausted. I am starving, and I need to conserve energy between all these shifts, the healing, and torture.

I can almost feel myself slipping into a deep sleep, which is dangerous, but I cannot stop it.

I'm drained.

The storm wakes me, the roar of thunder rattling the cage bars as lightning brightens the room. I blame the lack of food for making me sleep for so long. I come to with a gasp and scramble to my feet, my eyes widening when I see Jai opening the cage door with a gun in his hand.

Fuck!

Looks like he has given up playing games. He will kill me tonight to end this. My nostrils flare as he comes at me.

I don't shift back, and when he pulls the trigger, I dodge the first bullet and leap at him, smacking him to the side. The gun skids across the floor, even as he throws me into the bars. I get up quickly, using all my energy to fly at him, and he falls back, his arms coming up to stop my teeth from sinking into his neck. I claw and kick at him, gnawing on his arms as he reaches for the gun with his hand. With a grunt, he kicks me off, and I go flying once more.

Landing on my feet, I lunge at him again as he grabs the weapon. This time, I bite the gun, crushing it, and toss it away before changing and pinning him with one arm across his throat. As I stab my claws into his neck, I watch him bleed, knowing I pierced the artery there. He stops struggling, and his eyes widen as he realises he received a killing blow.

Leaning in, I sniff him hard. "For someone who is part wolf, you truly hate your own kind." I push off him, pulling my claws out, and watch his blood spurt as he covers his neck. I leap at the cage door.

It bursts open, falling to the ground as Lucien and Vale stumble to their feet. I spare them a glare as I land on my knees and then race outside into the pouring rain. Lightning arcs across the sky, the ground shaking with the thunder as I jump up and over the fence and then plunge into the forest beyond, changing into my wolf as soon as I am within the shelter of trees.

My body is dragging with exhaustion, but I don't stop running.

For the second time in my life, I am running from hunters.

From Vale.

CHAPTER SEVENTEEN

"G o after her!" Vale roars, flying out of the open door.

I spare a gasping Jai one look and take off after my brother and Quinn, adrenaline pumping through me so hard, my heart races.

I had been in a deep sleep before the gun and the crash of the cage door woke me, but it didn't take long to figure out what happened.

I'm instantly drenched, the rain almost obscuring my vision as thunder rolls and lightning cracks.

"Go that way!" Vale orders as he sprints towards the other side of the forest. I hesitate only for a moment before hurrying into the trees, stilling at the clear paw prints I see in the mud, leading deeper into the forest. My hunting instincts kick in, and I follow the path easily, even when it twists and turns, leading me astray until I find her.

My head jerks up as a growl splits the air and she slinks from the trees, leaping up onto a huge boulder. Her head is lowered in a threatening posture, and her paws are spread. She's ready to pounce.

There's a snap deeper into the forest, and she glances away for a moment. It gives me my chance, but I don't move. I just stare as rain streams down my face, chilling me to the bone as my clothes plaster against my body and lightning cracks overhead, illuminating her dark fur.

The wolf turns back to me, her blue eyes blazing. I have my gun, I could kill her, but for a moment, I see Quinn, not the wolf, and like my brother did all those years ago, I step back.

Her snarl subsides, and she cocks her head, no doubt wondering if it's a trap. I don't blame her. I don't know either.

"Now we're even," I tell her and turn away, letting her leave. When I meet Vale back at the front of the old mill, his blue eyes narrowed, I shake my head.

"I couldn't see her. She must be long gone."

"Fuck!" he roars, tugging at his hair until we hear a cough and we spin.

Jai stumbles from the mill, clutching his throat as blood pours through his fingers. Water slides down his pale face as he crumples to his knees. "Help me."

I'm there in an instant. I lift him and carry him inside, laying him on his cot as Vale rushes over, first-aid kit in tow. "Let me see," he demands as Jai shakes his head, his eyes wide and terrified.

He has the look of a man who can see his death.

We have seen it too many times, and we all know how vicious a wound like this is. He doesn't have long, and Vale and I exchange looks—we both know it.

"You idiot," Val says, his voice softening. "Now let's save your life so I can kill you myself for losing our best bet."

Jai's hands drop, covered in his blood, as he swallows rapidly, causing more to pour from the jagged wounds on his neck. His eyes roll around in fear as he pales further. Swearing, Vale packs the wound, and I do the same, both of us staring at each other above him.

It's fatal.

"My fault," Jai croaks, swallowing as he shudders in the cot.

Blood and water drip to the floor, the sound loud even above the thunder and lightning. "I let my hate win."

"Shh," I say as I look at Vale. "What about the pixie—"

"It won't work." I see his thoughts flash across his face as he thinks, trying to come up with a plan, and when his jaw grinds, I know he doesn't have one.

"No, we have to do something." I search the kit and push Vale's hands away. I sprinkle the last of the stolen pixie magic across the wound before covering it.

Jai coughs. "Kill them all. Promise me."

"Shut up for once," Vale replies. "You aren't dying tonight, not yet. You'll kill the fuckers yourself."

Something flashes in Jai's eyes as the moon moves from behind the storm clouds and lights up the mill, and for a moment, his eyes reflect it and shine inhumanly bright. I blink, wondering if I'm seeing things, but it disappears.

"Hold it there," Vale commands, and Jai's eyes shut. "No, stay with us!" he roars, and we watch in horror as his head falls lifelessly to the side.

Vale leans down, pressing his ear to his chest, then he lifts his head, his eyes wide in horror. "He's . . . He's dead."

"No." I lift my hands and step back. Jai is a pain in the ass, but he's one of us. He's like a little brother to me, even if he's a fucking psycho.

Quinn killed him, and I let her go.

Horror washes through me as Vale screams, turning and throwing the table over, scattering everything as thunder rolls. My eyes stay on Jai's lifeless body, watching his blood drip down his arm which hangs over the side and to the ground.

Suddenly, his chest lifts.

I move closer, wondering if it's an illusion, but I hear him inhale, his chest rising and dropping again. "Vale," I whisper, but he's raging and doesn't hear me. "Vale!" I shout, and he turns, crossbow in hand, no doubt to hunt Quinn, and heads over.

"Let's go," he starts, but he stops when he sees it too.

Leaning down, he peers into Jai's face as he parts his lips and takes a big breath, his eyes opening.

They are a bright, supernatural blue before they shut again.

Vale and I both stare, standing stock-still, before Vale throws the packing off the wound, and we watch it knit back together. The claw marks are scarring over.

The killing wound is healed.

It can't have been the pixie magic.

I stumble back and sit heavily on my cot, Vale joining me as we stare at Jai's still body, watching his chest rise and fall.

Covered in blood and rain, I lean closer to Vale. "He shouldn't have survived that," I whisper.

"I know." Vale looks at Jai. "I wonder . . ."

JAI

I can hear them.

"He shouldn't have survived that."

"I know. I wonder . . ."

Everything roars into clarity, and when I blink my eyes open, the pigments in the air are clear, twirling and dancing with the dust. My hearing pops, and it's like they are right next to me. My nose twitches, the coppery scent of blood and fresh rain filling my lungs as I rub my hands into the cot.

Everything feels new.

Did . . . Did she turn me?

"His eyes," Lucien comments. "They were blue, like hers."

"It could have been a trick of the light or the pixie magic moving through his veins. It could have healed him. He's always healed fast," Vale reasons, his voice too loud, making my eyes shut as my head pounds.

Every inch of my body is aching, even the tips of my fingers.

"Or she turned him," Lucien murmurs.

"No, not like that. It requires a bite, right?" Vale asks.

"I thought so, but what if we were wrong?" Lucien hisses. "Then he'll be one of them."

"Then we'll kill him ourselves, but for now, let's just watch him and not rush to make assumptions. He's alive, and that's all that matters. We'll watch him tonight and make a decision tomorrow," Vale orders.

"And Quinn—" Lucien cuts off at Vale's curse.

"Let her go. She'll be too far away now anyway. Our promise is up tomorrow, so we can hunt the pack then. We know they are here now. First, let's make sure Jai is okay."

I groan. Their loud voices are like jackhammers in my head. My body starts to heat, and it feels like I'm going to explode.

It feels like something is moving inside me, ripping me apart from the inside, and when it cuts, I scream. The sound must be trapped inside my own head since neither Vale nor Lucien react.

I silently fight an unknown entity, my body locked and still.

It is a battle I fought before all those years ago, and I won't lose now. I won last time, and I will this time as well.

The internal claws finally stop, and whatever it was slinks deeper inside me, but the wounds feel fresh and raw—a reminder of what I am.

A monster.

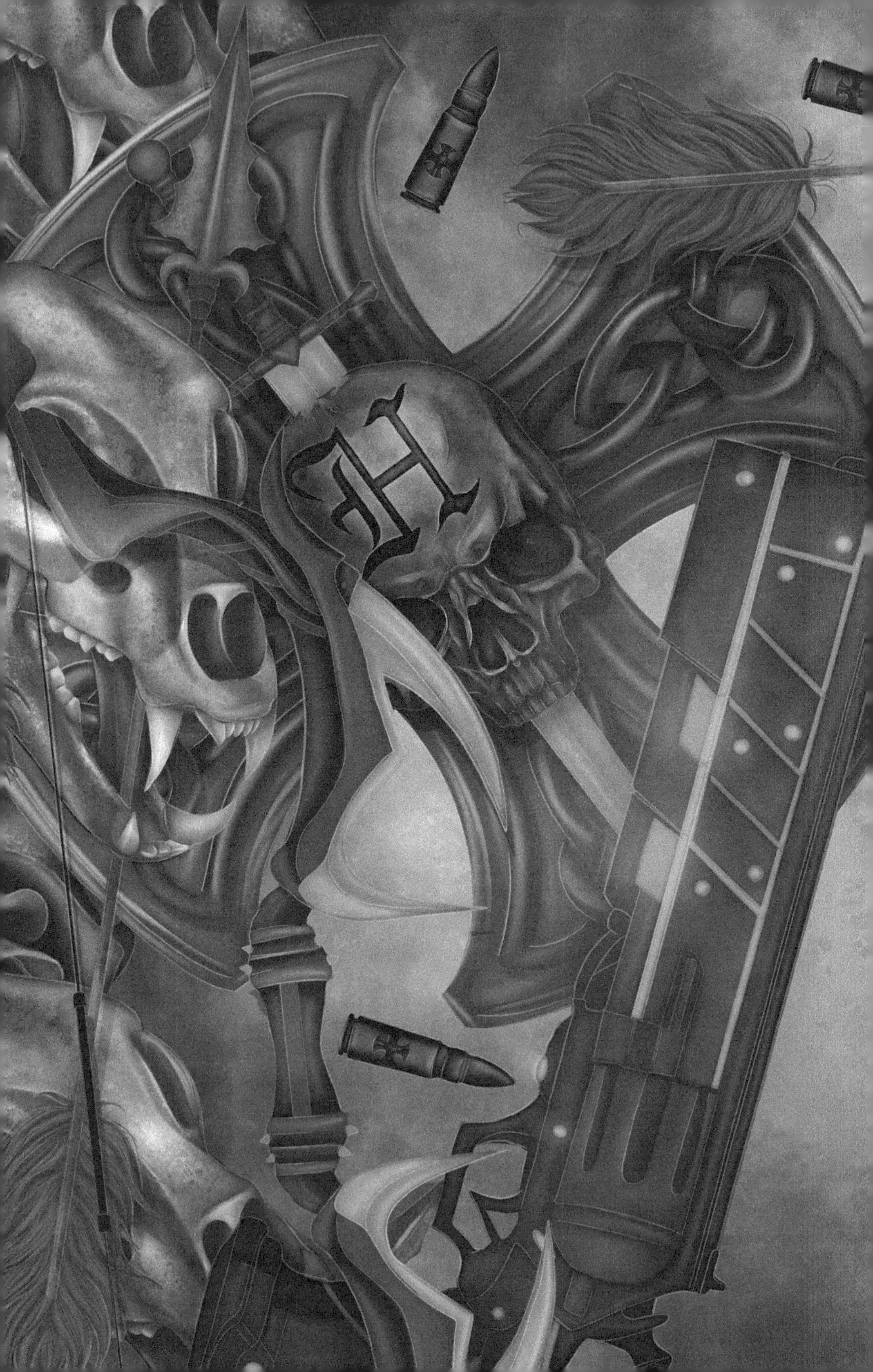

CHAPTER EIGHTEEN

The night drags on, the thunder and lightning only letting up in the early hours, but Jai still doesn't wake. We wash him clean as much as we can and redress his wound, and he still doesn't move.

He's alive though. There isn't a fever or anything, and it's like he completely passed out.

My eyes keep going to the wicked scar on his neck. It looks weeks old. I don't have a clue how he survived, and that worries me. I don't like what I can't understand, since it's usually monster related, but what I told Lucien was true. We will wait and see.

We spend our time tidying up, and for a moment, my eyes scan the empty cage, missing the weight of that stare.

No, not missing, annoyed.

Turning away, I ignore Lucien's gaze and check on Jai again. He's fine, so once we finish cleaning, I cook, needing the rhythmic motions to let my mind wander. How did Jai survive? Was it her? Is he turned? I guess only time will tell, but if he is, can I really kill him?

What do I do about Quinn?

As I stir the pasta, my hand stops. Those eyes . . . I keep thinking of them and the familiar way she watched me, like she knew a secret I didn't. It can't be her, it just can't be, but now I will never know, and part of me is angry at my own foolishness for never asking her.

If it was her, though, would that change anything?

I saved that girl that night, and in the end, it cost me everything. She is the reason I became a hunter. I always told myself that if I found her again, I would rectify the mistake I made that night. If it was Quinn, I will kill her. We will hunt her pack, and even with her warning them, they won't be safe. They won't run or abandon their pack land like that. I know that much.

It's about magic and the source of their powers.

No, they won't run. They will fight, which means before this is through, I will stand toe to toe with a pack while Quinn leads the charge. I should have weakened them and killed her, since she was clearly important, but I cannot change what happened now.

"Is it done yet?" Lucien grouses, annoyed and tired.

I look down and swear. "Yeah, sorry." I quickly serve it and grab two waters before sitting. I poke at my food, my stomach turning from the seriousness of everything I know is to come.

"Quinn will warn her pack," Lucien starts as he eats.

I nod. I was thinking the same thing. "It will make it harder," I add as I take a bite, barely tasting the food as I chew, glancing at Jai to see he's still motionless.

It's quiet for a moment, and then Lucien clears his throat. "I wonder what happened to the wolf you saved when you were a kid." My head jerks up, and he grins. "I was there, Vale. I'm not an idiot. I helped cover for you. You were just a kid—"

"It was a mistake," I hiss.

"True." He nods. "But I wonder where she is."

Does he know? Is that why he's asking?

"Probably dead." Or will be soon.

He watches me carefully before going back to eating, and I force myself to eat, knowing I will need my strength. When I'm done, I sit back. "Whoever she is, she will be dead soon. We will hunt them all, no exception. We owe it to our race, to our people."

Lucien is quiet for a moment. "Do you ever think that they aren't monsters, but nature's will? That we should coexist?"

I slam my fist down, and he snaps his mouth shut. "I tolerated that talk when we were training, but you know better now. Just look at Jai or the countless other men and friends we have lost over the years. We hunters are all that stand in the way of the annihilation of our race."

"I agree that there are monsters out there, but maybe it's like humans, where not all of them are evil. Some seem to just want to be left alone." He swallows at my dirty look.

"Are you backing out of your oath as a hunter?" I ask cautiously. "Answer carefully, brother, because we might be related, but I will not tolerate you betraying our kind."

"I'm just saying, it's something I wonder." He sighs. "You know I will go where you go, hunter or not. I just don't want to be on the wrong side of history." He stands, staring at me. "I don't want to become the monsters." He steps away.

I stare at him, wondering how much Quinn fucked with him to have him talking like this. I never should have left him alone with her. She clearly used her wiles against him, which is more of a reason for us to hunt and kill the pack and get him back on the right course.

Once she's gone, he will be back to normal, and then we can go back to our usual routine and hunts.

The day drags on. I get in a couple of workouts and a shower before I clean and strip our weapons, but Jai still hasn't woken. Lucien is also ignoring me, lost in his own world as he pushes his body to the limit in gruelling workouts before searching around the mill to check for any lingering wolves. We don't know how long it will take Quinn to get back to her pack, and they could already be coming for us.

We need to be sharp, and once Jai is awake, we'll move locations, dismantling this one and leaving them a nasty surprise—just in case.

After all, wolves are excellent trackers, and even if Quinn doesn't remember her way back, she will remember the smells and trails. She will come, and so will her pack. We must be ready, so I keep myself busy and start building the trap.

I place some wood above each door and entrance with spikes that will slam down when triggered, the tips covered in wolfsbane. It adds to the tripwire we already set around the outer perimeter, since Quinn seemed to easily avoid that.

Once I'm done, I'm covered in sweat but feeling better. It's my job to protect Lucien and Jai and I failed. It's also my job to lead them, and I'm failing at that as well.

Maybe I shouldn't lead them. Maybe I'm not strong enough. If Lucien is questioning his conviction . . . I don't think I could do this without him or Jai despite him being a crazy bastard. We have survived through thick and thin together.

We are soldiers, we are hunters, and we are brothers.

I cannot lose that, so if I need to be stronger, then I fucking will be.

No wolf will take either of them from me.

As the sun starts to set, I'm heading over to check on Jai once more when he suddenly sits bolt upright, his eyes snapping open and landing on me.

What the fuck?

CHAPTER NINETEEN

I run faster than I ever have before.

I know they aren't chasing me, but I need to warn the pack, gather them, and attack. I refuse to lose any of my family to these hunters. I cover the ground until I barely feel my paws, all while keeping a mental map to return. We are on the other side of town, farther away from the pack than I have ever been. It takes me at least three hours to cross into pack territory, and only then do I relax a little, but I still don't stop running.

By the time I skid into familiar pack land, I'm panting, and when I change back, I actually stumble. I've run more before, but due to the lack of meat and nutrients, I'm exhausted and stumbling across the uneven grass, heading towards the pack house which is lit up like a beacon.

My memories claw at me like weapons, recalling the boy who saved me and the man who saved me tonight.

No!

I hit the door with a thud, my limbs shaking, but that animal part of me knows I need to get inside and warn them, and it keeps me going as I fumble with the doorknob and slip inside. I stumble down the hallway until a familiar shadow steps out of his office.

Dark circles surround his eyes, his hair is a mess, and his clothes are stained.

"Dad," I croak as I drop to my knees, finally feeling safe.

"Quinny!" he roars, sprinting towards me and catching me as I fall.

The sound of rushing footsteps fills my ears, along with other familiar, comforting voices, and I close my eyes and relax. I'm home. I'm safe, at least for now.

They have me.

***

I'm on Jang's sofa in his office, wrapped in a thick quilt, the room crowded with worried pack members. All eyes are on me as I devour the feast before me, ripping into the bloody meat.

I need to feed since I'm weak from days of not eating properly.

Jang and Marie watch me worriedly. Jang leans forward, his hands hanging heavily between his legs, and Marie watches me with her hands over her mouth, so I make an effort to slow down and not worry them as much. They wait until I finish eating to question me —Jang's orders, and no one dares question our alpha. Not when he looks feral.

The betas of my pack line the walls, and I run my eyes over them, noting they look just as exhausted. Was everyone out searching for me?

"You're alive," White comments.

"Of course she is. My girl can survive anything." Jang huffs and leans closer still. "Quinny, what happened? The last we saw of you was you in a cage, being taken away by hunters."

Wiping my mouth on the back of my hand, I swallow the meat, knowing this is more important. I have time to rest, but I need to inform the pack, so I sit taller, not allowing any emotion to invade my thoughts. I am a beta and the next alpha. I will not break down. I am safe, and they are in danger.

They need to know.

Clearing my throat, I meet Jang's eyes. "There were three hunters—two brothers and one other member of their team. They set traps just beyond our border. I smelled a feral inside one. They also captured Sarah. I freed her from the trap and tried to cover her escape, but I realised they would follow us back, so I stayed to fight and give her time to get back." I pause as Marie whimpers. "However, they had weapons, which electrocuted my wolf, and the voltage eventually paralysed me, and then they drugged me. When I came to, I was caged in an old mill to the south of town. I know the exact location and can lead you back, but they are smart, and they will move. However, I do have their scents and can track them. They questioned me . . ." I swallow the truth, not wanting my pack to think I'm a traitor. "I did not turn back, and this evening, one of the team members lost his patience and entered my cage. I managed to kill him and escape."

"Quinn." Jang sighs, rubbing his head. "Did they hurt you?"

"Their methods did not scar or affect my wolf. I'm okay." His eyes narrow, and he knows what I am not saying—they tortured me.

"They kept me starved to keep me weak, but I managed to make it back."

"Of course you did," someone in the pack says, and they whoop.

"But Alpha, I must speak to you," I implore. "It's important."

He looks into my eyes and nods, and then he whistles. The pack clears out at the betas' urgings, and I overhear them say they can see me later.

Once the door shuts, I lean forward. "They moved their base here. They are all actively hunting wolves, and they know there is a pack. Although I believe this team didn't tell the other hunters yet, they will. They will come for us, so we must shore up our defences."

Jang's nostrils flare. "I will need to know exactly what I am up against."

"Of course. They use wolfsbane and bewitched blades. They also have access to pixie magic. They are well trained but still human and sentimental. I believe we can win. We have the home ground advantage, and if we don't spend time tracking their trail like a wild goose chase, which they will expect, then we can set traps and wait. They will come for us. In the meantime, I suggest we pull everyone back from the village because everyone is in danger. No one leaves the pack. Double patrol. I would also warn the other packs and even the ferals."

"All very good ideas." He grins proudly. "Even half-starved, you think like an alpha." He stands and heads my way, giving me an uncharacteristically hard hug. "Rest, Quinny. Eat. We'll talk tomorrow. For now, know I have it in hand. They won't harm our pack."

Nodding, I watch him go as Marie hurries over and wraps me in her arms, kissing my head. "I was so worried, as was Jang. He has barely slept or eaten. He's been running the forests, searching for signs of you. We even trapped some hunters." She pulls back, wiping the meat juice from my face. "I couldn't . . . I don't know what we would have done . . ." She turns away, and I hug her tighter.

"I'm okay, I promise. I'm too strong to kill," I tease.

"That you are." She pats my shoulder. "Thank the moons."

Swallowing, I search her gaze. "Mum, the men who killed my parents were hunters, we know that, but why didn't Jang ever go after them?"

She jerks back, her eyes wide. I never speak about what happened that night. I had nightmares every night, and Jang would sit at the end of my bed, protecting me. I know they went to my house, which burnt down, and there was nothing left of my parents to even bury in a moon shadow ceremony, which horrified me. Their souls will remain trapped here, never being able to join the moon and stars once more.

"We had to protect you. He wanted to," she whispers, "but I begged him not to. I couldn't lose him, and you couldn't either. You had just lost your entire world, and you clung to him like a lifeline. If he didn't come back, I would lose you too. I couldn't do that. So he stayed, even though it killed him. He chose to protect you and help you heal rather than get vengeance, but don't think for one moment that he didn't want it. Your parents were our best friends. Jang and your dad were like brothers, but we all know your dad would have wanted him to stay alive and protect you."

"I miss them," I admit. "And sometimes I feel so guilty thinking that because I have you."

"No." She holds my face tight. "They were your parents. You are allowed to miss them. I can tell you stories whenever you wish. Never feel guilty for loving them. Loving and missing them does not change how much you love us. I am secure with my heart, Quinny, and I know I am a mother to you just as she was. Your heart is big enough to love us all." She pulls me closer. "I'm sorry being with hunters brought this all up. I'm so sorry, Quinny, that we weren't there to protect you. Both that night and this one."

"It's not your fault," I tell her, holding her tight. "I'm a survivor."

"That you are." She nods, kissing my head. "My fighter, you always were. Your dad used to say you should have been born a lion." She chuckles, pulling away and wiping at her eyes. "You were so fierce and strong even as a kid, and now look at you, my beautiful, strong girl."

I hold her hands as she stares at me. "You remind me so much of your mother. You look more and more like her as you grow up, and sometimes I forget and for the moment, I see my best friend. I'm so grateful I get to see her in you every day. You have the best of all of us, Quinn, never forget that. You are our past and future, and you are our hope. We will get through this just like we do everything —together."

"Thank you for loving them and me," I tell her, kissing her hand. "They were blessed."

"As are we." She nods, wiping her eyes again. "I'll stop crying at some point."

She stands, smoothing her clothes as if they are out of place, but I know it's because she's hiding her emotions.

"Are you still hungry?" she asks. "I'll get more food and bring it to your room." She hurries away, and I watch her go before getting to my feet and moving around the desk. I sit heavily, reaching for the framed photo. Lifting it, I see a copy of the one I have under my pillow.

I'm smiling brightly in front of my dad, and Jang stands at his side.

I forget what he looks like sometimes, same with Mum, and guilt eats me alive. I survived that night thanks to them . . . and Vale, but hunters killed my family, and I cannot owe any loyalty to anyone other than my people.

I don't have time for revenge, even if it's all I wanted when I was younger.

Nothing will bring them back, but I can save my family now, and I will.

CHAPTER TWENTY

Quinn

That night, at Jang's and Marie's urgings, I stay in the pack house. The truth is, I don't want to be alone either. The familiar smells and sounds settle me as I lie in the large, wooden bed in my old room.

The wooden beams have fairy lights on them, giving warmth to the space, and the room itself is decorated with handmade wooden furniture from Daio, a pack member who is very talented. The moon shines through the huge bay windows, which have a cushioned nook before them, looking out at our pack land. The door for the en suite is slightly ajar and throwing warm, white light across the carpeted floor.

The old glow stars on the ceiling catch the moon's rays and light up softly, causing a familiar, nostalgic sadness to fill me.

I'm exhausted but unable to sleep, so I slip from the wide bed and pad to the window, sitting with my knees pulled to my chest as I look out at the dark forest below. I can hear the howls of our wolves and see the lights in the cabins throughout our territory, and above it all hangs the moon.

As a wolf, we crave comfort and companionship. I often appreciate my solitude, but my wolf likes to be warm and pressed against other bodies, and it's a constant battle—one my wolf won today. My concern, anger, and thoughts of the three hunters mix and make me volatile.

Is Jai dead?

If he survived, then my guess would be right—he's part wolf.

I smelled it on him the first day but could never quite figure it out, not until that night when I saw the beast in his eyes, as if waiting to be freed. I dealt a killing blow, and if he were simply human, he would be dead and Vale and Lucien would hunt me to the ends of the earth, but if he survived, then it proved the hunter is hunting his own kind.

Does he even know?

The widening of his eyes told me he at least suspected it deep down. He might be my enemy, but causing chaos within their ranks can only help us, and knowing there is a werewolf hunter? Brilliant.

Sighing, I lean my head against the cool windowpane, letting my eyes sweep over the trees. I wonder if they are out there right now, watching.

For a moment, memories fill my head.

I see the look in Lucien's eyes. Why did he let me go? He could have called out to Vale. Hell, he could have shot me. He did none of those things, though, and instead, he let me escape. He said it was so we were even, but for what? For saving his life? It didn't feel that way, but I'm not naïve enough to think he'll do it a second time. If I see them again, we'll try to kill each other.

I wonder when that will be because we will meet again.

I'm a wolf, and they are hunters.

We are destined to fight, and if it comes down to it, I will always protect my pack, no matter what Vale and Lucien did.

For a moment, my wolf purrs inside me, her dominance leaking into the air. The familiar power comforts me as heat throbs deep in my core. Shit, I forgot about my heat. I mentally work through the dates and relax. I have a month left until then. I need to make sure the hunters are dead and gone before that so I can lock myself away.

The most common time to confirm matings or pregnancies is during our heat, and I want neither. I've survived the demanding, red-hot desire many times, since it comes every year. I simply lock myself away in the cages like every other female who doesn't wish to ride out her heat with someone.

I get many offers, and the smell of my wolf in heat attracts many wolves from far and wide, but like always, I will spend this one alone. It's like a countdown in my head, reminding me that we need to be safe and sorted by then, which means there is no time to spare.

For a moment, I close my eyes, and a pair of bright blue orbs fills my mind, so I snap my eyes open with a growl. Why the fuck am I thinking about those idiot humans? I owe them nothing! Nothing! We are enemies.

So why does it feel like I'm missing their looks?

I must be so exhausted, I'm delirious.

I force myself back into bed and close my eyes, telling my brain to calm down and think of anything other than the three humans who tortured me.

Masochists.

"Little wolf."

The familiar taunt makes my eyes snap open. Grey, steel bars are before me, and Vale crouches there. His mocking blue eyes are locked on me, and Jai and Lucien linger behind him.

Fuck!

I climb to my knees. I thought I was home. I escaped, didn't I?

Fuck, was it all a dream?

Was I just missing home so much that I imagined it?

"You are finally awake," Vale scoffs. "I thought wolves were supposed to be strong, but you are so weak."

Nostrils flaring, I take in their familiar scents. This is real. I'm back. The concrete scratches my knees, and my skin is covered with goosebumps due to the cold.

"Time to talk, little wolf." He smirks as he moves around the cage, and I spin to watch him, wondering what the hell is going on.

My head is groggy. Maybe from a lack of sleep and food?

Either way, I don't know what day or time it is, but my confusion bleeds away as the lock drops to the ground and the gate opens.

I scramble to my feet but not fast enough. Vale's hand wraps around my throat, and he lifts me into the air. He walks me backwards then slams me into the bars as I snarl and growl.

He pins me there, and arms come through the bars behind me, holding me tight, as Vale tilts my head back until I meet his cruel eyes.

"You know, you're not bad looking for a monster," he sneers. "If you won't talk from pain, then maybe you will through pleasure."

My eyes widen in horror.

His head comes down, his lips above mine. "Isn't this what you want, little wolf?" He smashes his lips onto mine as I thrash, but they only hold me tighter, his hand gripping my chin and holding me still as he kisses my lips.

The pain makes me gasp, and his tongue sweeps in, tangling with mine even as I fight.

I bite down, and he pulls back, laughing as blood drips from his lips. "Keep fighting, little wolf. We both know you want this."

Growling, I kick out, and he flies backwards. I yank myself from the hands and pin him to the cage floor, my hands gripping his head to smash it into the concrete as he grins up at me.

"Kill me, little wolf. Oh wait, you can't, can you?" I freeze above him. "Go ahead, kill me," he taunts, and when I don't move, he grins and leans up. "Or better yet, fuck me. I bet we would be explosive. Don't you think, little wolf?"

I jolt awake with a growl, my heart racing. My hand lifts, lingering on my lips as they throb, even though it was a dream.

Moons, what is happening to me?

CHAPTER TWENTY-ONE

I shouldn't have said what I did to Vale. I know very well why we do this, why he is a hunter, and I will follow him anywhere, but sometimes I cannot help but feel like a monster myself.

If it takes a monster to stop the monsters, though, then isn't that worth it?

It's what I worry about all day, besides Jai and the idea of Vale finding out I let Quinn go. I can already sense his concern for me, and I can't handle his disappointment or, worse, losing his trust. To outrun my racing thoughts, I push my body to my limits until I can't take any more.

When Jai wakes suddenly, and I mean suddenly, we both rush to his side.

"Jai, are you okay?" I ask, searching his body as he sits bolt upright, his eyes an unnatural bright blue. He slowly turns his head to face me, and I see Vale reach for his blade, so I shoot him a glare. "Jai, can you hear me?"

He blinks, and his eyes are back to normal. "What happened?" he grumbles, slumping back, and Vale and I stare at him.

"Erm, we managed to heal your wounds," I lie. Until we know what's happening, I don't want to worry him, but he seems completely normal as he sighs and slides from the cot, standing on unsteady feet.

"I'm starving," he says, moving over to the kitchen, and we both follow him.

Vale clutches his blade behind his back in case Jai turns. Standing a safe distance away, we watch as Jai rips the fridge open, downing some milk before grabbing some cooked chicken. When his head turns, he freezes, his eyes wide.

"What?" he asks around a bite before swallowing and wiping his mouth.

"Here, think fast," I say, throwing water at him as Vale moves closer.

Jai blinks, and the water hits his chest. It was too fast to catch. "Dude, what the fuck?"

"Sorry." I shoot Vale a glare as Jai turns away. He opens a cupboard next, and when he doesn't rip the door off, I relax. New wolves cannot control their strength or change, and it's not something he could hide.

Jai is still human, or at least I'm betting on it.

Vale obviously thinks the same because he relaxes, sheathing his blade. We'll keep our eyes on him, but he seems okay. It must have been a trick of the light or something Quinn did to him. Yep, that's what happened. Once he finishes eating, he heads to shower, and when the water's running, I move over to Vale.

"He seems normal."

Vale nods, keeping his eyes on the door. "We'll keep our eye on him, but you're right."

"So what do we do now—" I stop as Vale's phone rings. Only one place calls that number.

He plucks it from his pocket, staring at it before he answers, "Yes?"

I can't hear what the other person is saying, but he hangs up soon, sighing. "A meeting has been called. We can't afford to miss another or we'll draw suspicion. Tell Jai, and let's get ready. It's probably good if we aren't here anyway in case wolves descend. Move everything back to the motel. We can keep checking if they trigger the traps."

Nodding, I move to my bags and quickly pack, although most are already prepared, ready to bug out. I pack the tools we used on Quinn, and by the time Jai is out of the shower, the trucks are loaded and ready to go.

There is no trace we were ever here bar the cage and traps.

It's like it never happened, but as blue eyes flash in my mind, I know it did, and I know nothing will ever be the same again.

The meeting room is overflowing with hunters, and there aren't even enough chairs. I've never seen so many of us in one place, nor this riled up. They are all angry.

We linger at the back, leaning against the wall, not only to give us space but to avoid the fury in the room.

We don't need anyone asking questions right now.

We've been lying to our own people, and every time someone looks at me, it's as if they know it, so I plant the familiar glare on my face and cross my arms. It's a giant sign saying *fuck off*, and I see some of the new recruits changing direction when they were clearly about to approach us.

Jai leans by my side, playing with his knife, and Vale stands at attention on my other side. We look every inch the perfect hunters, our jackets displaying the emblem, yet we are all hiding our secrets.

The commander clears his throat as he takes to the stage. "You may be wondering why I called you here." No shit. As usual, he wanders around the stage with his hands behind his back like he's presenting an invention. "The attacks in which human flesh has been consumed have increased. We are unsure of the type of monster at the moment, but it's clear this is our priority, so I will cut to the chase."

"Thank fuck," Jai mutters, making me and a few others around us who heard it chuckle.

The commander focuses on us and glares until everyone hushes. "I'm glad you think this is funny. Vale, you are no closer on the wolves, correct?"

I wince as all the hunters turn to us. He's trying to embarrass us, but Vale simply inclines his head, and I watch the commander's mouth twist in annoyance at the lack of response from my brother.

"Then the rest of our teams are going to be reassigned for now to deal with the imminent threat. Vale, your team will stay on the wolf matter. Oh, and Vale? Find the wolves or don't come back. The attacks have pulled back, so find a way." He focuses on the rest of the meeting as I watch Vale's hands ball into fists at his sides.

The attacks have pulled back because Quinn is home and they are protecting their pack. She has to know we won't give up though. We can't, especially now. If we fail this mission, we'll lose our jobs and our father's legacy.

Despite my mixed feelings, I will not put that in jeopardy.

Not for anyone.

"The rest of you, come to me after the meeting to check your new zones. I want everyone on high alert. We cannot let any more innocent humans die. This is our job. This is our duty."

We all repeat our mantra.

"We stand between the darkness waiting to consume this world and the light of day. We always will. Let's remind the monsters of that. Dismissed."

The hunters slowly get to their feet, complaining about skipping out on hunts while Vale strides from the room. I exchange a look with Jai, and we quickly follow.

It's clear the commander is annoyed with us since we have been avoiding him and keeping secrets, and he decided to punish us.

We have one chance to stop our lives from crumbling apart, and that one chance means putting a bullet in Quinn's head.

CHAPTER TWENTY-TWO

Bright sunshine warms my face, and with a contented sigh, I roll over to soak it in. My bedding tangles around my frame, and the long shirt I climbed into bed with is raised, exposing my stomach and ass. I'm comfortable, happy, rested, and fed. I can feel my wolf stretching in happiness, the energy pouring through my restored body. The dominance I usually carry is stronger than ever.

I'm back, I'm home, and I'm safe, and that's what gets me to force my eyes open.

After the strange dream that plagued me last night, I tossed and turned a little before finally passing out, and it's clear I slept until late morning, which is strange for me. Even stranger is that no one has come to wake me. I guess they assumed I needed the rest. I wouldn't be surprised if Jang is camped outside my door, glaring at anyone who gets too close.

I cannot sleep forever, though, no matter how comfy my bed is.

There are things to do and plans to put into motion.

But first, pants.

Sniffing the air, I decide maybe I should shower first. That's one downside of enhanced senses: you smell every little thing. With a groan, I slide from my bed and pad to the en suite, stretching as I go. Unlike the cold, sterile shower cubicle I used when I was held captive, this one smells of the forest and relaxes my muscles as soon as I step inside.

Greenery overflows hanging pots, climbing down the walls and almost obscuring the edges of the LED mirror. The sink below is a copper one I fell in love with at a market and insisted they install for me. The walk-in shower has a wooden bench, but it's the huge, claw-foot tub with copper legs that always calls my name. It's set before a window with a view of our land, my half-finished books and candles placed around it, but as tempted as I am, I turn to the shower instead.

I need to get out there and show my face. I can't let them think I'm weak, not when I'm going to be the next alpha. Stripping off my clothes, I throw them into the hamper and step into the stall. I press the touch screen at the side and let the waterfall showerhead come on as well as the side sprays. I hit the temperature button, increasing it until it's almost scalding, and then I turn on the music. Folk music fills the air, and I step into the spray, closing my eyes.

My skin starts to wrinkle, so I wash my hair three times to get everything out of it before scrubbing my skin and turning the shower off. Wrapping a towel around my hair and body, I move to the sink, brush my teeth, and do my skincare routine. I don't bother adding any makeup because I have a feeling I'll be shifting today, and for some reason, makeup always becomes weird during the shift. Maybe because it's not a natural part of our body so the shift rejects it. Instead, I save it for when I know I'll be staying human.

Rubbing my hair as I move to the wardrobe, I drop the towel and let my long locks air dry. I can't be bothered with drying it since it takes so long. Opening the wooden doors, I peer inside, happy to see someone has been keeping clothing here for me. I don't mind nudity, none of us do, but I feel the need to cover myself today.

Selecting some loose linen pants, I tuck in a white stretchy shirt before calling it good. I don't bother with socks or shoes since I like the feel of the grass underfoot.

I turn to leave when there's a hesitant knock at my door. I cock my head and listen, hearing an anxious heartbeat on the other side, and a familiar scent wafts under the door. Shaking my head, I open it and grin. "Hey there, cupcake."

Toby and Sarah stand with their heads down. Toby wrings his hands before him and is almost flattened against the wall opposite.

"We just wanted to see for ourselves that you were okay," Sarah murmurs, raising her eyes to meet mine to show her affection before they drop again out of respect.

"And apologise. I never should have sent you out there." Toby winces.

"Nor should I have been out there alone. It's my fault," Sarah adds, taking the blame for the omega, making me grin.

"It doesn't matter. It's my job as beta to protect you. I did that, didn't I?"

I don't realise my dominance has slipped into my tone—a habit with wolves in the pack—until Toby drops to the floor, prostrating himself to the alpha.

Sighing, I crouch and lift his head. "It's done, over. Come on, I'm hungry."

I sling my arm around their shoulders and drag them with me. After all, it's not their fault. Yes, Sarah should have known better, but I'm betting she has been chastised enough and feels bad as it is. It's the hunters' fault, not hers.

They are clearly still worried, but they let me drag them into the dining room where the pack is. All noise stops, and every gaze turns to us.

Rolling my eyes, I grin. "I know I'm beautiful, but how about we stop staring?" I call, and I hear some chuckles. "I'm truly fine," I say, answering the unspoken question.

"But did the hunters follow you?" someone asks and then ducks.

I seek them out, making sure to hit every eye as my expression goes dead serious—Jang calls it my alpha mask. Heads duck and wolves whine as my dominance leaks out, making it hard for them to breathe.

"I would never put this pack in danger. I was very careful on my return. The alpha will brief the pack shortly on what's happening, so until then, let's not speculate or spread rumours that could be hurtful to our people."

"Yes," they reply.

I drop the dominance and see some of them sucking in shuddering breaths. "Good, now let's eat." I grin.

Walking the perimeter of our territory, I search for any trace of hunters. I'm worried, not that I will show anyone else that. They are looking to us for protection and hope. They are scared after a beta was captured, and we don't need them to panic for no reason, but we also need time to discern the danger.

However, that is Jang's job. As beta, it is my job to keep us safe and report to the alpha, so here I am, searching for any signs, but I find none. They didn't manage to follow me like I expected, the storm keeping them at bay, not to mention Jai's wound. I knew they would choose him over hunting me, or so I hoped.

We are safe for now.

They were drawing closer, though, and that's concerning.

I'm just running back when I smell something in the air. "Tetrim," I snarl. "There is no point in hiding. I can smell you."

He saunters out from behind a tree a few feet away, no doubt following me. I'm completely alone but not scared as I lean back into a tree and wait as he moves closer. It's clear he wants something, and it's better to get this over with out here. I'm sick of the shit he's pulling, like I'm his and he has the right to follow me.

It is time he learned his place.

"What do you want?" I ask, spreading my legs slightly and dropping my hands, prepared to defend myself. I infuse my dominance into my tone and watch him flinch as he stops. His chest heaves as he fights it, so I pump more out of me. He falls to his knees, trying to fight it, but he's weaker.

"I wanted to check on my future mate," he spits.

Snarling, I feel my eyes flash as my claws extend, and I move so swiftly, he flinches back. I grab his neck and force his eyes up to mine, letting him see my wolf there.

"I will never be your mate. Do you need a reminder?"

"You will be," he grits out, his own wolf flashing in his eyes even as he shakes from the force of fighting against my control. He will always be a beta and nothing more.

I kick him, and he flies through the air, hitting a tree. Before he can recover, I slam my foot into his back, putting all my strength into it as I pin him there. When I remove it, he flips to his knees and glares at me.

Leaning down, I grip his chin as he snarls, holding him immobile despite the fact he is three times my size. "Don't forget your place ever again. You are not an alpha, and you are not my mate. You are just another wolf, one I can easily beat." Throwing his chin away, I watch in satisfaction as he ducks his head. "This is your last warning. I will not tolerate your disrespect again. I am your beta. Remember that."

With that last warning, I walk away, showing him my back in the ultimate gesture of disrespect.

CHAPTER TWENTY-THREE

The rest of my day is spent tracking deep into our land. I push it and run as far as the other traps were placed. The trails there are old, and any other traps were destroyed by the pack during their search for me.

I head back and inform the others of what I have found before collapsing into my cabin for some much-needed rest. My body is still healing and regenerating. After a nap, I shed my clothes once more and slide into the lake before my cabin, submerging myself as the sun heats it.

My eyes close as I sink to the bottom, and I let nature show me the way as it has so often before.

I reflect and heal.

I have hidden my talents for so long, very few know of my abilities. Jang calls me moon blessed. We do not know why my powers came or how, but the day after I woke in Jang's house after the death of my family, I felt my head burn, and when I came to, I could heal. It took a long time to train myself in how to control it.

It's not that I don't trust the pack. It's that it's another thing that makes me an outsider. The moon blessed me, even as this world took from me. I'm not sure how I feel about that because the exchange for these gifts was my family's lives.

One day, others will know. It is part of me, a part I should not be ashamed of, but for now, I hide it, even as I feel the markings light up across my forehead as the water surrounds me.

I am tied to our land, and I am part of it. I am inconsequential, and I am everything.

I am a wolf born of nature. I am the magic here.

My eyes snap open, shining brightly within the darkness, a warning to those who would stand against me and try to take this land from us—land gifted by the world itself. Hunters are evil beings, and I will remove them from this world before they scorch it with death and blood, but a whisper in the water stills my heart.

Death is coming, prepare.

Standing at Jang's side with the other betas, I look out at the gathered pack. We don't gather like this very often, and it's clear they are worried about what that means. Many whispers meet my ears, so it's hard to tell who is saying what. They are spread amongst the grass behind the pack house, the mountains behind them as a backdrop. Some are sitting with their families or on a mate's lap, while others sit on blankets or chairs.

All five hundred members gathered from far and wide.

My hands press to the base of my spine as I stand tall under their watchful gazes, not showing an inch of weakness since they will all be looking for it. I need to get used to this, but every time I stand here, I find it daunting. I don't know how Jang does it.

He steps forward, and everyone instantly becomes quiet, bending their heads in a sign of respect.

"As many have heard, Quinn, our beta, was captured recently by hunters." At his declaration, the noise starts again. "Enough!" he roars, and the silence is deafening. "Quinn was captured while saving a trapped member of our pack, and she took her place to spy on the hunters for us."

Nice, but not true. I don't correct him, however.

"She has come back with vital information. The hunters are drawing closer. They are searching for us, and when they find us, they plan to kill us. I won't lie to you on that. I am your alpha, so it is my job to lead us and keep you all safe, but I will never hide the truth from you." Their fear pumps into the air. "We will not be cowed or chased off our own land. We have faced hunters before, and we will again. We won't be an easy target, and for this exact reason, we have come up with some temporary measures. Quinn will now explain." He looks at me, and my eyes widen slightly as he nods.

He's letting me address the pack. He's showing them that he trusts me to lead. He's giving me a chance to be an alpha.

I will not fail him.

I step forward. "Thank you, Alpha. It's true, I was captured, but don't be afraid. The hunters are just humans, nothing more. If we stand together, we won't fail, but to keep us safe, we must do all we can. All those who work in the closest city or town will pull back." I hold up my hand to stop the frustrated protests. "Just for now, until the threat is gone. Those who live elsewhere will move back onto pack land where we can protect you. We are doubling patrols and pulling back on our lines. We will ride this out together."

"For how long?" someone yells. "We cannot stop our lives forever."

"I hear you," I reply, "but I have faced these hunters, and they will stop at nothing to get to us. They are not above using bait or hurting those they can get to. This is the way we'll keep you safe. I cannot give an estimate on when life will resume, but now, as your betas and alpha, we are doing everything in our power to stop this threat. We need your cooperation for this. Alpha Jang has never led us wrong." I meet every eye I can. "He has led us through worse, and he will once more. As someone who lost their family to hunters"—I feel the crowd's shock and sadness because although everyone knows, I have never brought it up publicly—"I cannot stress this enough. This threat is real, and I won't let one more wolf lose their lives to the human scourge. Trust us, and as one, we'll stand together like always."

"As one," someone calls, and it's taken up by the pack until it's bayed at the moon hanging above us.

I step back, but Jang takes my hand and pulls me forward until I stand at his side, and he looks down at me with a smile. "You were born to lead, Quinny," he tells me, pride shining in his eyes. "Let them see that. Remind them of who you are." Squeezing my hand, he looks out over the pack. "My child, our hope for a better future." His eyes land back on me. "The next alpha."

CHAPTER TWENTY-FOUR

We have a deadline, and worse than that, we have an ultimatum.

Either we find these wolves and bring their heads to our organisation or we lose everything we have worked for. I am nothing if not a hunter. It's all I know. I cannot be anything else. I was born to kill, and killing is all I'm good at.

We cannot fail, and it's clear the others know that.

We are tense as we head out. "Let's check the traps first, then we are going to land registry. The pack is here somewhere. We just need to find it," Vale snaps.

I follow them silently. No, I cannot afford to lose my family and job. I may as well have died that night if I do.

The traps are all empty. Our fellow hunters were right—the wolves have pulled back, no doubt due to Quinn's return. They are not hiding, but they are waiting. I can sense it in the air. Even the forest seems alive with it, threatening us for daring to invade nature.

Instead, we try a different approach, spending hours reading and combing through archives within the city council office. It has to be here somewhere. If they are in the area, then they must have some kind of permit for land registry, but nothing here is digitised.

It's all unorganised paper, and the man who showed us to the storage room laughed and wished us luck before leaving.

We'll need it.

It will take us weeks, maybe even months, to get through this all.

"Let's discard anything in the last five years. It's clear the pack is old, so we need to check the older records. Nothing within town limits. Break it down and work together. We have no other option." Lucien sighs and starts handing out boxes.

I settle in for the long haul, even as my mind itches for more, reminding me what I am.

A killer.

A hunter, nothing more.

"Jai!"

The wail of terror has me waking.

Slipping from my bed, I hit the wooden floor with a bang. I blink, trying to wake and clear the fog from my head.

"Ahh!" The shriek of pain has me pushing to my feet and tripping from my room, out onto the landing. I slide across the wood floor and stumble over the white rug, which has something red spilled across it. Heart hammering, I glance over the banister.

The front door hangs open at a strange angle, the sofa is tipped over, and claw marks mar the wooden stairs Dad just repainted. At the bottom, my father lies in a heap.

I watch a pool of blood grow around him when a black shape suddenly emerges from the shadow of the dining room right next to the stairs, and I watch in silent horror as it grips my dad's unmoving legs and tugs him away.

I stumble back as his body drags through the blood before sliding out of sight.

"Help me, please!" The scream echoes around the house, and I turn.

My gaze lands on the partially open wooden door of my parents' room.

I hurry down the hall, grabbing the golf club my dad forgot to put away on the way. Swallowing hard, I press my shaking hand to the wood and push.

The hinges creak as the door swings inwards, and my stomach churns at the sight before me.

My mum is on her once pristine white bed, which is now covered in blood and gore. The wooden post my grandfather hand carved before his death is covered in scratch marks as she holds onto one, her eyes wide in fear.

Above her is a beast that's ripping into her body.

I numbly realise it's eating her as she screams.

I must make a noise because the feasting stops.

"Run," Mum croaks, her eyes closing as her hand drops from the post.

The beast lifts its head, its muzzle covered in my mother's blood.

A wolf.

It's not a beast. It's a wolf.

Grinning viciously, the wolf leaps at me as I scream and fall backwards.

I wake with a start, my heart hammering as something moves through my body, drawn by my fear and anger. It almost bursts from my skin as I gasp and fight against it, until it disappears and I can relax.

My mum's screams still echo in my head. I lost them both that night. Police called it a freak animal attack, but I knew the truth. I saw it with my own eyes, and when the hunters found me, I went with them willingly. My only thought was to get revenge and kill the beast responsible for slaughtering my entire family and changing me.

Lifting my head, I scan the room, seeing Lucien and Vale sleeping soundly in the motel room. We moved here since the wolf knows the other hideout. We stumbled back and crashed after spending all day pouring over documents, and I barely remember falling asleep, but now I'm wide awake.

My mind races, and pain stabs at my heart.

I don't want to lose my friends.

It's clear from the way they watch me that they don't trust me anymore and they blame me.

They are right to since it's my fault we are in this mess. I need to make this right.

I fucked up our chances because of my own madness and need for blood.

Maybe it can save us as well.

Sliding silently from my cot, I grab my bag and coat, tug on my boots, and then head out to my truck. I'm ready to prove to my team and myself that I can be better.

I start the truck, and when the headlights shine across the rows of rooms, I hesitate for a moment. My gaze goes to the darkened window of our room, the bag of scent blocker clear from the window even as much as we tried to hide it.

If they wake up and I'm gone, they will be mad, but if I can come back with something, anything to prove that I am still one of them, then they might forgive me for everything.

My hand comes up of its own accord, gliding across the rough, raised scar on my neck. My own concern of how I healed sweeps through me before I pull out of the parking lot and turn onto the empty main road.

The streetlights of the tiny town fade the farther I drive into the forest. The moon hangs high in the sky, and the stars shine around it thanks to the lack of pollution around here. I follow it until I can't drive anymore, and then I park.

Leaving my truck, I sling my coat and bag on, palming my blade since you can never be too careful, and then I lift my nose and ignore the guilt that eats at me as I sniff.

Nothing, just nature. Keeping my footsteps as quiet as possible, I head deeper into the forest, searching for a wolf.

Luckily, my sense of direction is top-notch, and I leave myself markings with my blade to remind myself of the way. If the pack is here, it will be deep within the forest, closer to the mountains, and it's dangerous here at night. There aren't many wild bears but there are some wild wolves, not to mention the snakes and spiders.

These woods, which run for hundreds of miles, seem to be a hotspot for the supernatural, so I keep my eyes peeled. It's only an hour or so later when I realise I never turned my torch on.

How the fuck am I seeing in the dark?

The trees here are thick, almost obscuring the moon's rays, making it dark and shadowed. Swallowing against my sickness, I force myself to move forward. If I'm right and I'm changing, it's good that I'm away from my brothers. At least I can take some wolves with me as I go.

I keep walking, and as if my senses or my imagination conjures it, I hear the first growl. It comes from behind me, and I freeze, slowly turning as a black wolf steps from the trees. It's big, and I know instantly it's a werewolf.

Another growl sounds, and another, and I turn to find myself surrounded.

Fuck it.

Cracking my neck, I pull another blade and grin. "Bring it, monsters. I'll take you all with me," I roar as they leap at me.

In a flurry of claws, fur, and death.

CHAPTER TWENTY-FIVE

Quinn

"Quinn." My hissed name and shaking wake me, and I come up swinging, only stopping my claws inches away from Dom's neck.

He grins. "I love it when you're feisty, but we have bigger issues."

I blink, glancing at the moon. It's late or early, depending on which way you look at it. "Did the hunters attack?" I scramble out of my bed, and he follows me to the cabin door where I pull some shorts on.

"No, well, not really." I turn to face him, and he smirks. "We captured one."

"One?" I frown, still half asleep even as my wolf prowls inside me, as if knowing something I don't.

"A hunter. Patrol found him searching for us deep in the woods. They were going to kill him, but Jang was with them and decided against it. They want answers, an eye for an eye for torturing you. They brought him back."

A hunter? It can't be one of them, can it?

"Let's go." I hurry from the cabin, bursting into a jog, and he follows me, jogging at my side. "Where are they keeping him?"

"I'm not sure. Jang told me to wake you and meet him in his office."

I change direction as we hit the grass, seeing a lot of people awake from the commotion. Tents have been constructed for those displaced to sleep in, and I see some peeking out. I take the time to slow down.

"Everything is okay, go back to sleep," I call, watching them duck away as I stomp up the stairs to the pack house, heading to Jang's office. My heart thunders in my chest, and the entire time, I wonder which one it is.

Vale or Lucien?

Jang and all the other betas are waiting as I step into the office.

"What happened?" I ask, wearing nothing but brown checked pyjama shorts and a crop top.

Jang gestures for me to sit, but I cross my arms, and he smirks. "Out on patrol, we encountered a trail, so we followed it and found a hunter. He was wearing the symbol you told us about and had guns and plenty of weapons with him." He gestures at a bag.

It's a familiar bag, one of the black ones the guys used. Is it a hunter's bag or theirs?

Fuck, why do I care?

I decide I don't and that I'm just curious, so I focus on Jang's words once more.

"We attacked, and he fought." I notice some of them are bleeding. The wounds aren't deep, which means they must have shifted a few times to heal. "We got the better of him, and I decided to knock him out and bring him here for questioning. Since you saw some of them, I want you to—"

"Of course," I interrupt. "Where are we keeping him?"

"So eager." Tetrim huffs, and I shoot him a glare.

"These men tortured me and are now threatening my family, so yes, I'm eager to spill their blood." The other betas nod as I focus back on Jang. "Alpha, I request access to question the prisoner."

"I was hoping you would say that. He's yours." Jang nods. "We will have guards on him at all times. He's being kept in the moon cages."

I frown, but it makes sense. The cages were built for new wolves who are unable to control their shift or ferals we need to question. They are deep underground, way past the pack house, and not for the faint of heart. It also means no one will find them easily and none of the pack can see in or disturb whoever is there.

I incline my head. "Then I shall go."

"Quinn," Jang calls as I turn away. "Find out as much as you can then kill him. Don't let him make it personal. Keep calm and get what we need."

"Of course, Alpha." I nod, but I know he's wrong.

This is very fucking personal, and I'm going to make them hurt and bleed like they did me.

The door is hidden well, the metal frame shrouded by trees and plants. It was designed by one of the pack members who is an architect and built by our construction crew. I open it and hurry down the metal stairs, the door slamming shut and locking behind me.

The air is always slightly warm down here despite the ventilator, and when I hit the bottom, I nod at the three wolves standing guard.

To the right are the video feeds for the cameras we set up across our territory. This is also our base, so it has our computers, confiscated weapons, and artefacts that have been found on our land. The guard scans his handprint at the door, and it swings open. I step inside, letting it shut behind me. I ignore the cages for a moment and the shrouded figure I see in the very last one.

The wolf leans against the first one but straightens when he sees me, lowering his head. "Beta."

"Any issues?" I query.

"None," he answers quickly, and when I move closer, he bends lower, showing his respect.

"Good job," I tell him, watching him brighten as I move to the cell and finally look inside. Shock fills me.

Sitting with his knees drawn up, his head back against the stone wall is Jai. His dark eyes watch me. I see the usual madness in his gaze as he smirks, pulling on a slash mark across his cheek. I smell his blood and see his torn clothes, telling me he is worse for wear.

"Surprised I'm not dead, she-wolf?" he asks.

"Disappointed," I reply, leaning into the metal bars. "Foolish hunter, wandering our land alone. Where are your brothers?"

He doesn't answer, just stares at me for a moment. "Settled back into your pack, have you?" he comments as he pushes to his feet. Wincing in pain, he limps closer and wraps his hands around the bars. "Do they know the truth?" he mutters quietly.

I feel the wolf in the room looking at me, but I won't rise to the bait. "I have no secrets from my pack." Surprise flashes in his eyes, but I told him a lie. "So, hunter, shall we begin?"

"What? No names? I thought we were friends," he sneers.

"Friends?" I grin. "We were never friends, Jai, enemies for sure. Shall I remind you?"

"If you dare, she-wolf." He steps back, spreading his arms wide.

I smirk, holding his gaze. "Open the cage."

"Beta, we have been ordered . . ." The wolf hesitates.

I turn my gaze to him, and he withers. "I said open the cage." I let my power flood the room, and he whines as he drops to the floor, crawls to the panel, and hits it. I look around as the cage door swings open, and then I step inside.

He moves back, hitting the wall and watching me with that arrogant smirk. "I can taste your power." He cocks his head. I let my claws slide out, and his eyes drop to them. "I remember those well."

"I bet you do." I grin, looking at the wound on his neck. "It's a shame you survived, but don't worry, you won't this time."

I lunge at him, but he just waits with his arms at his sides. He knows he has nowhere to run.

He welcomes me like death welcomes its lover.

He's not easy to break, I'll give him that.

I cut up his body until he's nearly dead, his organs on the outside, and then I heal him and do it again. He doesn't scream once, nor does he answer my questions. When I grow bored, I let others join.

After all, many have history with hunters.

I've tried, and so have many others as I watched. He has countless wounds and is passed out on his side, barely able to move, so it surprises me when his voice comes. The room is empty bar us, but I'm unwilling to walk away before I get what I need.

"What you said," he says roughly, lifting up on his shaking arm, his pale face covered in blood as he turns his gaze to me. "That I hate my own kind. What did you mean?"

Leaning forward on my chair, I rest my chin on the top as I meet his eyes. "You know what I meant. You might be too afraid to admit it to them or to yourself, but you have always known."

His dark eyes stay locked on mine. "I'm a wolf."

"Or part." I shrug. "I'm not sure. I smell it on you, and the only way you would survive that"—I nod at the wound on his neck—"is if you were one of us."

He nods like he expected that, and I tilt my head, watching him.

"You didn't tell them, but they have to suspect, so is that why you walked into the woods to find us alone?" He swallows, and I know I'm right. Jai would rather die than admit he's a wolf or something like one. "How did it happen?" I ask. "You must know."

"Ferals attacked my house one night. They killed and ate my parents. I survived, but only because neighbours heard the screams and called the police. They shot one of the animals. They called it a freak attack. No one expected me to survive the wounds, but I did." He stops and watches me hesitantly, but if he wants answers, he knows he needs to talk. "I never changed. I didn't even know that was possible, and the hunters took me in and trained me, but I always felt this . . . other thing inside me demanding blood. Training helped, but when I got angry or overstimulated, it became hard to hold it back, and that's why they call me mad."

"Wolves' emotions are heightened, especially if changed by a feral. They crave blood and death. Wolves crave the hunt, and they need to work out those natural instincts. If you have been denying yourself that, then you have slowly been driving yourself mad and towards the brink of becoming feral. I don't know why you haven't changed. I have never heard of it. Either you change or die. There's nothing between. Maybe your will not to was so strong or something went wrong. Either way, there is a wolf trapped inside you, hunter."

I stand and peer down at him. "You are not human. Think about that. You are hunting your own kind and hiding from humans. They will find out. You're hated by both your own race and the race you wish you were. You are completely alone, Jai, and nobody will care when you die."

I walk away, but when I reach the door, his voice stops me. "I know, so do me a favour when you're done—kill me and put me out of my misery. I should have died that night with them. Let me die, Quinn. Please."

It's the first time I've heard Jai not only say my name, but also the word please.

It rings in my head as I open the door and head to Jang to report.

I'm unsure what to tell him. Jai's eyes follow me until he can't see me anymore, but there is one thing I know—Lucien and Vale won't be far behind.

CHAPTER TWENTY-SIX

I sit upright as someone hits my shoulder. "Vale, wake up. Jai is gone."

I blink, trying to figure out what's happening, bringing a worried Lucien into focus. He stands anxiously above me, highlighted by the sunlight streaming through the curtains.

"What?" I groan, rubbing my face. "He probably went to get food."

"No, his bed hasn't been slept in and his gear is gone, so is his truck."

That gets me up. I rush into his room, seeing Lucien is right, and turn to him. "You don't think—"

"He went to hunt the wolves himself?" Lucien nods. "The bastard is crazy enough to do so, and he's been worried ever since he woke up. I think he did. I think he went to track the wolves."

"Then we need to find him before they do." I grab some clothes and throw them on as Lucien does the same. I pick up my bag, and we both rush downstairs to our truck. Once inside, I drive out of town.

"Which way did he go though?" Lucien grumbles, scanning the trees on either side of us.

"Check the truck GPS," I remind him softly, knowing Lucien isn't thinking clearly. For all his bravado, he loves Jai like a little brother. As someone who protected me when we lost everyone else, he takes our safety seriously.

As do I, but I brush away the concern and focus on logic, on what I can control. Lucien was never able to do that.

"Fuck, I didn't even think of that," he mutters as he yanks out his phone and logs into the GPS. Both trucks have them. Lucien suggested we all get one implanted too, and I regret not doing that now. We know it will likely be too late if we are hunting for one another, but we can't give up hope.

Jai is one of the best hunters in the world, so he has to be okay.

I head towards the forest as he looks, knowing the general location he would have gone since we've been looking around here.

"Got it." Lucien shows me the location, and I nod.

It's far into the forest, and the roads turn into dirt tracks that throw us around even in our huge truck. I grip the wheel to keep us straight as Lucien presses his back to the door and holds onto the *oh shit* handle. When we finally emerge from the trees and into a dead end an hour later, the truck is right in front of us.

I pull up behind it, withdrawing my knife and gun. I leave our truck running with the doors open just in case there are any wolves around. We easily fall into formation, with Lucien watching our backs as we head towards Jai's truck. When I come up alongside it, it's empty, and sitting in the middle compartment are the keys and Jai's phone, the idiot.

"He left it behind." I peer into the forest. "I don't see any movement." I touch the hood as we round it. "Engine is cold, so he's been gone a while. We didn't go to sleep until midnight. Let's say he waited an hour or two to make sure we were asleep, then it took nearly two hours to get here. He would have started on foot around four in the morning, and it's only eight now."

"You can get far in four hours," Lucien reminds me softly. "Especially in these woods."

He's right. It's a maze of unmapped wilderness.

Thinking through our options, I peer around. "He'll head towards rock since that's the pack name. If you draw a line between here and where we trapped Quinn, the she-wolf, then he'll be heading east. I say we head that way and see if we find any trails and go from there."

"And if we don't?" Lucien asks, looking at me for a moment.

"Then we come up with another plan." Clapping his shoulder, I move back to our truck, turning off the engine and grabbing my bag. I sling it over my back and chug some water before locking up. "Don't worry, we'll find him eventually, and then you can kick his ass for being so stupid."

We hike for two hours. We found some trails leading into the forest and followed them, but as we got deeper, the trails seemed to disappear until there was nothing for us to follow.

We are deep in the wilderness now, no doubt in wolf territory, and it has us both on edge.

"We should head back," I admit in defeat.

"We have to find him." Lucien would hike forever, even right into the pack, to save one of us, but we need to play this smart.

"We will, but not like this." When his shoulders slump, I know he understands. We are crawling around in the dark forest, practically ringing the dinner bell for the wolves. We need to be smarter about this. We need a location we can go off of so we can form a plan of attack.

We need the upper hand.

"We could spend years combing through this forest," I mutter with my hands on my hips. "No, we need a faster way." I turn away. "We are going to find that pack and now."

"How?" he asks as we start to head back to the car. Luckily, we left markers that make it easier to navigate.

I smirk. "We ask nicely of course."

We become quiet after that, keeping our eyes peeled on our surroundings. We find evidence of wolves—either wild or pack, we don't know—and it has us speeding up. Two of us versus a whole pack would not end well for us.

We reach the truck in record time. Grabbing some paper, I pin a message to Jai's truck in case he comes back. I write it in code so the wolves can't understand it, and then we head out.

We need to find a better way and fast.

CHAPTER TWENTY-SEVEN

Jai

This she-wolf is a lot stronger than I first thought. She easily gutted me, torturing me with cold precision that even made my sick ass proud. Despite her healing, however, I'm exhausted and unable to move.

Instead, I stare at the door she left through.

The other wolves don't return. Either they are changing guards, which they do at random times so I cannot get used to it, or they simply think I'm too injured and weak to do anything. They aren't wrong. Right now, every inch of my body hurts. She didn't heal her latest round, and my skin is covered in claw marks, cuts, burns, and more. I can feel every single one.

My hatred and anger pale in comparison to the agony, and the worst bit?

I cannot blame her. If what she said is true, that I am a wolf or part wolf, then I have turned against my own kind and killed and slaughtered them. I can understand their anger, their need to protect their people by any means necessary. After all, didn't I do the same thing to her to protect my family?

So no, I understand her, and that makes it worse.

Rolling onto my side, I try to find a comfortable way to lie. I wince at the pain that shoots through every inch of my body. Despite the other wolves enjoying hurting me, no doubt taking their hatred out on me for my kind, she was never cruel.

Unlike how I treated her.

I have been hiding from myself since I can remember, running far and fast and denying these feelings in me. I've been hiding under the guise of being a hunter, but the truth is, I'm a coward. I'm too much of a coward to face the truth of what I am—that I could be anything like the beasts that killed and ate my parents.

I'm tired of running, though, and here, surrounded by the very beasts I hate, I have no choice but to face the truth. I want the truth, I realise, before I die, and I will die here. No one can save me. I'm a hunter, and they are monsters.

We are sworn enemies, so they will kill me. I just hope that Vale and Lucien aren't dumb enough to get involved. I would hate it if they were hurt because of me.

Swallowing hard, I close my eyes for a moment, letting that night fill my mind.

They told me it was a wild animal, but I knew it wasn't even then.

I feel the wolf tearing into me where I lie, pinned in the doorway of my parents' room. My blood pools around me as I stare into my mother's dead, empty eyes as I'm ripped apart.

I tried to stop it.

It was too quick, and I knew the moment it hit me, I was dead.

Good, at least I won't be alone.

My ears ring, and I can't even feel my body anymore or get it to work. Its muzzle is coated in my blood, and my skin is caught between its teeth. For a moment, the muzzle lowers until those eyes are all I see.

A flash of intelligence shines in those orbs, and it steps back, releasing me with just the claw and bite marks it has already inflicted upon me.

Its head lowers, as if it's waiting for something.

My eyes sweep around, searching for anything I can use to keep it away. Sirens cut through the air, and with one last look at me, the wolf growls. I scream as it lunges, but it simply flies over me, skidding across the hall and smashing out of the top window in the hallway.

Flopping onto my back, I watch the broken window as blue lights flash across the house, lighting it up.

Why didn't it kill me?

Opening my eyes, I swallow hard, my throat dry.

Did it sense something in me? Is that why it turned me and didn't kill me? Did it realise I was evil like them? Why else would a feral forgo a meal and turn its prey? I often thought the police saved me, but I was wrong. It was backing away before they arrived.

The feral chose not to kill me.

Why?

I guess I'll never know, but I can find out what I am. Quinn looked at me with pity, while the hunters looked at me with disgust and mistrust, all because of what hides deep inside me. The thing that drives me now, as Quinn explained, is probably the feral instincts running through my veins.

The very thing I hunt is inside me.

Closing my eyes once more, I curl my hands into fists, digging my nails into my slick palms. The sharp pain makes me gasp, and the instinct to kill rises.

This time, rather than satisfying or hiding it, I follow it.

I let it wash through me, filling all those dark holes and cracks inside me.

With a gasp, I open my eyes and watch as my skin seems to knit itself together, and only a slight pink mark remains where the claw marks once were. The exhaustion in my body is replaced by energy before it recedes, and when I close my eyes and dig deeper, I find an open, rotting wound deep within my soul.

Something slides past it, something cunning, dark, and angry. Usually, I recoil, pull away, and push my body until that retreats, but this time, I open my arms and I let it wash through my body.

I'm safe here, and I can't hurt anyone.

I reach towards the thing hiding inside me. I rip open the wound and dive into the pool of bright red blood. My hand reaches deep inside, and something reaches back—something sharp and furry.

A paw.

My back arches, and a scream lodges in my throat as that animal pours through my body. I feel my bones breaking and my skin ripping, and I wouldn't be surprised if I woke up in wolf form, but then it seems to recede.

It settles into my skin, as if it can't break through that last barrier, but it lingers on the surface.

I called them beasts, but as my eyes open, I realise I am the beast.

CHAPTER TWENTY-EIGHT

As I cross the grassy plains of the pack, the sun warming my skin, I ponder what I just learned.

Jai was attacked, and his family was killed. It's rare, and yes, ferals can kill, but they're mostly animals, and the closest pack handles them. For ferals to kill an entire family, something must have gone wrong. We allowed innocents in our own community to die, and because of that, Jai, the hunter, was born.

I cannot doubt his story. I could feel his pain, worry, and sincerity.

Is Jai a wolf? Has he somehow repressed it with his own hatred?

I don't know, but it's clear we need to find out. If ferals were turning people and letting them loose in the human world, then it affects all of us—not just by exposing us to humans and hunters, but by ignoring the very rules we live by.

No human will ever know the truth.

We don't kill or hunt outside of the pack.

We are bound by our code and the moon. We are blessed with these animals because we stick to them and don't spill unnecessary blood. We respect this earth and the power it holds, but if that is disrupted, then it could mean the end of wolves.

Swallowing my worry, I scoop up a pup who races past me and toss him around as a frazzled woman heads my way. I think her name is Inia. "Thank you, Quinn. I'm so sorry. He's a handful."

"Weren't we all?" I chuckle, handing over her son.

He struggles in her grip, yipping and laughing. I leave her to it as I head to the pack house. I wave at those who greet me, but I don't take the time to talk. I open Jang's door and step inside, sitting opposite his desk as he finishes a call.

He nods at me to let me know it's okay, and I wait, scanning the room.

"Will do, thank you, Ferra." He hangs up, and my eyebrows rise.

"Ferra?" I question. Ferra is alpha of the second biggest and strongest pack this side of the world, located a few hundred miles away. We often work and trade together, and when summits occur between the alphas, Ferra and Jang usually side together.

Rubbing at his face, Jang nods. "I was letting him know about the hunter issue so he could keep his eyes open. They are most likely just around here, but you never know."

"Any problems there?" I ask.

"Not from hunters, just some recent feral attacks, nothing out of the norm, but he will keep his ear to the ground. He also offered to lend us some of his best hunters and trackers."

"Wow, that's kind." I bring my knees up.

"It is, but not important right now. We might need them later. However, it's good to have open communication." He rubs his eyes again, and I tilt my head. He looks weary. His eyes are bloodshot, his mouth is drawn, and his face is pale. His hair is also a mess. If I didn't know Jang was worried, that would be enough to indicate his emotions.

"You look tired," I comment. "Have you slept?"

"An hour or two," he admits. "Don't tell my mate, she's all up in arms this morning."

Chuckling, I place my chin on my knees as I watch him. "A scary prospect for sure." I grin and then sober up. "I'm just coming to report on the hunter." I almost slipped and said his name, and that wouldn't have gone over well. If Jang realises the hunter in his cells is one that didn't only capture me but also hurt me . . .

Yeah, Jai wouldn't stand a chance, and we need answers before we kill him, so I keep it to myself.

"And?" he prompts. It isn't accusatory. He's simply curious about how it went. It isn't the first time I have been in charge of interrogating someone, so I know he trusts me.

"Not much yet. He didn't break." That has Jang's eyebrows rising. "I know, it shocked us. I'm going back after I change, and I will get the information we require."

"Be careful," Jang warns, looking worried. "Something feels off about this. I cannot put my finger on it, but my instincts are screaming at me."

I bet. Jang is the smartest man and wolf I know. He can sense something is different. Given time, he would sniff out the truth. Besides being an amazing alpha, Jang is a force of nature, and when it comes to his pack and his family, he can be brutal.

There is a reason he is able to control such aggressive, powerful shifters.

As I stare into Jang's eyes, I debate telling him what Jai told me, but something about it feels like betraying a secret. Stupid, I know. Jang is my father, my alpha, but I need to learn the whole truth before I go to him. If Jai is a feral, it will affect how we deal with this, so I need to be sure before I tell him.

I shelter Jai's horrible past and tell him everything else.

Jang is worried enough as it is, so I need to take as much off his plate as I can.

Once I'm done telling him everything, I let my feet hit the floor and lean forward. "I will handle this. We are all doing our part. Get some rest." I grin. "Or I'll tell Mom."

"You wouldn't dare," he mutters, and the big bad alpha actually looks scared.

"I would." I leave him to debate if he fears the hunters or his wife more.

We both know it's his wife.

———

After checking in with the patrolling betas and the pack as much as I can to ease Jang's burden, I head back to the cells to confront Jai.

I need answers, and I need them now.

I cannot let my pack suffer, regardless of him possibly being a wolf.

There are no wolves inside the cells this time, so they clearly think he isn't worth the effort, but even as I approach his cell, I know something is different. It's not even in the slight change of his scent, the musk almost rich and spicy. It's in the glow of his eyes.

He's less human and more beast.

It's in his voice, which is deeper and more of a growl. "Little she-wolf," he greets me.

Leaning back against the cell opposite, I look him over, seeing his wounds have healed. Only shifting or my healing ability could have done that. Surely, they would have noticed him shifting, even if they didn't notice anything else.

"You shifted," I comment, confused. He isn't stuck in his wolf form, which usually happens when ferals first shift, nor was I gone long, so what happened?

"Not exactly." He cocks his head, and it's definitely more animalistic.

He blinks as he climbs to his knees, gripping the bars, and I see them dent. I hold back my horror and shock as I stare into the abyss of his gaze.

Jai is absorbing his wolf, his feral side, and it's only made him more dangerous.

He's a hunter mixed with a beast.

It would be like turning into a serial killer. I know you cannot show fear or back down with an animal. After all, I am an alpha.

"What does that mean?" I ask, fusing some of my dominance into my tone.

His chin lowers slightly. Good, his animal recognises the leadership in my tone as well as the pack rank. That will help a little. Sometimes, ferals can abandon all thought and reason, even ignoring an alpha's command. It's what makes them so unpredictable.

"You were right. There was something in me. I let it out," he replies, his eyes going dark with his wolf. Most become brighter, but Jai's turn black.

They used to call it a sign of the devil.

He's feral, that's for sure.

Fuck.

"I didn't shift. I could feel it wanting to." His tongue drags along his lips as he looks at me. "I could feel it expanding in my skin, clawing to be set free, but it was like it couldn't."

"A trapped wolf," I murmur, watching him. They are usually the worst. The pain and short lifespan don't help, but it's at least good for us. "It happens when you aren't changed properly. You have the wolf, but not the ability to shift. You will have more strength than a human but less than a wolf and heal quicker, but not as quickly as a wolf. You will never be able to shift, and it will eventually drive you and your wolf mad . . . well, madder."

He watches me for a moment. "So I will never be a wolf?"

"No," I answer honestly. I'll admit I feel a bit of pity for him.

"Not human enough to be a hunter, too human to be a wolf." He laughs bitterly, the maniacal sound raising the hair on my arms. "I'm screwed."

"You won't leave here alive, so you don't have to worry," I say, and he looks at me.

"You don't seem happy about that. I thought you would after

what we did to you. I thought you'd want my death after how I treated you," he muses, clearly curious.

"You did what you had to do, and I'm doing the same. I understand duty," I admit. "Yes, you are clearly unhinged and enjoyed my pain, but I understand where that comes from now. They say when you know your enemy, you always care for them. I wouldn't go that far." He grins a slightly crazy smile. "But I also don't hate you or want your death. It's simply—"

"Duty." He nods.

"Duty." I nod as well. "Tell me about the hunters, about Vale and Lucien."

"I cannot betray my brothers," he replies seriously, "nor the hunters."

"You owe them nothing. They left you to die."

"No, I left to die. There's a difference. The hunters might have shunned me, but they are still my people. I will not betray them no matter what you do," he replies, and I sense the ring of truth in his words.

Jai will never break and betray his people for nothing, not even after they looked down on him.

He's a far better man than most, but it won't save him.

"They will try to break you, even if I go back and tell them I can't," I admit. "Tell me something, Jai, anything, so I can work with it. You understand duty." I step forward, lowering to my knees until we are eye level, my hands covering his on the bars. "Please, this is my family too, and I cannot lose them." I swallow. "Not again. My parents were killed by hunters." He flinches, his eyes wide. "I was a kid. My younger sister died, as well as my dad and mum. This pack took me in. I cannot lose them too."

I let him see my true fear. It won't matter because he'll die here.

"I can't—" I swallow deeply. "I cannot lose anyone else I love to hunters. Please, Jai, wouldn't you do anything to save your family?"

"Quinn, I cannot." He sighs. "I'm sorry about your family—"

"Did you know it was Lucien and Vale's father who killed them?"

He stops breathing then, watching me. "I did, and I still saved him. I still healed Lucien. I didn't kill them. Their father's sins aren't theirs. If I promise not to hunt them, will you tell me something I can use to keep my family safe?"

"Why wouldn't you harm them if that's true?" he asks suspiciously.

"Because I don't blame them." It's the truth. I might hate what they are, but I don't hate them. "I will do anything not to let a repeat of my story happen. I was too little, too weak to save them then." I know he understands that. "I won't be now. If I have to hunt Vale and Lucien to get answers, then I will. I won't save them this time. Please, Jai, if not for me, then for them."

"Quinn," he murmurs, his fingers twitching under mine as I plead with him.

"Do you want me to tell you how I had to watch my little sister die? Or how I had to watch my pregnant mother be ripped to pieces by your weapons?" He flinches, trying to tug away, but I make him face the truth. "How my father sacrificed himself to save me, staying by his dead wife and kid until the end even though it meant death? You know now that we aren't animals. We aren't bad. We are just here like you. My family didn't deserve to die. My father was innocent, my mother was innocent, and my little sister was innocent. Her name was Filly, and she wanted to be president." I grin. "She would walk around in suits my mother sewed for her. We would watch action reruns together, and my father would fix cars, always smelling of grease. We were not evil, we were just a normal family, and because of those people you are protecting, they are dead and the only time I see them now is in my nightmares because you hunters stole even my dreams of them. I don't remember the way they smiled or the way their arms felt around me. I remember their screams for help. Your people slaughtered children, an innocent family. Why are you protecting them? No matter what you say, you aren't evil. You hunt because you have to, because you feel like you protect innocents, so what about me? Am I evil? Was my little sister evil?"

"Stop." He tries to tug his hands away, but I grip them tighter. If he chooses to protect them, then he doesn't get to ignore the evil they commit.

He cannot have both.

"Was my pregnant mum evil? Were your parents?" He's breathing heavily, and his eyes are pitch black. "Is Vale? Is Lucien? There is only one way this ends, Jai, and it isn't good for either of us. Many will die, including Vale and Lucien, unless we can stop this. We don't want their deaths. We just want to be left alone. Surely you see that now."

"We can't stop this, even if we want to," he croaks. "We are just tools, Quinn. Don't you see that? We are just the blades in a century-long war. We cannot change the tides. No one can."

"We can try," I argue. "I have to try. Innocents have to stop dying. I cannot live with blood on my hands. My nights are already filled with nightmares. I don't have room for anymore."

"You are so optimistic." He sighs. "Like Lucien." He debates my words, staring into my face. "If I tell you something to keep your pack safe, will you leave Lucien and Vale alone?"

"If I can, but if they come here, I can't keep them safe." I won't lie to him, not right now. Right now, we aren't enemies. We are just two souls on the wrong side of the line.

He nods. "Understandable, but if you can, don't kill my brothers. Unlike me, they aren't killers. Vale acts like it, but he hates killing. He does it because of his father. Lucien hates it more but does it to keep Vale safe. Both of them are caught in their own cycle of respect and love."

I can feel his fight. He wants to help and stop his brothers from getting killed, and he knows there is only one way—working together with me. "If a hunter were to redirect them, telling them there was no pack here, then they would leave. We move HQs all the time, or if there were a bigger issue than the wolves, we would have no choice but to give up the hunt. They don't know where you are. At least, they didn't when I left."

I sit back, watching him. He could be lying but at some point, we have to trust one another. It's the only way this will end without bloodshed. "Could you do it? Could you call them off?"

"Me?" He laughs bitterly. "No, she-wolf, they hate me, even before this." He jerks his head at himself. "They never trusted me. I guess they knew the truth, even when I didn't. They would trust Vale, but he would never help you, not now that he thinks you have captured and killed me."

Nodding, I sit back and debate my options.

I lean into the cage as he does, both of us caught in thought when his voice suddenly breaks through. "What's it like growing up as a wolf?"

I turn my head to meet his gaze. We are so close that I feel his breath waft over my face. I don't move away, though, because something about him being this close doesn't feel completely wrong. It could be my wolf reacting to his, or maybe it's because we are just two lost, orphaned souls.

While I was adopted by loving parents, Jai was pumped full of hatred and prejudice since he was young. No wonder he turned out the way he did.

But can people really change?

Can he overcome years of conditioning? I don't know, and the sad part is, I don't think he'll ever get the chance.

Jai was doomed to live a short, painful life devoid of love and happiness. It will end the way it began—in bloodshed.

"Happy." It's the first word that comes to mind, and I smile. "I was never alone, and I hated being alone," I tell him. "If it wasn't my new parents, it was one of the pack members. They were always there. They helped me through my shift and wiped away my tears when I was hurt. They fed me, and we celebrated highs and lows. There is just so much love everywhere. Being a wolf isn't just about shifting. It's about pack mentality. We are one. If one of us is hurting, we all are. We take care of each other. We all have our roles, and you'll always find help and caring hands. Even when I fucked up when I was a bratty teenager, they didn't punish me—well, not too badly. They showed me why I was wrong and helped me understand. Here, we watch out for all the different generations of our people, from pups to the elders. We all live as one big family. Obviously, it's not always easy. We do fight for our positions and shit happens, but we always have one another."

"Must be nice," he murmurs after I trail off.

"What was it like growing up as a hunter?" I ask, genuinely curious. It's not like I'll ever ask again. I'll never be this close to a member after this.

"Scary," he admits. "I never knew if they were going to drop me, but being dropped as a hunter means death. It means you don't qualify. It was a lot like joining the military, I guess. We had drills and training since I was a teenager, and you had to graduate, which meant you got sent out on a hunt alone. If you survived, then you were a hunter. It's all we knew. We were given teams, but no one wanted me. Vale and Lucien took me in, they saw something in me, and we set out to prove ourselves. You start at the bottom and work yourself up the ranks, but it was always scary. I never knew if I would die each day. We moved continually, never putting down roots. We couldn't have friends or relationships, not that I wanted any, but it was a very lonely life. We put up with it because we thought . . . We thought we were helping people—the last line of defence between monsters and human extinction." He laughs bitterly. "I guess in some ways, we weren't wrong. We did save people, and that only gave us more motivation, but the older I got, the more I realised some hunters did it simply because they liked killing." He turns to look at me. "Like me."

"Sounds brutal," I say. I guess I never thought about it. "It sounds almost like a cult."

"I guess it is." He chuckles. "I met a cult once."

"Really?" I find myself grinning.

"Oh yeah. We got sent there because they thought they were witches, but it was just a very real human cult." He shakes his head.

"Crazy bastards. We ended up turning them over to the authorities, but we went undercover first, and they made me look sane."

"Damn, it must have been crazy then." I wink as he grins.

We lapse into silence, and I swallow when I realise we just had a normal conversation. No hatred, no threats, just talking.

"I'll try to save Vale and Lucien." I feel him looking at me. "Vale saved me the night my parents died," I tell him. "And Lucien let me go when I escaped the night I tried to kill you."

"Well, shit." Jai laughs. "Bastards."

I grin again, and feeling awkward, I try to get to my feet, but he catches my hand. "Can you stay a little longer? I'm going to die soon anyway, so can you entertain me for a while?"

"I'm not your joker. I'm your jailor," I tease, my eyes going to his hand on mine. He lets go quickly, but I sit back down, not saying a word.

"How does it feel to change?" he asks.

"Like euphoria," I reply with a wince. "It hurts like hell the first time, but then it becomes as natural as breathing and it feels like you take a full, deep breath for the first time. You and your wolf become one. It feels like part of your soul, and the freedom you find running? There's nothing like it. Sorry."

"Don't be," he says. "I probably deserve this."

We lapse into silence again.

"I still hate you, she-wolf," he says randomly.

I can't help but grin and meet his gaze to see him smiling softly. "I still hate you, hunter."

Why does that sound like a good thing now? Like an endearment rather than a slur?

CHAPTER TWENTY-NINE

Slamming the man into his desk, I glare at him as he shakes and cowers. "Where is it?" I demand.

Ask nicely, Vale said, but this is nicely since he doesn't have a knife in his chest.

Clearly, the townspeople are protecting the pack or unknowingly doing so.

We don't have time to keep searching the records. We need to find them fast. The man behind city planning has to know. He's an older man with a kind smile and moustache, but when we tried to bribe him, he threatened to call the police, and there was a knowing look in his eyes.

Too knowing.

"I don't know what you mean. I'm going to call the police, you thugs! This is a nice town. Who are you—"

I slam him down again as Vale gets into his face.

"Outsiders, a big amount of them, where are they?" He might not know they are wolves, but he knows something. His eyes slide away, confirming just that, and I shake him before slamming my fist into his face.

"I'd tell. I can be reasoned with, but he cannot," Vale cajoles, playing the good guy.

The man shoots me a glare over his shoulder. "I suggest you leave."

"Motherfucker." I start pulling my fist back again, but sirens cut through the air, and we glance through the dusty windows to see the police pulling up outside. Someone must have called them.

Fuck. We don't even have time to get away, but I release the man and step back. "This isn't over. We know you know."

"Alright, gents, hands behind your backs. We'll get this sorted at the station." Luckily, they are chill cops, since it's such a small town, but when they see the moustached man bleeding, they get rough with us, grumbling the entire time about outsiders.

My eyes narrow as the police handcuff us. The hunters will have us out soon, since we have dedicated lawyers, but we'll lose precious time, which we could use to find Jai—not to mention the questions HQ will ask.

We don't have fucking time for this.

As we are dragged outside, I see the moustached man making a call.

No doubt he's warning the wolves.

<hr>

JAI

I watch Quinn. She must have been exhausted to fall asleep here. Her head rests on the hard bars. I should wake her or move away, but I can't seem to stop staring. She's beautiful. I never really cared or noticed before. Hunting is all my life has been, but as I stare, something stirs within me.

Her lashes are long, and her hair falls in loose, messy waves, long and thick. Her face is heart-shaped and adorable, just sharp enough to give her a slightly menacing look. She's tall with muscles and feminine curves.

She is beautiful, yes, but why can't I look away?

She's the enemy, but more than that, I never cared about women or men before. Hunting is all I know. So why now? Why this wolf? Why does something inside me soften and throb?

She sighs, rubbing her head with an adorable frown, no doubt trying to find a comfy spot against the bars.

Swallowing, I slide my hand between her head and the bars as she sleeps.

The animal inside me seems to purr at her presence, and her sweet scent wraps around me like a warm blanket. Is this the wolf? Is it because we are the same now?

Even in my denial, I know I'm wrong. I saw her before.

I fucking saw her, and I hated her for it.

Why can't I seem to now?

When she jerks up at a bang, I yank my hand back. She glances at me, blinking before climbing to her feet and moving away as a huge man enters. He's older and massive, carrying an aura of power about him. He glares at me, but when his eyes rove over her, they fill with love and worry.

Boyfriend?

For a moment, something like envy fills me, though I don't know why, and the wolf trapped in my skin wants to lunge.

"You have been gone for a while."

I get to my feet, glaring at the man, but she doesn't even spare me a look as she goes to him. My wolf claws at me, making me grunt, and I narrow my gaze on him.

"I apologise." She ducks her head slightly, showing respect as his eyes go to me. "Let's go talk—"

"So this is the hunter." He steps past her, not stopping until he's before the bars.

Just a little closer and I could rip his throat out—or his eyes for looking at her.

"Alpha," she says, heading my way, but he ignores her, gripping the bars hard.

"The one willing to kidnap my daughter and hurt my family." I startle at that, looking at Quinn. This is her father? Her father is the alpha of the pack? No wonder she cares so much. This is truly her family.

I keep my mouth shut, but my anger lessens. I don't analyse why.

"Well, have nothing to say?" He looks at Quinn. "Has he spoken?"

"Alpha," she begins, and he snarls.

She lowers her head, and something in me awakens at her bowing to him. I step closer, and when he turns back around, his eyes widen at seeing me so close. I keep his attention on me. Daughter or not, he might hurt her. I can't let that happen for some reason.

Only I'm allowed to hurt her.

"Why don't you ask me?" I offer instead, my voice level and calm.

"Like I would believe anything that came from your scum mouth," the alpha retorts.

"Jang." She touches his arm, and he softens as he looks at her. "Come on, let us talk."

"I think I'd like to talk with him first. Meet me in my office," he commands.

"Jang," she begins, and he growls.

She drops her hand and head. "Yes, Alpha. I'm sorry."

She shoots me a troubled, searching look before turning and leaving. I watch her go, and when I glance back, he's observing me carefully. I don't know what he sees, but he doesn't like it. "Open the gate," he roars, and the cell swings open immediately.

He steps in, taking up the whole space.

I step back, ready to fight when I realise I can't. This is Quinn's father, and whatever else I have, I won't hurt her in that manner. I can't seem to want to, even if, logically, I know harming the alpha might set me free.

Instead, I let his fist hit my face. I let him throw me into the wall.

I let him beat me, and when he stands over me, his chest heaving and eyes bright with his wolf, I meet his gaze. "Don't you ever look at my daughter. Do you understand me? She is all I have left. You will not take her too. I will be back, and when I return, I want answers, whatever it takes."

He slams the bars and storms off, leaving me bleeding and confused.

I hope Quinn will be okay. He's a tornado of fury right now and no doubt heading to her.

CHAPTER THIRTY

I worry the entire time I wait for Jang in his office. What did he see? What did he hear? Fuck, I even worry about Jai. Will he kill him? I don't know why I care. I got what I needed. I owe him nothing. So why do I feel sick?

When Jang storms in, the door bangs against the wall with his fury. Waves of dominance hit me, almost knocking me over as I get to my feet. He rounds his desk and leans against it, his eyes bright with his wolf, and I spot the blood on his knuckles.

His and Jai's.

My heart rebels at the pain that slices through me.

Traitor, I hiss at it.

"Jang," I begin, needing to tell him what I know.

"You will not be in charge anymore," he snaps.

I jerk in shock. Is this because I fell asleep? Did he see Jai touch me?

Does he think I've betrayed them?

"Father," I start.

"No." He slams his fists, making me jump. "This is final," he warns. "This is a command from your alpha. Do not even go near those cells. We will make him talk."

I swallow my rebuttal and my disappointment. What did he see? I can't even tell him what Jai told me because he won't listen right now.

"Whatever I have done to earn your distrust, Alpha, I am sorry." I lower to my knees, my head bowed. I feel pain in my heart from his anger as well as him relieving me of my duties I have worked so hard for.

"It isn't that I don't trust you, Quinn." He sighs. "Just do this for me."

"Yes, Alpha," I respond dutifully.

I hear him inhale in pain. "Quinny—"

"Am I excused, Alpha?" I ask.

There's a long stretch of silence. "Yes, you're excused."

Standing without looking at him, I turn and leave, hiding the tears in my eyes. My father, my alpha, doesn't trust me, and the worst bit is, I don't trust myself.

What's happening?

I hide in my cabin, ashamed and angry at myself. How could I have been so careless as to fall asleep?

As for talking to him? He is a hunter, and these are my people.

How could I?

Screaming into my duvet, I flip over, holding the ragged picture to my chest. Worst of all, I hurt Jang. I disappointed a man who saved me and raised me as his own. I am a fool. How can I be an alpha if I can't handle this?

Why is my wolf on edge and restless?

Fighting my tears, I flop my arm over my face. Everything is so fucking messed up.

There is a hesitant knock at the door, and I peer over to see Dom. "Need a cuddle?"

I nod frantically. Wolves need contact. The heat and smell of another body is comforting, and right now, I need that. I don't ask how Dom knows, Jang probably sent him, but I need this. It's not sexual as he climbs up and removes his shirt to let me absorb his warmth and scent. It's just natural as he wraps me in his arms, and I melt into his embrace.

"What would you do?" I mumble sometime later.

"About what?" he asks, kissing the top of my head.

"If you knew what you were doing was right but it would cause someone to mistrust you, someone you love more than anything."

He thinks it through. "I would do it and hope they love me enough to understand and listen to me." He holds me tighter. "You are smart, Quinn, and capable. There is a reason you will be the next alpha, and it's not because of who Jang is to you. It's because you have proven time and time again that you put this pack first. Even when others didn't believe you could, you stood against all odds and survived. Whatever it is, you must have a reason. I won't ask because you clearly don't want to tell me yet, but know we love and support you. You're family."

I needed to hear that, but as I snuggle into Dom, the scent seems wrong.

I need a spicier one.

Fuck!

CHAPTER THIRTY-ONE

"I can't fucking believe this," Lucien grumbles from the cell over. Luckily, in this tiny town, there is only us and a drunk sleeping off his fix within the jail. The security is lax, and we could break out for sure, but we need them to let us go. We can't hunt wolves if the police are hunting us, so we stay despite how angry we are.

Each second that ticks by is another moment where Jai will be hurt, and it's eating me up inside.

On the outside, I look calm, my eyes shut and arms behind my head, but they don't see the hardness of my muscles or my fists clenching under my head.

"Vale?" Lucien hisses. I don't even have to open my eyes to know he's pacing. It won't change anything. They are clearly buddies with the guy we assaulted and are holding us here to decide what to do. I even overheard moustache guy say he wasn't pressing charges, but the cops are still holding us.

Are they buying them time to warn the wolves?

Fuck!

I feel my jaw tick, my gums aching from how hard I'm grinding my teeth.

"We need to get out of here. Jai is in trouble," he spits, like I don't know that. The sound of a chainsaw snore interrupts him, and I hear him grumble and bang on the bars.

Footsteps head our way, and I crack an eye open to see two cops standing on the other side of the bars as Lucien grips them. "Let us out," he tells them, practically vibrating with worry, but they mistake it for anger.

Why wouldn't they?

Lucien is a six-foot-seven brick wall. He could smash them with one hit, and they know that. Their hands drift to their batons and guns as he stands before them, unarmed and locked away.

"Whoa, big guy, if you don't calm down, we'll have to tase you," one warns as Lucien grips the bars, practically foaming at the mouth.

That gets me moving. I slide silently from the cot and move to the bars. When they glance at me, they jerk back in shock, surprised to see me there.

"Do not threaten my brother," I warn them. "It won't end well for you. Lucien, stand down." I spare him a look to see him throwing the cops a sneer before he sits heavily on the cot, his own worry and guilt making him careless. "Now, about my phone call."

The one with a big, red, bushy beard, a pot belly, and a name tag reading "Miller" glares at me. "You'll get your call when I say so."

"Which is now, unless you want us to cause trouble, which I'm betting from your tiny town and perfect record, you really don't want," I sneer.

"You big city folk are all assholes. You came here and started beating on our people, and now you're demanding I do what you want? You sure have balls."

"More than you know," I tell him. "But we work for someone, and they won't be too happy to know we have been locked up without being accused of anything or given a phone call or a lawyer, so it's your choice. Let me call now or face the wrath of our employer."

It's a bluff, sort of. We do have a lawyer on retainer. Hunters get caught by humans all the time. Some are labelled as stalkers or peeping Toms. Monsters even use human law to stop us. It was easier to keep a lawyer on staff to get us free.

I see him debating his options as I stare him down.

Whatever he sees in my frosty gaze unnerves him, and he turns away. "Get him his call."

I grin the whole time they cuff me and lead me out of the cell to the wooden desk a few feet away. The other cop tries to push me down using my shoulder, but I arch a brow and resist. His face mottles and his eyes bulge as he uses both hands to try and push me down into the chair. When he gasps and steps back, I finally sit and point at the black, old-fashioned phone.

"This for me?"

"You have two minutes, make it quick," he hisses as he lumbers to the door and stands there with his arms crossed. I wink at Lucien, who shakes his head, then I pick up the phone and dial the one number I have memorised—the one number you never want to have to call.

It means you failed because it means you need help, something a hunter should never ask for.

The line rings for a while before a grumbling, annoyed voice answers. "This better be good." There's a pause then as their systems work. "Fuck's sake, the jail?"

"It's me. Vale." I sigh. "We have an issue. Can you get us out?"

"What are you in for?" he mutters.

"Assault, but they aren't charging us—"

"Then they will let you out sooner or later. It's probably just a pissing contest. Don't piss them off and they'll let you go." He goes to hang up.

"Wait, we need to go now. It's a time-sensitive hunt," I hiss.

"It always is. I've got three in for mass murder, even though it was on a troll, one in for desecrating a corpse, who was trying to stop a fucking zombie, and another for robbing a mortuary. I don't have time for this shit." He slams the phone down.

"Fucking lawyers," I grit out as Lucien sighs.

"Phone call didn't go well?" The cop laughs as he yanks me to my feet and thrusts me into my cell. The door slams, and I put my hands through for him to uncuff.

"You'll have to let us go sooner rather than later," I demand.

"Probably later. Now have a good sleep with old Tom there but be careful. He wakes up vomiting." The cop laughs as he ambles away.

Nostrils flaring, I spare the drunk in my cell a look before meeting Lucien's eyes. "Any ideas?"

"Not any good ones, and none that are legal, that's for sure."

I glance at the clock. "Give them two hours, then we'll make a move. One way or another, we are getting out of here and finding Jai."

"Got it." Lucien nods.

I sit once more, pretending to relax as I wait for them to let us go.

Only one of us will win here, and it will be us.

JAI

My arms are chained above my head in my cell. My wolf flashes inside me, clawing to get out and get at the men glaring at me, but all it does is cut me up deeper inside, making it hurt worse as they ram their supernatural strength into my body time and time again.

As soon as Quinn left with her father, four of them came in, telling me it was time to talk, yet they've asked no questions, only tortured me. It's funny. Despite them being monsters, they clearly don't know the finesse of this. There is pain, that's for sure, but I'm used to pain.

There is no threat, though, no genuine reason to be scared of them.

I'm more scared of myself.

People call me unhinged, feral, and psychotic, and maybe I am since I'm grinning through bloodied teeth as they work my body over. I taunt them each time, daring them to do more, watching their anger get worse and worse.

"Enough," a dark, familiar voice calls.

Quinn's father.

He steps into the room, sparing me a disgusted look. "Has he spoken?" he asks, and I watch the wolves shrink in size, bowing to their alpha. Interesting, they also did that to Quinn.

"Not yet, Alpha," one responds, his knuckles dripping with my blood.

"Then I will. Stand outside," the alpha commands as he heads my way.

"Alpha, we can do this—"

"I never said you couldn't." He claps a man on the shoulder. "But this is personal. He took my Quinny, so head outside."

"Yes, Alpha." They all hurry out, slamming the door.

I swing before the alpha, before Quinny's father. "Where's Quinn? Is she okay?" I have to ask. He was really fucking angry, and I don't know this man. Did he hurt her?

Why do I care if he did?

His eyebrow arches as he looks at me. "You will never see her again."

For a moment, my heart goes cold. He killed her?

She's dead?

"You hurt my daughter. Do you think I would ever let her near you again?" I actually slump in relief. She's not dead. He's simply protecting her.

Good.

His knuckles crack as he steps into the cell with me. "I won't lose my daughter like I lost my best friend." His fist rams into my stomach, making me gasp as I feel something break.

I clamp my lips shut to hold back my agonised screams as he hits me again and again. I feel bones break and skin rip.

When he steps back, I spit blood, but it dribbles down my own chin to my chest. My lungs ache as I cough. "Where are the hunters?"

I don't speak, but I meet his eyes boldly, letting him see the truth in my gaze.

I will never betray my family, no matter what I am now.

I don't know what he sees in my eyes, but he stops, narrowing his own. "You're not human," he murmurs. "Did one of us turn you?"

"A feral, years ago." I finally speak, and he steps back, eyeing me.

"You're a wolf who works with them," he spits. "Traitor."

I clamp my lips shut again, and it's like that truth releases something inside the huge, hulking alpha wolf. It's then I realise he was holding back so as not to kill my human body, but not anymore.

There's so much strength behind his punch that I'm surprised his fist doesn't slam through my body, leaving a massive hole. One even knocks me back into the wall. I feel nearly every bone ache or break, and then he steps back.

"Where are the hunters?"

I don't answer, biting my tongue until I taste blood. This time, his fists hit my face, blinding me. I feel my eyes pop, and a scream rips loose as he grips my face.

All I see is darkness, and panic winds through me as I choke on my bile and blood. "Where are they?" he demands, his warm breath wafting over my face.

Next, he breaks my nose, and I choke, gasping like a fish through my mouth.

He's good, but I won't speak.

I won't betray Lucien and Vale like that.

It goes on for hours, or at least it feels like it. I lose all sense of time. My eyes start to heal, but it's blurry and wrong, and he takes great pleasure in inflicting the most pain possible. This is personal. This is hatred for what hunters did to his daughter and his friend.

I know because I have that same hatred inside my heart.

"Alpha, your mate is calling you," someone shouts sometime later before the door bangs shut again.

Cutting the rope, he watches me fall to a heap on the floor, barely moving. "You're strong, I'll give you that. If you were a wolf, you would be one of the best, but you're a hunter who's stupid and bound to die. You will eventually talk, and when you do, I will kill every last one of your kind for laying a finger on my daughter's head." The cell door slams, and he stomps away.

I don't know how long I lie there, my wolf moving inside me as if trying to heal me, for all the good that does. When my nose heals with a pop, I suck in a desperate breath of air. One of my lungs is still deflated, but it's getting better.

He's right. I'd be dead as a human, but there is one undeniable truth—I'll die here and painfully. Either way, I won't betray my brothers. They'll realise that sooner or later. Lucien and Vale will blame themselves for my death. They'll get reckless and stupid, attacking the pack and probably dying.

Still, there is nothing I can do.

I lie in my heap, knowing I won't die yet but wanting to. Deep down, I won't betray them, but that doesn't mean I want to spend the next few days of my life in pain.

For some reason, though, Quinn comes to mind, and my resolve lessens. Wouldn't the pain be worth it?

Fuck! It's the wolf talking. It's fucking with me, and I hate it.

It's not me, right?

"Jai." The soft whisper has me jerking my head up as my gaze locks on the crouched figure.

Even with healing eyes, I would know her anywhere.

"Quinn?" I query as I drag myself to the bars. "You shouldn't be here."

"No shit," she mutters, and despite the agony in my body, I smile.

"How'd you get in?" My voice is slurred, and I see her wince as my vision heals a little.

She shrugs. "The guard wants to fuck me."

"Of course." I snort. "Why are you here?" I ask seriously.

We aren't friends. We are enemies, despite the comfort of the other night.

She swallows hard, looking me over. "I have a plan that might save us all, but before I decide, I need to know, Jai . . . do you still hate wolves?"

I debate her question, seeing the seriousness in her gaze. "I don't know," I admit truthfully.

For a moment, she peers at me until I see a challenge emerge in her eyes, but I don't know who is more shocked, her or me, when she yanks me into the bars. Her lips press down on mine in a brutal, harsh kiss.

My lips part in confusion, and she sweeps her tongue inside, tangling it with mine. She tastes every inch of my mouth as I stay stock-still. Shock gives way to anger and then desire as she pulls back.

"How about now? Still hate wolves?" she whispers against my lips.

My bloodied hand slides through the bars, gripping her soft, thick locks, and I jerk her closer. She gasps as her face hits the cold metal bars, but it soon turns into a moan as I slant my head and kiss her.

If I'm going to die, I want to taste heaven at least once more.

Inhaling hard, I narrow my eyes on her cloudy ones. "You smell like another man." I slam my lips to hers again. Jealousy swims through me, though I don't have a clue as to why.

There's a bang on the outside door, and she rips herself away. We both sit there, breathing heavily. The dare in her eyes is gone, replaced by shock and desire. Neither of us want this, but we can't seem to help it.

My hand drifts to my lips, and she follows the movement before scrambling to her feet. "Never mind," she says and hurries to the door.

"Quinn?"

She stills, not looking back.

"No," I tell her truthfully. "I don't hate wolves anymore."

How could I when she is one?

CHAPTER THIRTY-TWO

My fingers drag along my lips as I walk across the grass in a daze. I waited until I saw Jang leave, covered in blood, and snuck in. I had to be sure for this plan to work—one that will cost me everything.

It will be worth it, though, if my pack is safe.

I shake my head at my own stupidity for kissing him and swallow the desire inside me, one caused by his rough lips. It's wrong. He's a hunter. Both of us are playing the other, so why did it feel so right?

Shit!

I need to snap out of it. There is too much going on to be daydreaming about a stupid fucking kiss.

"Quinn."

I jerk around, seeing Dom heading my way. I slipped out of his arms during the night and despite that, he still grins warmly at me.

He also knows me well enough not to ask. "Hey," I say, somewhat shaken.

"You okay?" he asks, slowing.

"Yeah, fine." I clear my throat. "What's up?"

His arm slings around my shoulder. "How about we go for a run to burn off some steam?" He wiggles his brows, making me laugh.

"Sure, sounds good to me." A good hunt might just brighten my mood and remind me why I'm doing this.

"Come on." He takes my hand, and we jog to the perimeter of the trees where we quickly shed our clothes, stuffing them in a hollow log before changing. We slink into the trees, our paws hitting the ground as Dom gives me a wolfy smile then takes off.

His brown wolf is a blur. He's smaller than some but strong as hell. He's still not as fast as me, though, and he knows it. It's a game, and I give him a head start before racing after him.

The scent of rabbit fills my nose, and I war with my wolf's natural instincts to hunt, bloodlust making my ears and tail twitch. Dom smells it as well, and we turn. I go right, and he goes left. With my nose down, I hunt the rabbit.

Dom snaps a twig to get it to run, both of us used to hunting with the other, and then we are off.

With a leap, I land on the furry animal and quickly snap its neck to make its death humane. I send my gratitude into the earth that provides as I lift the bleeding rabbit in my jaws and show Dom as he pads into the clearing.

His tail wags for a moment, letting me know he's playing, and then he lunges at me, snarling. I drop the rabbit and meet him head-on. We smack into the ground and roll, our paws hitting each other. He tries to pin me, and I dart out of reach. His front paws slide out, pushing his ass higher into the air, as he watches me and then lunges again.

He's trying to roll me to get me to present under him.

It's a game, it's flirting, and we both know it. When he succeeds in pinning me, I shift back to my human form, as does he. Dom is naked and panting on top of me, his eyes blazing with desire as he drops his head and presses his lips to mine.

I grip his shoulders, digging my nails in as I widen my legs to welcome him. It's a familiar move, but the kiss seems wrong.

It's sloppy and not hard enough. My wolf almost rejects it, and I'm about to pull away when Dom suddenly vanishes.

I jerk upright to find a furious Tetrim standing above me, his hands balled into fists. He spares me a disgusted look, and then he, too, is gone.

Leaping to my feet, I race after them, coming to a stop in the tree line to see Dom getting to his feet on the grass as the pack gathers, no doubt hearing the trouble. "What the fuck, man?" Dom demands, but Tetrim doesn't stop.

He heads right to him, slamming his fist into Dom's face. Dom doesn't fight back, knowing the rules. This isn't a fight, it's an unofficial challenge, but both of them could be banished for it. In wolf form, it's fine, but as humans?

A challenge must be issued, and Dom knows that, so he's playing by the rules.

Gritting my teeth, I head their way, annoyed as both Dom's friend and as beta of this pack. I can't believe Tetrim would so easily ignore our rules and flaunt possessiveness over someone who isn't even his. Dom goes down hard as Tetrim continues to pummel him, never once protecting himself.

I catch Tetrim's fist midair as he goes to hit Dom again, his dark eyes coming to me. "I challenge you," I declare officially as I thrust him away.

Gasps ring out, and a crowd forms. No doubt Jang and the others will hear about it soon. I already see White and Filmea watching. They nod at me in understanding as I step back to face Tetrim.

"You dare attack another pack member unprovoked without issuing a challenge? You dare to taunt the authority of this pack and our laws? The laws that keep us safe? Do you think you are above the alpha?" I spit as White grabs Dom and helps him up. I spare him a look to ensure he'll heal quickly.

"Quinn," Tetrim starts, but I turn my glare on him.

"You just proved you have no respect for this pack or Alpha Jang.

You will be punished for so confidently flaunting your disrespect of our laws."

"Why, because I hurt your boyfriend?" he sneers.

"No, because you dared to strike a pack member without a challenge. You want to fight, Tetrim? Fine, let's fight." I offer no more words. After all, this has been a long time coming.

He's a pain in the ass but also strong, so I can't underestimate him. He must be stopped, however, and punished before he believes he's untouchable.

I make the first move. Ignoring the pack and the whispers, I fling myself at him. He steps back as I expected, and I sweep my leg out, knocking him to the ground as I look down on him.

"I won't hurt you," he tells me. "I don't want to embarrass my future mate."

"I have no such qualms." I slam my foot into his head, making him jerk up with a groan. Grabbing his chin, I yank him to his feet and drive my fist into his face, knocking him back down. When he stumbles yet again, I spin and kick, hitting him across the head and sending him flying.

"I don't even have to shift to kick your ass," I sneer at him, watching my words land like I expected.

There is one thing I know for sure about Tetrim—he wants to be an alpha male, which means he's unable to let anyone else, especially a woman, win. With a snarl, he leaps to his feet and grabs for me, but I dance out of reach.

"So you're okay hitting a beta who won't fight back, but you can't win against a girl?"

The crowd laughs, and it infuriates him more.

With a roar, he flies at me, and then there are no more words, just the challenge. I'm fast, but he's stronger. I need to wear him down, so I dance out of reach again and again. He only lands one hit that staggers me, but then he starts to slow. I see it, and so does he, and that's when I go in for the kill.

I slam my foot into his face and then his chest, sending him stumbling back. Stepping closer, I smash my fist right into his face. He blinks as he crumples to his knees. Flipping over him, I grab his neck in a chokehold. "Submit."

Growling, he elbows backwards, but I ignore the pain and squeeze harder, dominance oozing from my every word as his wolf rebels, trying to obey me. "Submit."

It's a fight of strength and dominance, and with a whine, he crumples to his stomach. Rolling onto his back, he exposes his belly despite his anger. I drop on top of him, one knee on either side of his body. I ignore the flare of lust in his gaze and grab his chin as my voice rings out.

"For the crime of an unprovoked attack without challenge, I mete out punishment in form of your fangs. You will be unable to hunt or attack until they regrow in a year." I force my thumb into his mouth and grip his exposed fangs. No matter his defeat, he cannot change them back fast enough, and I rip them out as he howls.

Blood sprays across me as I stand to show the now silent crowd. "Let it be known, I will not tolerate defiance to the alpha or this pack. Rules are rules, and if they are broken, you will be punished." I step off him as he covers his face and sobs.

Losing your fangs as a wolf is akin to losing a limb.

Good, let it hurt, let it be a reminder every time he changes and they are missing. Fangs take a minimum of a year to grow back, no matter how much you change, and I'm hoping in that year, he'll change his tone.

Otherwise, Tetrim is bound to die. He'll hurt someone or push too hard.

This was a warning, a chance to change, so we'll see if he takes it.

"What's going on here?" Jang booms as he forces his way through the crowd, his eyes widening when he sees me and the fangs in my hand.

I meet his gaze, dominance flowing from me in waves as I curl my hands around the stolen fangs. "I issued a challenge and won." I step over Tetrim's body and nod at my alpha before moving past him.

The crowd parts for me. Smirking to myself, I pocket the fangs, knowing Tetrim is well and truly defeated this time.

I strung the fangs on a leather necklace, and now I wear them around my neck—a reminder and a warning. Dom finds me outside of my cabin. I know Jang will find me sooner or later, but he knows I was in the right.

"Are you okay?" I ask him. His lip is still split, and he has a black eye, but he doesn't look bad.

"Fine, he hits like a baby. You were a badass though." He chuckles.

Sighing, I look back out over the water, knowing what I need to do as the afternoon fades but unsure I can. For a moment, I just enjoy the peace, knowing it might be the last time I do after tonight. "Why not hold the party for the graduates tonight?"

He frowns. "Tonight?"

"We need something positive to distract the pack from the challenge and the hunters. It's last minute, but it can work, don't you think?"

He blinks at me before smiling. "Sure, I'll go tell the others and get it sorted. See? This is why you are the next alpha, always thinking of us." He kisses my cheek as he jogs off, and I watch him go, wondering if he will still think that after tonight.

Especially after I just used him to get what I need.

I stay here a little longer, my feet in the water, needing the comforting warmth and magic to give me strength for what I'm about to do. That's where Jang finds me.

"What the hell happened, Quinny?" he demands.

Things are still tense after our last fight, and I don't have the energy to butt heads with my alpha or my dad right now. "I don't want to fight." Something in my voice gives him pause, and he softens.

"What happened?" he asks quietly.

I look at him, memorising his face. I need this moment of warmth because I don't know if he will still love me later.

"I handled Tetrim. If I didn't take a stand and knock him down, then he would have ended up dead. He would cross the wrong person or break the rules one too many times. Hopefully, he'll learn from this," I explain.

"You are thinking like an alpha. One choice to head off others," Jang says. "I'm proud of you."

"I hope you remember that," I tell him as I look back at the water.

"Quinny." He sighs. "It's not that I don't trust you." He clearly thinks I'm talking about our fight. "I'm just worried. I can't lose you, okay? I know how strong you are, but I almost lost you once this last week. I cannot lose anyone I love ever again, so know I trust you, but I needed to handle this to keep you safe."

I swallow my guilt and pain and let him wrap me in his arms as purple and red splash across the sky, the setting sun lighting us up. "I know, and I love you for protecting me," I admit before I pull away. "But I don't need you to anymore. We need to keep this pack safe, and I will do anything to make that happen."

"I know." He smiles warmly, gripping my cheeks. "You are every inch your father's daughter." I smile. "I mean your real father. I like to think there is some of me in there too, but you look so much like him today. You're going to be an incredible alpha, Quinny, just don't be in a rush to take it. The responsibility it comes with . . . I don't want to see you shoulder that burden just yet. I want you to be happy."

"I don't think we get that choice anymore, do we? The hunters have decided to come for us. Like it or not, I must grow up. I have to keep our people safe, and I won't lose anyone else," I say. "We under-estimated them once and they killed my family. I won't make the same mistake again."

I look back at the water, feeling his concern as his big palm lands on my shoulder comfortingly. "Enough seriousness for tonight. Go have fun. Drink and dance. Be young. Tomorrow is a new day, and we will figure out this thing with the hunters. The world isn't ending, Quinny."

Mine is because I'm about to betray everyone I love.

I don't tell him that though. Instead, I smile and nod, and he leads me away from my solitude and towards the pack. The music is in full swing as food and booze is rolled out and the day turns into night.

The pack will use any excuse for a party—a party that will be the distraction I need.

The party is in full swing. I sip a beer and make my rounds, waiting until everyone is too drunk to notice. Couples slip away to fuck, and people dance and sing. Even Jang and Marie are cuddled up together, drinking near the fire, and for a moment, I spare them a look, hoping that when this is done, they understand and forgive me.

Either way, I can't back out. I turn and sneak away while nobody notices. I know the border patrol schedule well, such as the times and who's there, and I need to make sure I time it perfectly if this is to work.

It has to work.

It's our only way out.

I force myself into the cells and stop before Jai. He's on his feet, having heard me approach, and something in my eyes makes him frown. "What's happening?"

"If I let you go, if I get you back to Vale and Lucien, will you convince them to turn away from the pack?"

He blinks, and I step closer. "If you don't, Jai, both of our families will die and you know it. This is our chance, our only chance, to stop a bloodbath on either side. You said you don't hate wolves anymore, so prove it. I'm trusting you."

"Why are you trusting me of all people?" he asks.

"Because we are both stuck here—a man who only ever wanted his parents' love and a woman who only ever wanted them alive. We lost everyone to each other's kind, yet here we are, being friendly. If it comes from you, then they will trust it, and we know that. If we don't do this, you will die, and when they attack, so will Vale and Lucien. Yes, we'll both suffer losses, and we need to stop that from happening."

"They won't give up the hunt so easily," he murmurs.

"Make them," I demand. "Or everything we did to survive will be for nothing."

That makes him flinch. I unlock the cell and step back. "Go west. The patrols change in two hours, so you have until then to get through and onto the road. Pass the abandoned mine, then go around the creek and the old church. That's the safest path. Move silently and softly. You won't change, so your hunters are not in danger, but remember you will be stronger and faster now."

"Quinn." He steps out. "They'll kill you for letting me go."

"Maybe," I admit, "but it will be worth it to save my family. I couldn't save them then, but I can now. I'm counting on you, Jai, not just for me but for your brothers. You were willing to die for them, so I'm taking a bet you're willing to live for them too."

For a moment, he just stares at me, and I step back.

"Go now, before it's too late. The guards have gone to grab a drink. You don't have much time."

He gives me another long, searching look before hurrying past me to the door. My shoulders slump, heavy with guilt and hate, until I'm suddenly spun around. Lips crush onto mine hard and fast.

My hands come up of their own accord, gripping Jai's shoulders as he demolishes my mouth before stepping back. Panting, I peer at him. "Why did you do that?"

Walking backwards, he grins. "I needed to be sure. Besides, we'll never see each other again, so why the fuck not?" At the door, he sends me one last look. "I'll try, Quinn. Stay alive." He darts out, and I watch him go.

I let a hunter escape.

I betrayed our pack. No matter my reasons, I'm a traitor.

I just hope it was worth it. I hope I put my trust in the right person.

I sink to the floor and wait for my crime to be discovered.

CHAPTER THIRTY-THREE

I sit with my back to the cell wall, the small window throwing rays of moonlight across the drab grey floor. Closing my eyes, I draw my legs higher and drape my arms over them. Vale doesn't want to break out if we can help it because it will draw unwanted attention and make our job that much harder, but as the hours pass, we are running out of options.

Jai could be dying right now, he needs us, but I cannot think of that.

Instead, my mind goes to other places, and before I know it, I've opened my mouth. It's only Vale and me in here . . . and the drunk, but he doesn't count. There isn't even an officer nearby, though I can hear one snoring through the open door to the office. Vale has been quiet for far too long, lounging back on the metal shelf they call a bed and pretending to sleep, but his body is too tense for that.

He could never fool me.

"Do you know who she is?" He jerks at my sudden voice, one eye opening to meet my gaze before shutting again.

"Who?" he murmurs, confused.

"Quinn." I watch his hand fist on his chest. "Do you know who she is?"

"Besides a wolf?" he mutters, his angry tone telling me to drop this, but I can't. I hate lying to my brother, and there are too many secrets between us right now. I need to discuss this. I need to understand. I have to. When I get out of here, if I'm to kill her and her entire family, then I need to know the truth about why he saved her that night and when that naïve innocence turned into hatred.

"Lucien, what are you talking about?" He turns his head, meeting my eyes, annoyance lacing his voice.

I could backtrack, I could say never mind, but I can't. I need to know what type of person I am and what type of person my brother is. I need to know why I'm doing this because I don't know anymore. I really don't, and that scares me. It terrifies me that I could slaughter people—because they are people no matter how much we fool ourselves—to keep my brother safe.

What if I can't? What if he's too far gone to save?

What if he always was?

But no, that little boy saved a wolf. I know he's in there somewhere. I saw it in his eyes when he really looked at her. I need to know. I need him to understand what is at stake here because it's not just the wolves' lives. It's also my brother's soul.

Can he hunt monsters if it makes him one?

I don't know if I can live with that.

No one else cares about us, about him, but I do. I would forsake my very life, my very soul, to save my brother.

"I was there that night when you let that little girl go, when you saved that little wolf girl from our father." He blinks slowly, his jaw tightening. "I never said a word. I saw her too, and I let her go. Did you know that was Quinn?"

He doesn't move, doesn't even breathe before he suddenly jerks upright, his eyes dark and angry as he glares at me. "You're lying," he hisses.

"No, you're lying to yourself. You know it too. You know it's her.

The wolf you saved is Quinn. You saved a little girl, against orders, and that girl grew into a woman. A woman we took captive. A woman we tortured and hurt for being born. I don't know when we stopped saving innocents, but I think we both know we did, so did you know? Tell me, Vale, I need to know. Did you know Quinn is that girl?"

He stands, moving to the bars between us and wrapping his fists around them as he stares at me. "It can't be. It's a coincidence—"

"You're lying to yourself," I mutter as I stare at him. "She recognised you. She knew it was you. She didn't run from that truth, even if you did. We spoke about it. She saved me because you saved her, paying her debt even after her family was slaughtered by us. Tell me you didn't know, Vale. Tell me you didn't know the girl you saved is the one you are hunting and that this isn't some petty revenge to rectify what you did that night."

"I never should have let her go." He grinds his jaw. "That night—"

"Yes, yes you should have." I stand, staring him down. "She was a child, an innocent child just like we were. All of us were scarred because of that night, her included. She was a child, Vale. Just a child. Not evil. Not a monster. We made her into one. She might never have hated us had it not been for our father, and before you start defending him, I agree that there are some good hunters and what we do is important, but tell me you don't see how it's been warped. Some hunt just for pleasure. Tell me, Vale, do these wolves deserve it? What have they done? What has Quinn done? I sure as shit don't know, but I do know it is not half as bad as what we have done in the name of justice and becoming saviours . . . in the name of our cause."

"Those are the words of a traitor," he mutters—it's a habit, not a warning.

"Maybe," I admit. "But they are what I feel. Don't you? Haven't you seen us change these last years? We started as heroes, saving our race from those willing to use us as cattle and fodder, but there are evil humans, Vale, as well as good. Why can't the same be said for wolves? What if Quinn is a good wolf, her pack is good, and we are the evil ones here? What if we are the bad guys and not the heroes?"

His chest rises rapidly, his eyes on the floor before he raises them to me, and I see the painful truth in his gaze—he knows we are the bad guys and he doesn't care. I stagger back.

"They have Jai," is all he says.

"He walked into their territory to kill them. Wouldn't we do the same?" I whisper. "Vale . . . I can't. I can't follow you into damnation. I thought I could, but I can't. I cannot let you slaughter innocents. I won't let you become our father."

The moon hides behind a cloud then, throwing his face into shadows. "Will you stop me?" His voice is dark and cruel. "Would you kill your own brother?"

"If I have to," I reply. "It would ruin me, and I would follow you into the grave, but I will not let you live to become a monster. I would rather you die a martyr, a man. I have followed you all this time." I walk closer and wrap my hands around his. "I have followed you to hell and back. I would die for you, and I would live for you . . . but do not ask me to become this. Do not ask me to kill my own brother. It isn't too late, Vale. It's not too late to do the right thing."

"Even if it means forsaking our family, our legacy, and everything we know?" he hisses.

"What use is a family or a legacy if it hurts us?" I mutter. "I couldn't do it. I couldn't hurt her. She's a wolf, and I let her go too, Vale. That night in the storm, I let her go. Will you kill me too?"

I feel him jerk under my grip.

"Can you kill me, Vale? Because that's what it will take."

"I don't see another way out," he replies slowly, his voice tight and desperate. "This is what Father wanted. This is what we wanted. There's no other way out. If it's not us, it will be them, and we will be dead anyway for betraying them. We have no way out, Lucien. We are trapped. We are the weapon they wield, and as soon as we crack or break, they will toss us into the inferno. I have been fighting every day to stop that from happening and keep us alive, together, and safe."

"I know, brother, but we have to change. I would rather die on my feet, proud of who I am than on my knees as a coward. It's time to let go of the past. It's time to move forward. Change is not easy, but it must happen. I have buried my head, and that's my fault. I never should have let it go this far, brother. Please, Vale, please. Don't make me into our father, don't become him. I can stand a great many things. I can endure pain no other can, and I can lift more than most others and withstand the storms coming our way, but I cannot stand losing you to a hatred born centuries before us."

"What if we try and it's not enough, Luc?" he asks as the moon breaks through and shows me his glassy eyes. He looks so young right now.

"What if we try and it's enough?" I counter. "It's better than never trying."

He searches my gaze. "Is this what you want? You would stand with the wolves?"

"No, I would stand with you, brother, until the very end. Let us die how we lived, like those two boys who, even at such a young age, understood innocence despite species. That would be enough for me. Wouldn't it be for you? Let us be the first hunters to truly live for the cause and upstand the values they all shirk. Let us become the men I see in you every day. The man who let that little girl go, the one who cried after every kill no matter how right it was."

"And Jai?" he whispers.

"He made his choice, and we must make ours. We choose where to stand." I clutch him tighter, pressing my head to the bars, and he copies me, tears dripping down his face as he watches me.

We are two brothers caught in their father's legacy of hatred and pain, forged into weapons for a war they did not start.

"Choose, Vale, and I will stand with you until the end. Choose, and I will be at your side, brother, forever," I beg.

I beg him to choose this for us, to choose to fight, even if it's not easy.

His eyes close. "I don't want to kill innocents. I don't want to be my father." That's what this boils down to. His eyes open, glassy and blue—the bright light in the storm, providing a way home. "Yes, we will do what's right, even if it gets us killed, brother. We will do what's right."

"Thank you."

We stay like that as our world changes around us with no one else the wiser.

When there's a clank, we break apart, turning as a bored, impatient guard heads towards us, unlocking both cells and jerking his head. "It's your lucky night, get out."

Vale and I share a look before glancing back at the sheriff.

"What's happening?" I ask.

"Something bigger than you, so go before I change my mind," he demands.

We do just that, knowing this is the universe rewarding us.

It has to be.

CHAPTER THIRTY-FOUR

Jai

The trees blur past me as I run as fast as I can, following her directions. I heard music and people, and I avoided them like she said. Part of me expected some wolves to jump out and for it to be a joke, but no one stops me, and when I'm far enough away not to hear them anymore, I turn.

I look back at the lights of the pack in the distance.

Guilt and shame muddle my emotions. Everything I thought I knew changed in those cells. I don't even feel like myself anymore. I am different, reborn, but can I do this?

I don't know, but Quinn trusted me, something no one else ever has, and I want to try because she's right. This won't end well for any of us. We have to stop this before it's too late. It's up to us—two enemies who became unlikely friends—because there is one thing I know for sure.

Quinn and her family do not deserve to die, not for simply being born as they are. They just want to be left alone and have peace. Why shouldn't they get that? I can do that. I can keep her and keep my family safe. We can stop this before it's too late. Taking a deep breath, I turn back to the woods and begin to run again, faster than I ever have.

It's up to me, the fucked-up half-breed.

Surprisingly, the trip back takes half the time. Once, I would have refused to look at why, but now I just glance down at my body and know it's because of the beast inside me. It's good because the quicker I'm back, the quicker I can save us, even if it means tapping into that prowling animal sliding under my skin.

Quinn was right. I'm faster. I can feel the strength in my body and the heightened temperature, sounds, and tastes.

Everything is brighter and more beautiful.

Everything is just . . . better.

I find myself outside of the motel. I don't even know if they are here, but even as that thought crosses my mind, some deep-rooted instinct in me screams. It has me lifting my head, and before I know it, I'm sniffing the air as my brain sorts through the sensory overload —exhaust fumes, paint, cigarette, weed, piss, cum, sweaty bodies . . . Bingo.

I can smell them.

I can smell Lucien and Vale, and it smells . . . fresh, though I don't know how I know that.

Finding my courage, knowing they might kill me now for what I am, I head to our room.

I left as a human, as Jai, their brother, but I'm coming back as something else and asking them to help me stop this. They will call me a traitor, and they will be within their rights to kill me, but a small part of me hopes they won't—hopes they still care enough about me to at least hear me out before they mount my head on a spike and parade it through the hunters' base as if to say you were right.

Lucien might, but Vale . . . Vale is unpredictable, and that's coming from me.

When I stand before the door, I take a deep breath, knowing it could be my last. I can hear their whispered conversation, but I don't bother to wait. I knock to give them warning, so they don't feel threatened, and then I step back, holding my hands up behind my head to show I have no weapons.

I can hear their footsteps, even though they try to keep them quiet. The soft tread on the cheap carpet is followed by silence, and I know they are checking through the peephole. I keep my face calm, and then the door rips open. An astonished Vale and Lucien peer at me, both fighting to get through the door.

"Jai," Vale finally whispers.

"Hey." I cough. "I don't suppose you could let me in?"

That breaks them from their stupor, and I'm yanked inside the room, the door slamming shut and locking. I watch as Vale quickly sprinkles the pixie herbs across the window and door to mask my scent. "I don't know how the fuck you got out of there alive, brother, but I'm so happy," Lucien booms, clapping me on the shoulder before tugging me into a hug. "So fucking happy. I thought we'd lost you." He pulls back, his face stern. "Don't ever pull that shit again, you psycho."

I can hear love under his anger, and my wolf laps it up.

I always thought I was so alone, so isolated, and that I didn't need anyone. I was just fooling myself. I glance at Vale. He's leaning against the door, watching me. "Which raises a good question—how did you get away?"

"I didn't," I admit shyly. "They let me go."

Vale's expression transforms from calm to panicked, his eyes widening. "Shit, it's a trap!" They both dive for their weapons as I sigh and sit on the edge of the bed.

"It's not a trap. Calm down," I order, even as they take up position. "Guys, it's not a trap."

They aren't listening. Vale is barking out commands as Lucien scans the perimeter.

Sighing, I let some of that unrest inside of me leak through. "It's not a trap!" I roar, and when they turn, I know my eyes are glowing and my skin is moving with my beast trapped inside.

I know what I must look like. In fact, I glance into the darkened TV to check my reflection and yep, glowing, haunting eyes and sharp teeth. My skin moves as if something is trapped inside and wants out. I even look bigger.

It's then, when they take a good look at me, that I scent their fear.

"Jai." Lucien's voice is low, careful, but I see his hand inching towards his cursed blade, and my heart splinters a little at the gaping hole in our brotherhood now. "What's wrong with you?"

Sighing, I slowly lift my hands and place them on my thighs. I splay them there and calm down, knowing my eyes go back to normal, and I glance between them. "We need to talk, and we don't have much time, but know this: if you still have any trust, any love for me as your brother, then you will trust me in this. I will not hurt you. I never could. You are the only family I have."

Lucien swallows but drops his hand. "Then let's talk."

"Starting with what the fuck happened to you," Vale demands, not releasing his hold on his weapon. That's okay. That's good. At least I'm not dead yet.

I won't fight them, and I won't hurt them. I will let them kill me if that's what they want. I always thought I could do anything and kill anyone—how foolish I was. I was so blind to my own feelings, but now the wolf inside seems to have connected me to them.

It's exhausting feeling this much all the time. I have no idea how they handle it.

"First of all, I need you to know I'm still me. In fact, this is who I have always been. I just didn't know it," I admit sadly. "You know about when I was attacked when I was younger. I thought I survived and was human, but that wasn't completely right. It seems the wolf inside me was trapped. I'm not quite human, not quite wolf."

"Well shit . . . ," Lucien mutters. "But what happened—"

"You walked your ass into that forest," Vale snaps. "We followed you, hunted for you, were ready to die to save you."

"I didn't want that. I had made up my mind. I was going to kill them, but they captured me. I was . . . held." I leave out the torture part since there's no need to piss them off. "And they freed the wolf inside me."

"Why?" Vale asks, his nostrils flaring. "To use it against us? To switch a hunter to their side?"

"No," I begin, but he's not listening.

"It is a trap," he hisses.

"Brother." Lucien sighs. "Remember what we just discussed?" He eyes Vale meaningfully, and Vale seems to lose all steam. "Jai, was it Quinn?"

The wolf inside of me fucking purrs at her name.

"Yes, she freed my wolf. She felt sorry for me. Apparently, I will never be able to change. I am stuck like this. Not fully human, not fully wolf."

"Shit, why would she do that?" Lucien groans.

"Because it was the kind thing to do so I could know who I was before I died. Her pack was going to kill me—not because they wanted to, but because I know their land. I was there, a threat to their family. Guys, I saw the pack." They don't seem happy, but hope blooms in my chest. "It was just . . . full of life. Kids and families were everywhere. Everyone was enjoying themselves. It's just a village out in the middle of nowhere. They weren't monsters roaming around. There wasn't torture and death everywhere."

"You would say that now," Vale mutters, but Lucien kicks him.

"It was just life, and they weren't evil. In fact, they didn't seem to take joy in me being their prisoner. Quinn and I spoke while I was there. We realised a few things. We aren't so different. We both just want to protect our families, and if this carries on, if we keep doing this, both of ours will die. There will be so much bloodshed and death. We have to protect our families, the people we care about." I look between them. "I have to protect you. If we go in there, we'll die, as will many innocents, and they are innocents. I know how that sounds, but I'm still me, still the man who hated wolves so much he dreamed of their deaths. I was wrong. I am wrong. They are not all evil, and if we do this, if we alert the hunters, then everyone will die. There has to be another way. We have to divert their attention and get them away from here. I don't think I could live with the fact that you had their blood and souls on your hands, and you would. You would follow orders, and innocents would die, and it would change you. I can take the pain, the darkness, but I don't want that for you. Quinn knew that. She saw it in my eyes, and she let me go. She gave me a chance to change the future, so I'm here, knowing you might kill me for simply existing, and I'm begging you, brothers . . . We have to stop this war. We have to save the innocents like we swore to do." I drop to my knees, something I swore I would never do. "Please believe me."

"Well, shit," Lucien mutters after a time, seeming tired, and despite what I am now, he crouches before me, taking my hand. "Had you come a day earlier, this would be a very different conversation, but while we were in jail—"

"Jail?" I query, but he just surges ahead.

"We decided the same thing. We can't do this. Orders have changed. I—we don't like what they have made us. We never signed up to kill innocents. We just want to save them, so if you say the wolves are good, then we believe you, brother."

I look at Vale, and he drops his weapon, his shoulders slumping. "So how do we do this? How do we save both sides?"

"You—you aren't going to kill me and start a war?" I blink, feeling confused.

Vale smiles softly and heads my way, dropping his hand to my shoulder and squeezing. "We're brothers," he tells me. "Where one goes, we all go."

Lucien's hand drops to my other shoulder, both of them holding me. "Brothers until the end. Now, let's save the world."

Something about the interaction has tears forming in my eyes. Vale kneels and tugs me into his arms, and Lucien wraps me in his from behind. Both of them hold me as I break.

"I tried so hard not to become this," I mutter incoherently. "I fought it every day, but I can't fight it anymore. This is who I am, and yet I was so worried I would lose the only family I have left because of it. That the wolf would steal another family from me."

"Never," Lucien replies gruffly. "We are with you until the end, even if your eyes glow like some weird-ass nightlight."

"Exactly. Besides, Lucien has always been afraid of the dark so it will come in handy."

I chuckle as Lucien huffs. "We'll have our very own torch." He chuckles, and I can't help it. I laugh. They join in, our arms locked together.

Three men, three lost souls are finally exposed to one another.

Save the world they said, but can we do it?

What will be left of us if we do?

CHAPTER THIRTY-FIVE

I know they will come to check on the prisoner soon, and they will find me.

Tugging my knees closer to my chest, I wrap my arms around myself. They could even demand my death because I have betrayed them in their eyes. They will never understand why; it isn't our way. The man and woman who took me in, who made me their daughter, will think I betrayed them.

It hurts, and I wish I could get on my knees and beg them to understand, but I'm not owed that chance. I knew the moment I let Jai free that I would die here. Ironic, isn't it?

My alpha owes me nothing. I am just another lost wolf, and I will meet my biological family sooner than I thought. I will be reunited with my sister, my mother, and my father.

I just hope it's enough to save them, and if that's my last act, then I can accept that.

I can die happily knowing they are safe and have a future.

Live or die, I did it for them.

As a wolf born of the moon, I will be absorbed into its rays, and there, I will find forgiveness.

I know the party is still in full swing, one I organised to distract them. Their love fills the air, the moon and earth rejoicing with them, and even as I sit here, breaking and hurting, I still smile. This is why I did this—to protect them from the hurt coming their way.

For a moment, my fingers rub my lips as I remember the warmth of Jai's mouth pressing to mine, the desperation and hatred morphing to want. Shaking those foolish thoughts away, I bang my head back against the wall, my body stiffening when I hear footsteps.

Here we go.

Sucking up every ounce of courage I have left, I climb to my feet. I won't do this on my knees. I widen my stance, hanging my hands at my sides in a peaceful position just as the door opens. The wolf there is a guard named Flint. He's a young man, but he's quickly rising through the ranks. When he glances from me to the cell, he frowns, a sad look in his eyes.

"What happened?" is all he asks as he steps closer. I expected panic, anger, and shouts for the betas and alpha, but he surprises me.

"I let him go." I tilt my chin back.

He nods slowly, his eyes roving over me. "Did he hurt you?"

"No." I blink. "I'm fine."

"Good, that's good." He shoves his hands into his pockets, looking exhausted.

"Aren't you going to ask why? Or sound the alarm?" My voice conveys my confusion.

"No, you must have your reasons." He smiles. "I can't say I understand them, but I trust you, Alpha."

"I'm not alpha," I say.

"No, but you will be one day. Everything you do is for this pack, Quinn. I've seen that a million times, so if you did this, then you had your reasons. I'm not saying everyone else will understand, but I do." He nods. "I'll still have to take you to Jang, you understand. I can't lose my position."

"I understand." I walk closer, and his hand presses to my lower back as he escorts me out. It's a comfort as well as a guiding hand. Touch is important for wolves, and for a moment, I allow myself to lean into it.

"Don't let them see you look defeated. Don't you ever drop your eyes," he murmurs as we move closer to the pack house. "You will be alpha, never forget that. Don't let them see you as weak."

I don't know when Flint became this smart, but in this moment, I'm grateful for the reminder, and I'm very aware of why he has progressed so quickly within the pack hierarchy. He's kind, smart, and obviously very capable, and someone I need to keep my eye on, but that's for a later date. Right now, I need to face the alpha and what may come of it.

Lifting my chin, I boldly meet everyone's eyes as they glance our way. They are still partying, oblivious to what's happening and the impending war. I wish it could always stay that way.

Once inside the pack house, Flint knocks on Jang's door and waits until we hear his rumble, and then we enter. I don't sit, not this time. I stand as Flint shuts the door.

"What's wrong?" Jang immediately asks, climbing to his feet and looking exhausted. "Quinny, is everything okay?"

The fact that his first response is to check on me, not as an alpha but as my father, makes my heart squeeze painfully. I trust this man with my entire life. I just hope he can trust me as much in return. He is alpha, however, so he has the pack to think about. My shoulders drop as I lower my chin in respect, my gaze on his scarred hands, which are spread on his desk.

I won't fight him. I won't fight his punishment.

"Flint?" Jang asks when I stay silent. I have my reasons, but I won't use them as excuses. I made my choice.

"The prisoner is gone," he replies calmly.

"What?" Jang roars, hurrying around the desk.

"I let him go," I say softly, knowing this doesn't fall on Flint. "None of the guards are to blame. The only thing they are responsible for is trusting me. I lured them away, and then I let the hunter go."

Jang just stares at me in stunned silence.

"What did you just say?" His voice is quiet and deadly, his bristling wolf shining through, and I wince from the raging power brought on by his fury.

"I said I let him go," I repeat.

"I will give you some time before I alert the betas," Flint murmurs. "Alpha, for what it's worth, everything Quinn does has a purpose." Even showing that level of trust and allegiance could get him killed, and he knows it, yet he remains unshakable as he bows and leaves.

Jang and I are alone, which offers us a chance to sort this out before the others are involved. I owe Flint my life. He didn't need to offer me that small act of kindness, yet he did, and I won't forget it.

"Why?" he asks. "Why, Quinn?"

"I have my reasons," I tell him.

"Why?" he roars. "You hate hunters more than anyone, even more than me, so tell me why! Why, Quinn?"

I lift my head, meeting his eyes. For a moment, I just immortalise his face in my memories—the man who saved me, gave me a home and a chance. How could I not risk everything to keep him and those I love safe?

I go to open my mouth and explain when the door opens with a bang and the others file in. I look them over one by one. White seems sad, Filmea is disappointed, and Tetrim looks angry, while Dom watches me carefully.

"What is the meaning of this?" Filmea demands.

"We were informed that the prisoner is gone," White mumbles.

"I let him go," I state, knowing they will find out sooner or later.

I wince when Jang sweeps his arm across his desk, his back heaving in anger after the crash.

"We must go on high alert. Check the borders, double the guards, and stop the party."

I ignore the planning going on around me. My eyes stay on Jang's back as he hangs his head in shame. It's clear the others want answers, but they are protecting the pack first and foremost—something Jang seems unable to do right now.

I am his weakness, and in this moment, I hate that.

"I have one request," I interrupt them. "Don't let Jang carry out my punishment." I meet his eyes for a second, stunned by the agony I see in them. "It would kill a part of him. I will accept whatever you wish, even my life, but don't make him kill his only daughter."

"Tell us why," White orders in the stunned silence. "Tell us why, Quinn."

"You wouldn't believe me," I admit.

"Try me!" Jang shouts, gripping my chin as he appears before me. "Right now, you're a traitor."

"That's fine." I swallow. "I will be whatever it takes."

"For what?" he demands, searching my eyes. "Please, Quinn, tell me why. Don't you owe us that much?" I flinch. "Good, let it fucking hurt. Why would you betray us after everything we did? Why would you betray your own family, the one here and the one the hunters put in the ground?"

"Alpha, maybe we should—" Filmea starts.

"Silence!" he roars as I wince. "I want her to speak. I want to hear it from her tongue."

"Maybe we should all calm down." White moves to our side. "Alpha, we need to alert the pack and prepare for an attack. If the hunter is free, then he will lead them straight here."

Jang peers into my eyes for a second more before shoving me away. I stumble but right myself. "Take her away, lock her up, and keep her out of my sight."

"Yes, Alpha." Filmea quickly grabs my arm, leading me from the office and towards the cells. Once out of earshot, she softens and asks, "What's the plan, Quinn? You have one, and I know it. Just tell us. You know we will be on your side."

I don't speak. I can't. I won't endanger them more. I took a chance.

Sighing, she leads me to the cells and locks me inside the one Jai occupied, and then she stands there, eyeing me sadly. "You are a great woman, Quinn, and a brilliant wolf. I have always thought so, but you need to know when to trust someone. We are your pack. Don't let this be your end. You are destined for a great deal more."

She slams and locks the door, leaving me here.

Sliding down the wall, I hang my head.

She's wrong. My destiny ends here. I just hope I don't take Jang and my mother with me.

Being a prisoner is surprisingly boring.

I know they will be patrolling, expecting an immediate attack. News will have spread, and all that I have fought for and built will be destroyed. I will never be trusted again.

I just hope I was right. I hope wherever Jai is right now, he's fighting just as hard, risking everything to keep our families safe. Otherwise, it was all for nothing.

I pass the time thinking through every option, what he could be doing, what our pack needs to do now, and what we could do if Jai fails. My mind is working overtime, leaving me with a headache, and my wolf growls in annoyance.

No wolf likes being trapped, after all.

There's a fumbling sound at the door, and I jerk my head up, hearing muffled voices beyond.

"That is my daughter! You will let me in there right now, White, or I swear to God I will rip off your balls and choke you with them. Move aside!" My mother doesn't outrank them, yet she is a terrifying force of nature, and the sound of her insistence and anger brings tears to my eyes as she fights her pack to get to me—and wins.

When she sees me, her anger fades, and she rushes to the bars.

"Oh, my Quinny." I press my head to her shoulder as she holds me as much as she can through the bars.

She says nothing. She just holds me with a mother's unconditional love, even knowing I'm here on Jang's orders.

"It's going to be okay," she whispers.

Something in me breaks. "I had to do it, Mum."

"Shh, I know." Pulling back, she smiles sadly, brushing my hair from my face. "My Quinny, you have always had such a strong sense of justice. You did what you did, and I trust those reasons, whatever they are. I trust you, Quinn," she promises, kissing my forehead. "Dad will come around. He's just worried about you."

Closing my eyes, I soak in her familiar scent and comfort as she holds me. "I never wanted to hurt anyone," I admit.

"I know. Sometimes we do things for those we love, things others will never understand." She looks at me knowingly. "Love doesn't make sense. It isn't logical; it's instinctive. It's a call deep inside that we cannot ignore. Love makes us crazy, but in the best possible way."

"Why are you telling me that?" I mutter.

"No reason." She smiles knowingly. "One day, you will understand."

The door opens, and Jang's scent hits us. Marie's eyes tighten, but she leans in and kisses my forehead. "Trust in your heart, Quinny. It will never lead you wrong." She stands and turns to face Jang.

Her arms are crossed, and her feet are spread as if she would fight the world itself to keep me safe.

"Leave, mate," Jang commands.

The bags under his eyes are pronounced, and his body bristles with his wolf.

He's angry—no, he's furious.

I don't bother climbing to my feet. I hate that I am coming between them.

"That is our daughter, Jang," she begins. "I don't know what you think—"

"She is a traitor," he says, but under his cold voice is hurt.

The sound of a slap makes my head whip up to see his face twisted. "Don't ever speak about our Quinn like that. You figure this out, and you figure this out now. I will not stand by and let you hurt our daughter. You may be alpha, Jang, but I will stand against you if you lay one hand on her."

"My love," he tries, but she steps back.

"Be the man I know you are. Don't let your anger blind you, for you will lose us both."

She departs, and we both stare after her.

"She's terrifying," I murmur softly.

"Utterly." He sighs. "But not wrong. Don't tell her I told you, I'll never live it down, but the woman is never wrong." We share a sad smile, and he sinks to his knees before the cell.

For a moment, we just stare at each other.

"When you were younger, you scared me to death. Did you know that?" he admits softly. I blink, unsure where he's going with this. "You were just always so fearless. I remember this one time when an older wolf had built a swing, and he and his friend were playing on it. It was up on the bluff, and the drop was huge. You wanted to play with them, but they said no. They also called you some nasty names. So what did my little Quinny do? You climbed up that bluff and used the swing, dropping into the water below. They were so terrified after, they were shaking, yet you stood there, dripping wet and smiling brightly." He chuckles painfully. "So fucking fearless. In that moment, I was terrified because I knew you would always do what you thought was right, regardless of anyone else."

"I was utterly shitting it," I mutter. "I was so scared I thought I was going to puke, but I didn't like the way they were talking about you. I wanted to make you proud and prove to them why you had taken me in."

"You never had to prove anything to anyone, Quinn. When are you going to learn that?" he mutters.

"That's where you're wrong." I lean into the bars. "You're Jang, the baddest alpha in this country. Your kids were supposed to be the next leaders of our world, and then I came along and ruined it. They thought I was weak, a traitor for surviving that night. They turned on you, they spoke about you, and I hated it. I might not have needed to prove myself to you, but I did to them. I wanted them to look at me and understand why you loved me so much, and maybe understand why you did myself."

"I love you because I could do nothing but. Even when your father was around and you came with him, I loved you. You just . . . have this aura, Quinn. I couldn't do anything but love you. You looked at me, the giant, terrifying alpha that others feared, and you smiled. You held my hand and you smiled. I was always just Jang to you, and from that moment, you had my heart, and I swore I would always protect you, but I can't protect you this time, Quinny."

"I know." I smile. "I don't want you to. I knew the consequences of my actions, and I still did it."

"But why? Please, help me understand. Please, Quinn."

For the first time in my life, I see my alpha, my father, beg.

The plea in his voice is my undoing. I don't want him to fight his people for me. I thought not telling him would make it easier, but staring into his eyes, I know I can't. I owe him this much. I owe all of them the truth.

"I did it for the pack," I admit. "The hunters will find us. You know this, Jang. I saw it in your eyes. This time, it's different. We both know full well what they are capable of, and I couldn't let another family go through what I did. I couldn't allow them to create any more orphans. I saw a way out for us, a chance, and I took it, knowing it could backfire, but you once told me all we have is trust. I had to trust this man and his love for his family, the same love I have for mine. I took a chance, Jang, that after showing him what he truly was, he could go back and try to help—not for us, but for him. He knows if they come here, a lot of them will die, including his brothers. He knows it's wrong."

Taking a deep breath, I stare into his eyes. "Maybe it's naïve or foolish of me, but I trusted him. We were both stuck on the other side of a line drawn between us, forced into a battle neither of us wanted. The hunters are coming either way, so I figured why not take a chance that we can stop this before it even starts?"

"Oh, Quinn." He sighs, scrubbing his face. "What if it was all a trap?"

"What if it wasn't?" I counter. "I saw this man in action, Dad." He jerks at the name. "I saw his past, I looked into his eyes, and I saw the truth. He didn't want this, not anymore. I could have killed him here, but what would that have achieved? I wanted to prevent further loss of life if I could. I had to try, Jang. I had to. I can't—" I hiccup. "I can't lose anyone else I love, so if it means you have to kill me for my crimes against the pack, then I can accept that, but I cannot accept losing anyone else."

"Did you ever consider that I can't accept that either?" he booms. "To lose my daughter, to lose my entire fucking world?"

"You have your duty, and I have mine," I remind him. "I made my choice."

Jang frowns. "You truly think he will try to convince them to stop?"

"Yes, I do," I answer. "I think he'll do anything to protect the men he loves. The hunters don't know where we are yet, but it's only a matter of time. I think he might be able to stop it."

"He was a feral—"

"Exactly. No one had ever trusted him before. They disregard him because of his past. I didn't. I saw the value this man could have and trusted in him."

He goes quiet for a moment, and I stare.

"So what happens now?"

"I don't know. I really don't," he admits, sounding exhausted. "Some are saying your time as their captive warped you and that they used magic to make you betray us."

"I don't care what they say, only that you know the truth," I reply. "I will face the punishment."

Nodding, he stands. "I will speak to the others. They will push for a trial in hopes we can explain." Turning, he clenches his fists. "I hope you're right, Quinn. I really do. I envy you for being able to trust and hope in this world after what you have seen. I just hope it's not your downfall like it was your father's."

"What does that mean?" I ask as I stand.

"He had hope too, hope we could live peacefully with the hunters, and look how it ended for him," he murmurs, glancing at me. "You are your fathers' daughter, both his and mine, too strong and kind for your own good."

"I don't fear anything but losing you and Mum," I say. "It's okay, Jang. I will face this with the dignity bestowed upon me by being your daughter."

He rushes to me, kissing my head, and I feel his tears drip to my skin. "Foolish," he croaks before storming away.

I heard the pain and love in that one word.

My heart breaks along with his.

CHAPTER THIRTY-SIX

"So what now?" I mutter. "We are saving the wolves, but how exactly do we do that?"

"We need to get the hunters away from the area by giving them something worse to hunt," Lucien murmurs. "We need to change their direction and fast."

I huff. "They won't like it. Wolves are at the top of their list."

"Not the top," Jai murmurs, eyeing us. "Remember when we snuck into their restricted library—"

"You snuck in," I interject. "We came to stop you from getting killed."

"Semantics." He grins, and it surprises me. Jai has always carried pain around like a weighted blanket. It made him raw and crazed. I'm not saying he's not a little crazy now, because he definitely still is, but it seems he's finally accepted who he is. It's nice to see him even a little happy.

He came back for us, and that tells me all I need to know.

Jai is our brother through and through, and we will follow him until the end.

"But my point is, remember that list we found? Well, wolves weren't at the top."

Oh yeah, still crazy. His smile is slightly chilling. "You can't be serious."

"Deadly." His eyes twinkle.

"Care to fill me in?" Lucien asks. "I was on door duty, so I didn't see the list."

"There was only one word above the wolves—the biggest monsters around. Both monsters and hunters hate and kill them," I mutter. "When they can catch them, they are crazy, unpredictable, and the deadliest creature to ever walk the earth—necromancers."

"And I happen to know there has been blood magic around here, not to mention the graves," Jai adds.

"You think it's a necromancer?" I mutter. "Impossible. They are all dead."

"Don't be foolish. You can't kill dark magic. It's a necromancer. I know it. If we turn them onto that, then they will forget about the wolves for now."

"It might buy us time, but eventually, they will come back," Lucien mutters.

"Which will give us time to either pretend to kill the entire pack or say they moved so we hunt them elsewhere." Jai nods.

"Fine, so how do we convince them of the necromancer?" I shudder at the name. They are nothing but dark magic, and they crave pain and death. They are darkness incarnate, a perversion created by bringing a dead white witch back to life, or so I've read.

"We follow the trail of bodies of course." I smirk. "We are hunters, after all. We just need proof."

"Then let's get hunting." Jai jumps to his feet, blurring, and we step backwards. "Oops, sorry, still getting used to this new speed."

"Sure, erm, just don't do that in front of humans, okay?" I wince.

"Sure, sure." He grins, grabbing his bag and ripping it. "Oops."

Sighing, I glance at Lucien to see him smiling.

Fucking wolves.

"This is the third graveyard," Lucien grumbles. "Surely the necromancer has to strike here tonight. I can't think of any others."

The one we are in is about two hours outside of the motel. It's small and in the middle of nowhere, but we found one of the bodies here at the beginning.

"Let's hope so." I sigh as we move through the forgotten gravestones, searching for any signs of dark magic. We are rapidly losing hope and steam and all the while, I'm questioning if this is the right decision or not.

Jai and my brother believe in this, though, and they are right. We don't want to be the bad guys, so here we are, trying to save the wolves by tracking dark magic. Fun.

Two hours later, and we are still trawling through the graves and starting to lose hope when something lurches in the shadows.

I pull my knife and squint into the darkness. The shadows created by the trees near the older graves are almost pitch black, but there is an old iron fence running across the back, so whatever is there will have to come this way.

Carefully, so as not to spook whatever is lingering there, I let out a whistle to alert the others. Despite their best efforts, I hear them heading my way, and whatever is hiding in the shadows does as well. There's a hair-raising growl, one that doesn't sound human, and then it bursts from the cover of darkness faster than I thought possible.

My eyes widen as I get my first look at the thing lurching towards me faster than it should be able to since it's rotting and all.

It's a fucking zombie. Its eyes are sunken in, pure white, and bloodshot. Its skin is melting from its bones with some poking through, and its old-fashioned suit is in tatters. The smell hits me next, brought by the breeze now wafting through the cemetery.

I repress a gag even as I step back. Its head tilts before swinging my way, and its mouth opens, showing yellow and black teeth. It lets out another roar before ambling my way.

"Motherfucker," I hiss. "Oh, let's go track dark magic, that sounds fun."

"Vale!" Lucien hollers. "Zombie!"

"Yeah, no shit!" I yell, stepping back slowly.

It tracks my movements and follows, hunting me.

There is no way I'm letting that rotting motherfucker put its mouth on me. I don't plan on being anyone's meal—well, maybe the wolf. *Shit, no, focus.*

Just then, a blur shoots past me, and I stumble back. When I finally bring it into focus, I see Jai pinning the zombie down, its arms and legs tied with rope, cutting into its skin. It bites at the ground, emitting that low, hair-raising growl.

"Shit, man, you're fast," I mutter, covering the fact I nearly screamed.

He grins over at me, his eyes bright with his wolf. "Guess this shit proves there's definitely a necro."

"For sure," Lucien replies as he stops by my side. "Why didn't you stop the zombie?"

"Oh, I don't know, maybe because I didn't want to get eaten," I retort. "I'm not into the whole rotting flesh thing."

"Really? So just fur, huh?" he jokes, and I snap my gaze to him. He holds his hands up and moves over to Jai to help haul the zombie up. It snaps at him, and Lucien falls back with a yell, his arms windmilling before he hits the ground.

Chuckling, I walk past him. "Not so tough now, are you?" I mock as I drop my bag and grab the gag. With a wince, I shove it into the zombie's mouth, tightening it at the back. I gag at the scent filling my nose and the feel of its slimy, cold skin. Wiping my hands, I nod at Jai. "Let's get this back to HQ. They will have to believe us now and direct their attention to hunting down the necromancer, not the wolves. Just, erm, maybe stop the glowing eyes."

"Oh, right." He drops his head in embarrassment and blinks. When he looks back at me, they are still glowing but not as bright. "Is that better?"

"Maybe just stay in the car." I crinkle my nose as Lucien laughs.

CHAPTER THIRTY-SEVEN

"Roll down a window." I kick the zombie as he lunges at me again. "Stop it, asshole."

"They are open." Jai grins back at me.

"No, they aren't!" I growl. "Why did I have to sit in the back with this stinky magic bastard?"

"You lost wolf-vampire-witch." Jai shrugs.

"You know, you were a lot less annoying when you were an angry, psycho human," I mutter.

He lets out a full belly laugh that makes me smile. "Yes, but then I couldn't have saved Vale's ass tonight."

"I didn't need saving," Vale mutters as he drives.

"You definitely did," Jai and I say at the same time.

"I had it under control. I was leading it where I wanted it," Vale grumbles.

"You were running away like a damsel in distress." I kick his seat, and he throws me a glare in the rearview mirror before he very purposely rolls up every window back here.

"Asshole." I push the zombie off me again as it falls, struggling to get to me. "Stop trying to eat me. Jesus, at least buy me dinner first."

That makes them both laugh, and I can't help but smile. We did it. We just need to convince the hunters now and send them on a wild goose chase, then Quinn and her pack will be safe. Maybe we shouldn't feel so good about lying to our own people, but knowing we are doing the right thing for the right cause is also making us giddy.

"Is that what it takes to fuck you?" Jai jokes. "Guess Quinn had no chance. She tends to eat her meat raw."

Rolling my eyes, I look away.

"Oh, come on, it's not like we're hooking up with Quinn," Vale scoffs, and Jai goes suspiciously quiet. We both glance at him as we linger at a red light, the zombie groaning away. "Right?"

"Well, we might have kissed," Jai admits.

My mouth drops open. "How? Like, how? She was keeping you prisoner."

He shrugs. "Maybe I like chains."

"That was another joke. This is freaking me out," I mutter.

"You kissed Quinn." Vale blinks.

"Yes, then she kissed me, so I guess we kissed twice," Jai says and then looks between us. "Oh, come on, don't give me that look. I might have been an asshole, but I wasn't blind. You both wanted to fuck her too."

Vale and I blurt out our protests, and he laughs.

"Such liars. I saw the way you looked at her. She looked at you too. Don't be angry just because I kissed her and you didn't."

"I didn't know it was an option," I admit. "We're enemies."

"Not anymore," Jai offers helpfully.

"Shut up," Vale mutters, his hands tightening on the wheel. "She's still a wolf—"

"A very hot one," Jai interjects.

The zombie growls as if in agreement, and none of us can deny that.

"You're both just jealous," Jai says as Vale guns it.

Shit, is he right?

Maybe.

***

We did, in fact, make Jai wait in the car. He just can't control his new strength and glowing eyes well enough not to give himself away, and walking into the hunters' HQ as a new half-breed? Dumb.

We leave him there as we drag the zombie in like a trophy and throw it at our commander's feet when we reach the command room. He blinks and looks down at it before his eyes widen. "Is that a zombie?"

"Yep, we caught wind of a necromancer while we were hunting wolves, and we found this in a cemetery outside of the city along with remnants of a casting—blood magic. It looks like there is a necromancer out there, which is undoubtedly behind all these killings and the monsters running rampant," Vale says, his arms crossed.

"Well, shit, we hoped it was just witches, but a necromancer makes more sense." He sighs, no doubt he had been wondering too. "This complicates things a bit. A rogue necromancer isn't good for anyone."

"We should move units out and start to hunt whoever is responsible," Vale begins.

"We will after," our commander replies.

"After?" Vale frowns, not understanding. Meanwhile, I'm glancing around.

HQ is in chaos. People are running everywhere, weapons are being passed out, and armour is being strapped on.

What's happening?

A bad feeling wells inside me, and my intuition, which has kept us alive so far, blares an alarm. I nudge Vale, but he's focused on our commander.

"What could be more important than catching a necromancer?"

Vale snaps, noticing the buzz around us. "They are the biggest threat—"

"That's where you're wrong," he scoffs, looking far too happy. "We'll get the necromancer, but first, we are finishing off the wolves."

"There aren't any, and the necromancer needs to take top priority," Vale argues.

"Oh, there aren't? Then why do I know the pack's location? Weapon up, we are attacking at nightfall."

"What are you talking about?" Vale demands, his voice hard as he steps closer.

Our commander eyes him angrily for daring to question him. "You aren't the only hunters, Vale, and you clearly couldn't get the job done. You haven't been as dedicated as before, so fall into line. We got our own information from an inside source. Now, will you be with us, or do I need to terminate you?"

Vale's jaw grinds. "And the necromancer?"

"Will be dealt with after." The commander claps him on the shoulder. "It's time to make history, Vale. It's time to live up to your father's name and get revenge for him."

Vale meets my eyes as my heart stops.

They know where the wolves are.

They are going after Quinn and her pack.

Tonight.

CHAPTER THIRTY-EIGHT

I am to be presented to the pack this evening to face the music. By now, what I did has spread, and I'm sure the truth has been distorted. They might very well hate me and think I'm a traitor. That's fine. I don't regret my actions.

Not if it saves them.

I have visitors all day. Dom keeps me company, and then Filmea and White. All of them ask me why, but they don't seem angry. Instead, they seem sad that we are in this situation. It hurts as much as it helps that so many of them care about me to be on my side despite what I did, but they cannot save me. The pack will decide what will happen to me. They could demand my death or banishment.

That would be worse than death.

Either way, this evening won't be easy, not for Jang and Marie. They will watch their daughter and their next alpha face the music, and I know it's breaking their hearts. My father is stuck between duty and love, and I cannot blame him for what he must do. I never resented that the pack is above everything with him because it's how it should be. I know he will do what's right to keep them safe, and that gives me solace as I await my punishment.

What I told him is true—I will face it with dignity.

When the door opens and Jang stands there, his expression cold but eyes filled with pain, I know it is time. I get to my feet and meet him at the door. He cuffs my arm softly, reminding me he is here with me. We stop at the steps. "Remember, whatever happens, you are still my daughter."

"It's okay," I say honestly, then I lean up and kiss his cheek. "You cannot always save me, Dad."

He closes his eyes. "I'm supposed to."

"Not this time," I reply. "I love you, Dad. You have saved me so many times throughout the years. You gave me a happy life, and you gave me a family, a purpose, and a home when I had nothing. I don't regret anything, nor would I change anything. Whatever is to happen, I am proud to be your daughter."

He glances down, his eyes glassy. "And I'm proud to be your father."

His arms wrap around me, and he squeezes me tightly. I soak in his warmth, comfort, and safety before pulling away. He cannot stop this any more than I can. He would if he could, Jang would fight the world for me, but I won't let him.

Not this time.

"I love you, Dad," I tell him as I face forward again. "That will never change. I'm ready."

"If I told you to run, would you?" he asks.

"No," I answer. "I will not run, not now, not ever."

"My fearless, foolish girl," he whispers. "You were always too special for this pack." He leads me outside to the waiting betas.

I meet their eyes boldly, and they drop their gazes out of respect, one last showing. I will never be alpha now. I bow in return as they form a protective ring around us and lead us towards the gathered pack.

"Give them hell," Jang whispers as he leans down. "Know I am with you, *we* are with you, my daughter. We will always be inside your heart. We are one. We are infinite." Jang steps past me and onto the grassy hill, and the gathered crowd becomes silent. I blow out a deep breath.

"We have called a meeting," Jang booms out. "I am betting by now you have all heard the rumours. Know that rumours can be dangerous, and we are only interested in the truth." His voice is pained. "And we will always give you the truth. As your alpha, it is my duty to protect the well-being of the pack above all else." He takes a deep breath. "Quinn has committed an act against the pack. She had her reasons, and we will get to that, but that's the truth. She let the hunter go." The crowd stirs, and shouts are thrown out, but he waits until they calm. "It is my duty to take your wants and deliver punishment, but in this, I cannot. I cannot be unbiased and do my duty."

"Jang!" I gasp.

He stands taller. "I will happily stand down if that is what you wish, but I will not put my duties as alpha above my love for my daughter. The integrity and the heart of our pack has always been family, and Quinn is my family. She is my daughter no matter what she has done, and I cannot judge her as an alpha. I will take the punishment with her."

My eyes burn as my heart thunders in my chest.

"No," I hiss, stepping forward, but he doesn't even look at me as he kneels.

The alpha is on his knees, a place he should never be, with his head bowed.

If I didn't know how much Jang loved me before, I do now. I fall to my knees at his side, gripping his hand. "Stand, Jang. You don't belong on your knees, not ever, not for anyone."

"I would gladly die here for you, daughter," he replies, meeting my gaze. "It is where I belong, at your side."

Tears slide down my cheeks unchecked. "I made my choice!" I beg.

"As did I. You truly thought I could live if I didn't stand with my daughter?" He smiles. "Foolish girl. I am your father above all else."

"And my mate." My mother drops to my other side, taking my hand. "The sin of one, as they say." She winks and looks past me. "I love you," she tells Jang.

"And I you, my mate," he whispers.

"Silence!" White roars as the pack tumbles into chaos, and then he looks at us. As the oldest beta, it is his duty now, and he sags under the weight. "We are here to decide Quinn's fate, Jang."

"I know, and I accept it with her. I will also endure what is done to her."

"As will I," my mother says, and I have to bite back my sob.

I was ready to endure it all, knowing they were safe, but how could I now? They will suffer with me just because they love me.

"White, please, let me speak," I request.

He frowns before nodding and stepping back. I climb to my feet, still holding their hands, and face the pack I love. "I know you all have questions, and if any of you still believe in me or trust me, then I beg you to listen. I was ready to endure whatever you wished to happen to me, but I cannot stand idly by and let my punishment be inflicted on my parents. Jang is your alpha. He has led with dignity and respect for years. My mother is your heart, and she has looked after your children and fought at your sides for years . . . as have I. When my family was killed, I came here and found a home. I learned to trust and love again. You showed me that, and in return, I pledged my life to you, working to become the best alpha I could and be like my father." I look at Jang. "Or as good as any man or woman could be to measure up to this man. Everything I have ever done is to try and keep you all safe and to protect the home that protected me." I see some softening towards me—those who grew up with me, who helped heal me.

"All I ask is this. Please listen to this once, and if you still wish to punish me—us after, then I will accept it with nothing but love." I stand taller as the sky brightens with oranges and pinks, the sun setting as night takes over. "I did what I did. I let the hunter go. It's true."

I let them react before I carry on. "He was the hunter who took me hostage. His name is Jai, and when he was a kid, his family was killed by a feral and he almost died. He is a half-breed—part wolf, part human—and in him, I saw a chance to stop a war before it started. I saw a chance for hope and a better future. The hunters were coming, and all that would be left were flames and death. I have seen it firsthand, and I couldn't let that happen here. I couldn't stand by and lose another family, so I made a choice. I chose to believe in hope, in second chances, and I let him go in hopes he could stop the hunters. I did what I did out of love, never malice, but I understand your anger and mistrust. I ask you to look at my actions up until today and judge me based on them. I ask you to think about everything I have accomplished and given to this pack. I ask for your understanding and forgiveness, like you have given me so many times before. I do not beg for my life. I beg for theirs."

I swallow anything else I might say then, peering into the pack I call family, and I let them see my truth. I would die for them. I would suffer for them. I would do anything for them if only they would let me.

I kneel again, and Jang looks at me with pride shining in his eyes. "I'm so proud of you, my girl. You have grown into a true leader."

The moonlight kisses along his face when White steps forward. "We need to vote. I know where I stand, as do the betas, but we must agree as a pack—"

"Quinn!"

My name is screamed so loudly, it echoes around the trees. I push to my feet, searching out the source. It can't be. It can't.

"Quinn!" Another voice.

"Dammit, she-wolf!"

My eyes narrow on the tree line, and I gasp as Vale, Lucien, and

Jai stumble from the darkness within, panting and covered in dirt and sweat. "What—" I step forward, my brow furrowed as Jai waves his hands.

"Quinn! They are coming! The hunters are coming!" he shouts.

Chaos erupts at the declaration.

CHAPTER THIRTY-NINE

"Dom, bring them here now," I command. "Keep them alive."

Dom and White surge into the pack at my order. Jai and Vale try to resist, but Lucien allows them to drag them closer. I watch them struggle, refusing to shrink under the growls and threats that come from the pack as the hunters are pulled through.

They are pushed to their knees before us as Jang gets to his feet. "Hunters," he hisses.

I step in front of him before he can order anything, and I meet each of their gazes. "What are you doing here?" I ask.

"Warning you, obviously, she-wolf," Vale snarks, shoving White's hands off him. "If he touches me again, I'll gut him."

A growl goes up, and I sigh. "Enough," I command, and the growl cuts off. "You said the hunters were coming."

Vale grinds his teeth and nods his head.

"You brought them here?" I look at Jai, my nails changing to claws as I press them against his throat, tilting his head up until I meet his eyes. He doesn't fight me or argue, just waits.

Part of me is hurt that he would betray us.

"He didn't," Vale replies. "He found us and convinced us to help you and your pack and get the hunters off your back. We found traces of a necromancer in the area and captured one of its victims, and we took it to them to redirect their focus, but they said they had inside information on where the pack is located. They are attacking tonight. You need to prepare."

Just as he finishes, a howl goes up in the distance—a warning call.

"They are here," I whisper, looking into Jai's eyes. "You didn't do this?"

"No," he promises. "Never."

Swallowing, I search his gaze.

"We cannot trust them," Jang protests.

I have a choice now. I step back but don't sheathe my claws. "I trust them. They didn't have to warn us." I look at Jang. "They are telling the truth." I raise my voice. "Get the women and children inside. This is not a drill. The pack is under attack!"

Despite the ongoing trial, they jump at my orders. Drills and years of practice make it smooth despite everyone's panic and fear. Women and men alike grab pups and hurry to the safe houses while others prepare. I watch as a wave of werewolves get ready to fight, standing guard as I peer back at Jang.

"If you trust them, then I trust them," he tells me before grabbing the back of my head and kissing my forehead. "I know you tried to stop this. You did all you could. Now it is time to fight for our people, for our land. You take the south, and I will take the north."

"Father—"

His eyes close, and he kisses my forehead again. "So proud of you, my Quinny. Now show the pack why I chose you as alpha. Let us keep our people safe."

Nodding, I step back, and he turns, his eyes turning bright amber. "Change! Kill any hunter on sight. Protect the safe house. We hold the line. We fight tonight for our families, our pack, and our land!"

Howls echo through the air as Jang tips his head back and joins in. I feel my eyes shift, and I let out a mournful, angry howl along with them.

When I drop my head, I meet Vale's, Lucien's, and Jai's eyes. They slowly climb to their feet.

"We can help," Lucien offers.

"How?" My voice is a growl. I know my fangs have lengthened, and my power flows through our land.

Everything I did was for nothing. They are coming, and no one is safe, but I will never let them hurt my land or my pack. I would die first.

"We are some of their best hunters," Vale scoffs. "We know all their strategies, moves, and weaknesses."

"Then speak fast," Jang commands.

"We answer to her, not you," Vale snarls, going toe to toe with Jang despite him bristling and sprouting fur. He doesn't back down and eventually, Jang smirks and turns to me.

"I like him. Find out everything quickly." He storms away to ready our people, making sure there is no chance for any of them to slip through. Luckily, they can only come from the front and sides. If they wanted to go around the back, they would have to clamber through streams and over the mountain, which is impossible for humans.

"They will come in two waves. The first will be a distraction, attacking head-on to draw your attention. The next will circle to the sides or rear to catch you off guard and sneak up and slit your throats. They won't play fair. They will use wolfsbane, silver, and guns. They will also have snipers in the trees," Vale quickly informs me.

"Anything else?" I ask.

"Yes, many will die," he grits out.

I nod and hurry to Jang, who is barking orders. "We need our best climbers waiting in trees for their snipers and more blending in on both sides for when they try to sneak up on us. Warn everyone there will be wolfsbane and silver. They need to be fast and to move without hesitation. Let us use our advantage. We know this land. We can lead some to the gorge and others to the cliffs, and we are faster and stronger. I'm the fastest, so I will lead as many away as I can and come back."

"No, Quinny," Jang begins.

"Yes, Alpha. You know it's the right move."

He looks at me with so much sorrow and pain, I cannot help but clasp his hand. "I've got this, trust me. Let us end this tonight."

Marie comes up then, her expression hard and ready. "She's right. This has been a long time coming. Tonight, we'll fight or die for our pack as a family."

She grabs us both, hauling us into a hug, and for a moment, I soak in their warmth before pulling back. "I will use the hunters as well."

"Okay, you do what you think is right, Quinn." Jang catches my hand as I go to turn away. "Stay safe. I cannot lose you, Quinn. Do you understand me?"

I smirk. "They'd have to catch me first."

"That's my girl." He grins.

Marie kisses my cheek. "Kill them all," she whispers before moving to take her position at the front of the line where she belongs like the warrior she is.

I hurry back to Vale, Lucien, and Jai, who are strapping on their weapons, a bag open before them. "Don't hurt any of the pack or they will kill you. We have marked you as friendly for now, but get in the way and they won't hesitate."

"Got it." Lucien hauls up a bag. "I've got some fun toys in here. I'm going to plant them as far away as I can to stop some of them."

"Wait." I grab his hand as he goes to leave. He looks down at it then back at me, and I swallow hard. "Take a wolf. That way we'll all know where they are and can avoid them."

He bristles, clearly hating having a wolf watching his back, but he finally inclines his head.

I let out a whistle, and Dom hurries over. "Go with Lucien. If any hunters sneak up on you, kill them. Warn the others where the traps are through the pack bond so we can avoid them."

"Are you sure about this, babe?" Dom murmurs, eyeing the hunters.

I see them all stiffen at his endearment, but I tug Dom into a quick hug. "We don't have a choice. Go."

Dom kisses my cheek, and I ignore the glares I feel aimed at me, unsure why I'm suddenly uncomfortable with Dom touching me when we have done much worse. "Stay safe, babe."

I watch him and Lucien hurry into the trees, and then I turn back to Vale and Jai.

"I'll stay with you two," I say. "For now, I plan to lead some away. Can I trust you to watch my back while I do?"

"We're here, aren't we?" Vale snaps.

"Yes," Jai answers.

"Good." I move closer and press a claw to Vale's neck. He freezes. "If you hurt any of my family, I'll rip your pretty throat out and eat it."

He glances down to my lips, and it's my turn to freeze as his voice comes, low and almost flirty. "Pretty, huh?"

Rolling my eyes, I tug my hand away. "Just stay out of my way and make yourself useful or I'll kill you myself." I glance at Jai, who's grinning in that crazy way he does. "Both of you."

"Aww, don't be like that, Quinn." He winks. "I came back, didn't I?"

"You weren't supposed to." I snort as I step back and grin. "Fools, but it seems we are on the same side for now. Try not to shoot me."

I grab my dress and rip it over my head before shucking down my panties. I stand before them naked, eyes glowing and claws out. "And try to keep up." I transform.

They've seen me shift before, but when my paws hit the ground, Vale seems shocked as he watches me. I roll my eyes, snap my teeth at him, and head past.

I don't know how long we will have before the humans arrive, but I'm betting not long if they are as fast as Vale and Lucien. My heart aches for what we could lose tonight, but I cannot afford to think like that, so I try to push it away as I trot towards the other wolves who are preparing to defend our pack, two hunters following along behind me.

What a strange day.

CHAPTER FORTY

I don't know how long it will be before the hunters get here. It took us far longer than we wanted to escape their notice so we could warn the pack. They were already prepared and heading to the vehicles when we slipped away. Luckily, Jai knew the way, and we managed to get here before them, but they are tight on our tail.

We've chosen a side, and now we have to fight for it.

Regret haunts me for the friends I might have to kill, innocents just trying to do their jobs, but I know I have to. The kids and families I saw gathered tonight in the pack solidified my decision. They are innocent too, and they don't deserve to die.

That's how I find myself being followed by a way too happy man—er, wolf. Crouching, I dig the holes as fast as I can, laying the explosive traps and then moving on. He seems to mark each one, though I don't know how that works. We've set them back as far from the pack land as we can get in hopes of slowing the hunters down or deterring them.

All the while, the wolf watches my back. My hand twitches, wanting my gun in case he decides to attack, but I force myself to relax. Quinn marked us as safe, so I have to trust in that for now. Otherwise, what is the point of all of this?

It doesn't mean I'm not on edge, though, because I'm a hunter and he's a wolf.

We are enemies, but he doesn't seem to care as he whistles to himself, watching me work. I need to fill the silence, but for some fucking reason, the first thing that comes to my head slips out, and I want to kick myself.

"So you and Quinn are together?" I ask as I dig my hands into the wet soil before planting the trip mine. I cover it gently and mark it for us before moving onto the next area, but the wolf, Dom, is already there.

Smirking, he slams his claws into the earth and digs it up in a second, whereas it would have taken me minutes. "Every now and again."

"What does that mean?" I ask, unable to look at him.

"Why, hunter? Are you jealous? Does someone have a crush on a wolf?" He snorts.

"No, just curious. Forget I asked," I grumble.

"Oh, I can't—" He stops, and I lift my head. His eyes are narrowed as he looks around. "Humans," he hisses.

I stand quickly, pulling my gun and putting my back to a tree. There are gaps on either side in case I need to move, but it means no one can sneak up on me. Dom looks back at me, grinning with teeth that seem to sharpen as I watch. "Keep back, hunter. I promised Quinn I'd keep you safe."

He shifts. I don't think I'll ever get used to that. One minute, there's a man before me, and then with an audible snap of bones, a huge brown wolf stands before me, the hair on its back on end as it growls.

I check my gun and crouch in case they come out shooting. It's a few more minutes before I hear the crunch of booted feet and the whisper of talking hunters. They must think they have time before they reach pack territory because they don't seem to be paying attention as they stumble to a stop before the wolf, who doesn't hesitate to attack. Before they can get their guns up, Dom leaps.

He lands on one and rips his throat out before tackling the second, biting him as he screams. The third begins to bring his gun up, and I hesitate, but Dom is there, biting off the man's hand. The gun falls, and the hunter yells, staring wide-eyed at the stump on his arm.

Dom uses that distraction to knock him to the ground and start to eviscerate him while he's still alive, tugging at the body. I look away, bile in my throat, and that's when I see it. Both of us were so distracted, we didn't even notice them sneaking up. Their shock and horror are the reasons we are both still alive, but they are focused on the wolf now.

I fire, and the wolf turns, his wide eyes and mouth dripping blood. The two hunters who were sneaking up on him lie dead behind him.

I saved his life.

I saved a wolf and killed my own kind.

My hand drops, and the wolf glances from them to me before sniffing the air, and a moment later, a very naked Dom stands before me, covered in blood. "Good shot, hunter." He grins. "Now finish planting your bombs, we don't have much time."

Nodding, I holster my gun and drop to the ground, both of us silently digging holes as we move along, planting as many bombs as we can before we step back.

"Do you think it will work?" Dom asks.

"I hope so. We'll find out before long though."

Nodding, Dom turns back. "We better return." I follow him, and he glances at me. "Thanks for saving my life. You're not so bad for a hunter." He claps my shoulder. "I'll make sure to tell Quinn of your heroics."

"Dom, don't you—" I sputter, but he just laughs.

Wolves.

When we get back, there is a line of wolves waiting at the tree line, all in formation and clearly anticipating an attack. The many houses spread around are now dark, and everything is almost silent. The moonlight shines across the beautiful land and the red mountains beyond.

Standing in the middle is Quinn in wolf form, with Vale and Jai behind her. Jang is in human form at their side, his jaw clenched.

"They are set. We came upon early scout hunters, so the rest won't be far behind," I inform them.

Jang nods, and I'll admit there is something about the alpha that almost makes me want to follow his every command to make him happy, and I'm not even a wolf. Jai was right. He's a huge bastard and scary as fuck, but when he glances at Quinn, there is nothing but love and protectiveness in his eyes.

"We are ready."

"When they come, there will be casualties," Vale starts, but Jang cuts him a look that silences even my fearless brother.

"We know, and we're ready. Are you, hunters?"

"Yes." Vale nods. "We are with you, but please, not everyone who is attacking is bad."

"They are here to kill my family, so I will do everything in my power to stop that. If you don't like it, leave," Jang growls.

Quinn huffs and moves over to the wolves near the tree line, ignoring us and gazing into the distance. Jang watches her go, his face softening.

He observes for a moment then glances back at us. "No matter what happens, keep my daughter safe. She has already lost so much. Promise me that. We started as enemies, but I see the truth. Now, vow it. Vow to save Quinn no matter what."

"Why would you ask us?" I retort, needing to know.

He meets my eyes with a knowing look. "We are all but creatures of moonlight, born into destinies we know nothing about. This world is a huge, mysterious place, yet there are three things I know for certain. One, I was meant to be that girl's father. Two, she will be the most magnificent alpha this world has ever seen. Three, you do not betray your own people for just an ideal. You do it to save someone you care about. Now, you might not have realised or even admitted it, but it's the truth. Destiny is guiding your hand, and now I have to ask this of you."

"We will do everything to keep her safe," I respond gruffly.

"Good, that's good." He nods. "She won't make it easy. She never does." He grins. "She has always been so brave and strong-willed. She takes after her father that way, but she has her mother's kind heart. I miss them terribly, and so does she." I wince at that, as does Vale, and Jang smiles sadly. "We cannot undo the past, but we can change our future. We can atone for the sins of our fathers and make them right, even when we don't think we can." He changes before our eyes, becoming a huge black wolf—one we saw chasing after Quinn when we kidnapped her. He gives us a sharp, knowing look and heads to his people.

"He couldn't be more wrong," Vale scoffs. "We are doing this to save our souls."

I nod, but my eyes cut to Quinn, wondering if he was right.

Since the moment I met her, all I seem to do is defend and save her where I can, like there is a tether between us that has always been there, even when it shouldn't.

Is that destiny or a heart's desire?

CHAPTER FORTY-ONE

Quinn

The trees rustle before me, and I snarl, prepared to leap, but it's our advanced team, our warning system. They spring through the tree line, sliding to a stop, panting and covered in blood.

There are only five.

There were twenty.

Fuck!

"How far?" Jang barks, changing back to human form to engage with them.

"Right behind us," one answers as he changes back. "Maybe a couple of minutes. They killed everyone else."

Jang growls and turns to us. "Ready yourselves! For our pack! For our people!"

We tip our heads back and howl once more, a last warning for them.

They might be hunters, but we are wolves.

We remain silent after that, waiting under the full moon for the hunters to arrive. What should be a happy night of running and hunting was already ruined, but now, before it dips below the horizon and the sun rises, everything will have changed.

I feel it in my gut.

I keep my breathing even although adrenaline and the need to hunt makes me impatient, and when I hear the first hunter, I almost yip in victory. They are trying to be silent, but we can hear them as they spread out.

Like Vale predicted, they try to climb trees. I know because there's a scream and a thud, which sounds like a body falling, and then more follow. Suddenly, the hunters burst from the tree line, their guns up and ready to fire. When they see us, their eyes widen, but I don't focus on them.

I attack. They are my enemy.

Screams ring out as we leap at the hunters coming to kill us. More pour from the forest, the ones who make it past those in the trees. Guns fire, the smell awful and noise loud. I hear a wolf whine, but I don't have time to look.

I have to focus.

The first hunter I hit is an older man with a scarred face, and he goes down hard way too slow. I taste his blood before I hear his scream cut off. It gurgles as I rip out his throat and turn, leaping at the next hunter, slashing my claws across him as he falls back.

I hear more shots, one whizzing above me, and I jerk my head around to see Vale holding a rifle, firing at the incoming hunters above me. I nod in thanks and turn back just in time to dodge a hunter coming towards me.

I bring my head up, ignoring the gun so close to me, and bite the hunter's cock. He screams as he falls forward, but I rip through his trousers, tasting blood and skin, and when I tear my head away, his cock comes with me. I spit it out with a growl and leap at him, digging my claws into his chest, and then I bite his face off before rolling away from another shot and coming up behind a young hunter struggling with his gun.

I headbutt his legs, and he falls just as his head explodes. I glance over to see Jai with a gun pointed right at him, and he winks at me before turning to punch another hunter trying to get past him to the wolves.

"Traitor!" I hear someone yell, but I tune them out.

Instead, I nip at a hunter's side. The middle-aged man glares at me, wielding a knife, and I back away, my head lowered as those around him notice and turn to me—a woman and four men. Perfect.

I continue backing away.

"I'm going to gut this one and use its fur for a rug," a woman with the fierce face hisses.

I stick my tongue out at her and back into the trees before turning to run. "Hunt her ass down!" I hear someone yell.

I slow so they can keep up, their panting loud. Bark explodes on either side of me as they fire off shots, yelling as they chase me.

Fools.

I lead them away from my pack and towards the gorge, rolling over fallen logs and avoiding their guns but remaining slow enough so they don't lose sight of me. It's almost too easy. I'm barely breaking one of my slowest jogs, but I pretend to pant and panic.

They fall for it hook, line, and fucking sinker, and when I skid to a stop before the gorge, they laugh as they converge on me.

"I won't even use my gun for this one," one of the bearded men jokes as he withdraws a large machete. "I'll wear her like a fucking coat while I kill her pathetic family."

I step back, and they follow until I'm hanging over the edge. Only then do they seem to notice, and then I leap over them, faster than they can see, and ram into them. Luckily, they are so close that they tumble over the edge as one big mass of screaming humans.

Standing on the edge of the gorge, I watch them plummet to their deaths, but then a scream cuts the air.

My head snaps back, knowing that wolf's scream, and I burst into a sprint, heading back to the pack.

I slide to a stop just inside the tree line, taking in the chaos.

Human bodies litter the ground, but even more are still fighting, firing, and engaging wolves with everything they have in them. There are a few wolves littering the ground, dying or dead, and my heart aches as I memorise every single one.

I grew up with them.

It's like losing a limb.

There's so much blood and death.

Claws, fangs, and blades clash, and growls and shouts mix together as the moon illuminates the hatred and desire to kill one another.

I spot Jang in wolf form, taking on at least twelve hunters alone.

Jai is crouched, firing a rifle while kicking hunters away. Lucien is fighting hand-to-hand with two others, while Vale spins through a mass of four of them with a silver chain. My mother is making her way to Jang, fighting through the hunters and bleeding from one arm, but otherwise, she's fine.

I see White barrelling through their masses, while Filmea rips apart any who get too close. Dom, who screamed, is back on his paws and fighting with everything he has.

A warm droplet of rain hits my eye, and I shake my head, looking up at the moon as more fall. The ground turns slick as hunters scream in both agony and victory around me.

Rain pelts the ground as if feeling our pain, our anger, and Mother Nature reflects it. It obscures some of the hunters' vision and wets my fur through, but I don't stop.

I throw myself into battle, ripping through as many as I can reach. I barely feel the sting of their blades, ignoring it in favour of fighting, because each one who dies is another step closer to my pack's safety.

"Keep pushing!" I hear a human shout.

A scream has me whirling around to see more pouring from the sides where they must have escaped the traps. There is an explosion in the distance—Lucien's traps—but more try to box us in. Luckily, the wolves we stationed there leap down after them, trapping them within their own snare.

Jang transforms back for a moment. "Quinn, the house!" he roars.

I glance at the house to see at least five hunters heading towards the building filled with women and children. I nod and push off, kicking a hunter who gets too close. I pass Vale, and he quickly snaps the neck of a man turning to me before grabbing a gun, falling into step next to me.

When I glance back, Lucien is sprinting after us, and then Jai bursts into action, coming to my side with a wicked grin, his eyes alight. "Great night for death, isn't it?" He's covered in blood, almost as if he has been ripping them to shreds with his hands.

How people could think he was a human is beyond me.

I don't have time to dwell on that, however, as I hurry towards the safe house some distance away, my paws hitting the wet dirt hard before I race through the open door. I still then, the sound of water hitting the wood floor loud, but I hear no screams or growls.

They haven't found them yet.

Tilting my head, I follow the sound of quiet feet and look upstairs. I glance at Vale and then the stairs, and he nods. He points his fingers down, and Jai and Lucien move past him before he heads to the stairs. I trot after him, and at the top, he points left, so I go right, talking without words. It's strange how right it feels, but as I come upon my first hunter, I don't bother to think anymore. I slink through the open bedroom doorway, where he is ransacking the room, and quickly change back.

On silent human feet, I step behind him, grab his neck before he can make a noise, and snap it. The thud as he falls is loud, and I wait, but no one comes. There's a grunt, and I stride down the hallway, only to still. Vale smashes his foot into a hunter, sending him flying through the plaster wall, all while a second one has a sword to his throat, cutting it. His arm wraps around Vale and hauls him back.

"Fucking monster loving traitor. We'll gut you for this," he hisses, even as Vale snaps his head back, busting the man's nose. He slides from under the blade, twisting one in his own hand, and buries it so hard into the man's neck that it pins him to the wall. Next, Vale turns and spins around the man climbing through the wall, locking one arm across his neck and placing the other on his head as he slowly sits him down. His face turns purple and then blue as he struggles, trying to breathe before finally giving in.

Vale lets him go and lifts his head, his eyes narrowed in fury. For a moment, I just stare at his heaving chest and the trickle of blood running down his neck, and then I'm moving. The moon streams through the window behind him, bathing him in shadows and light until he looks every inch the capable killer he is. He meets me half-way, our bodies clashing together.

His hand slides through my hair, gripping the wet tendrils and yanking my head back as his lips crash to mine. His teeth dig into my bottom lip before I give as good as I get. I pull back, both of us panting.

His thumb runs across my lower lip, pulling it down before gliding down my chin and between my breasts, leaving goosebumps in his wake before his lips are back on mine. His hand in my hair, yanking me close. My own grip his shirt, holding him still as I assault his lips.

My fangs pierce his lip, and I taste the copper tang of his blood, which only makes us more feral. My back hits the wall hard enough to dent it, and his hands grip me firmly enough to bruise.

A hunter comes upon us and smacks into Vale's side, knocking him away. Snarling, I bury my claws into his chest then rip them free, offering Vale my hand. With a confident smirk, he slaps his into mine, and I haul him up effortlessly.

For a moment, we stare at one another before he leans in and kisses me again, softer this time. It's almost comforting.

His hand slides down my bare back to grip my ass, tugging me forward until I'm pressed against his body. I feel every inch of him, including the metal pipe prodding my stomach.

"Fuck." He groans against my lips, the sound husky and so fucking sexy. "Why do you taste so good?" He licks my lips, rubbing himself against me. "Like the freshest fruit. Forbidden." He nips my lip. "Do you taste that sweet everywhere?"

"You'll never find out," I tease, nipping his lip again.

"Want to bet, she-wolf?" he murmurs before deepening the kiss.

A yell makes us rip apart, both of us panting. I change back before he can say a word and leap from the top of the banister, landing on the floor below.

I blame my wolf's bloodlust, but that never should have happened, and when he joins me downstairs, I don't bother looking at him. What is happening to me? I've kissed two hunters now!

Shaking my head, I growl as I prowl into the living room where a group of hunters have Jai and Lucien on their knees, their guns aimed at their heads.

"There's the fucking beast," one snarls, glaring at me. "Is this the one who made you betray us?" he demands, looking at Vale. "She must have a good pussy to turn you against your own kind. Didn't realise you liked to fuck monsters, Vale. Do you do it doggy style while she's turned?" he taunts.

"Why? Is that what you want to do?" Jai smirks. "It sounds like it. Someone has a thing for bestiality, do they?"

One of them slams a gun into his head. He falls back with a groan but quickly sits back up. His nose and lips are bleeding, but he's still smiling crazily. He glances at me as he licks his lips, tasting his own blood.

I position myself behind the one with the gun aimed at him and glance at the one aiming at Lucien. He dips his chin slightly, and when I burst into action, slamming the human to the ground, he snaps up, grabbing the man's arm and breaking it before he even sees him move. I change back, grab the gun, and fire into the man's head before spinning to fire at the others, but Lucien is already there. His fist is covered in blood and gore as he holds one off the floor by the neck and slams his fist into the other. Vale just watches with an arched brow, but when the one Jai disarmed tries to run by, Vale kicks his leg out, tripping him, and Jai descends on him with feral delight.

I sit back and watch as Lucien pummels the man into a pulp before turning to the one choking and clawing at his hand with a growl worthy of a wolf. Lucien snaps his neck one-handed. I glance at Jai to see the man dead beneath him despite him still attacking.

"Well, shit, I guess there's a reason you're hunters," I remark.

"The best." Vale winks as I toss him a gun.

"We need to get back. How many more can there be?"

"At least a hundred—" A howl freezes my heart.

It's one I know better than my own.

"Jang!" I roar as I burst from the house, changing mid-run.

CHAPTER FORTY-TWO

I sprint as fast as I can, following the howl. Marie screams my name, but I ignore her, blinking through the rain as I slide to a stop just outside the ongoing battle. Wolves are falling, their howls of death breaking my heart. The sound of guns firing makes my ears ring as I frantically search the mass of bodies before me until I find him.

He's no longer in wolf form. I don't know why or how he changed back, but his eyes shine bright amber and his claws drip with blood even in human form. His huge naked body is covered in bleeding wounds, including bullet holes.

"Jang," I whisper.

He is surrounded by hunters, all of them brandishing weapons and intent on felling our alpha as if they know his worth.

Our betas are busy fighting, trying to get to their alpha, but no one seems to notice him slowing.

The wounds are taking their toll.

There are at least ten hunters surrounding him. Jang might be an alpha, but he is one man.

One beast.

My heart stutters and then stops for a moment as he stumbles under the weight of holding them off. I push towards him through the throng, whirling as something catches my shoulder. I growl, ignoring the pain, as I try to carry on, but a hunter stops in front of me with a wicked grin.

Ignoring his mouth and the words he's going to speak, I slam my claws through his neck and out the other side before removing them and kicking him away. My gaze locks back on Jang as he stumbles to one knee before getting back up with a shout.

No.

No.

No.

I leap over a wolf pinning a screaming hunter to the wet earth, still fighting to get to him. My nose twitches with the scent of gasoline, and when there is a whoosh of heat, I glance back to see flames licking at the pack house as hunters hurry away, laughing.

For a moment, I hesitate, but there's another pained grunt.

Jang.

I focus on him, slowed by the battle raging on around us. More hands grab me, trying to gut any wolf they can find, but I ignore them. Something inside of me knows that if I look away from Jang, it will be the end.

With a mighty groan, he falls to his knees, his arms raised in an X to stop a blade from heading for his throat. Instead, the blade slices through his arms. I watch his eyes flare, but he holds strong until a hunter kicks his back.

"White! Dom!" I scream, but I know they are too far. "To our alpha!"

I pick up a fallen blade and throw it. It embeds in the hunter, forcing his blade lower, and Jang staggers before stumbling to his feet. The scent of his blood reaches me even through the rain and fire eating away at our house behind me.

I'm the fastest wolf. I'm the fastest wolf—

Arms grab me from behind, lifting me, and a warm mouth meets my ear. "Not so fast, beast."

I throw myself backwards with a shout, fighting them, but more arms grab me until each of my arms is held in a hunter's grip, and they force me to my knees. I don't look at them. I can't look away from Jang.

He falls again, a bullet tearing through his side. He tries to climb to his feet, and I chant for him to do so, but he's weak. Wolfsbane. He falls again as the hunters laugh.

No!

"Get up!" I roar. "Get up and fight!"

I struggle against the hands holding me, trying to get to him.

Another bullet rips through him, this time his arm, then another in his thigh as he roars. The sound raises the hair on my arms. He still doesn't give up. He fights to get to his feet—to win, to protect his family, to protect this pack.

He's a true alpha.

There are too many of them though.

Another bullet tears through his chest, and a hunter steps closer to him, raising a blade above his head, ready to carve off Jang's head.

My father's head.

"Jang!" I scream helplessly. "Father!"

Like he hears me, his head snaps around to me, his eyes locking on mine even though he knows his death blow is imminent. "Look away, princess," he mouths.

"No!" I roar, and with renewed urgency, I kick away the hunters holding me, scramble to my feet, and dive for him, but it's too late.

The blade falls, and I watch in horror as it slices through his throat. His eyes are wide as they bring the blade out and back down, cleaving off his head.

It rolls across the grass as I fall to my knees, unable to look away from his open, lifeless eyes.

Jang . . . Father.

Arms grab me once more, but I ignore them.

Grief fills my body, taking it over until I cannot breathe.

I shatter.

My scream echoes to the moon, shaking the earth with its fury.

Everything around me fades.

I no longer feel the pain of my body or the hands holding me, nor the heat of the burning pack house.

All I feel is a bone-deep abyss of agony consuming me.

My body is slick with the rain, my hair hanging in drenched ringlets around my face. Our house burns as Marie lets out a grieved howl somewhere behind me.

My own head falls back, my scream ragged as I bellow my pain to the moon.

The lick of flames heats my skin, and I could be burning for all I know, but I don't care.

I hear the echoing cry taken up by the wolves as they turn to see their fallen alpha.

Jang.

He's gone.

It's my last thought as something hard hits the back of my head. I fall forward into wet, muddy grass and my eyes close.

My heart and soul are torn apart.

I welcome the darkness beyond.

Let them kill me.

Let me join both my fathers.

I will not live in a world without my family.

Please, I whisper to the darkness, *take me away.*

CHAPTER FORTY-THREE

The last thing I remember is an agonised scream that tore apart my heart. Quinn was on her knees, bleeding and soaked, shouting as her father was killed before her eyes. I stopped what I was doing, my own horror and pain ripping me apart until I stood stock-still with the rest of the wolves.

It was my downfall.

Pain splinters through my head. Either I was drugged or knocked out. I don't know why they didn't just kill me on the spot, but they must have their reasons. Part of me doesn't want to wake up.

We failed.

We failed the pack.

We failed Quinn.

The house was burning, and we were trying to put it out. It will be nothing but smoking cinders now, along with her father's body. She lost her family once, and I saw her pain when she spoke about it, so to lose her family again?

I cannot even begin to think about how she will go on—if she's even alive.

That makes my eyes open. I have to slam them shut instantly

because the pain turns to agony, which turns my stomach and has me gagging. Breathing through it, I count slowly until it becomes a dull ache, and then I slowly flutter my eyes open once more. My vision is blurry at first, but it slowly comes back.

All I see is scarred grey concrete.

I'm lying on it, my body shivering from the cold, my side aching from lying still for too long. Blinking once more to clear my vision, I roll my eyes up to see bars—cell bars.

A cage?

Prison?

My mind can't seem to work it out. With a groan, I push myself upright, my arms shaking until I'm on my knees. I reach back and run my fingers over my head, wincing when I prod a huge lump. I wasn't drugged. I was knocked out.

Motherfucker.

Lifting my gaze, I glance around, trying to figure out where we are. It's not somewhere I have ever seen before. It smells damp and old, and there isn't much light. It's almost fully dark except for some candles spread around the room. There are partially fallen wooden beams, and moss and rot are growing everywhere. It's cold, with a hole in an outside wall letting the wet breeze in.

It's still dark, which surprises me.

My eyes land on a cage opposite me, and my jaw drops.

Jai lies with his back to me, unmoving. Climbing to unsteady feet, I wrap my arms around the bars. "Jai," I rasp, my voice hoarse. He doesn't move, so I try again. "Jai!" He groans, and I sag in relief.

The cage is huge, big enough for at least ten grown men, and when I glance to the side, I see an unmoving Vale. My heart stops.

"Brother." I grip the bars harder. "Brother!"

He rolls over, his arm covering his face. "It's too early, and it hurts. Shush."

Pressing my head to the bars, I grin. "I bet. Wake up, you're not hungover. We're in trouble." That gets him upright, and he blinks like I did. There's a bloody gash on his forehead, and he winces, but his eyes widen as he looks around before his gaze stops slightly to the left.

"Quinn."

I whirl around, spotting a cage attached to mine like Vale's is to Jai's.

She's slumped against the bars, her arms and legs lying at funny angles, as if she were thrown inside without care. Her hair is dry but matted and falling through the bars. Her eyes are shut, and her mouth is slightly parted as if she's asleep, and for a moment, I watch her chest rise and fall, thankful she's alive.

Blood covers nearly every inch of her naked body, as does mud, and I don't know what's hers and what isn't.

"You think she's okay?" Jai asks, and I glance over to see them both standing.

"She's breathing," I murmur.

"That's the best we can hope for," Vale mutters, tugging at the bars. "Jai, look for a way out. You too, Lucien. We need to get out of here and fast. I don't like this."

"You think it's hunters?"

"They took her too, so I'm betting so," Vale replies. "I don't know why they didn't just kill us. They probably want answers, so we need to get out of here before they return."

Nodding, I turn to my cage to search it for weak spots, but my eyes keep going back to Quinn, the memory of her scream still haunting me.

I almost choke on her pain even now, like I feel the agony that fills her unconscious body, which is insane. Swallowing, I force myself to focus on checking the bars. They are too strong to bend or break, so instead, I check their welding points, top and bottom, for any weaknesses.

The cage itself is ten paces long and wide, and there is nothing else in it but me.

The top is also bars, and I grip them, lifting myself up and using my full weight, but it's no use.

"Anything?" Vale calls.

"Nope," I reply.

"Nothing." Jai sighs, tugging at his cage with his wolf strength before hissing. "The bars are infused with something that burns."

Frowning, I grip them again but feel nothing. It must be for wolves, but I don't say it out loud.

"So what now?" I ask worriedly.

Vale sighs. "We have no choice. We have to wait."

VALE

It's been hours. The ache in my head is still there, but it's nowhere near as bad as it was when I first woke up. They caught me trying to get to Quinn, the grip of the gun hitting my head hard. I can feel it scabbing, so I don't touch it, letting it heal. Lucien's eyes are on Quinn, as are Jai's as he paces. He's never been one for sitting still.

It's freezing in here, but I don't complain. How can I when Quinn is lying there, still passed out?

I let her heart break. My own broke with hers, like a fragile echo of what happened to her.

"What if she doesn't wake up?" Jai mutters, shooting her another worried look.

"It's better that she rests," I say, propping my arms on my knees as we wait. "When she wakes, she will only feel heartbreak and have to face his death. He can still live in her dreams."

"I felt it," he admits. "I felt her break at the sight."

I look at him. "Me too. I don't understand how."

"Me either." Lucien sighs. "But it was like someone thrust their hand into my chest, grabbed my heart, and squeezed until it crumbled to dust."

I nod. I felt the exact same thing. My gaze goes back to her again. "It will destroy her when she wakes. I don't know how she will cope."

"I wonder what happened to the pack," Jai whispers. "Are they all dead? Is she the last one?"

"I don't know. I hope not. I don't think she could survive that. We need to give her hope to keep her alive. She's our best bet of getting out of here."

"Don't be so selfish," Jai hisses.

"I'm not," I growl. "If she can get us out, then we can get her back to her pack, her family. We can try to help her—"

"What? Bring her father back?" Lucien snaps.

Just then, there's a small whimper, and we all stand and turn to face Quinn as her eyes open.

For a moment, there's confusion in her gaze before reality sets in, and those bright orbs fill with so much pain, I'm surprised her body doesn't tear apart from trying to hold it in.

I don't know how she is able to breathe around it when I simply fall at the sight.

Everything hurts. Not just my head, but my heart. When my eyes first opened, I couldn't figure out why it hurt. I thought I was back with Vale, Lucien, and Jai at the mill, taunting them.

So why do my eyes burn?

Why is my heart shattered and tearing me apart from the inside?

Why does every breath hurt?

"Easy," Vale says, and I cling to his voice like a ship in a storm, seeking out his bright eyes. He watches me carefully as I suck in desperate breaths. "That's it, just breathe, Quinn."

For some reason, his words give me power to breathe, and the lightheaded feeling dissipates. Panic and grief still claw at me, my wolf howls in mourning, and my head hurts, but I can't figure out why . . .

Is Vale in a cage?

Yes. Lucien is next to him, and I turn my throbbing head to see Jai next to me, all peering at me worriedly.

We are in cages. Why are we in cages?

Why is my body sluggish and cold?

"Why does my heart hurt?" I whisper, and Lucien winces as he glances at Vale. I look at him, but he just swallows, watching me. My eyes find Jai then. "Why does it feel like something is missing inside me?"

"Quinn . . ." He licks his lips nervously. "Do you remember what happened?"

"You came to warn us." I work through my sluggish, jumbled thoughts. "There was an attack," I say. "It was raining really badly, and we were winning, but fire . . . There was a fire? Was I hurt in it?"

"Anything else?" Jai prompts.

Squeezing my eyes shut, I rack my brain. My thoughts escape my like wisps, and there's a small voice telling me not to look, but I delve deeper, and my eyes open with a cry.

"No, no, no, no." I don't even realise I'm chanting it at first, my ears popping. My body vibrates as my wolf howls louder, and I understand now.

How can I still be breathing? How can I still be alive when everything inside me is gone?

I choke on my grief, screaming inside my head as I bow from the agony inside my body.

Jang is gone.

My father is gone.

Maybe my mother too.

Maybe my entire pack.

"Babe, focus on me," the voice calls to me, kind and soft, but it just makes me whine in agony. "Quinn . . ."

"Quinn, fucking stop it. Snap out of it." The sharp tone pierces my pain, and I lift my head, blindly searching for a lifeline. My gaze lands on familiar bright eyes.

The voice belongs to him.

Vale.

I can barely see through my tears as they track down my face. "You have to be strong. You have to because right now, we are surrounded by hunters who want to rip you apart for fun. You can fall apart later." I watch him close his eyes for a moment. "Right now, we all need each other, we need you, so swallow it."

"I can't." I whimper.

"You can and you will," he roars. "Do it with me. I did the exact same thing. Take all that pain, all that grief, and shove it into a ball. That's it, now swallow it. Bury it so deep, you cannot feel it anymore. It will sting every time you take a breath and will be waiting for you, but you'll be able to think."

I do as he orders. It eases a bit, but my heart aches, and every breath is still hard. "Why? Why do you do that?"

"You might have hated my father, and he might have been a monster, but he was still my father, and when he died, it broke me," he admits softly. "It's how I survived it. We cannot afford for you to break now. We need to get out of here."

"Why? What's the point?" I slump into the bars as if my strings were cut.

All my energy and fight are gone.

"I fought so hard, I tried so fucking hard, and for what? Everyone is dead." I meet Lucien's glassy eyes next to Vale. "Everyone is gone, and I'm all alone."

"You're not alone," he vows, searching my gaze. "We are right here. We are with you."

I snort, holding myself tighter as if that will prevent me from breaking.

Jang is gone.

Nothing else matters.

For the second time in my life, I have lost my family, my reason for living. When there is so much death and pain, then what is the point of going on?

I don't know how long I stare into space, replaying the last minutes before I was knocked out over and over again. I try to figure out a way I could have stopped it, could have saved him.

All it does it make me angry and so fucking sad, I want to drown in a river of my tears and never come up. I debate turning my nails into claws and ripping out my heart so I can be with them.

I'm so tired of fighting when it gets me nowhere.

Three sets of eyes won't let me though. They hold me prisoner more than any cage, keeping me alive and forcing my next breath, even when I don't want it.

"Quinn." Jai has tried to talk to me a few times, but I can't seem to care. I don't have the energy to respond. He sighs. "It's going to be okay. We'll get out of here and—"

There's a groan, the sound of a huge door opening. They all snap to attention, while I lazily lift my head, and then there are loud footsteps.

"Hunters," Jai hisses, sniffing the air.

"Pretend to sleep," Vale commands, hissing at me. "They want you to be awake, so sleep for now, please, Quinn."

I roll my eyes to his, my expression feeling heavy and wrong. "Quinn, please," Lucien begs. "They'll kill you if you aren't. Just close your eyes, beautiful. Just close your eyes and imagine you are somewhere good, where nothing hurts."

His words pierce the haze around me, making me whimper before I squeeze my eyes shut, turning my head away to hide my horrible acting skills. I tricked them when I was in their cage, so I was good at it then, but I don't feel so good anymore.

I feel like my every movement is wrong, and I can't seem to control it.

"Good girl," Vale praises. "No matter what, keep your eyes closed."

There are more footsteps then some strange dragging noises, but I keep my eyes locked shut, trying to calm my breathing to fool the hunters.

"Vale," a male voice calls.

"Commander," he retorts. "What's with the cages?"

"We keep them for feral animals like you," the commander replies. "Or traitors. So you are with the wolves now? I've got to say, your daddy would be disappointed. I knew something was wrong, but I had no idea it was this."

"What you are doing is wrong. Not every monster is evil. These were innocent people," Vale argues, which shocks me to my core.

"They are all beasts!" the commander roars, panting heavily. "Just monsters, and we hunt monsters. You took an oath, and you broke that. You warned them and because of you, we lost many of our ranks—friends of yours, people who fought at your side."

Vale is quiet for a moment. "I regret that." There is pain in his tone. "But I couldn't stand by and let you hurt innocent people."

"You never cared if they were innocent or not before," the commander snaps. "I suppose a little beast pussy got you all twisted up." I feel his eyes on me and want to snarl, but I bite it back. "I can see the appeal, but you're weak, Vale. You always were. Your daddy knew it, and so do I. Now, all of our kind does. Don't worry, though, you won't be leaving here alive. Any of you."

"Then why wait? Why not kill us now?" Lucien growls.

"Where would be the fun in that?" the commander replies. "Because of you, many are dead, and people are out for blood. They want their pound of flesh and they will get it, and the she-wolf? Well, she was just in the wrong place at the right time. We managed to snag her, and it will tide us over for now."

"What do you mean?" Vale asks.

I hear footsteps coming my way. "I wonder, did you fuck her as a wolf or a woman? Maybe I'll give her a try before we end her. It's probably all she's good for, breeding like the animal she is."

I bite back my growl, relaxing farther into the bars.

"Don't fucking touch her," Jai growls.

"So the rumours are true. Look at your fucking eyes." The commander laughs. "You always walked that line, and that's why I kept you so close. I knew you would fall one day. I'm going to take great pleasure in gutting you and putting your head on a mantle."

"Try it," Jai snarls. "Step into the cage."

"No, I don't think I will," the commander replies casually—too casually. Even in my pain, I can hear the trap in his words.

"But I do have a little present for your wolf. It's a shame she's asleep. I guess I'll just leave it here for when she wakes up." There's a snap and then a grunt. I hear someone's gasp of horror, and my eyes flutter open before I slam them shut.

It's a trap.

I ignore it, but a familiar scent hits me.

Jang.

I'm up before they can say anything, pressed to the bars, and for a moment, I feel hopeful that he's alive.

"Quinn, no!" Jai roars, but it's too late.

My eyes land on the thing before me, and my head screams for me to turn away.

There's banging and more shouts, but it all fades as it finally clicks in my brain.

"Don't look," Lucien barks, trying to reach through the bars to cover my eyes, but I can't do anything but stare.

It's Jang. It's my father.

His eyes are open, locked in cold horror, his skin is a strange colour, and his hair is covered in blood.

His head . . .

It's piked on a cross.

His body is underneath it, his hands and feet pierced through like some macabre religious iconography.

I throw up everywhere, tears streaming down my face as I sob.

"I'll just leave that here for now. See you later, wolf," the man calls, but I just keep screaming.

My hands claw at my eyes as if I can get rid of the image.

"Quinn, Quinn." They are all shouting my name, but I can't hear it over my own screams.

I try to pluck my eyes free. His scent, the smell of his blood, still surrounds me.

I hear cages rattling, their shouts getting louder, but I don't care.

I need it to stop.

My head lifts, a dark idea coming to mind, and before they can react, I slam my head into the bars of the cage. It dazes me, my wolf whining at the pain, but I push through it and do it again and again. I feel my skin split, my eyes going spotty, and still I slam my head into it.

Finally, the darkness claims me, leaving me unable to see it again.

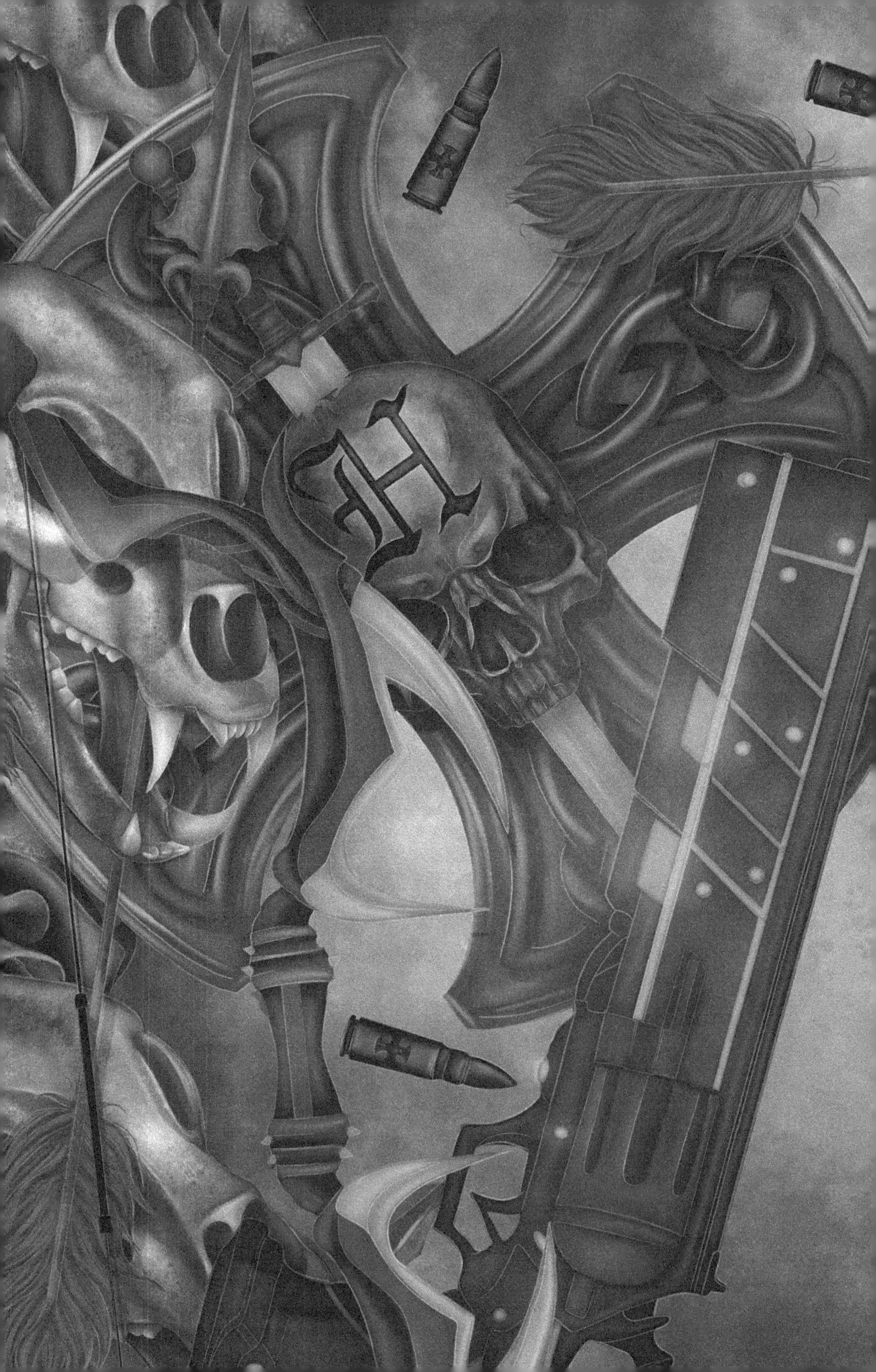

CHAPTER FORTY-FIVE

I can't pull my eyes from Quinn.

She woke up a few hours ago. The wound on her head was already healing, but her powers cannot heal the open wound in her soul and heart.

It doesn't help that they leave the body right in front of her cage.

It's torture, and she has no choice but to smell him. If she turns her head, he's there. She curls into a ball to try and ignore it. At least she isn't screaming anymore.

The scent of her vomit makes my nose twist. I can't imagine what it's doing for her senses, but I can't seem to care. I move closer, trying to reach for her, to comfort her, but she doesn't move or react. It's as if she's sunken in on herself.

It's like she's given up.

"You have to keep fighting," I snap.

"Why?" she replies so calmly that it chills me. Quinn is many things, but she is not a quitter. She doesn't even look at me.

All that time we held her captive and tortured her, she never gave up. She never stopped fighting, taunting the world to give her more.

I won't let this break her. I can't.

Not the woman who challenged me and made me more.

Not the woman who made me see who I am and trusted me when no one else did.

I'm beginning to realise I cannot exist in a world without Quinn, even if it means she hates me. We were destined to clash, my moon and me.

"Your pack could still be alive, and if they are, then they need you. If not, you need to honour everyone who was lost and keep going. You cannot just give up."

"Quinn," Vale warns, his voice hard as he tries to get through to her like he did before, but she ignores him too.

We watch as, second by second, we lose another piece of Quinn —the woman who has come to mean something to all of us. I spent all that time tracking and hating her, when I really just hated myself, but I couldn't stop myself from going back to her time and time again.

She gave me purpose, a family, and hope.

"Let it hurt." Lucien's voice comes steadily. "Let it thread through you and tear you apart until you can't breathe. Don't turn away from it. Feel it, feel every horrible moment of that pain, beautiful. Don't choke on it. Feel it. Cry. Scream. Throw up. Just don't numb yourself to it because it always comes back. You can't ignore this, but you also cannot give into it. Your father, the man who raised you, wouldn't want that. He fought until the very end, and your pack needs you. We need you. Grieve, Quinn, and fucking hurt until you feel like you cannot live through it, and then dust your ass off and do it all over again because life doesn't give a shit. I won't let you or my brothers die in this hellhole. You are being weak—"

"Fuck you," she hisses, jerking her head around. Her gaze goes to Jang for a moment, and she shudders before focusing fully on Lucien, and it's the most emotion and action we have seen out of her in hours.

"Good, anger is good." He stands, gripping the bars. "Hate me if you need to, Quinn. Swear to get revenge, but don't give up. It is not your style. You aren't weak. You are the strongest person I know. You live for your family and your pack, so keep doing that. This isn't the end, so don't you dare close the book. Turn the fucking page. We make our own destiny, Quinn. It isn't easy, but we walk that path, and we don't stop and sit down on it."

"It hurts," she sobs, her head pressed to a bar.

"I know, baby." Vale sighs. "I know it does. He's right. Even now, my grief is still there no matter how much I choke it down. It's always there, and it doesn't go away, no matter how much I wish it did, but don't dishonour your father."

"He thought you were an alpha," I add, standing. "All of the pack looked to you for guidance. I heard it while I was there. They need you, trust you. Be the woman your father knew you were, the woman we know you are."

"What if he was wrong? What if I'm not strong enough?" she asks, her voice so soft, I strain to hear it. "What if they were all wrong? What if they all died for nothing?"

"Don't be so selfish," Vale snaps. "They died for you, so fucking live for them."

She lifts her head and meets his eyes. "Why did you save me the night my family died?"

He swallows, searching her gaze. "Because when I looked into your eyes, I saw the evil reflected back at me and knew I didn't want to be that. Even facing death, you were so strong as a kid, and I knew this world needed you. You were just a child, and so was I. I was taught to hate; we aren't born with it. We learn it, and for one moment, I didn't want to hate. I wanted to do something good. You haunted my dreams every night for years. You still do. Every life I took, I thought of you, wondering if you would be angry at me. You kept me alive, either with hatred or hope, for so many years, so let's keep you alive. Let me save you one more time, like you saved me that night."

She's quiet for a moment. "I want them all dead."

"Then we will help you," I reply without hesitation.

"They aren't our people anymore," Lucien explains. "Anyone who could do what they did . . . No. We'll help you get revenge."

I watch her straighten, anger changing her expression. "Quinn is gone. She's dead. She died with him." She looks at Jang. "I'm going to rip them all to pieces and feast on their blood. I'll do whatever it takes, and if you can't handle that—"

"We can," I state strongly, meeting her eyes. "I'll be right there with you."

"Then we need to get out of these cages." She glances at her father once more, her lip trembling for a moment before I watch her swallow and lift her head.

That's my fucking girl.

"We will, and when we do, we'll make them all pay," Vale vows.

"Good, but don't say I didn't warn you." She turns away, and I wonder what she meant.

There was power in her words.

What does she know?

CHAPTER FORTY-SIX

I let rage fuel me. I let it blind me to anything else.

I let it numb the pain that will live inside me until the day I die.

I was a child when I lost my family, and I grieved as a child does, but now, as an adult, it is all too real. I have lost my family, but I still have one to fight for. Moreover, I have revenge to get. I don't care what Jang would think because he isn't here, and I'm going to kill all of them.

I tried to be nice.

I tried to change the world, but sometimes you can't.

Sometimes, you cannot stop evil without becoming evil yourself.

I feel them watching me, the men who pulled me from the darkness with their own anger and hatred.

Maybe I needed an enemy. Maybe I needed them to hate me to fill me with something other than grief.

Maybe I always needed them.

I pace my cage, warming up my muscles and coaxing my wolf to the forefront until my hands and eyes are changed. I know they are watching, Jai's eyes glowing with his wolf that will never be free, and it gives me an idea.

It's a horrible idea, one that could doom me, but it's all I have.

If I get the chance.

Hours pass, but I don't sit still, not for a moment. I hear them trying to plan how to break free. I ignore them and wait, knowing men like their commander will come back. They have no other joys in life, and they only want to cause pain, so he will want to witness ours.

Soon, I hear the boots again.

I'm at the bars when he stops before me. He looks exactly like I'd expect a hunter to look—scarred, old, and filled with hate. He peers at me with a smirk. "How was your talk with your dear old daddy?"

I just stare.

"What? Nothing to say? Have we broken you, wolf?"

A smile creeps up my lips, and his eyes narrow. He doesn't like that one bit.

His hand darts through the cage, gripping my hair. I let him. He slams my face into a bar, and I feel my cheek break then start to heal. I ignore Vale's shouts and focus on him. "Look at him. Look at your father," he sneers.

He made a mistake.

Turning my head, I sink my teeth into his wrist so deep, I feel his blood burst across my tongue. He screams and tries to pull back, but I grip the bars, using my superior strength to hold on, gnawing on it until a gun is pressed to my head.

Chuckling, I step back, releasing him while his blood drips down my chin.

He pulls his hand through the bar and cradles it, his blood hitting the floor as he stares at me in shock while the hunter with him holds the gun shakily. Licking my fangs, I wink at him. "You taste just like steak."

His nostrils flare, and his teeth grind. "Let's see if you're so cocky tomorrow." When I just stand there, he snorts and looks around. "All of you are to be our entertainment. We voted and figured it's the best way."

My eyes follow his to the giant penned ring at the bottom. It's raised so everyone can see inside, and a domed cage sits atop it so no wolf or human can escape.

As we watch, three feral wolves are thrown inside.

"All of you will face them, starting with our very own traitor hunters, only you won't have any weapons. You like the wolves so much, boys, then you can be ripped to shreds by them." He laughs.

I laugh with him, and he looks back at me. "After I kill them, I'm coming after you next," I promise, licking my teeth again. "And I'll eat you alive."

"If you're so hungry"—the hunters close in on Vale's and Lucien's cages—"then let's feed you. Just try to leave something for the ferals."

I watch as ten hunters drag Vale and Lucien out. They walk calmly, eyeing the hunters and looking for their chance, but they don't have one. My cell door swings open, but I don't move as they shove them inside and slam it shut once more.

The idiots just gave me what I wanted.

"Move the body," the commander grits out, looking at my father. "She can watch while the ferals eat him tomorrow." My eyes track my father's body until it's out of sight.

Turning away, the commander stomps off. "Until tomorrow. Get your rest!" he shouts.

His hunters follow him, not taking their eyes off me as I stand there, my mouth and chin coated in their leader's blood.

CHAPTER FORTY-SEVEN

Quinn is watching us in a way I don't like. Lucien and I are leaning into the bars that lead to Jai's cage, where he's pressed to the other side. She's on her knees, watching us. Her eyes are bright blue with her wolf, and blood still covers her lips and chin. As I watch, she drops to her hands and crawls towards us.

"Quinn," I warn, but it ends on a gasp as she crawls up my body and perches right on my lap, her heated core grinding down on my cock, and despite the circumstances, I start to get hard. I try really hard not to, focusing on the blood on her face, but that only makes me groan, my hands fisting at my sides. "Quinn," I admonish, but it's more of a pant.

She lost her father, so she's not thinking clearly. She's more animal right now—

Her hand grips my chin, jerking my head back until it hits the bars with a resounding crack, the slight pain fading as she lowers her head. I try to pull away, but the strength in her one hand puts me to shame, and I realise she can easily overpower me.

She's just been playing with us this entire time.

This is the true Quinn and the strength she kept hidden.

This is the beast.

When her lips crush against mine, I don't even protest. I lose myself in her like I did the other night because I'd be a liar if I said I don't want it. I crave her touch as much as I hate it. Even when we were enemies, I wanted her.

Her mouth is sweet, tangy with blood, and I groan as she grinds her hot little cunt against my hardening cock.

"Shit," I hear someone whisper, but I don't care.

I lose myself in her kiss, in the heat of her body against mine as she dominates me, nipping and eating my mouth until I almost spill in my jeans.

She pulls her head away, leaving me dazed as she turns her head, grabs Lucien, and drags him over. She kisses him hard, and I jerk in shock. I should be disgusted because that's my brother, but I can't be when she's grinding her hot little body against mine as she kisses him.

He's winding her up as he threads his hand in her hair, deepening the kiss, and she moans as I pant below her.

I need her attention. "Quinn."

We might die tomorrow, or even tonight, and I cannot seem to care about all the reasons I've told myself I can't have her. I want her, and she wants us.

This might be grief, anger, or even just animalistic need, but I do not fucking care.

I want Quinn.

It's almost freeing to acknowledge it, and my hands slide up her hips as she moans into Lucien's mouth before she lifts her head, her lips bruised and bloody. Lucien looks as dazed as I feel, and then she rises and kisses Jai through the bars, linking us together in need.

She reaches down as she slides her hips off me, her hand covering my length and sliding up to my buckle. She deftly undoes it while still kissing Jai, but my hand captures hers. Even in my desire for her, I have to be sure.

"Quinn, we don't have to do this. We know you're hurting—"

"Don't, don't think, don't ask. It's sweet that you want to protect me, but right now, I just want to feel, so shut the fuck up, Vale, and fuck me like you hate me. Fuck me like I'm still your enemy," she whispers, kissing across my face to my ear.

It's my turn to snarl like an animal. She tugs my trousers down until she can get her hand around my length. It jerks under her soft touch, and she hums. "So big, so thick, I've never had a human. Can you fuck me like I need you to?" She strokes me the entire time before bending down and sucking the head of my cock into her hot mouth.

Gripping her hair, I groan and lift my hips, unable to resist her.

With laughing eyes, she pops her mouth free of my cock and glances at Lucien. "It might take all of you. Wolves have a big appetite."

"What?" Lucien asks, blinking. "I—"

"Don't think." She grabs his hand and slides it down her body. "Just feel. Just for tonight."

I hear him swallow and know she's hard to resist. My cock jerks in her fist as if to agree. She taunts me, licking the rim of my cock before sucking and teasing until I can't take it. Gripping her hair, I yank her off me.

"On your knees," I order. "You want to be fucked, she-wolf? Then fine, we'll fuck you like the animal you are."

Her eyes dilate.

We don't have much time before they come back, not enough for me to taste that sweet pussy until she screams for me, but I can't resist leaning down and having a taste as she presents herself to me.

Her groan echoes around the room, her hands curling into the concrete as she pushes back for more, but she wants me to fuck her like I hate her.

She doesn't want tenderness. She wants pain.

She wants to lose herself in this never-ending agony we seem to be locked in together.

I can give her that. I can't change what happened, but I can make her forget, even for a moment.

My hands find her hips, yanking her higher onto her knees as my other hand slides down her spine and presses her face to the concrete. "You want to be fucked, she-wolf? Fine, then hold on and I'll show you just what humans are capable of."

Next time, I'll take my sweet time tasting those little cherry nipples until she's whining for me—wait, next time?

I shake that away, my own anger flaring over how much I've always wanted her.

I take it out on her just like she wants. My hand comes down on her pussy in a hit, catching her engorged clit. She cries out, pushing back for more.

I reach up, fisting her thick hair and using it as a handle as I lean over her and lick her ear. "Scream for me, she-wolf."

"Make me—" Her words end in a cry as I line my cock up with her tight, wet entrance and push inside, forcing her to take every inch of me despite the fact she's not wet enough. It has to hurt as I work my way in until I'm balls deep, but her body writhes on my cock and her cries get louder. Her channel grips me so tightly, I almost spill as I fight back the pleasure. All the while, I force myself deeper inside her, knowing it hurts.

Our she-wolf likes pain, and I have to remember she isn't human.

She can take whatever I throw at her.

It's like that thought removes the last thread of control I have.

Fuck what I should do. I'm going to take every inch of her until I taste her blood and cum.

Pulling out of her tight, wet cunt, I slam back inside, pushing into her as she groans, wiggling her ass to take me deeper. The sight nearly makes my eyes cross, and I can't stop watching my cock, covered in her cream, hammer into her stretched channel. The sight is so fucking hot, I'm lost, just pounding into her cunt as she cries for me. My hands are brutal and hard, denting and bruising her skin as I use her body like she wants me to.

I slide my fingers down her parted cheeks, circling the rim of her asshole. Her cunt clenches on me as I chuckle. "You like it dirty, she-wolf? You want us to claim every hole and pump them full of our cum? You want to be fucked like you are still our prisoner?"

She groans at my words, trying to get me to fuck her harder. Her nails lengthen into claws and scratch the concrete as she pants, her lithe body moving desperately for me.

"Vale," she begs, and hearing my name on her lips is my undoing.

I lick the sweat from her spine as I yank her back until she screams.

My hand slides from her hair to her throat, cutting off her air as I hammer into her, giving her everything I've got. I take her body so hard that it hurts when we slam together.

Her perky ass pushes back, taking me harder and faster as she laughs, fucking me like the animal she is as I groan. Yanking her up, I don't stop moving between her thighs as I turn us and push her down into the bars none too gently, the clank loud above our pants. Jai is there, watching us, his pants tented at the front.

"Take him out," I order.

She scrambles, reaching for him through the bars, and frees his length, making him groan.

"Suck him," I demand.

His eyes move to mine before she drops to all fours for us, and I know he can't resist, just like I can't. She hums happily, pressing against the bars.

Jai feeds her his cock before gripping the bars, then she sucks him as best as she can as I hammer between her silken thighs. I yank her back onto me, feeling every tight, wet inch of her cunt while she moans, sucking Jai's cock as his head hits the bars. His chest rises and falls rapidly as he watches her like she's his saviour and damnation, and he wouldn't be far off.

I feel the exact same way.

I watch her hips move, her pink cunt dripping. She shines brightly, even here. My nails cut into her skin until I feel her blood.

All the while, she swallows Jai until he's moaning loudly, his hips hitting the bars as he tries to get closer.

Something about it drives me even wilder. My hand slides from her hip to her clit, pinching and twisting it meanly until she clenches around me again.

"Fuck!" Jai roars. I don't know what she did, but his eyes roll back into his head. His hips move so fast, he's a blur, and then he roars, his hips snapping to the bars so hard, he would have snapped a bone if he were human. She groans, swallowing his release before turning her head and opening her mouth, showing me his cum on her tongue.

I yank her back to me and hammer into her, my heart thundering so loudly, I cannot hear anything else. All blood rushes to my jerking cock, and my balls draw up as pleasure arcs through me so hard, it feels like fire is burning through my veins.

"Vale," she growls.

I can't take it.

I come with a bellow, one she echoes, clenching around my cock so hard, I see stars. My release fills her as my hips snap, forcing it deeper into her until I pull out and fall back.

She looks over her shoulder, her eyes bright with her wolf and desire written across every inch of her face.

"Brother, help our she-wolf," I rasp.

She turns her head, seeking Lucien, her little pink tongue darting out to lap at her lips as he hesitates. Her head tilts, and she leaps at him, pinning him down as he gasps.

She claws at his clothes, yanking his trousers down as his hands fight to stop her. With one effortless flick of her wrists, she gathers both of his hands and presses them above his head as she frees his cock and sinks down onto his length. He tosses his head back, his eyes closing with a groan as veins bulge in his neck.

Good, if she didn't take control, he might have talked them both out of it, but we all know they want this—need this.

She doesn't let him think. She takes what she wants.

She pins my brother down and rides his cock, rocking her hips faster and faster. Her hard nipples beg for attention, and Lucien finally snaps.

He sits up, sliding his hands up her back and over her shoulders, using them to push and pull her down onto his length. His mouth closes around one of her breasts, his teeth digging in as she screams for him.

He bites down so hard that when he pulls away, there's a bloody imprint of his teeth around her nipple. He does the same to her other one as she cries out, her claws sliding across his body, nicking his skin as he gasps. The scent of his blood fills the air as she rides him shamelessly.

"Quinn," he growls, licking and biting her nipple while one of his big hands slides down and grips her ass, urging her on. "I can feel how close you are. You're gripping my cock like a vice. Fuck, baby, you feel so good. All that soft skin and muscle, so warm and wet for me." He groans, licking her chest as she leans back and closes her eyes, but they snap open when he bites down.

"Eyes on me," he tells her. "I want you to see me when you come on my cock."

My eyebrows rise at my brother's order, but she does as she's told, and their lips meet in a tangled kiss before he breaks away.

"Come for me," he demands.

She listens once again, her hips jerking as she finds her pleasure in his body.

She howls her release, and the ferals echo the howl.

He groans and hammers into her body. I watch her breasts bounce from the force, her lips tilted in a victorious smile, and my cock jerks at the sight.

When he roars his release, she sighs happily and then slips from his body and lies next to him, panting heavily.

I'm still sprawled on the floor like my brothers as she licks her lips, our cum dripping from her cunt.

I'm helpless when it comes to her, and my body reacts again despite the fact I'm exhausted.

Like she knows it, she lifts her head and looks at me like I'm her next victim. I would gladly accept. I have a feeling I will never get enough of Quinn.

Rolling to her hands and knees, she crawls towards me, her eyes bright and intent.

She slides up my body once more, and I see something different in her eyes. "I'm going to turn you," she tells me casually, and I startle, my eyes widening. "It's the only way," she explains. "If we stay like this, then we'll all die. If I turn you, then you might live and be strong enough to get out. It's your choice—turn into a monster or die as a pathetic human."

My heart stutters, the truth of her words sinking in, and pleasure turns to ashes in my mouth.

"If I say no?" I ask.

"Then I'll let you die as a human." Leaning down, she licks my lips. "Say yes. You promised you would be at my side for revenge, and the only way you'll survive the ferals is as a wolf."

"If I survive the change," I snap, annoyed now.

"True, but you're strong, Vale, so you'll survive. I know it, but it's your choice." She sits up.

"Vale," Lucien snaps.

I debate it, discarding all the ideas until I come to one conclusion —she's right.

We'll die in that cage tomorrow. We aren't getting free.

We need a way to win, and this is our chance—becoming a monster we hunt.

I nod my head. "Then turn me. I'd rather live as a beast than die as a human."

She pins me as I struggle, a knee-jerk reaction, and shows me her real strength. "This is going to hurt," she whispers. "Try not to scream too much, baby."

"Vale!" Lucien shouts, but then her teeth are in my chest, sinking into the muscle above my heart, and my own screams fill the air.

Red-hot agony pumps through me, along with her purrs vibrating in my chest.

What have I done?

CHAPTER FORTY-EIGHT

Lifting my head, I gulp down his blood as Vale jerks beneath me, bleeding from the deep wound. It's not a killing one, but it's pumped full of my venom. I feel his blood drip down my fangs as I turn my gaze to a horrified Lucien.

"What have you done?" he whispers.

"It's your turn," I purr, climbing from Vale, who groans. I injected more venom than I should have since I've never done this, but I also need them to change quickly. I need them to be in control and ready for tomorrow, and I'm trusting them to survive this.

If anyone can, it's them.

"Wait, Quinn," Jai begins, but I snarl, filled with alpha power, and he lowers his head, his wolf reacting.

I don't stop until I'm licking Lucien's lips, and he recoils at the taste of his brother's blood. "Choose."

His eyes dart to Vale, who starts to scream, the change coming on.

"Quickly," I purr. "Die like a human or live like your brothers and me as a wolf."

He swallows. "I don't have a choice. I never did. I follow where they go."

"I'm giving you a choice," I promise, kissing his lips again. "I will try to protect you as much as I can tomorrow, but I cannot guarantee your safety. None of us can. It is your choice, Lucien. It has to be."

I watch thoughts flicker through his eyes as Vale quiets down. "Turn me. If I'm going to die, I might as well do it by taking as many of them down with me as I can as the very thing they hate."

I don't waste time, knowing he could change his mind. It's cruel, but none of us will probably live through the next few days anyway.

"Fuck it," he mutters. "Turn me."

Despite my own thoughts, I hesitate. I wait for him to change his mind, but his eyes harden.

"Turn me, baby." He grabs me, kissing me hard. "Make me like you. Make me strong enough to keep you safe."

I swallow as I pull back, and he turns his head, offering me his neck.

Leaning over him, I hear Vale grunt behind me, and I know I need to be quick. Gripping his throat in one hand, I strike quickly, not giving Lucien the chance to back out.

He groans, the sound vibrating against my mouth as I sink my fangs in deeper.

His hand grips my hair even as he grunts and falls back. His body writhes beneath me as I pump my venom into him, forcing it into his blood like I did with Vale. He cries out but still holds me, stroking my hair as I turn him.

I pull back, his blood dripping from my mouth as I watch him. He's pale, his eyes are squeezed shut, and his mouth is open in agony as he writhes. I slide from him and kneel between them, looking between the brothers.

Vale is deathly still now but sweating, the bite on his chest bleeding. Lucien starts to scream, his back arching as he thrashes, and I can do nothing but stare. Jai grips the bars, his eyes haunted.

"Mine was never like this," he whispers.

"You weren't fully turned," I reply softly. "I forced the venom straight into their hearts to speed up the process. I've never turned anyone, but I've heard that alphas have the power to create more powerful wolves," I admit, and Jai nods.

"What if—"

"They will make it," I assure him as I look over them. "If anyone can survive this, it's them."

I settle in to wait.

The screams stopped a few hours ago, but it doesn't mean they won't start up again. They keep changing between screaming agony and sweating silence. I don't know which is worse. I dampen their skin with the rain hitting the cage and wipe them with my shirt. I stroke their hair and speak to them as Jai and I stand sentry.

They haven't uttered a word, nor have their eyes opened, and as the time passes, they seem to slip away, as if their bodies are giving up the fight, giving into the venom rather than mutating with it like I need them to.

I've never turned anyone, but I've heard enough about it as beta to know this is the most important time. Either they are strong enough to accept it, changing every inch of their DNA, or they die. More often than not, they die. Human bodies just aren't made to accept the wolf, but I know they are different.

I feel it in my bones. They are our only chance.

Gritting my teeth, I head to Vale. I feel him slipping away. Tightening my hold on his cheek, I turn my head and tear into my wrist with my fangs until it bleeds, and then I swallow a mouthful and lean down, pressing my lips to his parted ones and spitting my blood into his mouth.

I infuse my blood with my alpha command to heal, to adapt, to change and live.

I leave my lips there, closing my eyes as I summon my healing magic.

I push it into him, and his whole body lights up in agony. Bones crunch and snap, skin tears, and organs split. I push as much power as I dare before pulling away, and I'm relieved when I look down. He has more colour and seems more relaxed, so I move over to Lucien.

I do the same to him. He isn't as far along, but it's clear he's in agony. I wish there were something more I could do, but I sit back, resigning myself to watch. Every now and again, I smear my blood on their lips and push more healing magic into them, trying not to drain myself at the same time.

"Don't overdo it, you are going pale," Jai comments. "Don't kill yourself. You need to be able to fight."

"I'll heal quickly, don't worry. I'm more concerned about these two," I tell him, guilt and resolution warring inside me. They made their choice, and we had no other way out. I keep telling myself that.

"For all your bravado, you care if they live," he remarks, and I jerk my head up, meeting his eyes. "Just stating a fact." I growl, and he smirks. "Just saying, she-wolf, you might have changed them for your own reasons, but you still want them to be okay. Maybe you don't hate us as much as you used to."

"Shut up," I mutter, not examining the truth in his words. "I need to hold onto my hatred right now."

"And when you don't need to, when the hate is gone, then what will be left, she-wolf? Just your desire for them, for us, and you're not ready for that, but you will be one day, and we can speak then."

"I liked you better when you were an asshole."

"So you keep saying." He chuckles. "I think you just like me a little crazy."

"Maybe," I admit, and then there's a groan. Both of our eyes snap to Vale. He shudders, gripping the floor, and as we watch, claws burst from his nails, dragging along the concrete.

"It's happening," I murmur.

Their scents slowly change from hunter and human to something deeper, muskier . . .

Wolf.

CHAPTER FORTY-NINE

Jai

I watch as Vale's back bows, his mouth open on a silent howl. His teeth drop from his mouth, and in their places, huge fangs start to grow, making his mouth open almost impossibly wide. Deep black hair sprouts on his arms, continuing to grow, and his trousers start to burst at the seams. Even Quinn seems entranced by what's transpiring.

"Don't fight it," she calls. "Embrace it, Vale. Embrace the wolf. I know you crave control, but give it up. Let it fill you. Embrace the wildness and the power it holds," she commands, and she growls when he thrashes again. "He's fighting it."

Heading his way, she grips his thrashing arms and leans down, her eyes flashing so brightly, they almost blind me. "Accept it, stop fighting," she orders, her voice filled with so much power, I want to give into her command and it's not even aimed at me.

His mouth opens wider, and she slides backwards as he bursts out of his clothing with a bar-rattling roar.

A wolf now stands where Vale once was.

He's huge, bigger than any wolf I've seen, and when he lifts his head groggily, he opens his eyes, revealing bright blue orbs that match Quinn's.

She's grinning widely at him. "Good boy." Her hand drags along his back, and he purrs happily, leaning into her. "That's it, rest. When you wake, you will change back, and I'll teach you." She strokes him as the wolf slumbers, the change no doubt draining him.

For a moment, jealousy fills me before I tamp it down.

There's a groan, and we jerk our heads to Lucien.

He seems to be going through the same process, and Quinn moves to him. Unlike Vale, who fought it, Lucien seems to embrace it. His clothes tear as his teeth fall out, and his hands change to claws and then paws as hair sprouts across his body, covering him as I hear bones snap and his yell turns into a howl.

The big wolf shakes off the tatters of his clothes, trying to stand on shaky paws before collapsing.

I thought Vale was big, but I was wrong. Lucien is enormous, easily the size of a minivan. His eyes open. One is bright blue, and the other is almost black, as if Quinn's magic is infused in one and the other is his. He's a deep black, almost like a shadow, and the only colour on him is a blue circle on his forehead as if reflecting Quinn.

"Beautiful," she murmurs, stroking him. "You did so good, baby. Now rest, I have you."

His tail flickers and then he wraps himself around her protectively, growling at nothing, but the sound turns to a purr when she giggles and pets him. He partially covers her human body like a giant boa constrictor, but she doesn't seem to mind.

Finally able to relax now that they are both through the worst, I turn my back to their cage to hide the jealousy in my eyes. I have a wolf trapped inside me, and it's still there, baying and wanting out with his brothers.

I'm still an outsider, even now.

There's movement behind me, but I don't look, not until a gasp is dragged from my lips as a hand tightens on my hair and tugs. It's dragged back until I'm peering up at bright blue eyes. She smirks down at me, her fangs still hanging over her bloodred lips.

"Stop it," she orders, her voice infused with her power. I shudder at the feeling. "I can feel you spiralling. You are still one of us, still important, and we need you no matter what. You are my halfling, Jai, the best of both worlds. Don't ever think otherwise."

"Quinn, they are wolves now. They won't need me—"

She snarls, cutting off my words. "I need you. I saved you, Jai, and for good or bad, there is something between us. You were right about that. I need you, don't you see? You are—" She leans down, pressing her lips to mine upside down. "You're the only one who understands."

The words are whispered.

I swallow it, loving being needed by her. "Okay." I relax, turning so I can kiss her properly. She sighs and sinks into it, the bars keeping us apart. "So what now?"

"Now, we let the wolves sleep, and when they wake, we teach them how to change so they have the element of surprise in the fight tomorrow. We are going to rip every hunter here apart. I want to bathe in their blood. I want to eat their fucking hearts and drown in their screams."

I pant at her bloodthirsty words, even as her claws prick my head, drawing my blood.

"I want to show them just what a beast I can be."

I can't tear my eyes away from Vale and Lucien. They are sleeping peacefully as wolves, and the ferals in the ring at the bottom have quieted down now. It's almost too quiet here. I dare not speak. I just sit here with my eyes trained on them.

I've already lost them. They aren't hunters anymore. They are wolves. I am nothing, and despite what Quinn says, I will never fit in with my brothers again, even if we survive past this moment.

I know what the hunters have planned for us, but I also know the look in Quinn's eyes.

I wouldn't dare stand against her, even if I were still a hunter. In her blue depths, I see death. I see a stark hunger for revenge, as if she has let go of all the reins on her beast side. Sitting in that cage with an innocent smile on her face, she is not the Quinn I have come to know and care for.

She is a monster who will bathe in blood before this is through.

The sight shouldn't make me hard, but it does. What can I say? Crazy likes crazy, and my brain has never been right. I appreciate pain, I love death, and I thrive on bloodshed, so seeing her like that? Yeah, I'm as hard as a rock, and now is not the fucking time, but my cock doesn't seem to care.

Her eyes drift across me like she feels my need, and I practically shudder under that look. She isn't even touching me, but it doesn't matter when it comes to Quinn. I ache to feel her claws ripping at my skin, making me bleed. I ache to have her use me.

"Jai." The way she caresses my name has me pressing to the bars, begging wordlessly for what I know only she can give me.

She crawls across her cage, her hips swaying from side to side, a predator even in the state she's in. She doesn't stop until she presses against the bars, mirroring how I'm sitting, her head tilted as she watches me.

"I can smell your need," she murmurs, licking at the air as if tasting it. I grind my cock into the hard bars, the pain making me hiss. Her eyes dilate at the sound, looking down my body and back up as I gulp.

Her eyes land on my bobbing Adam's apple, and a gleam enters those shining depths.

Slipping her hand through the bars, she grips my shoulder and tugs me impossibly closer until I'm squeezed against the metal.

"I want to taste it," she whispers, forcing my head back, her lips trailing down my chin and stopping on my neck as I pant, swallowing hard at her proximity.

Her sharp teeth close around my Adam's apple, and slowly, so fucking slowly it drives me mad, she starts to bite down. I feel the moment her teeth break through my skin, the sharp pain followed by blinding pleasure as I groan. My cock jerks from my desire as I feel my blood slide down my neck.

Moaning, I thrust into the bars as she bites me, tasting the fire in my blood, her hands holding me prisoner.

"Baby," I plead.

"Hmm?"

When my voice comes, it's hoarse. "I've behaved. I've been a good boy. Please, please, Quinn." The words flow out of me, uncontrolled. I barely know what I'm saying, but I don't care, not if it gets me what I want.

It's a type of pain that only someone who understands agony can provide, and it sets me free.

Most would think it strange and morbid, but pain has been my constant companion since my parents died. It's what keeps me moving, keeps me feeling anything other than the rage inside me. Pain is what allows me to cope, to be free, and I know Quinn can give me that release.

Her teeth dig in harder, until it feels like she will rip my throat out. The agony is pure bliss, and my eyes slide shut with ecstasy. I slump against her, giving her control over my body and soul. I let someone else take away all that darkness inside me, and instead, I just feel.

I feel every sharp point of her teeth.

I feel the slow, seductive flow of my warm blood down my skin.

I feel the hard bars rubbing against my muscles and cock.

I feel the pounding of my heart, the warmth of her body, and the softness of her curves.

Quinn is a beast, she was born that way, but I was made into one.

My head falls back as pleasure explodes through my body, dragging me with it, and with a guttural moan, I come in my own trousers just from her teeth.

I mewl when she pulls her fangs free and licks the wounds, lapping away my blood before pressing her stained lips to mine and forcing me to taste my own blood and submission. I kiss her back, limp and satisfied, willing to do anything else, but it quickly turns hard.

Our teeth clash as desire storms through me, stoked back to life by her touch until we are both groping each other through the bars, needing more.

Breaking away, she drops her eyes to my rapidly hardening cock. "Quinn—"

We both still at the shuffle, a noise from one of my brothers. We wait and slowly relax when it doesn't come again.

"Later," she promises just as there is a very human groan behind her.

"What the fuck happened?"

Vale.

CHAPTER FIFTY

I release Jai and turn to Vale. His eyes are wide and panicked. He's swaying on his feet, looking paler than normal, and when he glances down to find himself naked, he balks and stumbles back so fast, he falls on his ass.

The commotion wakes Lucien, who stretches and smiles sleepily at me before blinking. He glances down at his hand as he makes a fist, his eyes widen, and then he looks back to me and then his brother, his own panic becoming evident.

Fucking hell.

"Calm down," I order them. I can see them bristling, their muscles rolling with the need to change, and if they don't get that under control soon, then we are all dead.

"Did we turn? Did we make it? Why do I feel so full?" Vale places his hand on his racing heart. It's thumping so fast, I can hear it. His legs shake, his claws lengthen, and hair sprouts on his arms. He yelps when he sees it.

Lucien climbs to his knees, eyeing his body warily, his panic silent but there.

The stench of their fear makes my nose twist as I hold out my hands like they are wounded animals. "Breathe, relax, you are okay."

"This is not fucking okay," Vale snaps, his panic talking despite the fact he made this choice. For a moment, I eye the mark on his chest, my bite mark, before pressing my hand to my chest.

"Watch my breathing, slow and steady, in and out," I murmur, my voice soft, but it doesn't seem to matter.

They are spiralling and turning along with it, ready to burst out of their human forms.

Nice Quinn isn't helping, so let's try mean Quinn.

"Stop it," I snap, and my venomous voice catches their attention, their gazes swinging to me. "You have to calm down," I tell Vale. "Your wolf reacts to heightened emotions, and any new wolf, even turned, is susceptible to that. You feel too deeply and your wolf senses it and rushes to the front to protect you. If you don't calm down, you are going to keep turning and eventually be stuck like that. To master your wolf, you must master your emotions. Feel them and let them wash through like a trickle, but don't feel that fire. Don't fan the flames, and don't be afraid of the wolf. The more you are, the more it will fight back. Accept it. It's part of you. Welcome it, let it fill your body. You are the same now." I show him my breathing. "That's it, slow breaths. Fighting yourself will not help, and we don't have time for me to teach you six to twelve months of puppy training, so listen up."

I look at them, meeting each of their gazes, and make sure they are listening. "The first few times you change, it will be slow and hard. It will hurt like a bitch. Don't fight that. Let it hurt because the less you fight, the quicker it is. We need you to practice your change as many times as you can before they throw you in with the ferals. The split second it takes for you to change is enough for them to gut you. You are weak and vulnerable when you shift, and if you're slow, you're dead."

As I've been speaking, Vale and Lucien have stopped hyperventilating. Their eyes are still wide, but they are breathing slower, and their change seems to have halted.

"Just breathe for a moment, and when you are ready, I will walk you through the change. We don't have time for me to hold your hand and play nice. They could be back any minute. This is going to hurt, and it's going to suck, but you wanted this, and this is how we survive."

Vale nods jerkily, closing his eyes for a moment. I swing my gaze to Lucien, who watches my chest rise and fall and seems to copy my breathing.

"It feels like I'm too full, like my skin is too tight," Vale whispers.

"That will go away in time. You have been forcefully changed so quickly, your body doesn't know how to feel. Everything will be enhanced, and it will take some getting used to. I'm sorry. I wish I could give you more time, but I know you can do this. You are so strong, both of you, so just breathe for me." I press my hand to Vale's chest and then Lucien's, keeping track of their heartbeats.

Vale lets out a low purr and then seems shocked as I chuckle.

"Don't worry, that's normal too."

Lucien's chest rumbles with a possessive growl, and I roll my eyes. "That too."

I just breathe with them until they are relaxed enough. "Okay, so we have no time. I need you to change. I'll start with Vale. I have a feeling you'll be the hardest since you have such a stick up your ass about emotions." I pull away from Lucien, who chuckles and leans back into the bars to watch the show.

"What do I do?" he mutters.

"Change, duh." I wink. "You need to feel to call your wolf. Feel anything and he will come. I'll teach you control if we survive this, but for now, it's enough to bring it forward fast and hard."

"He's too good at controlling what he feels," Jai remarks. "He removes himself from it. Look at him."

He's right. In the short time since he woke up, Vale has detached himself from his panic, anger, and confusion. He's cold and calm, which isn't the best for a change, but there is one thing that makes him angry—me.

"Okay, I need you to feel something, so get angry," I command Vale, my hands on my hips. He simply watches me, his eyes cold as always. "Jesus, I don't know, think about your dad." That has him growling, but he still doesn't change.

Rolling my eyes, I mutter as I move closer. "We don't have time for this." I swing, punching him right in the face with my full strength since I don't have to hold back anymore. His head snaps to the side before it slowly turns back towards me.

A growl fills the air, his eyes brighten, and his fangs lengthen. "Good." I punch him again, and his snarl gets louder. Gripping his chin, I pull him closer. "Every time you want to turn, think about me hitting you. The wolf you hate, the one who turned you."

"He doesn't hate you. It would be easier if he did, but he never did. He wanted you, and he hated that about himself. He saved you, and he hated that he did. He hates that you made him weak," Lucien scoffs behind me.

Vale's nostrils flare, his whole body vibrating. "Shut up." The words are growled, almost jumbled, but I understand them.

A sore point, I can use that.

"Did big bad Vale want to fuck the wolf who got him all twisted up?" I taunt, pouting my lips as he glares down at me. "When you threw me in that cage, were you keeping yourself safe from me? Did you want to come in there and fuck me, even though I fought you? Did you want to keep me for yourself even when you knew you should kill me?"

"Stop."

"No." I lick his lips, cutting my tongue on his fang. "Feel it. Stop holding back. Stop being in control. You wanted to fuck me so badly, even when you were a hunter, that you locked me in a cage to keep me safe from you, didn't you, Vale? When I screamed, when you tortured me, did it make you hard?"

The growl he lets out is pure wolf. I see it shifting in his eyes.

"There he is. Let him out to play, Vale. You know you want to."

Vale is pure control, but his wolf?

His wolf is feral and all emotion.

As it erupts from his skin, I step back. The change is slow and sluggish, but the wolf shakes it off and heads my way on unsteady paws. I smile, reach down, and stroke his head, letting him get used to it. "Now shift back," I command, infusing it with my alpha power.

His fur stands on end, and a growl erupts from his lips as he warns me not to control him, and that has me blinking with shock. He truly is an alpha, and a strong one at that.

Fuck.

That makes this so much harder, so I grab his fur in warning. "Now!" I roar.

With a slow growl, the wolf lies down, and with popping bones, Vale emerges. It's faster this time, but still too slow. I let him catch his breath before he lifts his head. "That sucked."

"I know." I reach down and kiss his lips gently. "Now do it again."

"Masochist," he sneers.

"Asshole," I respond with a tilt of my lips. "Do you need me to make you mad again, or can you handle it?"

He grumbles, climbing to his knees and closing his eyes. "I'll just picture you pissing me off . . . or maybe on your knees." He smirks at me.

"Focus," I mutter, but I can't keep the amusement out of my tone.

His eyes close, and I watch him struggle, his skin rippling before he finally sighs. Before he can ask, since I know that would wound his pride, I slap his face hard.

He snaps his eyes open, angry and annoyed, but it's not enough. He's still holding back, so I turn, grab Lucien, and yank him down for a kiss.

Lucien blinks before sinking into me, grabbing my waist, and dipping me as he nips my lip. I can taste Vale's jealousy. Wolves are not good at sharing what they claim as theirs, even temporarily.

A growl splits the air moments before we are ripped apart. I stumble back, watching as Vale stands before me in his wolf, shifting faster than I expected. A growl trickles out, as if he's threatening his brother.

"Easy," I murmur, stroking his back. I wouldn't dare to touch any other wolf this way, since they would take it as a sign of aggression and snap, but something tells me I can get away with just about anything with Vale, though I'm not sure why.

He turns back to me, nudging me, and I kiss his head. "You did good. Now change back, and I'll let you rest for a while."

This time, he changes back to his human form, and before I can react, he kisses me hard then steps back.

"You'll be fine as long as we piss you off before the fight," I mutter. "Now, it's your turn." I clap as I turn to Lucien.

Unsurprisingly, Lucien is easier to help. He's emotional, and he doesn't let it hold him back, nor does he fear it. He seems to take it in stride, accepting this is who he is now, and doesn't reject the wolf, making it easier for him to shift, much to Vale's chagrin.

"Good. Again," I command, leaning into the bars as Lucien hangs his head with a groan, his naked human body shuddering from exhaustion, but I need to keep pushing. It will be dawn soon, and they will come.

They need to be ready or they will die. A small part of me doesn't want them to, and I tell myself it's so we can all survive, but I know that's a lie.

"I'm tired," he mutters.

"Aww, poor baby." I whine. "Tough shit. Again."

"You're a mean alpha," he mumbles but does as he's told, shifting quicker and quicker each time.

"So I've been told." I wink at his massive wolf. He's the biggest I've ever seen, even bigger than Jang. Pain pierces my heart, and for a moment, I sway with it. When I come to, Lucien's wolf is wrapped around me protectively, whining with my pain as he holds me up.

"I'm fine," I whisper, sinking my hand into his fur to ground myself. The warmth and comfort settle my grieving wolf, just like any wolf's touch would.

Breathing through the pain, I smile down at him and bend over slightly to kiss his head. "Thank you, baby. Okay, change back. We'll go again."

Vale chuckles. "No rest for the wicked."

"Or the beasts," I tease.

CHAPTER FIFTY-ONE

Being a wolf is strange. I can see every little detail of this room, even in the shadows in the corner where a family of spiders seems to live. I can smell the wet, old fur of the ferals, the stench of the mould, and under it all, I smell her.

She's sweet, musky, and mine.

I feel stronger and faster, as if I could do anything, yet lingering under it all is something wild. It slides through my body every now and again, the feeling almost uncomfortable. It's like I'm walking on a wire and could fall into its waiting jaws at any time. I grit my teeth against it, forcing myself to walk straight and tall.

Quinn explained that shifting takes a lot of effort and energy, but when we are fresh, we take on a feral edge of adrenaline and power, and we can also shift whenever if we are not careful.

She pushed us all night, only giving us an hour to rest. I know why. Despite the fact that she's trying to hide it, she's worried we will lose the fight and they will turn their attention to her. It's not just her life she worries for, though, it's ours.

She doesn't want us to die.

It makes warmth bloom in my chest as I watch her stroke

Lucien's back where he lies with his head on her lap. My arm is wrapped around her, holding her to me, as a strange possessiveness rolls off me in waves. I feel the need to constantly touch her.

Under that, though, is a deeper need to mark her.

Her bite on my chest burns with the thought, and my wolf purrs, but it wants to return the favour. It wants to see her skin marked for everyone to see and know whom she belongs to.

Wait, *belongs* to? What the fuck?

I don't have much time to dwell on it, though, because I hear footsteps heading our way. They sound like they are next to me, but it takes a few minutes before I see the hunters.

We all stand, and they do a double take at us being naked. Honestly, it would have bothered me too before I changed, but it doesn't seem to disconcert me as much now. I'm warm, and there is something almost freeing about watching their shock and embarrassment for me. I might never get used to it, but I pretend I am as I stare at them.

"Is it time, boys?" I ask.

Quinn leans into the bars, half facing them, half facing me, and she winks at me and turns her head. "Isn't anyone going to play with me?" She wraps her hands around the bars, dragging her tongue up one before laughing. "I could take those ferals with my eyes shut."

"That's exactly why you're not going down there. You're going to watch your little hunters die," one of them hisses. I think his name is Mark, or maybe it's Matt? He was never very memorable, but as the five of them move to the cage door, I step back.

I need to at least pretend to fight or they will think it's suspicious.

They open the cage door, and I step back. They have to come all the way in to get us, which they hate. They keep their gun trained on Quinn the entire time, but when I swing, they swear and converge on me. She winks and moves to the gate, doing something before stepping back when one turns to check on her.

I hold my strength back as much as I can, trying to keep my

movements sluggishly slow, and I curse when they capture us and drag us out. The cell door slams shut, and as they haul my writhing body towards the ferals' cage, I turn and drag my feet.

Jai calls out to us, real worry in his voice because we know this is a gamble. We are new wolves, and they are ferals, but I've been killing monsters since I was a kid.

This won't be any different.

I have something to lose now though. My eyes go to her, and she nods at me. She believes in me. She thinks we'll be able to get their guard down enough so we can escape and kill them.

My wolf growls approvingly at that, baying for their blood.

Swearing, I fight harder the closer we get to the cage like they expect, not wanting them to question why I'm calm. I hear Lucien doing the same, and when we are tossed inside, I check on him. His lip is split, he has a cut across his cheek, and his knuckles are bloody, but he grins at me before glaring at the hunters as the gate closes.

We hear a clap, and we see the commander stepping closer, ready to watch.

Asshole.

"Here, one weapon." Matt smirks as he tosses a tiny blade through the cage, watching it land near my feet. I glance at the ferals to see them snarling and lunging at the bars, not realising we are here yet, but then one sniffs and turns to me.

The ferals begin circling us, and I grin. "I don't need one. I am a weapon."

I turn my back to the gate and share a look with Lucien. He can turn easily, but I'm the one who will need help. I loosen the reins on my anger, but it's like a squeezed fist that I can't unclench. I can feel my wolf snapping at my insides, trying to burst out and protect us, but something is always holding it back. Something I can't control.

"Vale, you asshole!" Quinn shouts. "God fucking damn you, you weak fucking hunter dick. Your brother was better anyway." She laughs as I snarl. "Stupid, pathetic—" I turn when there's a groan.

Her lip is bleeding, and my heart stills as I watch the hunter slam his baton into the bars again, hitting her side.

Fury like I have never felt before blasts from me, and one second, I'm a human, the next I'm a wolf lunging at the bars for him daring to hurt her.

She grins at me with burning bright eyes, licking the healing cut on her lip. "Kill them for me," she orders. "Kill them."

"What the fuck?"

"He's a wolf!"

I hear the hunters scrambling and yelling, but it's not like they can come in here with us. Glancing back, I see Lucien changed too, and I slink over to his side as we face off with the ferals. Their heads are lowered now, scared by what they see, but unlike most animals, there is no rational thought there.

They attack, confused and angry, but my hunger is bigger than theirs.

I want to taste their blood. I need to show my mate my strength.

Mine, mine, mine.

It's a feral chant that I give into as I leap at them.

My jaws close around a feral's shoulder, but he bucks me off. I roll over him, hitting my side, but I'm back up on my paws, and as he turns, I catch his tail and bite down. He yelps, but I'm barrelled into by another and knocked down. Claws rake down my side, making me howl, but I kick out, knowing better than to let them near my belly.

I give into my instincts and just move.

Lucien roars in victory, and I glance over to see him coated in blood with a wolf under his paw, its neck ripped open as his head tips back in a triumphant howl. Snarling, I leap at the feral and pin it. It tries to flip us, but I bite down on its neck.

I taste blood, and I yank my head away, feeling it rip out, and then I glance at the other feral who is backing away.

Spitting blood through the bars at the horrified hunters, I prowl left while Lucien stalks right. We work silently as a team, pursuing the feral. It's only a matter of time before I'll taste its blood. It hunkers down, ready to run.

Only, it flings itself at me in a last-ditch effort to survive.

We roll, and I nip at Lucien as he tries to help. My claws dig into the feral as it whimpers and cries out, and I tear through its skin, feeling blood hit my fur as we continue to roll until it's under me. Its back leg manages to get free, and it kicks me off.

Lucien bites its tail, dragging it, and then he throws it at the bars. I watch the hunters scatter away as I get to my feet.

I'm pissed now, and my wolf is furious it got away from me.

I want its blood.

I want its death.

Growling in warning, I stalk it around the cage. Blood trails behind it as it limps away from me. When it stumbles over the body of its friend, I pounce.

I use my weight to knock it against the bars and rip into its side with my teeth as it yelps. Claws rake against me, but I ignore the pain and keep ripping through his body.

I tear through its bone and muscle, gripping its heart in my teeth before biting down as its body jerks and then dies. Tugging my muzzle free of the gore, I lift my head and give the hunters a grin as I press my paw down, kicking the body as I watch them.

They are next.

My eyes lock on the wolf sneaking up behind them, and I laugh.

CHAPTER FIFTY-TWO

Vale and Lucien are destroying the ferals.

As I watch them, shock, awe, and desire curl through me. They move faster than I anticipated, like they have been wolves their entire lives. Their instincts are strong, and they are better fighters than most of my pack. The hunter at my cage is distracted, so I drag my gaze away as they tear through the ferals. No matter how much I want to watch them, I have a job to do. I wink at Jai as I wrap my arm around the man's throat from behind. He is unable to scream, but he struggles.

I drag him back and laugh in his ear. "They can't hear you. They are watching the fight. They don't care that you're going to die," I hiss, and then I snap his neck, dropping my other hand down his body to grab the keys. I slide them back through the bars and dance over to the gate.

Unlocking it and opening the cell, I step out and turn to Jai. I unlock his door and then crack my neck.

"Get them out when they are done. The hunters are mine," I snarl, and then I turn and run. I leap into the air and change, landing on all fours as I sprint at them.

Vale is giving me a wolfy grin from in the ring, and a hunter who is farther back turns—the one who tortured Vale. He yells, trying to bring his gun up, but it's too late. I land on him, taking us down to the floor as I tear out his throat with my teeth. I leave him there, choking on his own blood, as I race towards the others. They are screaming and scrambling, unsure where to go. A few guns go off, but I dart out of the way, avoiding their clumsy bullets since they weren't on guard.

I hit the two of them like a bowling pin, knocking them down before digging my claws into each, ripping into their stomachs as they scream. I glance over my shoulder to see Jai head-butt a hunter and grab his gun, blowing out his brains before blowing me a kiss.

"Stupid fucking mutt!" the commander calls, stomping my way with his gun raised.

I snarl and lean back, ready to attack, but there's a click, and then he grunts.

Eyes widening, he stumbles back and looks down at the bleeding hole in his shoulder. We both turn to look as Jai steps up next to me with a deadly expression. "That was a warning shot. Don't fuck with my girl." He lifts it and fires again, hitting his other shoulder as the man shouts. "That's for messing with my brothers."

He fires again, hitting his left leg, and the commander crumples to his knees. "That is for corrupting hunters' values." Another shot to his other leg. "That's for daring to hurt us."

He raises the gun and aims at his head. "And this is for her father." He looks at me. "He's all yours, beautiful."

Turning back with a wicked grin, I slink towards the bleeding hunter. He crawls backwards to escape me. I taunt him, pretending to lunge. His arm comes up, and I keep walking. He stops when he hits a post.

"You stupid fucking mutt—"

I lunge.

He never gets to finish his words because I clamp my muzzle around his jaw and bite down. He screams as I yank back, taking half his face with me, exposing muscle, tendon, teeth, and bone. His eyes roll around, and I let him suffer as I spit his skin onto his bleeding knees, and then I slice my claws down his chest, deep enough to hurt but not to kill.

I drag it out, making him suffer like my father suffered.

The last thing he sees will be me.

He will die of terror for harming my family.

He's still screaming and bleeding as I cut his entire body, tearing him up until I finally bite down on his neck and slowly shut my jaw, letting him feel every agonising inch as I decapitate him.

Ripping off his head, I drop it to the ground and turn back, changing and getting to my feet.

I see Lucien and Vale prowling towards me as wolves, Jai at their side with the stolen gun in tow. He whistles at the body as I drop the head. "That was a masterpiece." He nods.

"There are more. I can smell them over the blood," I begin, my voice hoarse, and then an alarm blares, alerting any hunters who are left in the building. With a grin at Vale and Lucien, I turn and shift, racing towards the incoming stampede of feet. I hear them growl and burst into a sprint behind me, heading towards them as well.

I glance up and see Jai climbing the cells before crouching, his gun up and aimed at the open steel doors we cannot see from our positions.

I charge as they march through the door, the alarm cutting out, but their screams now fill the air as three wolves hit them. I feel blades slicing at my side and bullets whizzing by, but I don't care.

I give into my bloodlust.

The echo of my father's screams and the sight of his dead, empty eyes spur me on.

I want more death and blood.

I drown in their screams and bathe in their agony. I wash away my pain with theirs.

One tries to crawl away, but I drag him back even as a net wraps around me. I don't stop, instead tearing through him and eating him alive while he screams. The net gives, and I glance back to see Jai with a machete, and with a wink at me, he spins.

I watch the artist work, and I'm glad we aren't enemies anymore. He's part animal, part human, and he uses that.

He slices throats and guts them, watching as their intestines fall to the floor, and he laughs the entire time.

Lucien throws a hunter into the air and catches him with a leap, ragging his body side to side. Vale is facing down four and holding his own, and I know this is where they are supposed to be—at my side.

Turning back to the hunters, I growl and leap once more, throwing myself into the fray. I use my grief and pain to fuel me until I cannot move without being weighed down by the bodies I have killed.

Spinning with a snarl, I eye the corpses, searching for any that might move, but every single hunter is dead. Jai walks through the bodies, shooting them in the heads just in case, and I head over, searching for a target.

I need more, but they are dead. We killed them all, and I have to bite back my disappointment and anger.

I finally turn around, elegantly stepping over missing limbs and blood until I stand at their sides, eyeing the massacre before us, and that's what this is—a massacre.

Even with their weapons, they didn't stand a chance against us.

Not after what they did.

"Now what?" Vale asks, all of us covered in blood and naked bar Jai.

"Now, we send a message." I turn back around and wade through the bodies and gore to pick up the head.

CHAPTER FIFTY-THREE

Usually, we would burn the building down to cover our tracks, but not today. We want it to be found so they know what we did and understand who they are fucking with. Quinn carries Jang's body, refusing to let any of us help. Vale carries the commander's head, and Jai collects weapons as we go until we step outside into bright sunlight.

I wince, my eyes watering, and I glance around, wondering where we are. Frowning, I turn back to the brick building and head to the side. My hands still drip with blood, so I drag them down the brick, ignoring the abrasion.

Hunters beware—kill an innocent and you are next.

"Subtle," Jai scoffs and quickly scribbles underneath.

Don't fuck with wolves.

Laughing, I turn back to see Quinn nod.

She glances down at her father and swallows. "We will need to run. I know how to get back to the pack, but there is somewhere we need to go first." It's clear she's worried about what's left of the pack, but we simply nod. We will stand at her side no matter what.

I know her people—if there are any left—might reject us, but they will have a fight on their hands. Unless Quinn tells me to leave, I'm not going anywhere.

She is my home now, my reason to fight and live.

She gave me life, and now I will use that life to protect her until the very end.

"I need . . ." She swallows.

"Anything," I vow, stepping closer.

She smiles sadly. "When I turn, can you lay his body over my back? I won't leave him here alone, not even for a moment. He goes home with me. My father never got a burial, but Jang will on pack land. He will be honoured."

"Quinn," I begin.

"No, it is my duty. Please," she begs.

I nod, and she gently places her father's body down, but his head rolls a little. She winces, closes her eyes, and breathes through it. I can almost taste her agony.

Sitting back, she changes and gets to her paws. We take our time placing his body on her back so he doesn't slip, and when she nods, we change too. Vale carries the head in his mouth, and with Jai on human feet, we set off into the forest.

We walk in a slow trot so Jai can keep up. Despite being human, he doesn't complain, and when we stop, she turns back into her human form, laying her father against a tree. "Where is your HQ from here? You mentioned there was one."

"It's north of town," Jai answers.

"So not far," Quinn mutters. "We are north, so we'll pass it. I want to leave them a present." She glances at the head. "Lead the way."

Jai nods, then she shifts back, and we set off once more.

We march towards HQ, and once we arrive, we shift. "There will be too many inside. All of the hunters will have been called in," I admit.

"They are not my target, not today. I need to take my father home, but I want them to be afraid. I want them to know I'm coming for them. I want them to understand they are nothing." Taking our commander's head, she walks into the carpark, naked and covered in blood.

She grabs an old, forgotten pipe and pierces one of the cars' bonnets, stabbing the engine and making it smoke. Next, she spikes the commander's head on top and turns back.

She doesn't run. She walks back towards us, her eyes hard.

Quinn carries her father's body the entire way back to the pack. Even as exhaustion wears on and day gives way to night, she doesn't stop or falter.

It's hours before we reach familiar trees and land, and once we break through the tree line, she walks straight across the grass.

The bodies are gone, as is the blood, as if the area were washed clean.

The moon shines brightly down on us, illuminating her like an angel.

Her pack house is gone, burnt to the ground, and for a moment, it's silent until I see wolves and humans step into the clearing, drawn by her scent. A howl goes up, a call, and my throat vibrates with the need to join, but I don't.

She doesn't stop as her pack filters in, joining her and crying out. I see her mother rush across the grass, her hands covering her mouth as we head her way, grim and determined. Quinn doesn't stop until she is before her mother, and then she gently lowers down, catching her father before she lays him at her mother's feet.

She shifts and kneels before her mother, her head bowed.

Her mother swallows, and tears flow down her face before she sinks to her knees, her hands hovering over her mate before she turns and embraces her daughter.

The pack mourns as howls echo around the burnt land, the remnants of the pack house standing behind the grieving woman.

Hands reach for them, showing their support, until the whole pack is crowded around them, touching each other.

We step back, lingering at the tree line, knowing we don't belong, but when she lifts her head, her gaze seeks us out, and she relaxes when she sees us.

It's in that moment that she steals whatever is left of my heart and soul.

CHAPTER FIFTY-FOUR

I can see them trying to blend in with the trees, but like it or not, they are part of us now. We usually have to vote new members in, especially if they were turned, which is very rare, but they saved my life and fought by our side. In my books, they're already pack.

When my mum pulls me to my feet, embracing me again, I find them once more, silently demanding they don't leave.

Pulling back, my mum cups my face, tears still streaming down her cheeks. "I thought I'd lost you too. I thought I'd lost my entire family."

"Never," I murmur, kissing her hand. "I'm sorry, Mum. I couldn't save him. I tried—"

She covers my mouth. "I know. We all do. We saw you. You tried to save him, but you couldn't. If anyone could have, it would have been you, but he died fighting for his pack, for his daughter, and we will honour that." There is so much pain in her voice, I'm surprised she's standing.

Losing a mate is usually a death sentence, but my mum stands tall, shouldering it. I know her soul is fractured because when we mate, we give pieces of ourselves to our mate. We hand over our heart and soul, so when one perishes, it usually takes the other.

You cannot live with half a soul, but here she stands.

"How is everyone?" I ask.

"Let's walk and talk." She peers down at Jang, and I see her composure crumble, so I wrap my arms around her, holding her up.

"I'll carry him," I promise, kissing her cheek. Leaning down, I hoist my father up and glance at Vale, Lucien, and Jai. "They are with me. Welcome them and show them to my cabin, then feed and clothe them." I meet their eyes. "You will be there when I return."

I turn away, carrying my father as my mother walks at my side.

He will need to be prepared for the ceremony. I head to a small cottage nestled between the trees. It is our holy ground, and the door is already open. A solemn-looking wolf stands there with his head bowed.

I walk past and carefully lay my father down on the wooden bench. I right his arms and legs, not looking too carefully at him, but my fingers linger on the holes in his palms—palms that held my hands so many times.

Swallowing, I lean down and kiss his forehead. "I love you, Daddy. Thank you for everything. I promise to keep this pack safe for you."

I turn away before I break down again, and Marie and I embrace each other and cry, sinking to the ground.

For a moment, nothing else exists but our shared pain.

Our loss.

We talk as we walk, moving down the path towards the lake and my house. I see the chimney pumping out smoke, and I can smell the guys inside which relaxes me. They are safe—for now.

"How is everyone?" I ask. My face is still puffy from crying, but I need to focus. I promised Jang I would look after this pack, and even if I will never be alpha, they have my loyalty. They are lost, and I need to make sure they are taken care of and led correctly.

A pack without an alpha is like a body without a heart.

It cannot function.

"Grieving, lost, and scared. We worried the hunters would come back," she admits, holding my hand, the moon lighting our way.

"Tell me what happened. I don't know anything after I fell, and I didn't exactly question them," I tell her, feeling shame.

"When you fell—" She licks her lips. "The pack rallied. The hunters were busy taking you and the others . . . the hunters with you. They started to fall back, realising they were outnumbered, and we drove them back as much as we could. We stayed vigilant all day and night. We put out the fires and collected our dead. It was then I realised Jang was gone. I was—am so numb. It was all moving so fast."

"I know," I murmur. "I couldn't even think, so I cannot imagine how you feel."

She nods, a tear rolling down her cheek, but she tilts her head back.

My warrior mother.

She swallows. "I've tried to lead as best as I can, but I was never meant to be alpha, not like you or Jang." She hesitates. "Filmea is dead. White was hurt, but he's recovering. We lost thirty wolves, and another thirty are injured. The pack house is gone, so I have spread everyone out. I have wolves on patrol. I wanted to send them after you, but I couldn't spare—"

"You don't owe me an explanation," I promise, squeezing her hand. "You did what's best for the pack, and that's all that matters. It was what I hoped. I thought . . . I thought I'd find nothing but cinders."

We are quiet for a moment, and we stop in front of the lake, looking out at the water. "So what happens now?" she asks. She's my mother, but right now, she is lost and looking to me for guidance.

After all, I was trained and prepared for this day, just not in these circumstances.

"Tomorrow, I will visit each injured wolf and heal as many as I can. I will put more betas on patrol and check in. The hunters are wounded, so they won't strike soon, which means we have time. We need to rebuild the pack house, but that can wait. Right now, we need to house everyone and give them stability so they don't flee. This is still our home. Tomorrow night . . . we will honour Jang and bury him and the dead. Then, we'll rebuild and prepare. I will select a willing alpha, someone we can trust—"

"Wait, why not you?" she asks. "Jang picked you."

"I betrayed the pack. I was on trial. I cannot be alpha. I will step up with the betas and help until we are settled, and then I will find someone suitable, someone who can earn their trust—"

"You can re-earn it," she snaps. "This is your land, your family, and your pack. For once in your life, Quinn, do not do the honourable thing. We need you. I need you. This pack needs you. Jang knew you were ready, knew you were the one, so don't dishonour that."

I stare out at the lake. "We will see. We have time before that."

I won't admit that I don't know if I can be alpha anymore. I made so many mistakes, ones that got people killed. Their blood is on my hands, and I don't know if I have the stomach or the strength to lead anyone through that, not when I blame myself.

She gazes out at the lake. "Do you want to know why I didn't simply follow him?" she murmurs.

My head jerks around, and I nod slowly. When I saw Marie alive and well, I thought she was a ghost.

"You." She looks at me. "I stayed for you. I will always stay for you, even if my heart is broken. I know he is waiting. He will wait for eternity if he has to, knowing I'm here looking after our daughter, so I tied myself to this world and to you, and when the time comes, I will rejoin my mate in the moon." She kisses my cheek. "I am here. I am at your side. Forgive yourself, Quinn. You did everything you could to save us. The world doesn't rest on your shoulders. Now, get some sleep because tomorrow is a new day, and we have a lot to discuss."

I follow her eyes to the cabin, seeing the three faces at the window before they drop out of sight. Rolling my eyes, I snort. "A lot. They saved my life."

"I know or they would be dead. They stood with us, fought with us." She squeezes my shoulder. "In old times, they would be bloodied in battle and celebrated as heroes of the pack. I won't ask why they are wolves—"

"I had no choice. We would all be dead if I didn't turn them, but I gave them a choice," I admit.

She sighs. "Then okay, we'll figure it out."

"They are hunters," I mumble.

"Were. Now, they are wolves, and they are here, Quinn, and that means something. They are here, and they fought for you and us because of you. Remember that." She leans in and kisses my cheek. "I'm tired all of a sudden. I'm going to rest."

"You can stay here," I start, but she chuckles humourlessly.

"I may have lost my home, but I have my memories, Quinn. It was just a building. My home is right here." She presses her hand to her heart. "He is with me wherever I go. I will sleep with the pack tonight and give you your space. Make sure to rest. We'll talk in the morning."

She starts to walk away, looking so lonely I call out, "Mum." She stills, and I take a deep breath. "Thank you for staying for me. I couldn't have dealt with losing both of you. I know it's hurting you to simply be alive without him, but thank you."

"I have fought for you every day since you were a child. I won't stop now, Quinn. Where you go, I go. I am your mother, your biggest supporter, and when the time comes, your father and I will be together again, and he will be so proud."

I watch her go and for a moment, I swear the moon's rays form the shape of my father walking at her side. She's right. He will wait for her. It's selfish, and I know she's hurting, but I'm glad she's still here with me. I don't think I could do this alone.

But I'm not alone, am I?

I glance back at my cabin and sigh, heading in.

The guys scramble, dropping into chairs. They avoid my father's chair as if they know, and I stare at it for a moment before sitting in it, breathing in his scent.

"They brought lots of food," Jai says, passing me a plate. "Eat, you need it."

I nod, staring down at the full plate. The fire crackles at my side, their scents invade my home, and I smirk. "I never let anyone stay here, not really. This is my sanctuary."

"We can leave," Lucien offers.

"No, no, I like having your scents here, and I don't want to be alone," I reply sadly.

"Then we will never leave you alone again," Vale vows. "Now eat, then we can sleep. I don't know about you, but I'm exhausted."

The shifts will do that to them. I eat quickly, not that I taste much, but I know I need to since I've missed meals and have been shifting and fighting, not to mention healing. Once the plate is cleaned, I head to the bathroom. I take a stinging hot shower, coming out in an oversized button-up shirt to find them waiting in my bed.

"Hope this is okay. There isn't much room down there." Lucien winces. "We can sleep on the floor—"

"No, it's fine," I mutter, climbing between them and lying down. "It will be your wolf instincts too. Wolves like to pile up and sleep close for warmth and comfort," I explain, since they don't know a lot.

"What's Jai's excuse then?" Vale chuckles.

"He's a perv." I smile softly as he grins at me.

"Too right."

I settle down then, forcing my eyes shut as they get comfy, and within moments, they are asleep, no doubt exhausted from the day. Their warmth invades the coldness that I haven't been able to shake ever since Jang died, but it's not enough to make me drift off. My eyes open, and my hand slides under my pillow.

I slide my picture out, peering at the familiar, torn image, but all it offers is pain, not comfort.

I listen to them snore. They move as they sleep, so I'm practically piled under them, but I'm still cold and my heart still hurts as if finally coming home has made it all that much more real.

He will never sit in that chair again.

He will never walk with me in the forest.

We will never run together.

We will never sit in that office again. Everything is gone, but Marie is right: his memories live on in me. I'm just worried what will happen when they start to fade. Will I forget the way he smiled? The way he laughed? His scent? The way his chair would creak as he turned to look at me?

I don't want to forget anything, and that makes it hurt all the more.

Clutching my picture, I slip out of their embrace and head to the lake, sitting on the shore. I let the water wash over my feet as I peer down.

I have lost so many. Only Marie is left now. I wonder how long it will be before this picture is just a memory and there will be none of us.

Moon, I feel so alone right now, so lost.

I'm home, but I've never felt more confused and unsure.

A noise has me jerking my head around, and I find Jai standing behind me.

"I felt you call for me," he murmurs softly.

I blink. Did I?

I guess, in my own way, I did. I hold out my hand, and he takes it, sitting next to me and looking down at the picture. "Are those your parents?" I nod, and he smiles. "You look like them. They seem happy."

"They were," I admit softly. "Now they are just memories."

"True, but they were here, Quinn. Nobody can take that away. Time is funny. They are gone now, but they were here. They influenced this earth with their time here, even if you don't see it. Your life is filled with moments of them, and they live on in those moments." He scoops water up and lets it trickle through his fingers. "Just like water, droplets are part of a whole. They will never leave you, Quinn." He tilts his hand, letting the water drip away, leaving a wet sheen behind.

Tears slide down my cheeks as I stare into his eyes. "What if I forget?"

"You won't. You love them, which means you'll keep them alive," he promises, getting another handful and then letting go so all the droplets splash back into the water. "Even when they are gone, you'll remember everything and love them for it. Nobody can take that away."

Nodding, I lay the picture down carefully on the shore far away from the water and lean into his side, allowing myself that weakness. "I don't know what tomorrow holds," I admit.

"Nobody does. We have tonight, and that's enough," he murmurs, kissing my head. "But if tonight is all I have left with you . . ." He tips my chin up with a finger. "I want to make it last forever."

My breath catches at the hunger I see in his gaze. "Jai—"

He leans down and kisses me, stealing his name.

He kisses me back to life and warms me to my soul.

In his kiss, I find redemption and hope.

CHAPTER FIFTY-FIVE

She tastes like heaven. She tastes like . . . mine.

She's hurting right now, and she's feeling alone and reaching for me. She can use me all she wants. I might only be a mutt, but I'm all hers. I lean back, pulling her down on top of me, knowing she needs to feel in control when everything else is a mess.

Her lips eat at mine until I'm tasting both of our blood from our fangs, her hands stroking my body hungrily. Gripping the back of her head, I pull her away and stare into her bright, narrowed eyes. Her lips are stained with my blood. Fuck, she's so beautiful.

"Use me, Quinn. Make yourself feel better. Use me in every way you want. You're not alone. I'm right here, baby, so use me."

She takes my offer, her lips sliding across my cheek to my neck where she bites, making me hiss, but I just grip her tighter as she slides her lips down my chest. I sit up as she pulls off my shirt.

My hands slide across the button-up she's in, and I rip it, feeling the buttons snap, and then I tear it from her body. My mouth dries at the sight of her golden skin, all bare and exposed to me.

I can't resist. I lean up, licking one cherry nipple as she groans, her hand sliding down my chest and pushing my trousers down so she can circle my hard cock and stroke it.

Desire storms through me, and I groan, barely able to breathe. I watch my hand span her chest, sliding across her toned stomach and down until I can grip her pussy. I feel her wetness for me as our lips meet again.

I swallow her moan as I slide two thick fingers into her channel and work them deep. Adding another, I smile as she shudders. I rub my thumb against her clit until she writhes and grinds, fucking my hand as I kiss her.

I kiss her like there's no tomorrow, the moon shining on us both. Water laps at our sides and overheated skin.

I swallow her moans of pleasure as I work her cunt, fucking her slowly with my fingers until she can't take it and cries into my mouth, her channel fluttering around my fingers as she comes for me.

Me. A mutt.

I am a nobody, and this moon goddess comes for me.

Her hand tightens around my cock, and I feel myself leaking, my own desire so strong I almost come, but she doesn't want that.

She lifts her head and pulls my fingers from her cunt, then she licks all three of them clean of her release. I watch her sweep her tongue across them until I remember the way her tongue felt around my cock, and I can't take it.

Grabbing her hips, I haul her higher until she's pressed to my cock, and with a wicked grin, she sinks down on me.

We both groan at the feeling, her wet cunt gripping me so tightly, it drives me wild. My wolf cries out for more, baying to mark her pretty golden skin as she starts to move. Her hands press against my chest as she rolls her hips, using her knees in the wet shore to lift and drop until she's riding me.

One of her hands lifts from my chest before tweaking her nipples.

"Fuck, Quinn." My head hits the shore as I groan, my cock jerking inside her.

She likes driving me wild. Her naughty grin tells me that as she speeds up. "You're so big, Jai. I feel so full. I'll even feel it tomorrow, and every time I move, I'll remember the way your big cock filled me while you looked up at me with those shining, desperate eyes."

"More," I beg. "Use all of me."

She growls at my words, her hands clenching my pecs.

Her claws pierce into my chest as she winds her hips. The sharp agony makes me cry out, even as my cock swells at the pain.

She's marking me, making me hers.

***

QUINN

His eyes narrow with agony and pleasure as he watches me ride him, my claws in his chest.

For a moment, all I want is for Jai to be whole, to be the wolf he so desires to be. I should have known better. The moon takes my intentions, my wants, and transforms them.

I fall off him as he screams, his back bowing. "Jai—" I reach for him, but his scream becomes deeper until it's a howl. He flips to his front, curling on his side, and a wolf suddenly bursts from his skin as if cutting its way out.

I lean back on my knees, my chest flushed and panting, as the wolf whines, shaking and climbing to its feet. There's still a scar down its eye, and its fur is a shaggy brown like his hair, but he has a crescent moon on his nose.

He's big, somewhere between Vale and Lucien, but lankier, and he quickly gets used to his body, his head swivelling to me. A hungry growl erupts from his throat as he watches me.

I fall back as he heads my way, a determined glint in his mismatched eyes.

I never quite know what to expect with Jai, but with a wolf, I definitely don't.

"Jai," I warn, scrambling backwards, but he keeps stalking towards me until I fall to my back under his wolf.

His mismatched eyes hold me prisoner as he leans down, sniffing my cunt. His paw presses to my stomach, pinning me, while his head nudges my legs open. My eyes widen in both worry and desire, but when his muzzle dips and his long tongue drags along my pussy, I cry out.

My wolf purrs in approval as he growls.

It's wrong, so wrong, but Jai's wolf doesn't care, and neither does mine as I widen my thighs, letting his head push closer. I feel his sharp fangs pressing against my intimate skin, the threat making me gasp even as my cunt clenches on his tongue as he forces it inside me, fucking me with it as I scream.

I cry out his name, and the pleasure that had been building comes back with a ferocious roar. His growl vibrates through me, and I know exactly what he's saying.

Mine.

His tongue pulls from me and lashes my clit, his wolf crouched before me. The sight is so fucking wrong, yet I can't help it.

I cry out to the moon, coming all over his muzzle. He growls in approval, dragging his fangs along my pussy as he tastes my pleasure.

"Please, Jai, I need you," I beg, and I do. Despite just coming, I'm still needy. My cunt hurts, and I need it to be filled.

His wolf snarls and sits back, and he seems to shrink, as if he can't quite change back just yet. I've heard of it before with turned wolves.

He's covered in hair and at least twice his normal size, his face is slightly elongated, and his eyes are purely his wolf. The stiff, throbbing pink cock jutting from his hips is huge, with a thick mushroom head and throbbing veins as his precum drips down it. He grips it as he crawls over me and pins me with little effort despite my strength. I'm weak as he lines up and slams into me.

My eyes cross in ecstasy and pain.

He's too big, so big I feel him buried through my stomach and so wide and thick it hurts, and then he starts to move. He growls the entire time, blocking out the moon until the half man, half beast is fucking me like the beasts we are, and I love it.

I drag my claws along his back as I wrap my legs around his waist, lifting my hips to meet his thrusts. His long tongue rolls out and laps over my face before forcing itself into my mouth. It's not quite a kiss, but it does things to me.

I clench on his insanely huge length, coming again, and he continues to fuck me, hammering into me like the beast he is.

Claws slide along my side until the scent of my blood fills the air, and then I'm flipped. He pushes my face into the shore roughly, and my hips are lifted, and then he impales me on his length again.

I scream, fighting against him as he holds me with a strength I didn't know he possessed as he ruts me. He pounds into me with quick, snapping thrusts that border on too much as my cunt flutters and my clit throbs so hard it hurts.

"Jai, Jai, Jai, Jai . . ." I chant his name, unsure if I'm asking for mercy or more.

I don't get a choice. His long tongue slides along my spine as he spears my cunt over and over. I feel my cream and his precum dripping from me, sliding down my skin as his claws slice me almost to the bone and hold me still for his attack.

The agony mixes with the insane pleasure until it's too much.

I scream again, clenching around his cock as I come, and he roars.

His massive length jerks and fills me, swelling impossibly big until it feels like he's blocked my channel off completely. He forces his cum so deep, I swear I can taste it.

The pleasure fades, leaving just pain, and it must pierce the haze. He starts to pull his huge length from me gently, but the thick head stretches me as he pulls out, and I cry out.

Human arms catch me, and I'm flipped to my back to see a worried human Jai.

"Are you okay?" he asks, looking concerned.

"Fine," I reply, and he sighs, relaxing back so we both sprawl on the shore.

I turn my head to meet Jai's grinning eyes. "Well, shit," I mutter.

"You freed me." He rolls over, kissing me deeply. "You made me whole. God, Quinn, I love you."

I swallow the happiness those words cause, knowing I don't deserve it, but I lap them up greedily anyway.

CHAPTER FIFTY-SIX

Quinn is still sleeping. I hold her tight, not wanting to move and wake her. I know she struggled to sleep last night, and when we woke up to find her gone, I had to fight to not go to her as well. Her call echoed in my heart, but seeing Jai so happy makes me glad I didn't.

We all know what happened last night—we saw and heard it— and I silently congratulate him as she sighs and buries her head into my chest.

My wolf purrs happily as I lie here as the sun rises—another change. I can actually feel when the moon disappears and the sun comes up. It's fucking weird, man. I don't know how long we lie here, but I never want to move. I want to be wrapped around her at all times.

She fits in my arms perfectly, and part of me thinks it's where she belongs.

A strange male scent hits me, and my wolf sits up inside me.

"Yo, beautiful," a male voice calls.

Three growls fill the space, all of us turning to the door and seeing a grinning man there who looks way too comfortable in her space.

Our space.

Instinct takes over as she sits up with a sleepy smile, and I climb the railing and throw myself over and down to the next level, landing on my feet before storming up to him. I wrap my hand around his throat and slam him into the wall while he just blinks at me.

"Shit, babe, call off your attack dog," he mutters.

"Lucien," Quinn snaps as she comes to my side, naked and unbothered. I move to block her body. Luckily for him, he doesn't look, or I would pluck his eyes out. "This is Dom, my friend and beta. Hell, you worked with him. Let him go."

"Mine," I snarl, more wolf than man as I get in his face.

Dom sobers. "Quinn, I would put some clothes on if I were you. He's serious. He's not thinking clearly right now. It's okay," he says, dropping his eyes to my chin. "I'll wait outside."

I let him go at Quinn's urgings, snarling as he slowly backs away and steps outside, shutting the door. I look at Quinn. She has her hands on her hips, and she's glaring at me. "Cut that shit out now," she snaps before turning away. "And go apologise." She stomps off as I glance up at Vale and Jai to see them watching me, their eyebrows raised.

My wolf retreats, and I'm left scratching my head. I'm wearing the borrowed jeans I slept in, so I head out, slamming the door behind me as I face the man on the porch. He keeps his distance, his hands spread as if in peace, and keeps his eyes on me as if I'm going to attack him.

Great, all this wolf shit is so confusing, but it's clear my wolf thinks he's a threat, and I don't know how to change that.

"What the fuck was that?" I mutter more to myself than him, but surprisingly, he answers.

He chuckles as he watches me. "That was your wolf staking his claim on her, which is surprising as hell and even more so since she let it slide. You didn't like my scent or wolf in what you have claimed as your den. It's natural. I didn't know. I'm sorry. I'm surprised your wolf didn't fucking gut me. Anyone else would have."

The door bangs open then, and Quinn shoots me a glare and then smiles at Dom. She goes to hug him, but he steps back. "Hell no. Sorry, babe, but I am not looking to die."

A growl trickles from my throat at the word "babe," and he grins at me. "Dude has power," he tells her. "He even made my wolf submit."

That seems to shock her, and she glances at me for a moment, evaluating me.

"What does that mean? Claimed you? Den?" I ask, needing answers.

Quinn's jaw works as she stares at me. "Wolves . . . mate. We get to pick who, and we are claimed during a ceremony if the male can prove himself worthy—"

Dom snorts. "Which no one ever has to Quinn."

She glares at him then looks at me. "But some wolves are born with an instinct that, when they meet certain wolves, comes to light. They call this fated mating, and although they still go through the ceremony, they claim the other beforehand, or at least their wolf does."

"So my wolf has claimed you as his," I say slowly.

"So it would seem," she mutters, sounding unsure. "I need to visit White and see everyone. Dom, can you show them around and give them the rundown and layout? I'm hoping that showing people they are helping might go a long way in the pack accepting them."

"Are you sure? He still looks like he wants to rip me apart," he says.

"Please," Quinn begs.

"Sure thing, babe—Quinn." He coughs. "Go, I've got this."

She spares me another look and sighs. She put on some denim shorts and a crop top, and her hair is unbound. She heads my way, patting my chest. "Behave and don't kill Dom. He's a friend, a good friend." She waves at the others through the window and jogs off into the forest.

"Oh, this will be fun." Dom grins, rubbing his hands together.

Fun isn't the word I would use to describe this.

The wolf inside me hates even being near Dom. Something about him is rubbing the feral creature inside me the wrong way, and I have to swallow back my growls.

He was familiar with Quinn, very familiar, and it seems my wolf and I have claimed her as ours. It's giving me a headache, and so is his insistent, happy chatter as he leads us through the forest, pointing out the best areas to run, to rut—whatever that means—and swim. It's a lot to take in, especially when you've only been a wolf for a day and haven't even had time to fully understand what that means yet.

Everything has been happening so fast, but I can't deny there is beauty to this pack and its land—something that calls to a part of me, telling me I'm home.

When Dom lapses into silence as we walk, I find myself eyeing him. I suppose he's attractive enough, albeit too happy, like a puppy. I didn't know that was her type. After all, none of us are like that.

As if feeling my gaze, he shoots me a smile and carries on walking. I know he told me they hooked up before, but I need to know what that means. "Are you and Quinn . . . mated?" I test the word, not knowing if it's the correct one. Two growls sound behind me from Jai and Vale.

Dom chuckles before eyeing me. "Oh, you're serious?"

I nod, biting my tongue until I taste blood. Jealousy wars with possessiveness, and my wolf wants to rip this man apart while the human in me knows he's important to Quinn and that would hurt her.

Blowing out a breath, he turns to face us, his hands on his hips.

"Okay, so you are new to being wolves. I should have realised that." He rubs the back of his head. "Yes, I have been with Quinn." He doesn't step back when we all step towards him threateningly, which makes my estimation of him go up. "I won't apologise for that. We were both single, and wolves crave comfort from sex. However, we are not mates. There is a difference between mating and mated. Mating is fucking. It's what every wolf does. We are sexual creatures, and we love the high, especially after hunting or running. Mated is a lifelong bond between two, um, usually two wolves." He spares Vale and Jai a look. "Though Quinn never did like to do things normally," he mutters quietly.

"It is a choice," he continues. "You choose whom to mate, and it's consummated under the moon before the pack, but under all that is a feeling, a pull, like being born to your destiny. Sometimes, mated pairs are just from love that is grown, and sometimes they are moon bound, as we call them. The goddess herself blesses it. Once mated, you are committed, like a human marriage, only much more binding. Your wolf would never accept another, even if your mate dies, which is another thing—if your mate dies, then usually, you would as well."

"Quinn's mother didn't perish," Vale muses softly.

"She's a strong motherfucker. She's alive for Quinn, but make no mistake, that woman has lost her soul and her wolf is grieving and broken. It's a miracle she is still alive," Dom replies seriously, then he seems to perk up. "So no, I'm not Quinn's mate." He gives me a grin. "I have a feeling that title has been taken. Besides, Quinn was always hard to get close to. She is so determined to be the best alpha she can be, she kept everyone at a distance, as if feeling too much made her weak. Or maybe she just worried about getting hurt again and losing them when she had already lost so much. I'm not sure, but don't let her push you away. Keep pushing, she's worth it."

"I know," I admit, begrudgingly liking him. "So the tour?"

He nods. "Ah, yes, come with me. Ignore the stares you'll get. We don't often have new wolves, especially turned ones. They'll get used to you eventually."

"They've probably never had hunters turned into wolves though," Vale points out.

"True, but Quinn has a lot of loyalty here. She has risked her life over and over for the people of this pack, not to mention she would take care of us every day. She genuinely wanted the best for us. She would help build houses or cook for the pups when the mums were pregnant. She would run with the changelings to help them get used to it. She's an incredible wolf and an even better alpha," he explains as we reach the grassy verge. The black remains of the pack house are to the right, and there are many wolves dotted around, starting to clean it up.

Even in the colder weather, they are wearing shorts and not much else, but then again, I've been hot since I woke up, so I guess that explains it.

Dom follows our eyes, and his expression turns pinched and sad. "We will rebuild. It was just a house." He sounds forlorn. "For Quinn, though, it was so much more. It was her home, her safety net after she lost everything. All her memories of her father were tied with that wood and brick, and now it's gone."

My heart skips a beat. I didn't think of that, and as I scan the burnt remains of the house, I see more than one upset wolf as they clean it up. It meant a lot to all of them, and we brought that destruction here. What if they never accept us?

What if we were made into wolves but we will forever be stuck as ferals, without a pack or a home, and hunted like we once hunted them?

"Come on." Dom waves us along and leads us into the tree line and onto a path. "Most of the pack lives here on pack land. They have their own space and houses. We have lawyers, doctors, midwives, you name it. Some work in town, and some even work in the big city and come back. Jang was good like that, but everyone has a place, and there is plenty of room here to be free. The cliffs behind us protect us from the back, as you know, and we have forests on either side for running and hunting with patrols on the outskirts of our land. What we take, however, we give back. If we fell a tree, we plant two more. We only hunt when needed, and we house and feed a lot of wild animals. Quinn even started an animal hospital for wild animals that were sick or injured." He points at a hut with a cross on the front and then to one next to it with a cross and a snake over it. "Wolf and animal." He chuckles.

"We all used to eat in the pack house, but for the moment, we have turned the gym into a makeshift canteen." We move through some wooden houses on a path. Some are one story, with cute little chimneys, and some are two or three stories, but each is built to give maximum privacy. We finally break into another clearing to see a large, two-story building. "So yeah, that was the gym and pool, and now it's being used for housing for anyone who lost their houses and food. Are you hungry?"

We all hesitate, looking at one another. I don't like being away from Quinn for this long, nor do I have any desire to mingle with wolves who will want us dead, and I can't blame them.

We need to make an effort though, if not for us then for Quinn, so I nod, and Dom leads us over. The double gym doors are open, and even from out here, I can hear the hustle and bustle inside. We follow him in to see mismatched tables and chairs placed everywhere. Even so, people are standing and sitting on the floor, eating as if there aren't enough places. The room is long and huge, with a basketball court—where the food is being served—and gym equipment. Skylights let the sunlight in, so it feels open and bright. It's beautiful.

There's a food line to the left with more wolves behind it, serving everyone, and Dom leads us over. I know when they first spot us. Whispers go up, and then everyone falls silent. Forks drop to plates, but I keep my head high, unwilling to make Quinn look bad.

The line moves quickly, but as I grab a plate and hold it out, the wolf glares at me before slapping down what looks like a casserole then turning away. I add veg and grab some bread and a water before turning to follow Dom to an open table. The three members sitting there get up and leave, but Dom ignores them, smiling happily and waving as he sits and starts to dig into his food.

My back is tense. Even as a wolf, I still feel like I'm surrounded by enemies, and it's hard to not reach for a blade as I sit here stiff as a board. Vale is no better, his eyes darting everywhere as his hand grips his plate so hard, it cracks. Only Jai is eating, completely oblivious.

The chatter slowly starts back up again, but it's tense, and my back burns from their gazes.

I force the food down, even though it's like swallowing cement, knowing I need to eat to stay strong. It's one of the tensest meals I've ever been at, and that includes meals with my father, which weren't exactly relaxed.

I can feel Vale getting stiffer and stiffer by the minute, so I nudge him. "Quinn needs us," I remind him, and he nods, blowing out a breath. We are here for her. Not only that, we are also wolves now. If we don't belong here, then we don't belong anywhere.

"How dare you." We all turn to see a lanky man glaring at us. "How dare you sit there and eat our food."

The woman at his side tugs at him. "Peter," she hisses, sparing us a look before dropping her eyes.

"How dare you sit there brazenly while we grieve for what we have lost because of you." The room goes silent. All eyes are on us, and the truth is, we don't have an answer.

It is our fault.

They have every right to hate us.

"I said they are to be made welcome. Are you going to make me a liar, Peter Jones?"

The familiar voice rings out like a threat, and my wolf purrs in approval as she steps into the gym.

Quinn.

CHAPTER FIFTY-SEVEN

Quinn

I ignore the bowed heads and glares as I make my way through the crowd and stand before Peter and his table. He works his jaw, trying to stare me down, but he finally drops his eyes. He's not strong enough to challenge me.

"Well?" I demand, my arms crossed. "Are you making me a liar?"

I heard the commotion outside while I was doing my rounds, and I'm glad I came. My wolf had been pulling me here to the gym, and I didn't even realise it.

"They are the reason Jang is gone," Peter hisses. "How can you trust them, never mind like them?"

My heart hurts at his words, and I look around to see the same expressions on many people's faces. They hate them. They will never accept them. I leap onto the table and prop my hands on my hips. "He's right. Jang is gone. He's never coming back, and I know you are all grieving his loss as well as the loss of every single wolf who was taken that night. Our land was scarred, our families stolen. It hurts, and you're angry. I am too." I see people nodding. "But you cannot fight hate with hate," I snap. "They are my guests. Moreover, they are part of us now."

"They will never be one of us!" someone yells.

I let out a growl that has them all whining and ducking. "They are, and they will be. They changed their minds, and they changed their allegiance. Have you ever considered the fact that they stood with us, fighting their own people for us? They had to kill friends and family just to do the right thing. They were raised and pumped full of hatred, yet here they stand, changed into wolves to keep us alive. We cannot blame them for their upbringing, not when we were all raised with love and acceptance, so let's show hunters who the real monsters are here. We will welcome these men—men who saved my life, who saved every single one of you here—with open arms."

There's silence as some relax and sigh. It will be a long road, but I've made myself clear.

"Does that mean they cannot be challenged?" someone shouts. I seek him out, finding a middle pack member named Harvey. He might be a problem, so I mark him.

"As with any new wolf, challenges are not to be accepted for one year." That causes an uproar. "Silence!" I shout. "These are our laws, and we will follow them. We are not animals. Jang would not want this for us. He accepted them, he fought at their sides, so do not dishonour your alpha."

"But he is gone," Peter protests, and I shoot him a withering glare.

"He might be, but his teachings and desires live on in every single one of us," I retort.

"They saved us," Sonia, a very pregnant wolf, calls. "I saw it. Without them, the kids would be dead. I say we give them a chance. We have to start somewhere."

I silently give her my gratitude as others nod. "I'm not saying you have to be best friends with them, but get to know them like I have," I plead. I need this to work. I cannot deal with any more heartbreak, and for some fucking reason, my wolf wants them. My eyes go to them, where they sit pale-faced and dejected. "Take Lucien, for example. He became a hunter to protect his brother after his father filled his head with hate. He didn't do it for fun. He did it for family. Jai's entire family was murdered by ferals, yet here he stands amongst wolves. Vale . . ." I meet his bright eyes. "Vale saved my life as a pup," I admit as shock rings through the room. "When my family was killed, I nearly didn't make it. I was in the tree line, running. I was young and surrounded by hunters, and then there he was, just a kid, yet he stood against his own family and let me go. He saved my life that night and did so again yesterday. Despite what he has done, he is a good person. They all are." I let that sink in. "I will not dishonour the men who saved me by turning them away when they need us most, nor will I reject our teachings for kindness and acceptance just because it's hard."

I look around.

"If anyone has a problem with my ruling, then you may challenge me now."

White moves to my side, even injured, as do the other betas. They stand with me, and for that, I'm eternally thankful, so much so I want to cry. "No?" When no one stands, I nod. "Good, then go back to eating. We have a lot of work ahead of us, so you'll need your strength." Hopping down, I thank White and the others and then walk over to the table where Vale, Lucien, Jai, and Dom sit. Grabbing a tray, I sit with them, even when it is common law that the alpha, even a temporary one, sits with the betas.

"Thank you," Vale murmurs.

"I only spoke the truth." I snag his bread. "But I'll take this as thanks."

Lucien smiles so brightly, I can't help but melt a little. I just stood up for them in front of my whole pack. I could have been challenged, yet I can't seem to care. "So, having a good tour?" I nudge Dom, who grins.

"They are a bunch of fun, so easy to wind up," he mutters, making me laugh.

I wink at Vale as he growls and turn as Jai thrusts his bread at me too. My eyebrows rise, but I accept it and eat it, knowing his wolf will be offended if I don't. He hums happily and goes back to eating, his eyes bright. He wears his wolf much closer to the surface than most, that is for sure.

"Quinn."

I turn my head and swallow, getting to my feet. "Sonia." I smile as she tugs me into a hug, and I melt despite the awkwardness of her belly.

Kneeling, I lean in and whisper, "Hey, little fellas, are you looking after your mum for me?" I feel a kick, and she laughs.

"They only do that for you," she says as she glances at the table. "Hi, I'm Sonia. I'm a lawyer in the human world but right now, I'm a breeding machine." She chuckles as I stand.

"And so beautiful." I kiss her cheek. "Sonia is one of our most accomplished wolves. Her mate, Patrick, is running the perimeter right now or I'm sure he'd be here growling at everyone."

The guys look confused, so she takes pity on them as I guide her into a seat. "Mates get very protective during pregnancy, especially in the last few months. I can barely leave our home without him growling at everyone. It's a wolf thing," she explains. "So, what are your names?"

I mouth, "Thank you," to her, knowing she is doing this on purpose. The pack trusts her, and she's showing them kindness. It makes even more wolves move closer, growing bolder, and I smile widely.

"Vale, Jai, and Lucien," I introduce, "this is Amanda." I point to a tall lady who works as a blacksmith on pack land. "She makes all our weapons, but also all our metal for houses and interior. She's very talented. This is her mate, Lily." I nod at the smaller curvy lady with a bright smile and vivid pink hair. "She's a vet." I chuckle.

The guys laugh at that. "I suppose that's a good job to have here," Vale remarks, making an effort.

"You could say that." Lily giggles, leaning into Amanda, who wraps her arm around her and kisses her head. "So if you ever need any help, I'm over in the clinic."

Amanda seems more reserved but nods in welcome, being kind in her own way. For the next half hour, there is a parade of wolves wanting to meet the hunters. I can see it's exhausting for the guys, but they try their best to keep all the names and faces straight, and when I finally rescue them and we head outside, I hear them muttering.

"Lily, pink hair, mole on her left cheek. Willa, big glasses—"

I smile. "Don't worry, you'll get used to it. I still get people's names wrong."

"They love you," Vale says seriously as we walk through the trees, giving us some privacy. "Every single person looked at you with reverence, and when they spoke of you, it was all good, gushing things. You are an incredible wolf, Quinn."

"Thank you," I murmur, blushing slightly, so I change the subject. "We won't have much time over the next few days so . . . want to run?" I wiggle my eyebrows as I walk backwards, gripping my top and tugging it off. "As wolves, I mean. We might as well make the most of your change." I shift and sit back, waiting for them.

Unsurprisingly, Jai is the first to change with barely any effort. His wolf is there, bursting from his clothes, then he trots over to me, rubbing along my side with his muzzle before dropping to his back and exposing his belly to me. Grinning, I rub his belly and turn to look at the others.

After a morning spent picking up the ruined pieces of my house and pack, I need a little fun, and watching Vale struggle from his clothes mid-shift is definitely that. He presses against me, rubbing his scent along me, before Lucien knocks me back as I giggle. He doesn't realise his own strength, and soon, I'm in the middle of a pile of wolves rubbing against me before I break free, trotting on all fours towards the trees before I glance back at them.

Lifting my rump, I wag my tail, knowing their wolves will understand exactly what it is.

A dare.

A hunt.

Catch me if they can.

I shoot off into the trees, not holding any of my speed back.

I hear them chasing me, their paws hitting the packed dirt as I shoot through the foliage. A bunny takes off, thinking I'm chasing, and I head away, sliding under a fallen log and through some boulders. I feel teeth near my tail and put on a burst of speed, grinning when I hear them growling in annoyance behind me.

I should have known better though. I slide to a stop when I see Jai before me. He cut through and around, and now they are corralling me. Vale comes up behind me. Where is Lucien?

I tumble to the ground, hit from the side by Lucien. With a grunt, I tug myself from under him and keep running, moving past Jai even as they work together to try and corner me. I manage to outrun them for a while, and I can taste their frustration. Maybe that's why I slow down.

I want them to catch me, and I'll let them after I make them work for it.

Adrenaline mixes with bloodlust, which soon turns to desire as three wolves pin me down.

The hunting lust turns to just pure lust, and desire forces me to cry out and rub against them, but I need more.

I need them.

I change back, landing on all fours as Vale's hands transform on my hips and he drives into me. My head drops back with a howl.

The pleasure and pain blend together as my claws dig into the dirt and leaves below me.

His hand slides up my back and grips my throat, his claws meeting at the front as he squeezes and yanks my head up. A growl escapes my lips, which is only echoed by him. He ruts me like an animal, his growls making the hair on my arms rise as I gasp, pushing back to meet him.

The smell of our desire is so thick it almost chokes me, but then Jai is before me, pushing his cock into my parted mouth. I widen it carefully so as not to nick him with my fangs, but he doesn't seem to care as he grips my messy hair and yanks me down onto his length. He claims my mouth with brutal thrusts that have his balls slapping against my chin.

A whine escapes my lips, even as pleasure builds within me, the feeling of being trapped, of being used, unusual for my wolf, who purrs inside me. The hussy. Their controlling hands yank me onto their lengths, and it gives me the freedom to just let go and feel rather than being in charge and dominant.

Their wolves snarl with need, and when I roll my eyes up, I see Jai's mismatched, glowing gaze watching me. This isn't Jai. This is his wolf. Just then, Vale's claws pierce my hips with the force of his thrusts, the sudden, sharp pain making me cry out around Jai's cock. The scent of my blood fills the air, and a hair-raising growl comes from beside me.

Lucien.

I see him, still in wolf form, pacing at our sides, his fangs flashing as he waits for his turn to claim me, but it's obvious he's getting impatient.

Wolves do not share well, and it's never been more apparent than when Lucien charges at us, barrelling into Vale and sending him flying into the forest. Suddenly, Lucien is human again, if not slightly bigger, and vibrating with his wolf's snarl, and then his huge length impales me. I choke and cry out on Jai's cock, his hand tightening in my hair as he continues to pummel my mouth, uncaring about the fight going on for my cunt.

Lucien claims my pussy brutally, forcing me deeper onto Jai's cock until I'm choking, tears escaping my eyes as I gag. There's a growl, and then Lucien is ripped away. I jerk from the force, and Jai releases me so I can turn my head to see Vale and Lucien tumbling around on the ground, their fangs and claws flashing. Lucien is bigger, but Vale is more brutal, and with a sharp right hook, Vale knocks his brother out and then turns to me, his eyes dark and narrowed.

He lunges at me, impaling me on his length once more, and I

scream before it becomes muffled as Jai slams back into my mouth. Both of them fuck me hard and fast until I feel my release growing stronger.

"Come for me," Vale snarls, his voice animalistic. Fingertips pinch my clit and send me over the edge, and I scream around Jai. My cunt clenches around Vale, and he roars.

His hips stutter before I feel him swell, so big it hurts, and then he's spilling inside of me. His wet, hot release makes me gasp as Jai slams all the way down my throat and comes, forcing his release deep into my stomach before he falls back with a groan, his eyes closed in bliss.

Spit and cum drip from my abused lips, which tingle as they heal. When Vale pulls from my abused cunt, I whimper at the pain. I feel his warmth behind me as he leans down.

"Shh, it's okay. You did so well," he says lovingly.

When he's free of my body, he lifts me and carries me over to his brother, who's groaning as he wakes up. Vale slams me into Lucien's hard, wet length.

I take over quickly, my eyes on Lucien below me. Lips tilting in a snarl, he grips me possessively as he helps me ride his cock, going from unconscious to awake and claiming me in seconds.

"Luc." I rock harder, my desire coming back with a flaming pain until I'm riding him desperately, chasing another release, and then I cry out as my release takes hold again. His gaze traps me as I shake on his cock, and when I slump, he rolls us, pushing me into the dirt as he fucks my limp body. He lets out a bellow and stills, spilling inside me.

Dirt covers my body, along with my blood and leaves, but I can't help but smile in satisfaction.

The best kind of fuck is dirty and bloody, and it seems my hunters have embraced all that comes with being a wolf.

Even the desires, and it's oh so delicious.

CHAPTER FIFTY-EIGHT

I'm laughing as we wander from the tree line towards the pack, a wicked grin covering my lips that matches theirs. I slide to a stop when I see a grim-faced White and Dom waiting for me. Instantly, I'm in alpha mode, all traces of pleasure and fun gone.

"What happened?"

"Tetrim is gone," White growls. "None of us realised he was missing during the chaos of the battle or the aftermath, but it's clear he's been gone awhile."

I try to think back to the last time I saw him. It was when I removed his teeth with a warning. I don't remember seeing him since, and although he usually sulks and licks his wounds, it is not like him to stay gone for this long. Between the battle, Jang, and coming back, I didn't even notice his absence.

"You don't think . . . ," Dom trails off. "You don't think he helped them, do you?"

"The hunters said they had an inside source. Could it be him?" Vale asks. "They knew exactly where to go—"

"It's him," I snarl. "I defeated him one too many times, and he decided to get his revenge. He betrayed the pack."

"What do we do?" White asks. Despite his age, he defers to my leadership, and I know he did it on purpose.

"We cannot track him down, not tonight with Jang's burial. Put out a notice. He's not allowed on pack land. If he's caught, he's to be brought to us, not allowed to wander free," I warn. "Then tomorrow . . . Tomorrow we will find him. Tonight, we grieve."

The reminder of what's coming sobers me. Tonight, I say goodbye to another father. Tonight, we send him to the moon and our goddess beyond.

No, there is no time for hunting today, but if Tetrim betrayed our pack, then he will die like a traitor.

***

The moon is high, and the pack is sombre. It is time.

My father lies on a stone bench in the clearing. Wildflowers dot the hill he sits on, which is as close to the moon as we can get. It shines on his skin, which a pack member has taken time to clean and make him look as peaceful as possible.

Our pack history, gifted by the goddess, lies across him. The black tapestry shines brightly with incandescent blue writing and drawings as it covers him from chin to feet, trailing to the ground on either side of him.

I take in the sight, allowing my heart to break once more. I feel every hard edge and let it wash through me and out into our pack.

I squeeze Marie's hand before taking my spot before him. For now, I'm acting alpha, and so it is my right.

Standing before the pack, I allow my voice to ring out true, albeit slightly warbled due to my grief.

"The trees bend in their grief for us, the land flows with forgiveness, and the goddess looks down on us, reminding us this is the end in this life, but not all." I swallow. "We are born from the moon and gifted to the Earth. We are creatures of beauty and history. Our life span is short, but we live so well, and Jang did that. He lived well. He lived for us, his pack, and for his wife, his mate." I look at my mother as she stands tall, tears rolling down her cheeks. "And for me, his daughter. Jang was a kind man, a good man, albeit a bit grumpy at times." There's some laughter. "But when he loved, he loved strongly, and what he claimed, he claimed for eternity. There is no other I would follow, no other I would bend my knee for. He is and always will be my alpha . . . my father."

I look out at all the faces, knowing they feel it too. "Tonight, we feel a grief so big, it seems insurmountable. We have lost so much, but we are still here, and as we are, so is their memory, their legacy." I glance back at Jang, throwing all my love into the look.

"Tonight, we consign him to the moon. We send them back to our goddess with our gratitude for such a pure, loving soul. We know that our love comes with a price—pain. We take it gladly, for it meant he was here, he was alive, and he was loved." I bow my head, kneeling before my father.

"We carry you always."

The chant is repeated through the crowd as the moon's rays fall upon Jang, making him glow brightly.

"We are one. We are pack," I add as the new words spread out like a prayer. "Tonight, tomorrow, and forever, we will keep you with us. Until we meet again within the moon, we carry you always." I bend my head, repeating it with the pack before I stand.

Marie comes around the other side, taking the edge of the tapestry, and I grab the other. Slowly, we lift it, covering his head. When we step back, it begins to glow brighter and brighter, and I kneel.

"We beg you, goddess, to take our alpha and keep him safe until we meet again. Goddess, keep him in your heart and moon, and make it so he hurts no more. Goddess, we beg you."

The lights grow brighter as we chant. I dig my hands into the mud, pushing my pleas into the earth. I pour everything into the ground as my pack does the same with me.

The ground bleeds with us, pouring out its condolences, and

when I look up, I see him shining so brightly, my eyes water. A bell tolls, and we all stop. The silence is loud, our hearts thrumming as one as I lift my head to see the tapestry melt to the stone.

Jang is gone.

The first time I saw this, I was shocked and had so many questions, but now I am thankful, for it means he has been accepted in the beyond with our goddess. I weep happy tears. "Thank you, goddess," I whisper. "Keep him safe for me, until I may join you again."

There is a brush of feathers across my skin. *Rest, wolf, I have him.* The words are whispered, and I shudder from their power.

No one else hears them. I have only heard the goddess two times in my whole life, but you do not forget the feeling. I know it is her. She protects our pack, and for some reason, she seems to talk through me, using me for healing and change.

The first time I heard her was the night my family died. She cried with me.

The second was when Jang announced he was training me for alpha. She was proud.

Now, I hear her grieve with me once more as the howls of my pack start up—a mourning howl, a song of love and loss.

I join in, my voice telling Jang and the goddess everything I cannot speak.

Some might see the celebration after a moon ceremony as morbid or wrong, but it is the opposite. We have grieved their loss, so now we celebrate their life. Stories are shared over campfires, food is given to help absorb the pain, and drinks flow to staunch our tears.

It is the way of our people, and the way Jang would want it.

I sit in the middle of it all, my hands warming my beer as I look around. So many were lost or injured in the battle. I didn't even get time to heal many today, but the scar the hunters left will remain for a long time.

I cannot bring them back, I cannot change what happened, but I can change how this ends. My need for revenge must be put aside. Jang is gone, and nothing can bring him back.

It fucking hurts.

I have a whole pack to think about, and I finally understand what Jang meant. The pack comes first, always, even over my own emotions. I must take care of them. I might not be alpha forever, but I am for right now. They need a leader, someone they trust, and despite my mistakes, it's clear they still look to me for answers, which means I need them.

I cannot let another battle occur like that one. We won't survive it.

I underestimated the hunters, but it will not happen again.

"You are thinking awfully hard," Vale murmurs.

I glance over at him where he sits on the log next to me. Jai is leaning back between my legs, far too comfortable, and Lucien is to my left. They never really leave my side, and I should hate that. I like my alone time, after all, but something about them being here to lean on makes my wolf and me happy.

I always thought I had to do this alone, but maybe I was wrong.

"Just thinking about the future and everything I need to do to keep these people safe," I admit.

"It will still be there tomorrow. Being a leader means being able to switch off when you need to," he murmurs. "Tomorrow will come all too soon anyway, so stop begging for it to come faster. Just enjoy tonight and this moment. Centre yourself in it. Right now, they don't need an alpha. They just need you to feel this with them."

I meet his searching eyes and look out at the crowd, knowing he's right. I was so lost in my worries and plans, I didn't see the children looking to me for how to act and the betas checking in on me rather than relaxing. Every wolf is looking at me, their alpha, and I'm sitting here as stiff as a board.

Sighing, I rub at my face and lean into Lucien as I sip some of my drink. "You're right." I nod before I down the rest. "Let's mingle."

For the next hour, I sit with different parts of the pack, listening to heartfelt stories of my father. He was a phenomenal man, and he has left some big shoes to fill.

I will never be the alpha that he was, no one ever could be, but every day they give me a chance, I will strive to be the best I can be.

CHAPTER FIFTY-NINE

I might have gotten a little tipsy last night, and the guys might have had to help me into bed, but luckily, alcohol burns quickly through our system. It takes a lot to get drunk, never mind stay drunk. So before the sun rises, I'm up and dressed. I leave the guys sleeping as I slip out and head towards the pack.

I have a lot to do.

I go to check on my mum first, but I find her serving food at the gym. I grab some toast, eating it as I watch her.

"She's okay," White murmurs at my side. "She needs to stay busy right now, let her."

"Are you sure?" I ask.

"I am. Come, let's walk." I follow him out as I eat the rest. "Did you know I was nearly mated once?"

My head swings his way, and he grins at my astonishment. "I take that as a no." He chuckles. "Most don't speak of it out of worry it will upset me. It was a very long time ago, and I was young, barely twenty years old. She was from a different pack, and we met at a summit. My father was alpha then, before Jang, and we had grown up together. I was supposed to be alpha, but I never wanted to be, so when I met her, it was like I found my place. I moved to her pack to be with her, and we were supposed to mate at the end of the year. She had just turned nineteen and wanted to celebrate her birthday. I was weak to anything she wanted, so I agreed. A few of us snuck out to a local human club. We drank and danced. It was the best night of our young lives . . . until it wasn't." I peer at him as he walks, seeing agony in his eyes.

"You don't have to tell me." I clutch his hand. Either way, I feel his need for comfort now.

He pats it, smiling sadly. "I do. Anyway, on the way back, we stumbled into a feral's nest. We didn't even know one was there. Her father did and was in the process of hunting them, that's why he kept warning everyone to stay home, but we were young and stupid and didn't listen." His hand drifts to his scar. "Only two of us made it out that night. I was one . . . She was not the other."

I swallow hard as we stop, the sun filtering through the canopy of trees and caressing us. "I took her body with me. I was so broken and numb. I tried to bring her back, I tried everything, but she was lost to me. I could have given in and died with her, but I knew she would have hated that. She was all about living, about experiencing everything, and she would have hated me giving up just to follow her. I had one year with her, Quinn, but it was enough to last me a lifetime. There will never be any other for me. How could there be when she took my heart with her?

"I will wait for her until the next life, Quinn. What is twenty more years? What I'm trying to say is, your mother will never get over her mate. She cannot, but she can live if she wishes to. It feels almost like a half-life, but it is better than nothing, so let her live, give her reasons to. For the first two months after, I spent every day building houses from sunup to well after sundown. Your father, my friend, never stopped me. He just understood, and most days, he would build at my side. He never asked, never complained, until one night, I just started crying and he held me. When the sun rose, he told me it was time to stop building now and start living, and I did, for him and this pack who supported me at my lowest."

He turns to me. "Your father was my best friend, he was my brother, and he was an amazing alpha, but more than that, his favourite roles were mate and father. He loved you both more than I ever knew anyone was capable of loving. That kind of love leaves a mark. He will always be with you, Quinn, and until the goddess claims me back for my mate, I will be here with you, at your side, where he should be. When you and your mum are ready to stop building, I will be here."

"Thank you." I lean up and kiss his cheek. "She was lucky to love you, even for a short time, and I have no doubt she is waiting for you on the other side, my friend."

He swallows, rubbing at my hair. "Go on, off with you. I'm sure you have a lot to do. I'll call the meeting you mentioned last night for later today."

"Thank you." I smile at him as I head deeper into pack land. His story reminds me why I'm still moving, still living.

My first stop is to the healers' hut. Our pack healer and doctors are busy at work, looking after those who were hurt in the battle, and it's about time I helped. The door is open, so I slip into the wooden building. Inside, there is a collection of wood and stone with a fireplace burning to keep everyone warm. The beds are separated by bright curtains on either side of the long room, and pack members bustle from bed to bed. Some are sitting up in their beds, while some are asleep and in worse shape.

"Alpha." A nurse named Toma bows.

"Don't let me interrupt." I wave him on. "I'm just here to help where I can."

"I'm sure simply seeing you will help," he replies. "Erm, if you'll excuse me . . ." He looks down at the bedpan, his nose wrinkling ever so slightly, and I nod as he hurries past to empty it. Moving deeper into the room, I peek into the first curtain.

There's a young female there. Her face is familiar, but her name escapes me. She is sitting up, though, and smiles brightly at me despite the bandage covering one eye. "Quinn—Alpha," she corrects, wincing, her smile dimming for a second before it grows once more. "It's a surprise to see you. I'm sorry about your loss." She becomes sad. "He was an excellent alpha."

"Thank you. How are you?" I ask, pointing at her eye.

"Ah, arrow to the eye. Hurt like a fucking bit—a lot." She coughs, wincing once more, which makes me grin. "They said they couldn't save it, but hey, I can wear an eye patch, right?" She looks at me hopefully. "It won't affect my wolf, will it? Never mind, I made the choice to fight. I'm okay and much less hurt than some, so please ignore my complaints."

Sitting in the vacant chair next to her, I grip her hand and smile. "I don't think it will affect your wolf, and you are not complaining. You were hurt protecting your pack. You did an incredible thing, choosing to fight, especially at such a young age. I can't change you getting hurt, but I might be able to help with your eye if you will let me."

She blinks, and I hear her heart skip a beat. "You can?" Despite her bravado, it's clear she's worried about losing it and what that means. "I heard rumours you could heal, but I didn't know—"

"Shh, let me?"

She nods eagerly, closing her other eye trustingly.

Leaning closer to her, I lay my hand across her injured eye, ignoring her slight inhale. "Relax," I command, and she does so.

I close my eyes, bringing that feeling forward and pushing it directly into her eye. I control how much, needing to keep some to heal others. It's a strange feeling. I can feel her eye, ragged and flat under the bandage, and it slowly starts to round out. When I pull back, she's gasping and crying. Her hands fly to the bandage, and she rips it off, waving her hand in front of her healed eye. It's a different colour than her other one, blue now, and I wince. "I'm sorry. I didn't know it would change colour. It's blue."

"Are you kidding me? You gave me my eye back!" She throws

herself at me, sobbing. "Thank you, thank you, thank you." I hold her as she cries, rubbing her back, and when she sits back, she's smiling brightly. "Besides, blue is epic."

Chuckling, I stand. "Glad I could help. I'm going to see if I can help any others now."

"Alpha," she calls as I turn. "Thank you. I don't regret fighting for this pack. I would do it again if needed. We all would."

"I hope it doesn't come to that," I tell her, "but thank you."

I move to the next bed. It's an older wolf named Sam. I've seen him around, and he's usually in charge of livestock. Right now, his entire torso is bandaged and he's sleeping, so I creep in and gently place my hand on his side. This time, I urge the healing to be soft and push him deeper into sleep so he feels no pain. It must work, and when I open my eyes, he's not as pale and he is breathing better.

The next bed is another man. His arm is in a sling, and he watches me warily. "Alpha." He nods, but he doesn't seem happy. "I heard you speaking to the girl. I don't want your healing. I will heal the old-fashioned way."

"Are you sure?" I ask, not the least bit offended. Despite us being born from the moon, most don't trust magic of any kind. Most even know of my skill, though they choose to either forget or ignore it.

"I'm sure."

"Very well." I bow and head to the next bed, watching the woman there. She is sleeping as well, and I can't tell where her wound is at first. I round the bed and have to cover my mouth. The entire side of her face is bandaged, and I can see burns extending down to her neck.

Oh moons.

I'm reaching for her when a commotion reaches my ear.

"Help! Someone, help!" Toma shouts.

Hurrying from the curtain, I glance over to see a wolf seizing on the bed. Toma is struggling to hold him down as the man screams and shouts, kicking and fighting. Fuck. Hurrying over, I try to pin him, but he's too big, so instead, I grab his face.

"Calm down before you change," I command, infusing my voice with my alpha powers until he has no choice but to listen. His wolf whines and retreats, and he slowly slumps and stops fighting.

"Thank you," Toma says. "He's been out since the fight and just woke up swinging."

"It happens. Glad I could help." I watch as Toma covers him in a sheet and lays a compress on his head. "Is there anyone who really needs to be healed?"

He blinks at me. "So the rumours are true?"

I nod, and he watches me carefully. "I don't know if he'll let you. He's an old, cranky bastard." He points down at the very end. "Had to move everyone away. He's delightful, but he's hurt badly, and I'm worried about his wounds."

"I can deal with cranky," I promise as I head down that way.

The curtain is pulled the entire way around, so I knock on it. "Hi, can I come in?"

"No, fuck off," a grumbling voice mutters.

Rolling my eyes, I pull the curtain back and peer in at the older man in the bed. He's not familiar, but then again, some pack members aren't and prefer to keep to themselves. He seems like the loner type. His hair is long and brown on the edges, with grey on the top. His mouth is pinched in both pain and annoyance, and his brown eyes are narrowed. He's a big guy, though, very muscular and built.

That's when I remember Jang mentioning someone like him. His name is Con, and he is an engineer for the pack but was always a loner.

"Hi, I'm—"

"I know who you are, child," he snaps. "Not to be rude, *Alpha*"—he sneers the word—"but kindly fuck off and let me die in peace."

"No." I sit down in the chair next to his bed, though it's clear he hasn't had visitors.

"No?" he snaps.

"No. I'm betting you're not used to that word, but you don't scare me, Con." I lean back. "How are you feeling?"

He eyes me. "Fucking peachy, can't you tell?"

I nod. "You look like shit," I agree.

He barks out a laugh, but it turns into a groan. "Gee, thanks, kid, and I was told you were the nice one in the family."

Leaning in like I'm going to tell him a secret, I smile. "Nah, that was always Marie."

"Marie? Nice? We are all fucked then." He huffs, eyeing me. "Why are you here, kid? You just lost your dad and were handed a pack. You have more important things to do."

"I do, yet here I am, but I'm assuming you won't let me heal you." His eyes narrow. "So how about we talk instead?" He groans, and I laugh. "Alright, how about we play a game or something then to pass the time?" He just keeps glaring, and I sigh. "Con, no one wants to die alone. If you won't let me heal you, then at least let me be here."

He grinds his teeth for a minute. "Suppose I can't stop you, nor could I stop you from reading that book there out loud." I glance to the bedside table to see a worn copy of Jane Austen's *Pride and Prejudice*. Grinning, I pick it up.

"I pegged you as more of a *Wuthering Heights* man." I open the book to the marked page and settle back, starting to read out loud. Sometimes, that's all you can do—sit here and be with someone.

Hours pass like this before I close the book and lay it on the side table. "I can pick up where we left off tomorrow if you like?" He was quiet the entire time, but he watched me, listening intently despite the pain he is in. It's obvious his wounds are extensive, though I'm not sure what they are since he's bundled up under the sheets.

He watches me as I set the book down. "You're not giving up, are you? Your father had that same annoying habit."

"I guess I'm more like him than I realised then." I smile. "I'm not giving up on anything or anyone. You are part of this pack, so how about you stop being so pig-headed and determined to do this alone and let me save you? That way, you can go back to scaring everyone and reading your books. There is more to life than waiting to die, just like you don't have to do this alone. I won't even tell anyone if you want. Just let me do this, if not for you than for me. I've lost enough. Do not make me bury another body."

It's a low move, but it's the truth, and he sighs. "Fucking family of yours." He watches me. "It won't hurt you?"

"No, I'll just be tired after, but I will recover quickly," I promise, and that tells me what type of man he is. He was worried for me, even as he's dying.

"Okay." He blows out a breath. "How do we do this?"

"Just relax. Can I take your hand?" He swallows hard and holds it out, wiping it on the bed.

"Sorry, it's scarred from years of—"

I grip it solidly, squeezing. "Close your eyes," I murmur. "When you open them again, then you will be back to scaring children."

He chuckles with a moan before his eyes close. Holding his hand, I close mine too.

I push my healing magic into his hand and down into his body. He gasps but holds on as I push it deeper, healing every wound I find, which is many. I don't know how this man isn't dead, never mind sitting up and giving me shit. It takes a while and lots of healing until I'm happy he's out of the worst of it.

When I open my eyes, I find him watching me. "You are incredible," he murmurs. "I saw the moon trapped in your skin. No wonder Jang picked you for alpha."

"Some people don't agree," I admit. "How are you feeling?"

"Better than I have in years." He sits up without a wince. "Thank you, Quinn, and ignore those fools. You might be young, but no one would have gone head-to-head with me, not even your father. You're a force of nature. Remind them of that when they doubt you." I stand then, smiling. "And maybe, every now and again, you could come by and read with me," he mutters. "Maybe I don't need to be alone all the time, and maybe you could use a quiet place to retreat to."

"I'd like that," I reply. "You can teach me the classics." I nod at his book. "I'll bring some of the new romance ones I read. I think you'll like them. They are spicy." I wiggle my eyebrows, making him laugh.

"Go on, kid. Go lead the pack and shit, and I'll see you later."

I leave, tired but with a smile on my face that no one can take away.

The meeting is taking place near the lake. My house is too small to host it, and we need as much privacy as we can get. I lean back into the grass, my eyes on the water, not wanting to look at the gaps in our ranks.

Jang, Tetrim, Filmea.

So many.

Speaking of . . . "Are we sure he is gone?" I ask, filling the silence. So far, we have spoken about patrols just in case there is retaliation from the hunters, but I think they will be too busy licking their wounds. We've talked about pack relocation and housing, all the boring bits that come with being alpha. No wonder Jang was always annoyed. We've been at it two hours and barely made any headway.

"Yes," Dom answers. "His scent here is old, and there is no sign of him. He's gone. We think he betrayed us to the hunters."

I nod, knowing he's right. "Which means he's probably still with them. He knows our defences, our routes . . . We need to change it up so he cannot inform them again. Switch routes around, add new defences, and make it so he's useless to them."

"Will do." White nods.

"We need to make sure he's there with them," I mutter as a plan comes to mind.

"We need to schedule the alpha ceremony as well as appoint two new betas," White reminds me.

"Later." I groan as I stand and stretch. "I'm going hunting for a traitor. I'll be back."

"You are alpha now," White says with a frown.

"And still the best tracker and fastest wolf. I'm just going to check, then I'll be back. I'll be okay. Keep the pack running until then." I hesitate. "After this is over, we'll deal with swearing in an alpha, even if it's not me, and also appointing new betas. For now, we need to survive."

Dom frowns. "You know we are all voting for you."

"It is not up to us. It's up to the pack. I will follow what they want no matter what. After all, they could be right."

"You don't have enough faith in yourself." White frowns. "But go, we will spread the word and sort the new defences while you are gone."

I hurry to the forest before they can stop me and change. Once in my wolf form, I push myself to run as fast as I can despite my exhaustion from healing.

I dip my muzzle in greeting at the wolves on patrol and then sprint past before they can shift and question me. Alphas are tied to pack land, we are the heart, and we are supposed to be there no matter what, but I refuse to make others do what I am willing to do.

I cover the distance to the compound in just under two hours, and once there, I sniff around. I keep out of sight, even though it seems to be quiet enough. Are they gone or resting? I guess time will tell. I'm just about to give up when I come across an old trail.

Tetrim, it's him. I'd know that smell anywhere.

I must have been too far gone last time to notice it.

Any wolf cannot resist shifting and running. We go mad if we don't, and it's clear he's been here. The trail loops around the compound a couple of times and then heads to a back door.

It's true. He betrayed us.

I bite back my snarl and turn away, happy enough to know that he's there and not hiding somewhere in pack lands, waiting to jump out. Forcing myself to head back to the pack before it gets too late, I race there as fast as I can, shifting once in the tree line as the sun starts to set.

Exhaustion sets in, making each step heavy. Between healing and shifting, I'm drained, and I find myself dragging my feet back to my house, needing rest more than I've ever needed anything.

I stumble back to my house, ready to collapse.

The door is open, and inside, I hear the voices of Vale, Lucien, and Jai, and despite the weariness lining my body, I smile as I slip inside.

CHAPTER SIXTY

We spent all day learning the layout of the pack, helping reset traps, and patrolling with Dom. It seems he's become our welcome committee, and despite the fact that we hate how close he is to Quinn, he's a good guy. He doesn't complain, nor does he care about the looks we get. After Quinn's speech, the hostility has eased, but it doesn't stop the glares.

We eat at her house and stay out of the way as much as possible as we wait for her to return. She was gone when we got up, which I didn't like, and we haven't seen her since, so when she stumbles inside, we all rush to her side.

"What happened?" I ask as I help her into her chair.

"Nothing, nothing." She sighs, waving me away, but she's pale and cold. "Just tired. I healed a lot of people and then ran. It takes its toll." She shivers. "I've been keeping back the aftereffects of the healing, but they're starting to kick in."

She's gotten stronger at healing, but I can still see it's taking its toll on her. I don't know if she's realised that the more she uses her healing abilities, the stronger she gets, but now is not the time to tell her. Instead, I grab a blanket and wrap it around her while Lucien prods the fire, adding more wood.

"Stay there," I murmur, kissing her head. I move back to the kitchen and pull the dish from the oven where I had been keeping it warm. It's nothing fancy, but I learned how to cook early on to keep us alive. It's a simple roast with vegetables, and I dish it up and take it over, but her head is lolling, and when she tries to lift her hand to grab it, she sighs.

Rolling my eyes, I sit on the arm of her chair. "Open," I demand.

"I'm too tired. Maybe later," she teases, eyes twinkling.

Huffing a laugh, I cut her a bite of everything and hold it to her mouth. She watches me for a moment before wrapping her lips around the fork and pulling the food off. She chews and swallows like it's hard, but I give her another bite, knowing she needs to eat.

I hand-feed her until she leans back. "I can't eat another bite," she says.

I finish off her plate and take it to the kitchen. When I glance back, Lucien has her in his arms. "Let's get you washed and dressed for bed, baby." While they head to the bathroom, I make her tea to warm her and then make the bed into a nest for her to relax in. All the while, Jai chops wood for the fire. When he comes back, he adds more so it will last the night, and I watch as she comes out, shaking in Lucien's arms.

He's worried, but he holds her with one arm while climbing the ladder, and then he lays her in bed, covering her carefully. I head up and hand her tea. "Drink it all," I order.

"Yes, sir," she jokes but downs it before handing it back. I put it aside and climb in next to her, pulling her into my arms. Jai moves to the other side, and Lucien props her up as she shakes, her eyes closing in exhaustion.

"Rest, we have you," I promise, kissing her head once more, unable to resist. I need to touch her at all times, it seems. I could blame my wolf, but I had this feeling before I was turned.

She slips into a restless sleep, but the aftereffects of healing creep up on her, leaving her body trembling in pain.

We hold her through the night, through the agony of the aftermath of her healing so many. She never once complains, suffering through it until she finally drops off to sleep a couple of hours before sunrise.

We leave Quinn in bed. She needs to rest, and if we are there, our wolves will demand we wake her up and claim her. Instead, we leave her breakfast warming in the oven, and we head out into the pack, trying to make ourselves useful. Dom isn't with us today, but there is plenty to do to keep this pack running and to help Quinn, and that's what we want to do—help her and make ourselves useful so she will keep us.

Not just in her bed, but at her side.

We run the perimeter with the others, checking for any signs of hunters since we are the best at recognising them. They slowly warm up to us, and once we are back, we don't bother putting on shirts since we run hot and are going to work up a sweat. I sling on some borrowed shorts and head to the rubble of the pack house.

Without waiting for an invitation, I start to help, and between the three of us, we begin to make a good dent. Lucien can lift a lot, and the others start to appreciate that. We never once stop, even as the sun peaks in the sky, making us sweat like hell. They stop watching or throwing glares, and I just focus on the rhythmic motion of clearing.

We bag as much as we can or put it in the wheelbarrows and drag it over to the pile they created. It's hard work. My muscles ache, and my throat is dry, but I carry on every single day and put in the work.

I'm sweeping some ash in the back corner when something catches my eye. Leaning down, I pull out a partially broken wooden photo frame and wipe the glass. The picture inside is a little singed and dirty, but I make out a young Quinn, Jang, and Maire.

"It was her birthday." I whirl at the voice to find Marie standing there. She thrusts a water at me, and I take it with a nod of thanks, draining it before handing it back. "The picture." She nods.

"Oh." I hand it over, and she smiles, but it doesn't quite reach her eyes, as if she cannot do that anymore. "It was one of the happiest days of the year. He had this in pride of place on his desk." She swallows hard, her eyes turning glassy with pain before she blinks it away. "Thank you for this."

I nod, unsure what to say. This is the mum of the woman I have fallen for.

I've never had to meet a girl's parents before, never mind when we are supposed to be enemies, so I'm unsure what to say. I'm not good at this stuff like Lucien or crazy enough to wing it like Jai. Luckily, she saves me from myself and peers into my eyes.

"Jang liked you, I could tell." She nods. "But if you hurt or betray my daughter, I will rip out your heart and eat it." I blink, astonished as she smiles kindly. "Now make sure to drink plenty of water. It will be hot today."

I blink at her for a moment. "Erm, thanks, I will." I cough, rubbing at my hair, which is growing long since it's been a while since I cut it. "Just so you know, I don't want to ever hurt Quinn again."

"Good, then we won't have any issues." She pats my arm as she heads out to hand out more water.

"I like her," Jai says as he leans on a shovel, covered in ash and sweat. "She's crazy like me."

Fuck, what kind of family am I in?

By the time we get back to Quinn's house, we are covered in sweat despite washing all the ash off hours ago. We started moving the wood over to rebuild. Surprisingly, Quinn is there, curled up in her chair with a mug in hand. She turns and blinks when she sees us.

"Erm, are you okay?" she asks, her eyes roving over our bare chests. "I'm not complaining—"

Jai grins and heads her way, grabbing her hand and dragging it down his sweaty chest. "No? Want to play?" She chuckles as she slides her hand lower, gripping his cock.

"You wish." She huffs as she pushes him away, her nose crinkling. "Now shower because you stink, and we are eating with the pack tonight."

"We can just stay here," I begin with a frown, but she glares at me in a way that makes my cock hard and lets me know she's going to get her way.

"No, we eat with the pack tonight. You are one of us now, so you better get used to it. Plus, the more they see you, the better, so go shower."

While Jai flirts with her, I claim the shower first. I'm almost too tall for it, so I have to bend my head, and after washing, I dress in more borrowed jeans and a shirt before letting Jai and Lucien claim it. In the meantime, I'm with Quinn, both of us happy to sit in silence. We find solace in each other.

"Do you regret saving me?" she asks, and I whirl around to see her. "When we were kids, if you hadn't, you wouldn't be here now. You'd still be a hunter, and nothing—"

I cover her mouth with my hand. "First of all, everything happens for a reason, and no, I don't regret it. For a while, I thought I did, but the truth was, I regretted not doing more that night. I hated who I had become. Like this, as a wolf, I feel . . . whole, happy, and free. You gave me that, Quinn." I remove my hand and kiss her softly. "I wouldn't want to be anywhere else."

"Still hate me?" she whispers against my lips.

"Sometimes." I smirk against hers. "Still hate me?"

"Sometimes," she admits, dragging her lips across mine softly before nipping my bottom lip. "Thank you for saving me that night."

"Thank you for saving me now," I murmur, sliding my hand into her hair and tugging her closer so I can deepen the kiss.

"If you two aren't fucking, can we eat?" Jai calls, and I pull away with a sigh.

"Come on, beautiful, let's eat." I offer her my hand, and she accepts it, holding it the entire way to the gym. I expect her to let go when we get there, I even try to step back, but she holds me at her side and walks in without an inch of shame.

Surprisingly, no one seems to bat an eye, and as we grab our trays, she leads us over to a half full table. Her mum is there, as are White and Dom. I sit next to Quinn and without even realising it, I put my bread onto her plate, making her grin, and when I glance up, her mum is smiling too.

Clearing my throat, I begin to eat as they talk around us, but Quinn nudges me. "You belong here," she reminds me.

Trying to make an effort, I glance at White. "Is there anything we can do to help with the new border security?" I'm sure that's what they were discussing, right?

"Oh, erm, actually, yes." He blinks, surprised. "We wanted to lay some new traps, but I've used all of ours. Do you have any experience with building some?"

"Lucien and I are very good at them. Believe it or not, hunters actually get sent to workshops for that kind of thing."

Quinn laughs. "Oh my god, is there a hunter summer camp?"

"Pretty much." I grin. "Though we learned spear making, archery, and how to gut animals for bait."

She laughs, her head falling back with the sound, and I can't help but watch her. She's so beautiful. I place my hand on her thigh under the table, needing to touch her, and she winks at me. "I'm just imagining you three at summer camp in little uniforms."

"I pulled it off." I grin.

"What else do they teach you?" Dom asks curiously.

"A lot." I shrug, but then I carry on, seeing that he's trying. "We attend school like normal, but sometimes we would be forced to miss it for hunts. We have to be taught all the skills by what they call senior hunters and pass a test before we can become a full-fledged hunter. The health benefits aren't great, but they had killer uniforms."

He chuckles. "I bet, and cool toys."

"The coolest." I nod.

"What about your family?" Marie asks.

I freeze at that, colour draining from my face, and Quinn leans into me, offering comfort. "His father is dead. He has no other family bar Lucien," she tells her mum. "Just like us."

Marie looks at me and nods before going back to eating, and I relax as much as I can.

"What's it like being a hunter?" Dom asks.

"Lonely," is the first thing Lucien says. "And tiring. You are always on the road. The people who should have your back sometimes don't. We got lucky with us three though."

"Do you pick your unit?" Quinn asks.

"Sometimes. Most don't, and they get thrown together. We got Jai because no one wanted the crazy bastard."

Jai just grins, but Quinn leans over and whispers something that has him smiling wider.

"And Lucien and I came as a packaged deal."

"So you're just given hunts and off you go?" Marie asks, but it doesn't sound mean.

"In a way. We were left on our own a lot. I'd never hunted wolves before. You are classed as the top dogs," I admit, which makes them whoop. "We hunted vamps, trolls, and witches, usually ones that killed a lot and drew attention. Do you remember the spree of drained bodies last year about four hours from here?"

"Yes." Marie frowns.

"We caught that vamp. He was a lone male draining them dry, a serial killer vampyr." I shrug.

"I see." She nods. "So maybe you're not all bad."

"We aren't all good either," I reply. "I can admit that. We've made mistakes, but we are trying to make up for them now."

"Everyone makes mistakes," Quinn murmurs. "You're trying, and that's all that matters."

I nod, my eyes on my meal, and it's only when her mum speaks that I let go of my shame. "I hate hunters. It's not a secret, since they hurt my family, hurt me, and stole my mate, but if my Quinn trusts you, then so do we. People can be more than one thing, and my Jang always believed in second chances, so here's your second chance. Embrace it."

"We will," I murmur.

"Good, and eat up, you're too skinny." She huffs.

White leans over the table. "That's her way of saying she likes you." He grunts when Marie elbows him, but I smile and continue eating, wanting to make her proud.

After all, I've never had anyone care if I was hungry or too skinny.

It's nice.

"Quinn," I warn.

She's walking backwards with a smirk as she plays with the hem of her shirt. "What, don't think you can catch me?" she teases.

Jai huffs. "We know we can."

"We just don't want anyone else seeing you," Lucien admits.

"Then take me home," she purrs, and within seconds, I close the distance between us, hoisting her over my shoulder. I run back to her home as she giggles. Slapping my hand on her ass, I hold her firmly, and as soon as we get inside, I throw her to the floor.

She teased us all night while we sat with the others with flirting touches, wandering hands, and hungry eyes.

It drove me wild.

Now, she gets to pay for that.

She moans loudly as I yank her head to the side and bite down on the skin there, my wolf urging me to. Her hands rip at my shirt, tearing it away with her claws as I lick and suck the bite. Her legs wrap around my waist as she rocks into me, rubbing her hot, little body against mine.

"Vale," she begs, tilting her head to give me better access, her eyes sliding shut in bliss. The moon streams through her window and caresses her skin like a lover, and I'm jealous of it as I kiss down her throat and across her chest, gripping either side of her shirt as I use my new strength and rip. She gasps as I tear it free and toss the shirt behind me. We both hear a groan and glance over to see Jai sniffing it as he watches us. Smirking, I turn back, kissing down her chest and stopping at her perky, beautiful breasts to pay them special care. My tongue wraps around her cherry nipples, licking and sucking them as her back bows, thrusting them deeper into my mouth as her claws stab into my back, holding me in place.

I hear her heart hammering against my mouth, and the sweet musk of her desire wraps around me and only gets stronger as I release her nipple and slide down her toned belly, licking the ridges of her abs before placing a kiss above the waistband of her shorts.

"Don't you dare," she warns as I go to rip her shorts, and she slides them off, leaving her in a tiny black thong.

Before she can protest, I rip it free and toss it aside, both of us watching as Jai catches it and shoves it into his mouth with a groan.

"See what you do to us?" I murmur, blowing a warm breath across her pussy as she shudders, her toned thighs parting to show me her pretty, wet cunt. "Driving us crazy all night, weren't you? You enjoyed teasing us until we were almost out of our minds with desire, and now it's your turn."

"Vale—" Her voice turns into a scream as I seal my mouth around her pussy and suck as much of her as I can, tasting the sweet cream of her desire. I slide lower, forcing my shoulders between her thighs, and then I sweep my tongue across her pretty pussy, ignoring her engorged clit. Instead, I lick and suck her lips before teasing her pulsing hole.

Sliding my tongue around it, I lap up her essence as she cries out, pressing her cunt firmly into my face. I torture her, dragging out her pleasure until she's wild with it, her legs shaking.

"Vale, I swear to the moon," she hisses when I pull away before she can come again. Chuckling, I prop my chin on her pussy as she lifts her head to glare down at me. "Fine. Lucien, come do what your brother can't—"

I seal my mouth over her bratty little pussy, sucking on her hard nub as her back bows and a scream erupts from her lips. Thrusting two fingers inside her, I curl them and rub, and within seconds, she comes.

Lapping at her release, I pull my fingers free with a smirk and lick them. "What were you saying, she-wolf?"

"Asshole," she growls, sprawled out on the floor.

"If you keep calling me that, then maybe I really should be." Her eyes narrow at the threat in my voice, and before she can mewl a protest, I flip her to her hands and knees.

The guys and I have worked together long enough that we can speak without words, and when I ram my cock into her cunt, Jai moves our way, sliding underneath her body as I pound into her before pulling abruptly out.

I part her plump ass cheeks and drag my dripping cock around her other hole. "Vale, don't you fucking dare—" I push inside her little ass, which has been driving me mad since we first met.

I slide past her clinging muscles. "Relax, she-wolf," I demand, my voice hard and leaving no room for protest. Her wolf whines for me, even as her body relaxes, and I work my cock in inch by inch.

It's my turn to pant, but when I'm buried balls deep, I lean over her and press my lips to her ear. "Who's an asshole now, she-wolf?"

"Still you," she snaps, pressing her head to Jai's chest, but despite the annoyance in her voice, she pushes back, taking me deeper into her tight ass.

Nipping her shoulder in warning, I grip her hips as I lean back. "Jai, get in her cunt before I blow in her ass. She's so fucking tight."

She turns those glittering eyes on me, a smirk playing on her lips. "I thought hunters were supposed to have patience."

"Nobody could have patience with you sprawled before them, their cock deep in your bratty ass. Not even a fucking god, she-wolf," I grit out, and she smirks, wiggling her ass, so I slap her plump cheek, making her groan.

Her groan soon turns into a whimper, and I lean back, watching as Jai's cock slowly stretches her pussy. I can see and feel it. She gets tighter on my cock, and I can almost feel him through the thin barrier between us.

"Good girl, you're doing so well, she-wolf. Shit, you should see how you're taking us both. You are stretched so wide for us, your greedy little cunt leaking around him. Does he feel good, Quinn?"

She nods, but I grip her head, yanking it up with a snarl. "Use your words, she-wolf."

"Yes, yes, he feels good." She groans. "So good, please."

"Next time, I think we'll play with you with some of my toys," I murmur. "I'd love to see you trussed up like our victim, our blades running over this skin." She clenches around us, giving her away. "Oh, she likes that, brothers. Our little she-wolf wants to be our victim, our prey."

"I do like it when she bleeds for us," Jai growls, lifting his hips to thrust into her. We work together on a fast, hard rhythm that has her crying out, stuffed full of our cocks.

"Of course you do." Lucien snorts. I expect him to reach for our girl's mouth—after all, there are three of us, and she has three holes—but he seems content to watch, and there is something dark in his eyes, as if he's planning something else.

I leave him to it, my eyes turning back to my girl. I watch my fat cock slide from her ass. My wolf howls in need and hunger, and my fangs ache to be buried in her skin, my claws pricking through my fingers to spill her blood.

I let them lengthen, knowing she can heal anything we do to her.

That old hatred resurfaces, mixing with my love for the she-wolf grinding back against us.

I slash across her back, and she cries out, arching despite the pain. Leaning down, I lick the blood rolling from the wounds before I widen them with my tongue, making them bleed more. I can feel the magic in her skin as it tries to heal them. Leaning up, I lick my bloodied lips.

"There, she's bleeding for you."

I peer down to see her blood dripping onto Jai, and his eyes are wild as he snarls and hammers up into her, all of our rhythm lost.

She screams raggedly between us, her skin slick with blood and sweat, and I can't take it. I meet Jai's eyes, and we nod.

I bend over her, my fangs lengthening.

My fangs pierce her neck on the left, his on the right, and she screams her release to the moon, dragging us with her. I can't hold back. It burns down my spine and bursts out of me as I bellow into her skin and pump my cum into her tight ass, feeling Jai do the same to her tight cunt. It seems to go on forever, and my eyes cross at the pleasure, her ass squeezing every drop of cum from me until there's nothing left.

I lie over her as my heart races, my cock softening before I pull out of her and slump back. Jai lifts her, his arms shaking, and she drops to her knees next to him. Her neck bleeds from both sides, her hair is mussed, and she looks so fucking sexy, my cock starts to harden again.

I will never get enough of Quinn. Not in this lifetime, not in the next.

Lucien stands then, eyeing her hungrily.

"Luc?" she whispers sweetly, her voice hoarse from her screams, but she recovers quickly, her knees spread as she kneels. Our cum drips from her as she blinks her big eyes at my bristling brother.

"Run, she-wolf," he warns. "Run fast because when I catch you, I'm going to fuck you until sunrise."

Her eyes widen, and I hear her heart skip a beat and then she's off, racing through the door. Lucien rolls his shoulders as he watches, giving her a head start before my brother stomps after her, leaving us with his parting words.

"Don't wait up for us."

LUCIEN

I can hear her. I can smell her.

She's being loud, her human feet pounding the earth, and their cum drips from her like a trail, the scent of her desire filling the forest as I race after her.

There is one difference this time though. Quinn wants to be caught. I can hear it in her laboured breathing and taste her excitement. When I spot her up ahead, I pump my arms faster, closing the distance with a burst of speed, and I catch her waist and slam her back into the nearest tree. The force dazes her, and before she can react, I wrap the hunters' rope around her wrists, flinging it over the tree branch above, and hoist her up.

"Luc!" she yells, kicking her legs as she twists. I keep going until I can wrap her legs around me. Her eyes are wide as she stares down at me in shock. I lick a line up her bloody, naked stomach.

"I caught you, my prey. Now I can eat you," I murmur, "like we all wanted to in that cage." Her heart skips a beat, and her legs tighten around me as I smirk, pricking her skin with my fangs. "You want to be fucked, Quinn. You want to be used, tied up, and forced. You want to be dominated, and that's exactly what we are doing, baby. Now, be a good little prey and scream for me."

Her mouth falls open, and before she can talk her way out of this or overthink it, I lift her higher and drop her onto my cock. I patiently waited for my turn, knowing I wanted to chase her and fuck her, the adrenaline of the hunt making me wild as I pound into her.

The tree creaks as she swings, but I move faster, using every ounce of my newfound strength and power until she screams, lifting on her bindings to help drop herself onto my cock. Her pussy drips down my length, tightening around me to the point of pain.

There's another creak and then a crack. The branch snaps, and I catch her, turning in the same movement and driving her into the ground as I hammer into her, pinning her bound hands above her head. My mouth closes on her breast, and I bite down until I draw blood like they did.

She screams loudly for me. It echoes around the forest, and I hope all her wolves hear and know I've caught and bred their alpha. My hips snap with such force, she slides higher in the dirt.

"Luc, Luc." She chants my name like a prayer.

"Eyes on me," I snarl. "Watch me as I rut you, prey."

She opens them, her gaze clashing with mine, and it sends me over the edge. My release slams through me with such force, my back bows. She cries out, tightening around me as she comes. I bury myself inside her as deeply as I can until my cum fills her cunt.

Dropping my head, I lick at the already healing wound. "Holy fuck," she rasps raggedly.

Grinning, I kiss over her racing heart. "You have five minutes, and then you will run again."

I want her screams to ring out all night so everyone knows Quinn belongs to me.

CHAPTER SIXTY-ONE

I'm walking to breakfast the next morning—the guys left early to help at the pack house, and I took my sweet time getting ready—but the noise has me speeding up. Dom runs past, and I grab his arm. "What is it?" I ask.

"Follow me."

I fall into line next to him and follow him to the tree line, where two betas, Terrance and Sandy, are waiting.

"What's wrong?" I bark.

"We found something on the outskirts of the forest, almost beyond pack land. You need to see it, Alpha." Terrance bows his head in respect, but not before I see the worry in his eyes.

"Show me," I order, and I change without a second thought. Dom and I follow them, and then I change and take a good look at what they found. The smell of blood undoubtedly alerted them and drew them out. I'm just glad it wasn't a trap.

It's a message.

There is a glowing, poisoned blade pinning a heart to a tree, which has a piece of paper behind it. I quickly tug the blade out, dropping it to the ground, and read the blood-soaked message left for us.

We are out for blood. You took our people, and now we will take all of yours.

Not very poetic, but they are hunters after all. It's a warning, a promise of what's to come, and all the happiness and security I've felt from the last few days vanishes. Crumpling the paper, I toss it away. "Call a meeting," I tell Dom. "We need to end this now."

I hoped we would have time, but we clearly don't. We have barely recovered from the loss of Jang and our packmates, but they don't care. They will return, and more will be lost.

Unless we take this war to them and make them all pay for what they did.

"It's suicide," White hisses.

"It's our only option," I argue. "If we wait, they will attack us again. We might be okay, or we might lose yet more wolves and solve nothing. We have to press our advantage. They are hiding right now. They are weak and pumping out threats, expecting us to hide and wait. We cannot do that!"

The gym is empty bar the twenty wolves I've called, all ones I trust, but a decision has to be made.

"She's right," Vale says slowly. "I know how hunters think. Right now, they are calling more reinforcements in, building more weapons, and biding their time until they attack. When they do, they won't retreat this time. They will kill everyone—children, women, and men. Our best bet is Quinn's plan, the element of surprise. We can catch them before they are ready and end this once and for all."

"And who goes?" Dom asks.

"Volunteers only. I will never force anyone, but know I will be going," I reply, waiting until the protests die down after my announcement. "If I don't come back, Marie will rule in my absence until another alpha can be chosen."

"No," Marie protests. "I lost my mate. I won't lose my daughter."

"You will lose me regardless. At least this way, we stand a chance," I tell her. "I won't sit here and wait like a coward. I will face them head-on. They are just humans, that's all. Despite what they did here, they are weak and powerless. We are creatures born from moonlight and pain. We are fangs and claws. We are wolves. It's time we showed them that." I wanted this to be a vote, but it's clear they need someone to take charge, so I stand tall, trusting my judgement like Jang taught me. "This is my ruling. This time, it isn't a joint decision. Spread the word, volunteers only. Gather as many as we can without leaving the pack undefended. Make it known we may not come back."

I watch as they file out, arguing amongst themselves. "Please, Quinny," Marie begs, her eyes glossy with unshed tears as she stops before me. "Don't make me stand by and watch as you walk towards death."

I grip her hand as I meet her worried gaze. "I have to do this. Please understand, I'm doing this for everyone."

"And what about you? What about me? My mate gave his life for everyone, and now you are going to do the same," she hisses, anger mixing with her pain.

"It stopped being about us the second they killed one of our pack members. I am alpha now, not just your daughter. I have everyone's lives to think about, not just my own. I cannot and will not stand by and let them ruin our pack. If they want a war, then I will give them one." I lean in and kiss her cheek, knowing she's hurting. "I know you're scared, I am too, but I have to do this. Don't make me go without your blessing."

In some ways, I don't envy my mother. She is the heart and soul of this pack, and although she will never lead, she has to watch her family do just that and die for it. All the while, she stands tall, keeping our people together despite her own agony.

She swallows, tears sliding down her cheeks. "You better come back."

"I'll try," I promise. "Look after the pack for me."

"Only until you get back," she retorts. "So come home." She steps back, looking at Vale, Lucien, and Jai. I don't even need to ask them if they will volunteer because I know they will come with me.

It's an unspoken promise.

"Bring my daughter home to me. Vow it," she demands.

"Mother," I warn.

"Vow it," she roars.

"I would die before I let anything happen to her," Jai states calmly. "I will kill every single hunter who dares hurt the woman I love, and we will do everything in our power to bring Quinn home to you."

My heart skips a beat at his confession. He loves me?

It feels right, and despite the circumstances, my wolf howls in happiness and approval.

Marie swallows and nods. "I guess that's good enough." She looks me over. "You are a brave fool, just like your father."

"That's why you love us," I reply.

"Sometimes love fucking hurts," she mutters before hugging me and departing. I watch her go, knowing she is struggling with losing her only tie to this world. I don't just need to return for my pack, but I also need to return for her. I know losing me would be her death, and I will not let that happen.

I'm coming back.

I have to, and when I do, I will bring peace.

They wanted beasts?

They've got them, and all the wilderness that lives inside our souls.

We are all aware tonight could be our last in this world. The pack is quiet as loved ones spend the night with those who have volunteered, making the most of the time we have.

I'm alone, staring at the lake, but I should have known I'm never truly alone—not anymore. I once craved silence and solitude, but I hate it now. I miss their taunts, their teasing voices, and the warmth of knowing they are next to me.

They haven't been in my life long, but I've come to depend on them when my burdens get too big. That should scare me, but if anything, it's a relief. I have looked after everyone else for as long as I can remember, but with them, I don't have to. They look after me. They take the weight and allow me to function.

I feel them behind me, giving me the space I need without letting me feel alone.

We might have started out as enemies, but we are ending as something much more, and if I'm going to be honest with myself, I wish we had more time to explore what.

Maybe it's the ticking clock I feel or the concern that tomorrow might never come, but I find myself feeling raw and vulnerable for once.

"I wish—no, I know that we could have been something great, maybe even mates in this lifetime. You never wanted to steal my power from me, you just wanted to be at my side as I led, and I've never had that. Maybe in another life, we could have grown old together. Maybe you could have been everything I didn't even know I was looking for."

"We can have all that," Lucien murmurs. "We can have it all, and we are mates, Quinn, whether there's been a ceremony or not. We are mates. We started out as enemies, but if we are being honest, our hate was far too close to love to have ended any other way."

I smile at that, my eyes still on the water, as if I'm afraid that when I look away, they will disappear along with it. "In another life,

Lucien, I would have loved you until the end." I look at Vale. "I would have spent years exploring all those scars and healing them." I glance at Jai as I swallow. "I would have taught you to be the wolf you always were."

"Then let's do that," Vale says. "If we make it through tomorrow, then we do that. We spend forever together. You already have us, Quinn. Even when we were enemies, our lives revolved around you —we hunted you, hated you, and hurt you—so let's spend the rest loving you."

"And if we don't have forever?" I ask, sad for once about that.

"Then we have tonight," he murmurs as he steps closer, the moon shining on him like a lover. "We'll make it feel like forever if you let us."

I meet his bright eyes, a soft smile curving my lips. "Then show me how forever feels."

He closes the remaining distance in one stride, his hand tangling in my hair as he kisses me. We sink to our knees on the shore, and he falls back, pulling me on top of him as we kiss.

I sink into him. I drown in him. I let him make me a believer, and in his name, I pray.

I pray tomorrow never comes as his hands slide down my body, claiming every inch along with my heart and soul.

His hand glides over my core, stroking as he kisses me. This moment is so soft, unlike our usual frenzied, animalistic fucking. He turns my head, and more lips meet mine—harder and slightly crazy.

Jai.

We kiss as Vale strokes my pussy until my hips roll, a slow pleasure building within me. Jai pulls away, and my head is tilted back so Lucien can kiss me upside down.

His brother drives me to the brink of release and then pulls away.

"Keep kissing him, beautiful. Let us love you until the end," Vale murmurs as he slides up my body. He grips my thighs as his warm, hard cock presses inside me, and tears fill my eyes for some unknown reason.

They are treating me like I am precious, and I want to weep.

Vale slowly pulls from my clinging cunt and pushes back in, his hips rolling against mine in slow, loving movements as his brother kisses me. Jai's hands sweep down my body, cupping and caressing.

I let them carry me away, and when I come, Vale follows me. The soft orgasm carries me on a wave until I wake up to Lucien slipping into me, his hand spanning my chest as I blink my eyes open. "Feel your heart, Quinn. Feel it beat for us. It's ours, and we are keeping it, now and forever."

I nod, feeling the beat of my heart matching his as he leans down and claims my lips once more. He kisses me softly, our tongues tangling as our bodies join. The water laps nearby like music, our breathing laboured and bodies slick with sweat.

"That's it, beautiful," he whispers against my lips. "Feel us, feel me. Let me prove how beautiful forever could be with us." He nips my lip as his hips speed up, making me moan loudly. "I love you, Quinn. I love you." He buries his head into my neck as he comes, pulling me with him.

I wrap my legs and arms around him, holding him as waves of pleasure spread through us before abating.

With another soft kiss, he rolls from me, and I turn and crawl to Jai, who opens his arms eagerly. I crawl up his body, and our lips meet in a hurried, slightly unhinged kiss while I push him back and sink onto his cock.

He holds me tightly, letting me ride out my worries on him. His madness and my uncertainties meet and melt into something beautiful.

The scarred, hateful hunter and the stubborn, strong wolf.

Together, we are perfect, and we come together just like it was always meant to be. When we find our bliss in each other's arms, I kiss his rapid heartbeat with a gasp. "I love you."

I love them all.

I want forever with them.

We watch the sunrise together, tangled in each other's arms, knowing what this brings, and I'm reluctant to let go of them.

I send up a prayer to the retreating moon.

Please give me a chance at the future they described. I promise not to waste it.

CHAPTER SIXTY-TWO

Jai

Morning comes all too quickly, and despite the bloodlust coursing through my veins, I keep my expression calm and reflective as we meet with the other wolves where the pack house once stood.

Thirty wolves against whatever is left of the hunters.

It might not work, but we have the element of surprise. Either way, we are doing this. My eyes go to Quinn as lovers kiss goodbye, wives and husbands hug, not wanting to let go, and family members beg for their loved ones to change their minds. Through it all, Quinn stands tall, watching every moment as if memorising it and letting it fuel her.

She will feel every loss today for the rest of her life. She takes everyone's safety personally, even though they made their own choices. It's just who she is. It's one of the reasons I love her, and I think it's one of the reasons she loves me.

She needs the edge of madness I give her.

I might have calmed down since embracing my wolf, as if I've healed the two sides of me, but the madness always lingers in my brain. She helps keep it at bay, but today, I'm going to let it out. I'll bathe in my own people's blood for my mate, and I cannot fucking wait.

"Quinn." We all turn as Marie, White, Dom, and another man she introduced as Con head her way. Her mother looks nervous but resigned, likely knowing there is no arguing with Quinn once she has made up her mind.

"Hey. It's early. Why are you all up?" God, Quinn is oblivious.

"For you, obviously. It's not for the fucking sunshine," Con grouses, making her grin.

"To see you off," White murmurs.

Marie throws herself at Quinn, hugging her tightly, and when she pulls away, she wipes at her tearful eyes. For a moment, I wonder what it would feel like to be that loved.

"Please, just come home," Marie says.

"I will. I'll be back in time for breakfast," Quinn murmurs, hugging her quickly.

"You better." White points in her face. I know they would have all volunteered as well, but she forbade it. She said in case she didn't make it back, the pack needed stability with the betas. "I mean it, we need our alpha."

"Got it." She turns to Dom, who hugs her quickly and steps back with a laugh as we growl.

Con grinds his teeth before he grabs her, hugging her abruptly. "Come back safe. You're the only person I tolerate and might even care about." He gruffly thrusts her away and turns and storms off.

"I like you too, Con!" she calls after him with a grin before looking at her mum, White, and Dom. "I'll be okay, don't worry. Just protect the pack while we're gone."

She steps back and releases a whistle, letting them know it's time to go, then she glances back at her loved ones. "I'll be back before breakfast, so make something good."

Today is going to be long. We aren't planning on attacking immediately, but not everyone can run as fast as her. We estimate it will take us three to four hours to get to the base, then we'll scope out any new traps they might have set around the perimeter so we can prepare.

By the time night falls, our howls will split the air and their blood will scent the night.

Without looking back, she takes my hand and leads us into the trees. She wants to save everyone's shifts as much as she can since we will need all our energy tonight, so instead, we walk.

My bag hits my side with every step. You can take the wolf out of the hunter, but not the hunter out of the wolf, so I brought toys.

Lots of toys.

When we pass the silent sentinels at the border, it becomes too real. I can smell the nervous energy of the other wolves silently following us—their worries, their fear, but also their determination. Whatever tonight holds, we all know it will change everything.

We walk and walk, Quinn never once breaking stride, her hand held in mine as we move for over an hour.

Suddenly, Quinn freezes. "What is it?" I ask.

"I felt something in the distance, something big, like pure power." She leans down, pressing her hand to the dirt. "Like the earth itself is being wielded." For a moment, her eyes glaze over. "It is, in a battle for the future." She blinks then stands. "It seems we are not the only ones defeating enemies today."

Sometimes, I swear Quinn is not of this world, as if the moon itself kissed her cheek and blessed her with knowledge beyond her existence, but it gets less odd the more I'm around her. It is just Quinn, and sometimes, she knows things she has no way of possibly knowing.

I simply incline my head as she takes my hand once more. "Come, we will reach the base by midday."

Quinn is right, my little smart she-wolf, because we reach the base around midday. We allowed for stops along the way, very aware of what we are walking into. Once there, we crouch in the tree line to make sure we aren't seen until we are ready.

There are trucks and cars in the parking lot, so they already managed to call in reinforcements. The truck Quinn speared the commander's head on is gone, which makes sense. The two-story building is dark, which is not surprising since they have tint on the window to make it look like it's abandoned. The top floor is mostly empty bar some bunks for hunters, the second floor is for supply and drop, and the basement floor is their command centre.

I meet Vale's eyes, and he nods, his fingers moving in a circle. We have hunted together so long that we can speak without words, and I understand immediately. "Stay here. We are going to check the perimeter and mark new traps and set our own." I kiss her and leave her with her wolves. Lucien goes left to wrap around the building, and Vale goes right.

Me? I go straight ahead.

I know the cameras' blind spots, since we helped fit them, and despite our best efforts, there are always blind spots. I keep to them now, and in the spots where they can see me, I crawl under cars. When I'm under one of the bigger trucks, I flip over onto my back and pull my bag closer, reaching inside for a toy. With careful, deliberate movements, I attach it to the undercarriage.

Once I'm sure it's set, I check the detonator before grabbing my bag and shimmying to the next car. Luckily the idiots park close to each other so I can just sneak under one after the other without anyone being the wiser.

Want to hurt a hunter? Destroy their pride and joy—their truck.

They live on the road, so they have no home but their trucks and cars. Yeah, they become an extension of themselves, so not only will this be a distraction, but a kick in the teeth.

I'm not sure how long I spend moving from vehicle to vehicle and planting our little toys, but I barely break a sweat. Once I'm done, I flip to my front under the last car, eyeing the short distance to the building when I see a tripwire. It runs the length of the front door, idiots. Like we are planning to just bust in and say hello.

Leaving it there since it's not important, I start the arduous task of crawling back to the tree line without being spotted. When I get there, Vale and Lucien are already waiting. "How did you do?"

I grin. "All rigged and ready to party."

Vale nods. "Good. I disabled the alarms at the back door as well as the security system."

Lucien grins. "I added some booby traps just in case."

"What about the roof?" Quinn murmurs. "Do they set traps there?"

"No." I snort. "No one is crazy or skilled enough to get up there without being seen."

"Until us." She smirks, and I groan as I rearrange myself, that smug sentence going right to my cock. "Okay, this is the plan—"

We listen and prepare.

It just might fucking work.

I can almost taste the blood in my mouth.

CHAPTER SIXTY-THREE

It's time. We waited hours for the sun to set because unlike us, they can't see in the dark. It leaves them vulnerable and weak. They will be preparing to attack, not waiting for one. That element of surprise will give us the win we need. I'm sure of it.

I turn to Quinn as she nods at me, grab her head, yank her closer, and kiss her hard. She gasps into my mouth before I pull away. "See you inside, beautiful."

"See you there," she rasps, watching me for a moment. I watch her right back before I nod at my brother. With Jai at my side and the fifteen wolves who chose to come with us, I start the task of moving through the trees to get into position at the back door, knowing timing is everything.

I see Quinn moving into position with her wolves and Vale, and we wait.

The moon is high in the sky, and when she gives us the nod, Jai pulls out the detonator.

He grins a mad smile as he mouths, "Boom," and hits the switch.

The first explosion rocks the earth, the flames of a truck reaching higher than the building.

Another one goes off a minute later as we hear the hunters run out front to see what is happening.

Jai winks at me. "There she is."

I turn to see Quinn racing from the cover of trees, and I send a prayer up to the moon.

Let this work.

While the idiots race to the explosions out front, we run to the side of the building. I watch in awe as Quinn flings herself halfway up the side before slamming her claws into the brick and using it to climb. I wait at the bottom as the fifteen wolves with us follow, and only then do I leap after them.

We are on the roof before the last explosion rocks the earth.

We wait for a moment to see if any alarms go off, but when they don't, we move to the skylights, spreading out across the roof. I tilt my head, listening, and the moment I hear the back door being slammed open by Jai and Lucien, I leap at the skylight I stand above.

I crash through the glass, effortlessly falling before landing on my feet on the upper level. Crashes sound all around us as the others follow suit. A hunter who stands at the top of the hallway, staring out the front window to see what's going on, turns.

He's too slow, too human, and the wolf closest to him grabs his throat and snaps his neck before he can so much as utter a word.

"Change," Quinn commands, her voice husky with her alpha power.

The hallway fills with the sounds of snapping bones and growls until, moments later, it's filled with snarling, angry wolves. Quinn winks at me and then changes while she throws herself over the stairway to meet the oncoming hunters, brought up here by the crashes.

I follow suit. I take off as a human and land on a hunter as a wolf, my jaws snapping around his head and crushing it as he screams. I rip it off and turn, seeing Quinn with a heart in her mouth, the hunter frozen before her with his chest ripped open.

She prowls closer, rubbing against me before heading down the stairs, wolves flowing down after us. I quickly catch up, wanting to be at her side to keep her safe, though she is more likely keeping me safe.

Reaching the bottom floor, we see the front door open, with some confused hunters trying to put out the flames, but then we turn when we hear fighting to find more filling the hallway, the basement door ajar.

We meet Lucien, Jai, and the other wolves in the hallway. They are fighting a mass of hunters, trying to push them back and out, but the hunters are so focused, they don't hear us coming up behind them. Their screams fill the air as we attack.

My eyes are splashed with blood, almost blinding me, and I ignore a searing pain in my hind leg as someone stabs me, but I feel them falling as Lucien pushes on, and within minutes, they are all dead, their bodies mutilated.

I turn to the basement and nod at Quinn.

This is where it will become difficult.

They will have heard us coming, so they will be prepared. Any hunters who are down there will shoot to kill, and we are their targets.

CHAPTER SIXTY-FOUR

Quinn

With Vale at my side and Lucien and Jai at our backs, we start down the staircase leading to the basement. The guys already explained that this will be the hunters' last stand, their fortress. It's not going to be easy, but if we clear this and get rid of them, then we are safe.

I hesitate at the bottom of the stairs. Something feels off.

A shot explodes through the plaster above my head, and I duck with a growl. They are shooting at the stairs, so we won't get through without getting hit. I glance at Vale, unsure what to do. I'm fast, but I don't know if I'm that fast.

I crouch down and peek around the corner as quickly as I can, jerking my head back as another shot rings out. There are at least thirty hunters lined up behind overturned tables, their guns aimed at the stairs.

Beyond them is a corridor that travels deeper into the building, leading to their meeting and security rooms, where there could be more.

The truth is, they have us trapped, but so are they.

They have to come out sometime or let their guard down, but waiting gives them time to gather more reinforcements.

I search Vale's eyes for an idea, needing something to break their ranks, when a human hand shoots past me. Blinking, I glance up at Lucien, and he smiles as he holds out a round object and winks at me. "Be ready." He pulls a pin and throws it.

I wait, but there's no explosion. There is, however, a bright flash, and he barks, "Go!"

We surge from the stairs, seeing the hunters ducking and rubbing their eyes, blinded by the flash, and I quickly take in the room for vantage points. They've created a bottleneck, but if we get over their flimsy defences, then we can get behind them.

We do just that, leaping over the tables like a scourge of wolves as they stumble back. Some fire blindly, and there's a wolf's cry, but I cannot spare a glance to see who it is. Pain fills my heart at the idea of losing one of our own.

Instead, I double my efforts, knocking a hunter back with my paws on his chest, digging my claws in. He attempts to bring his gun up, but I knock it away. Snarling, he buries a knife in my side. Ignoring the pain, I bite down on his neck and tear backwards.

Blood gushes across me as I turn to reach the blade, but it's stuck. Ignoring it, I leap at another hunter. He avoids me, grabbing the blade as he whirls around and yanks it free. I cry out.

Lucien is near me, and he hears the noise. Turning with a growl, he shifts, and with more strength than I realised he had, he grips the back of the hunter's neck, lifts him kicking and screaming into the air, and then throws him against the wall. He hits it with a sickening crunch, but Lucien grabs the discarded blade and rushes over, stabbing his chest multiple times. He's so focused on defending me, he doesn't see the hunter moving into the hallway, aiming a gun at him.

I lunge at him, smashing him into the wall as the gun goes off. Jerking my head around, I see Lucien is fine. Snarling in the hunter's face for daring to shoot what is mine, I bite his head clean off.

I growl down at him as I glance back to see my wolves holding their own. Jai has two bodies around him and a hand in his mouth still attached to a human who is punching him with his other fist, trying to get him off. As I watch, he spins rapidly, throwing the human across the room and right into the waiting muzzles of two other wolves.

Vale is backing towards me, dodging blades, so I hurry over to him.

Circling around the back, I split their efforts so they have no choice but to choose between him and me. They chose him because he's bigger. They think he's more of a threat.

They are wrong.

Faster than they can react, I clamp my mouth on one's leg, yanking him down. I rake my nails across his front, gutting him then leaving him there to die a painful death while I leap at the second. He jumps out of the way and right into Vale's mouth. Vale crunches his windpipe, and the hunter drops to the ground.

"Stop!" The human yell has me and Vale whirling around to see a young hunter, barely older than eighteen, wielding a shotgun. It's aimed at a human Lucien, where he was assisting in patching up a hurt wolf. Slowly, Lucien stops his ministrations.

"Lucien, please," the boy cries. Shit, he knows him.

I forget sometimes that these are people they fought beside.

How many people have they killed tonight that they knew?

"Ara, go," Lucien commands.

"You know I can't do that." He raises the gun. "You're one of them. You're a monster. You need to die."

"Ara, you're just a kid. I know you don't want to kill anyone—" The gun goes off, and Lucien ducks.

"Fuck, man, don't make me," the guy cries, aiming at Lucien as he walks towards him.

Lucien grabs the gun and jerks it to the side as it goes off again, and I watch in worried silence as he bends the barrel so it no longer works before he chucks it away.

"Go, Ara, now," Lucien orders and turns to the wolves behind him with a growl. They part, and the kid throws us a look before running through the throng and up the stairs.

Lucien sighs and glances at me. "He's just a kid."

I nod in understanding and look around, seeing all the other hunters are either dead or dying. Turning back to the hall, I prowl down it, only for Jai to throw me into a wall, stopping me. Growling, I nip at his side, and he nips back, jerking his muzzle down to an almost invisible wire I didn't see before.

A trap.

Fucking hunters.

Vale steps over it and makes sure everyone else does as well, then we proceed more carefully, our eyes peeled for traps, just as the lights go out. A emergency light turns on, bathing everything in shadows and bright red light.

Red, the colour of their blood splashed upon the walls. Red, the colour of my soul when I fill it with their deaths for what they did to my people.

They had no mercy. They had no rules when they killed my people.

Neither will I.

The corridor ends all too soon. All the doors are shut, and I smell nothing inside, so I don't even think to check. Too late, I realise my mistake when the doors open and hunters pour out.

Their smells are masked by herbs and magic, and they attack us from both sides.

Wolves cry out in pain as blades and bullets cut through their bodies, and I roar, leaping into the fray as we turn to attack them. They use the doors as shields, popping in and out, so I fling my body at one, knocking it off its hinges, and Jai surges into the room. Hunters' screams ring out, making me grin as I see Lucien and Vale doing the same.

The madness subsides, and our wolves regroup, seeing what we are doing and copying. I have to jump over a fallen wolf's body, and grief chokes me for a moment before I lunge into a room. It looks like what used to be a classroom, and there are two hunters reloading their guns.

Before they can finish and kill more of my people, I leap onto a desk and then onto them, clawing through one while I rip the other's throat out, watching blood spray over the forgotten whiteboard. Turning, I hurry back, grab a gun, and run into the corridor.

I might be a wolf, but Vale spent three hours showing me how to work one last night, so I take aim. I miss the first time. Blowing out a breath, I pull the trigger over and over, careful not to hit any wolves. I hit arms and chests, knocking hunters back to allow my wolves time to get to them without being shot. When I fire and one's head explodes, I blink but keep shooting.

No wonder hunters love guns so much. It's death in my hands.

Once the gun clicks empty, I toss it at a hunter coming towards me. It smashes into his face, bursting his nose as he yells, and then I throw my human body at him, riding him to the floor as my hands change to claws and I hit him with them. His head jerks to the side with each slash as blood flows across the floor and walls, and when he stops moving below me, I stand, my claws dripping with blood.

I watch a hunter drag his human nails across the floor with a scream as Vale jerks him backwards into a room, and his screams suddenly cut off into a gurgle. Stepping over the bodies, I head back to the room at the end of the death-trap corridor.

It's a huge room with chairs spaced out before a stage, which has a board and maps across it. There is a table of forged weapons and traps hanging from the ceiling. I see a door to the left, which is the security room if I remember correctly.

At the back of the room is Tetrim. He's in a cage, in human form, his eyes wide with anger and shock. "Quinn," he whispers.

"Traitor," I hiss, my nostrils flaring. "I'll deal with you later." I point a clawed hand at him as I spin and slice through the neck of a hunter trying to sneak up on me. I look back at the room, counting four hunters in here.

They are terrified but determined as they clutch their weapons. They stand near the cage, and in their eyes, I see the truth.

They know they are going to die.

Lucien, Vale, and Jai step up to my sides, and I bury my fingers into their fur as I smirk at the hunters. "Drop the guns and I won't make it hurt too much," I promise.

"Come closer and he's dead." One points his gun at Tetrim, whose mouth drops open.

"I'm on your side! I helped you!" he roars at the hunters.

"Kill him. You'll be doing him a favour because when I kill him, I am going to rip him limb from limb until he chokes on his own blood and pain," I purr as I nudge Lucien and Jai. They stalk into the room, Vale in the middle. The hunters swing their guns back and forth, unsure whom to aim at, and I snarl.

"Aim at me," I tell them. "Are you aiming at my mates?"

"They were hunters!" a big, scarred man snaps.

"And now they are mine," I purr. "But don't worry, I won't turn you. I'll rip out your heart and bathe in your blood."

He swallows, swinging his gun up to me, and my mates snarl in unison, their hackles rising.

"They didn't like that." I chuckle as I step farther into the room. "I think—"

I jerk with the force of the bullet as it hits me but quickly straighten, my eyes going to the hole in my side. I dig my claw into the wound, hissing as I fish out the bullet and drop it to the floor. The hole quickly heals, and he swears, firing twice more. One hits my arm, the other my shoulder. Laughing, I dig out the bullets and drop them, wiping away the blood to show the healed wounds.

"Hunter, I am a creature of moonlight. I am a beast, the monster you fear. Your bullets cannot kill me, but just for that, I'll make it hurt." I smile evilly. "Boys, make it hurt."

More wolves slink to my side as Lucien, Vale, and Jai leap at the hunters.

Their screams fill the air as my mates rip them apart while they are still alive for daring to hurt me.

I head straight to the cage. "You betrayed our pack, our people," I murmur, staring into his familiar eyes. No matter your differences, you do not betray family. "I knew you were a fool, but not how much. Because of you, our people are dead. Our alpha is dead."

He jerks at that, shocked.

"My father is dead," I yell into his face. "Why?"

"For you," he whispers. "It was always supposed to be you and me. I thought if I could get rid of those hunters and show you who I was, you would accept me. I didn't expect them to go so overboard."

"You fucking fool. Your own hate blinded you." I grip the bars. "I told them I would make it hurt, and I meant it. I will leave you here, surrounded by bodies, and you will either starve or go mad. Maybe even more hunters will find you, but you will be alone, remembering all the death you caused until your wolf is gone."

I turn away and walk down the hallway.

The hunters are dead.

It is done.

We won.

"Quinn, you can't leave me here!" he bellows. "I did it for you!"

I sneer as the wolves part for me.

"Quinn, please! Please, we are pack!"

My wolf bays, wanting his head, but I resist, knowing this is torture for him. To be left alone to go mad, cut off from a pack? His wolf will eat him from the inside out until he's begging for death.

I head upstairs, ready to double-check that the building is empty, but there is no noise bar my wolves following me.

The hunters are dead.

It's a promise, a massacre, to warn any who may come after us wolves. It's not enough, but it will have to do. I cannot hunt down every single hunter. I have a pack to run.

I turn to my wolves, smiling. "We did it! It's over!"

A howl of celebration goes up as I grin, knowing Jang is looking down on me with pride.

CHAPTER SIXTY-FIVE

The squeal of tires cuts our celebration short as we peer through the open front doors in time to see trucks full of hunters heading our way. A coughing laugh comes from behind us from a dying man.

"We were just buying time," the hunter sputters. "You're all fucked now."

With a snarl, Lucien smashes his foot into the man's face, crushing his skull and silencing him right before bullets cut through the air. Jai grabs Quinn, throwing her into the stairs where the concrete protects us.

I quickly roll into the open doorway with Lucien. Others rush backwards, but they get hit, their wolf bodies jerking from the force of the machine gun tearing them apart. Their pained howls make my wolf cry in agony.

We hide until the bullets stop, the sound of truck doors banging open loud as I peer at Quinn where she crouches in human form. She nods to let me know she's okay, and I breathe a little easier as I look around.

There's a whole fucking army out there, and at the front is the one man you never want to see.

Sergeant Black.

His mouth is cut into a sinister smile from a witch's blade, and he has more scars than any hunter alive, as well as more kills under his belt too. I've only met him once. He runs the entire northeast hunters guild, and he's a killer through and through. A fucking psychopath.

They called him in, and now we are all fucked.

"We know you are in there. We also know you don't have enough wolves to take us. You have two options—run with your tails tucked through the back door and maybe those who are fast enough will escape, or fight and die," he calls as their vehicles' headlights flood the parking lot. "You did a good job so far. I'm proud of how I trained my hunters, even if you are traitors, but it ends here, tonight."

"Vale?" Quinn looks at me, glancing at the back door. "They'll just hunt us forever, won't they?"

I nod, knowing she's right. They won't let us get away. They can't.

For a moment, her expression collapses, all hope fleeing before she rolls her shoulders back and blows out a breath. "Then so fucking be it. Tonight's as good a night as any to die." She looks at the wolves still left standing. "Anyone who wants to take that out, head through the back door now. Don't go directly to the pack because they will track you. If you want, you can stay and fight with us. I won't demand it since you have already given so much, and I cannot ask for more, but I also can't think of a better group of people to die with. It has been an honour to serve you, to lead you, and to fight at your sides, and know we will meet again in the next life."

My heart breaks, my soul screaming. I cannot lose Quinn. She deserves to live. She deserves a future. She deserves to lead her pack and find happiness. She deserves the things she wanted, they all wanted, before we brought this war to them, but we have no choice.

We are trapped, and we are going to die. At least we'll die together so I won't have to live a second without her.

She looks at me, licking her lips. "I'm sorry we didn't get forever, but you have loved me more than most get in a lifetime." She looks at Jai. "All of you, and I am honoured to have found you." She glances at Lucien. "Even if it was just for a little bit, know that I'm honoured to have been loved by you and to love you. However this ends, they cannot take that away. Fill your hearts with love, not hate, and let us go out the way we came into this world—flame and pain."

She stands. "We are coming out!" she calls.

"Is that the wolf I have heard so much about?" Black calls with a chuckle. "I've got to say, I saw the camera footage of you taking out all my men at the warehouse. You're good, but you're not good enough for all of us. However, I appreciate your bravery. I will make your death quick, I promise, to honour your courage."

Men troop towards the entrance to escort us to our deaths, but I see something happen before it actually does and almost laugh.

The idiots don't know about the tripwire, and I watch as the first line of their defence falls, grateful Jai didn't disarm it.

"Well, that took out some." Quinn changes and lunges into the chaos.

We chase after her, following her to certain death just like I always knew we would, but like she said, I'm not scared of dying, not after getting to love her. It is just another beginning for us.

"Don't waste your bullets. Kill them with your blades and make it hurt. They were leading us into a trap," Black orders as he steps back.

Snarling, I dive at them, but these are Black's elite hunters. They move faster than most humans, better too. It almost makes it impossible to catch them, and their blades sink into my sides.

I hear wolves screaming in agony and know we are losing.

The moon turns red with our blood, and I glance over at my mate, knowing it will be the last time I see her.

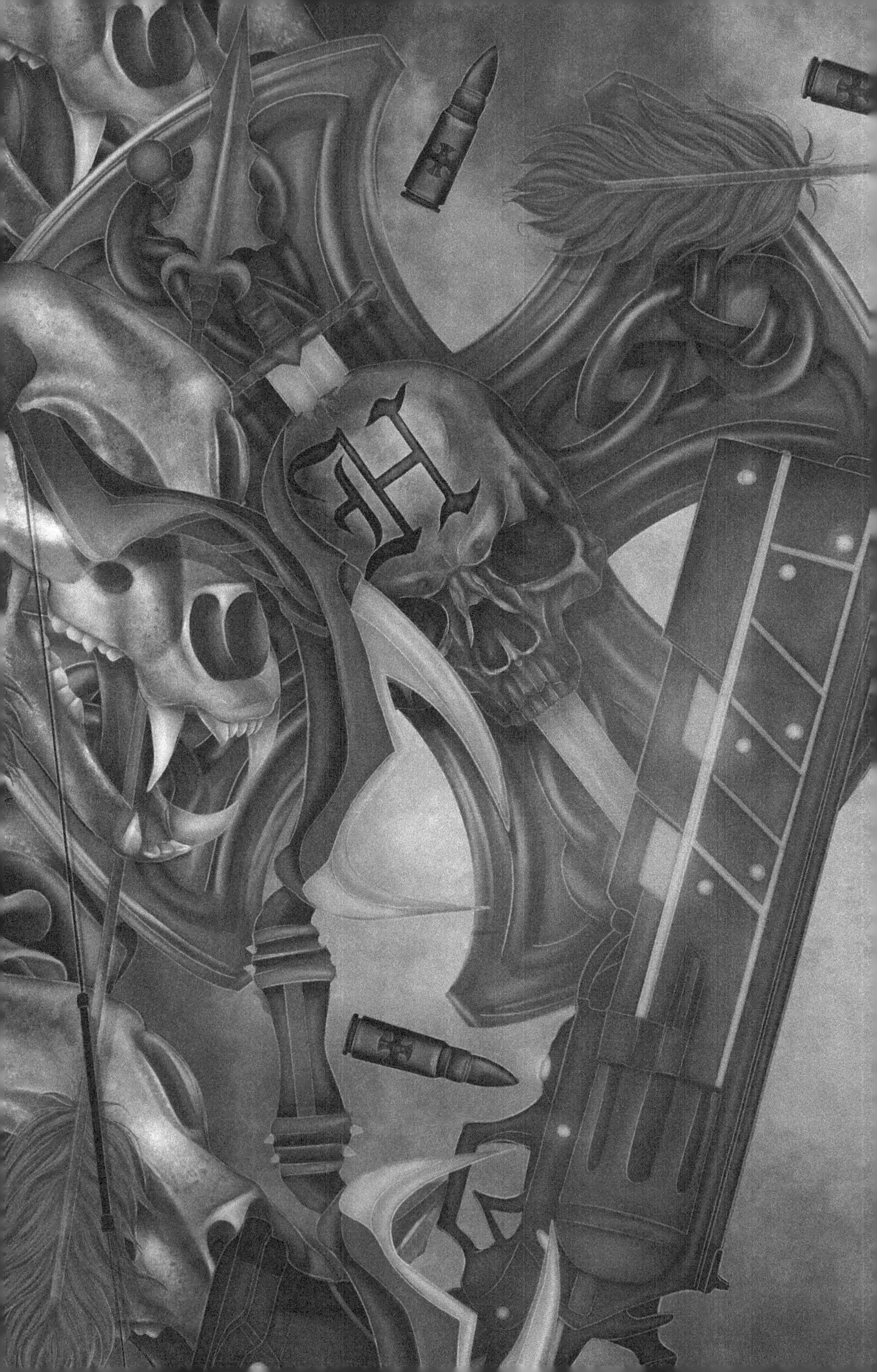

CHAPTER SIXTY-SIX

I roar in agony as a blade sinks into my back leg, rendering it useless as whatever poison they use spreads through my body, but I continue to fight at Quinn's side, trying to hold them back. All the wolves followed us, and so many have already died.

The bright lights of the trucks are only outshone by the brilliant red moon shining ominously above us—a sign of impending death.

Our deaths.

I will fight until they steal the last breath from my lungs, and the last thing I'll see will be my mate. My destiny was always leading me to her.

I should be scared to die, but I'm not—not when she's at my side because I know we will be together in this life and the next. Our love cannot be stolen by death. It is eternal. It will live on even when our bodies won't.

I didn't even believe in love until her.

We were enemies, but in the end, we are lovers.

There's a scream that makes my heart ache, and Quinn stumbles back with a blade in her chest. I leap at the hunter attacking her, knocking him away as I block Quinn, taking the blows meant for her.

Jai screams, and I glance over to see him in his human form with a needle in his neck. In horror, I watch as a hunter grabs each arm and breaks them. He falls back, roaring as they stomp on both of his legs, and even from here, I hear them snap.

My eyes find my brother who is looking at Quinn, even as a blade heads for him.

She is the last thing he wants to see.

I scream as another blade sinks into me, my eyes going to Quinn to see her in human form too. As I watch on in pained horror, she tugs the blade from her chest and tosses it away, her hands falling to the cement where she sprawls.

She's dying.

We all are.

Goddess, do not let her suffer. Make it last forever for me if need be, but do not let Quinn suffer.

JAI

I roll to my side as the hunters move away. Knowing I will be dead soon, they attack other wolves, leaving me broken on the stained concrete. Wolfsbane runs through my system, meaning I can't change back or heal.

I'm human. I'll die like I began.

My eyes find Quinn, and horror and heartbreak fill me.

My beautiful, strong Quinn.

She lies on her back in the middle of it all, hardly moving.

Blood bubbles on her lips as she coughs, her eyes blinking rapidly at the sky before she turns her head to meet my gaze. A sad smile curls her bloodied lips as she looks away from the hunter coming up behind her, their blade raised, ready to end her life.

I'm dying, yet I turn my head to keep her in view.

Groaning, I flip to my side and grit my teeth against the agony as I crawl to her.

I drag myself using everything left inside me, despite the pure torture it pours into my body. My body shakes as it shuts down, wanting to quit, but I force it to keep going, my eyes on her. I throw myself over her just as the blade comes down, piercing my body.

Her eyes widen below me, my name a rasp on her lips.

"I love you," I mumble, knowing it will be the last thing I say.

I love her enough to die for her, to take the blade meant for her.

Coldness spreads through my body, and I blink to keep my eyes open and locked on her until my last breath. I don't want to see anything else as she cries beneath me. Her hands cup my cheeks, but I cannot feel it.

"I love you."

I think I say it, but I don't know.

As I slip away from this life, her roar of anguish follows me.

I'm sorry, Quinn.

CHAPTER SIXTY-SEVEN

I stare up into Jai's eyes, and my heart breaks.

He's dying, maybe even dead, and I cannot feel anything beyond the numbing grief as my wolf screams. My soul darkens, and I lose pieces of myself until it feels like I'm being torn apart from the inside out.

Beyond him, I hear Lucien and Vale crying out and know they are dying too.

I'm losing them to the evil of this world, to the hunters who stole my home and family time and time again. They will not take everything from me again.

Despite my body dying, my soul fills with a rage born from my ancestors who were hunted for simply being alive, my parents who lost their child and then their lives, and my father who sacrificed everything.

Hate fills me with rage.

It builds so much, I cannot control it anymore.

It is an anger formed throughout the centuries from all persecuted monsters and hunted beasts.

Their souls bind with mine for one moment, filling me until my dying body cannot hold it anymore.

It explodes out of me, a scream filled with centuries of pain and suffering. It echoes into the night, and I feel it reaching into the deepest, darkest recesses of the world, touching creatures like me.

I feel their pain.

I see it.

My cry echoes it, and when I slump, a new energy fills me, one I know will leave soon, so I sit up, catching Jai and laying him down. I place a kiss on his unmoving lips, knowing if I focus on him, I will simply die next to him.

Climbing to my feet, I meet Black's eyes. "Pull back," he roars as his hunters race to his side. I don't know what he saw or felt, but for the first time tonight, he looks scared.

Terrified, actually.

"What are you?" he asks.

"Me? I am just a beast, just like those." I nod at the forest, guided by a deeper power, and together, we turn and watch as beasts pour from the darkened depths, called forth by my pain and anger. They surge into the clearing with their own battle cries.

Feral wolves.

Pixies.

Vampyrs.

Witches.

Ancient, wild creatures.

A huge, lumbering shadow of darkness that I have never felt nor seen before.

They rally and leap at the hunters with their own war cries, coming to avenge, defend, and save.

The hunters don't stand a chance. My gaze sweeps over the mismatched beasts, my eyes catching on the one who seems to be made of darkness and shadows. When I meet its bright red eyes, they are dead.

Ignoring the death magic within it since it answered my call, I focus on Black.

For a moment, I begin to look for Vale and Lucien, but my heart knows if they are lost, then I will simply collapse. Instead, I move over to the now terrified hunter. He turns to me.

"You did this," he hisses. "It dies with you."

I dodge the first bullet, then the next, until I stand before him, and then I smash my fist into his face. He falls back with a shout, his gun clattering across the ground as pixies giggle, yanking at his hair and face, leaving scratches across him as he screams.

"Enough, this one is mine," I order.

A small female pixie turns to me, her multicoloured hair shining brightly. "As you wish, moon child. There is enough flesh to go around." With a bell-like noise, she flies into the air, her horde following to eat and attack other hunters.

Black is bleeding as he clambers to his knees, panting as he glares up at me.

I stop before him, pinching his chin as I tilt his head farther back.

"You are right. We are monsters and beasts, so fucking what?" I sneer. "These beasts? We are going to rule this world, and nobody will remember you." Without further fanfare, I slice across his neck, stepping back to watch him choke on his own blood.

He deserved a slower, more painful death, but exhaustion is starting to kick in as whatever power kept me upright flees. I watch the beasts finish off the rest of the hunters before they wander back into the forest without a word.

"Thank you," I whisper after them, begging the earth to carry it to them.

Turning, I find Vale and Lucien at Jai's side, and I fall to my knees, my strings cut. Bleeding and hurt, I crawl to him like he crawled to me, and once there, I lift him into my arms, pressing my lips to his cold forehead.

"Wake up," I demand, infusing the words with whatever power I have left.

My tears blind me as I rock him in my arms.

"Quinn, he's dead," Vale whispers, his voice choked.

"Baby." Lucien reaches for me, but I jerk away, holding Jai in my arms.

He's dead. He's dead.

Jai is dead.

He's gone. I feel it. I feel his empty shell of a body. I push my magic into him to try and heal him, but it's too late. They are right.

He's dead.

His soul is gone.

My mate is dead.

My head drops back, and I roar with grief.

All of the energy that kept me alive up to this point leaves me.

My soul and heart are gone with my mate, my father, my mother, and my sister.

With all the loss I have faced over my life, I finally break.

We have won, but at what cost?

CHAPTER SIXTY-EIGHT

Recently, I carried my father back to my pack for burial. Now, I carry my mate. He's heavy in my arms, but I refuse to let Lucien or Vale hold him. Instead, they help carry our other dead. We lost fifteen wolves.

Fifteen souls including Jai.

Some were so badly hurt, we had to steal the hunters' trucks to transport them back. Only four, including us, are left fully standing.

I hold Jai on my lap the entire way home, and when we drive the farthest we can, I walk with him even though I'm nothing but an empty shell.

I keep walking.

One foot.

Left.

Another foot.

Right.

Again.

Left.

Right.

Left.

Right.

I keep going, the rhythm holding me together until we reach pack land. Still, I do not stop. I see wolves run towards us, reaching for their family members, gone or alive, and screams fill the air. The sounds are filled with so much horror and grief, I start to crack again before I push it all down.

Left.

Right.

"Quinn?"

Marie.

A hand reaches for me, but I avoid it.

"He needs to go home," I mumble.

"Okay, baby girl, it's okay. Let's get him home," the familiar female voice whispers at my side, and something about it makes me want to cry.

"Quinn, would you like me to take him?" Another familiar voice —White.

"Or I can," Con offers.

"Don't, she won't let him go. It seems to be the only thing keeping her upright," Vale mumbles.

"She's hurt," Marie whispers.

"Let's get him home, okay, my love?" Lucien mumbles at my side.

I nod jerkily.

Left.

Right.

I feel people at my sides, at my back, all waiting for me to crumble, ready to catch me. They walk in silence, mourning with me as I head through the trees towards our cottage on the lake. Once there, I sink down to the shore, still holding him in my shaking arms.

"It was a moon like this one when you told me you love me. Do you remember that?" I murmur to him, looking down. I brush his hair from his eyes, expecting his mismatched orbs to open.

They do not.

He's silent, like the grave.

"It was a moon like this one when you made me whole once more." I nod, lifting my eyes to the water. "It's fitting that it is a moon like this when you break me."

"Quinn." A hand grips my shoulder. "Please, we need to check your wounds, and Jai—we need to lay our brother to rest."

"No." I clutch him closer. "He'll be lonely. He hates being alone. It reminds him of his childhood."

"Okay, baby," Lucien says. He's bleeding all over me but doesn't seem to notice. "We won't leave him alone, okay?"

There's agreement behind me. "We won't, Quinn. We will stay with him the entire time, but he would want you to get your wounds checked, okay?"

White.

I nod, though I don't know how I find the strength to.

Slowly, Con extracts Jai from my arms, and when they are empty, I gasp and reach for him. "No, no, please, please don't take him."

"Baby." Vale wraps his arms around me, stopping me from attacking Con or hurting myself. "He's already gone. He's already gone."

"No." I sink into the ground. "No."

Something wet hits my chest—tears, I realise, as I watch Con, Dom, and White carefully carry Jai away.

There are so many wolves here—I don't know how I didn't hear them—and they all sink to their knees in respect, bowing their heads as he passes, and that is the last drop in the bucket.

It destroys me.

My hands sink into the earth as I scream, the sobs rattling my chest until I can't breathe.

Wetness touches my skin and hair as arms hold me—two sets, brothers.

We are missing our fourth. There is a hole where he should be, and that makes me spiral more.

I scream and cry.

"Baby, please, you're going to hurt yourself," a choked voice commands, but I cannot stop.

My vision fills with dots, blackening at the edges as I sob and scream.

Marie drops to her knees before me, her hands cupping my cheeks. "I know, my daughter. I know. It's so dark, empty, and painful that you think it would be easier to give in, but don't you fucking dare. He wouldn't want that. He would hate that. You have to be strong. You owe that to him, as well as your other mates. They need you. We need you."

"It hurts." I whimper.

Tears flow down her cheeks as her lips tremble. I blink my wet lashes, trying to bring her into view, but everything is wrong. "I know, baby. I know. Let it hurt. Let it hurt."

"Mummy," I sob. "Make it stop."

She covers her mouth for a moment. "I wish I could, baby. I wish I could. It's not fair that you didn't get any time with him and I got a lifetime. I wish I could, baby. I would do anything to bring him back for you. I would."

There is nothing anyone can do or say.

Jai is gone, and my soul and heart went with him.

I am just an empty vessel.

She wraps me in her arms. They should be warm, but the embrace feels cold and empty like my cracked chest.

I fall into the darkness with open arms, wanting it to stop.

In the darkness, I know I will see him again.

CHAPTER SIXTY-NINE

I don't know how long I sleep for. It feels like years, yet when I wake, I don't feel rested. I feel empty, cold, and tired.

My men are at my side, sleeping as well but restlessly, and when my eyes roll to the empty spot in the bed, pain cracks through me. I scramble upright, trying to stop it. My eyes drop to my body. I'm healed, but there is a jagged scar down my chest from the blade.

Good.

It should scar.

His death should scar.

I climb from the bed, knowing they are hurting too and worried about me, but I need time. I need to be alone. I dress quickly and head towards the pack before changing my mind. I cannot deal with questions or pity right now, or even blame from those who lost loved ones.

My house is filled with flowers and food, so maybe they don't blame me. Maybe that's my own guilt.

I sneak through the trees to the house I know holds my mate's body.

At the door, standing sentry, are Dom and Con. Their expressions soften when they see me, and they open the door. White stands at Jai's side. They aren't leaving him alone, just as they promised. I swallow, knowing I need to say something, but words don't come easily right now.

"Thank you," is all I can manage to rasp out.

"Of course." White nods. "We will give you a moment."

My eyes go to Jai, and I step back. "No, no, that's—no." I turn away, unable to look at his empty corpse. It is just too real, too cold, and devoid of the madness that makes him Jai. I cannot stand it.

I don't know how or why, but I find myself before the trucks we drove here last night. The seats are stained with blood, but I don't care as I climb in and drive away, needing space.

Even as I put miles between myself and my pack, it doesn't make me feel whole. I just feel even more alone.

I wonder if I will ever feel okay again.

I don't remember making the decision to come here, but I find myself back at the hunters' HQ. In the late afternoon light, the bodies and blood are stark. I wonder if the humans will find this when it starts to smell or if the hunters will take care of it.

I wander through the battlefield, remembering every horrible second.

I stand above a puddle of dried blood, and I know it's his.

Turning away, I head inside, down through broken doors, and over more bodies, then I find myself in the back room. Tetrim sits up in his cage, but I turn away. I am not here for him, and I do not need his vitriol right now. The closed door catches my eye, and with nothing better to do, I kick it in.

Maybe Tetrim senses something is wrong, or maybe he's given up, but he just watches me without speaking. The door splinters, and I find computer banks and monitors. Cocking my head, I step inside. I've never been great with technology, maybe it's the wilderness in me, but I know enough.

I scan through the laptop before I find what I need, what I didn't even know I was looking for, and I hit record.

"Last night, my pack and I killed every hunter in this area. We didn't do it unprovoked. Hunters came into my home. They burnt my family alive. They chopped my father's head off before my eyes. They killed so many, the blood cannot be washed away, even today. They also went after children, innocents who had never done anything wrong. Along with this email, which I am sending to every hunter whose email address is in this laptop, I will attach the videos I have found that show their crimes—not just to wolves, but to every beast, as you call us. You are hunters. You vowed to protect human life and innocents, but you are just using it to cover your sick tendencies, like rape and torture. You aren't soldiers, you are serial killers, and this is your warning. We will rise. We will not accept this anymore. Every monster will be made aware. You have two choices—die for your crimes or clean house. Stop the madness. Kill those who hurt innocents, not those who are innocents. I know from my mates, who were hunters, that you did not start this to be evil, but to help, so do that. Help. If you don't, if this doesn't stop, mark my words—I will hunt every single one of you down and rip out your hearts." I hit end and attach the videos before pressing send, then I turn away and depart once more, leaving Tetrim screaming my name.

***

The moon is high.

I avoided my other mates all day, knowing if I met their eyes, I would break. Jai sits upon the same stone that my father did a few nights before.

I cannot look at him. Instead, I look out at those gathered, knowing they are expecting me to lead, but how can I when I don't even have the energy to speak?

Jai deserves my words though. He deserves so much more.

"Jai was a feral. He thought he had no family, but he was wrong. He had us. We are his family." I lick my lips as more tears fall. "I always thought I had to do everything alone to be strong, to prove myself to you, but he didn't care. He barged into my life and stole my heart and soul. He made them his own, all while handing me his. He didn't believe he should be loved, but I loved him with every fibre of my being, and now he is gone and so is the love he brought into my life. I have lost everyone." I turn, falling to my knees. "I have lost everyone."

I look to the moon. "Please, please, I cannot live like this. I have won your war. I have followed you and served you tirelessly. Why are you doing this to me?"

I bow my head as I cry, and for once, I do not take solace in the moon.

I shun it.

I reject it.

CHAPTER SEVENTY

Death is strange. I was expecting, well, I don't really know—something. There is just darkness that I'm floating in. I can't feel my body or really think. I just float.

There is no pain.

There are no regrets or grief.

No love.

There is just darkness.

I don't know why that unsettles me, but before I can analyse it, that uneasiness is gone as well, washed clean by the darkness. I just exist in nothingness.

Suddenly, I have a very real body, and I am falling through the darkness. All that numbness is stripped away and fear, terror, and pain is all I know as I scream and try to stop my descent. The darkness parts, replaced by bright moonlight as I land heavily on a huge pile of leaves. Groaning, I roll to the side to see what's happening, and the leaves move with me, causing me to slide down the side with a surprised yelp.

The grassy ground races up to me, and when my feet hit it, I expect my legs to snap, but I just stop and stand, and when I glance back, the leaves are gone.

What the fuck?

Glancing around in confusion, I see some of the most beautiful landscape I have ever seen in my life, bar Quinn's pack—

Quinn.

Agony tears through my heart, and I gasp as I spin around, searching for her. If she's here, does that mean she's dead?

If not, is she alive?

"Breathe, my child." The feminine voice seems to reach deep inside me, loosening the constrictive vice around my heart and lungs, and I can breathe normally, the panic receding. "It is only you and me here."

Quinn . . . She's not dead, which means she's alive.

That's good, really good.

It means my death was worth something and for once, I didn't fuck up. It means my love lives on, even if I'm not there, and I know my brothers will love her enough for us all.

"I'm dead?" I ask to confirm, but I have to be sure. That's the only thing that explains this darkness and weird world, not to mention I remember taking my last breath, staring up into Quinn's watery eyes as she sobbed for me.

"You are," she answers, her voice echoing around me.

"And this is the afterlife?" I ask calmly.

Glancing around once more, I soak in the beautiful scenery. Rolling hills stretch as far as the eye can see, with wild wolves rolling across them and deer playing alongside them. Bunnies hop through the underbrush, while butterflies dance in the sky alongside glowing bugs. The moon is bright and so big, it touches the land in the distance. On either side of us, huge, ancient trees stretch into the sky. Some leaves are amber-coloured, some are covered in snow, some are bright green, and others have flowers on them.

It's as if all the seasons exist, but always at night under the moon.

"Not really," the voice calls again. "This is my land. I simply brought you here, the will of a god, you see. Plus, the god of death owed me a favour. I built his mate a garden sanctuary for their upcoming anniversary."

Frowning, I glance around with furrowed brows, trying to find the person behind the voice.

"Oh, forgive me. I forget how three-dimensional you Earth dwellers are." She chuckles, and my eyes cut to the woods as the trees bend and a woman walks from their midst.

Her feet are bare, her golden hair is unbound, and she is in nothing but a translucent white dress. She glows, as if the moon is trapped within her skin. She has bright white eyes, and although she doesn't possess irises, I can tell her gaze is locked on me. She is almost ten feet tall as well.

She peers down at me with a soft smile. "I'm sure you have questions, Jai."

"Why are you so tall?" It blurts out of me, and she throws her head back on a laugh.

It's musical, but it doesn't have the husky quality of my Quinn's.

"That is your question?" She grins as she looks at me. She waves her hand and suddenly, she is a similar size to me and we are sitting in a courtyard that appeared around us in the middle of the rolling hills.

She perches on a bench, and I force myself to sit on one opposite her, not wanting to offend whoever this mystical woman is.

"It was the first thing that came to mind," I admit sheepishly.

She grins wider. "I can see why my daughter likes you."

"Daughter?" I frown.

"My Quinn." She tilts her head.

"Erm, Quinn is your daughter?" I ask, confused.

"In a way, all the moon children are, but I blessed Quinn myself with some of my powers, knowing she would need them. That means I have a special interest in her life, and you, well, you interested me."

"Lucky me," I mutter.

It becomes very hard to breathe, and I find myself on my knees as she grows before me, glowing so bright it burns my eyes. "You will watch your tone, wolf. I am your creator. I am your god, and you are just a lost soul." She's smaller again and sitting down, smiling like nothing happened, and I'm left gasping, which is strange since I'm dead.

"Sorry." I cough. "No offense meant."

"Yes, you did, but that is okay. You have been testing limits your whole life, so I would be disappointed if you did not push mine. Yes, I see why my Quinn likes you. You are fearless, bordering on madness, even when faced with a god."

"Most just call me crazy." I shrug. "If you watch our lives, then you saw everything that happened. Why didn't you stop it?" I frown.

"It is not our duty to interrupt or change events. Everything happens for a reason, Jai, even the bad things."

"No, some shit just happens and there's no reason behind it—my family dying, Quinn's father's death. Bad shit happens and there is no reason," I snap.

She nods sadly. "Even gods have limits," she admits. "Sometimes, even when I want to, I cannot interfere. Just like you, my hands are tied."

"So why bring me here?" I ask, growing angry as I pace. "For a little chitchat? To measure up the man who loved your daughter?"

She sighs once more. "I will allow your anger since it's understandable—"

"Fucking thanks," I mutter.

"But do not make the mistake of aiming it at me, wolf. I brought you into this world, and I can end you just as well," she warns.

"I'm already dead!" I shout, turning to face her, and then I slump. "I'm dead, and she's alone. My brothers are alone when they need me most."

"You worry for them, not for yourself," she murmurs, watching me.

"Why worry for me? It's them I should worry about. They are alive and alone and probably angry and scared. Quinn has lost so much." My shoulders slump. "Is she okay?"

"She is hurting, but she is not alone," the god offers. "You have given a lot in your short life, Jai, to lead you here."

"I also made some terrible decisions. I wasn't a good person," I admit.

"But you have the power to be," she replies. "You already started to. Quinn healed you—not just your wolf, but your heart too. She took your hate away and offered understanding. She blurred the line between hunter and wolf. She did what was never done before. She loved without limits or restrictions, and that is the best type of love. Destinies are tricky business, but even I did not see you three coming. You changed everything for the better. I couldn't have done this in a million lifetimes, even if I wanted to. I'm tired, Jai, of watching my children be slaughtered simply for being blessed. I am so very tired."

"What are you saying?" I ask, beyond confused.

"We gods offer choices. Quinn is blessed, and that world needs her and the change she represents. It needs her steel backbone and soft heart, but she needs you. She is lost. Part of her is missing, the part that makes her so easy to love and follow. Even the strongest need someone to lean on every now and again, I'm beginning to understand. I have seen it myself, a revolution of love changing even the gods. Quinn's soul is splintered, and I do not like that. She needs to be whole for what is to come for her, so she may rise to the station I have chosen for her—to lead and keep our people safe. I am offering you a choice, warrior, for someone who has given so much in the name of love. You can go back. I will send you to be with her, at her side for eternity, but there must be a sacrifice. Death demands payment, and not even I can change that."

"Anything," I offer without hesitation before swallowing. "As long as the price is paid through me and nobody else."

"Even if it means your life? Think carefully," she cautions.

"I will not make the payment on behalf of anyone else." I nod. "I pay it or not at all."

"Then you are exactly the man I thought you were. Redemption, Jai, and second chances are so hard to come by, but you deserve one. No one else will pay, but you will. I will take your wolf from you. You will walk by her side, and you will be her human. She loved you as such before, and she will again, but you will never be one of us. When the time comes and you join us once more, you will be reunited with the beast inside."

I grip my chest. Even now, I can feel my wolf. He has been with me since my parents died, so in a way, he was my constant even when I didn't know he was there. I just found him, just freed him and found my place, but it means nothing without her.

"Yes." I nod, even as it pains me. "Take my wolf, just send me back to her. Even if I am half the man I was before, please just let me be there to love her."

"As you wish, warrior." She stands. "Brace yourself, for this will hurt. It will tear your soul into pieces."

I try to, I really do, but nothing could have prepared me for the agony of when she presses her clawed hand to my chest and digs, clawing into my soul and dragging out my wolf. My screams echo across her lands, my back bowing as I roar.

My wolf fights for purchase, tearing me apart as I feel my soul rip in two, and then she lifts her hand away, and floating in a glowing ball in her palm is my wolf.

"Sleep now, warrior," she commands.

The last thing I remember seeing through bleary eyes is her glowing finger pressing to the middle of my forehead.

I fall backwards and wake with a jerk.

My body is cold, and my eyes hurt as they open to see the moon, but this time, it's farther away. The air smells fresh, like it just rained, and sobbing reaches my ears.

For a moment, my body is just . . . quiet. I don't feel whole, and it is obvious my wolf is missing, as if there is a gap in my soul where he belongs, but the crying has me sitting up when I realise I am on the stone bench. I swing my legs out from under the tapestry that covers me, peering down at Quinn where she kneels.

My brothers kneel at her back, one hand on either shoulder, their faces also streaked with tears.

Stumbling from the stone, I drop on my knees before them. "Baby?" I croak.

Her head snaps up, her eyes widening as she stares at me. Those bright orbs glow with such pain, and tears stain her cheeks in a way I never want to see again.

Reaching for her, I cup her cheek, letting her warmth infuse me and bring me back to life. "Shh, baby, I'm here. I'm here, Quinn."

"No. How?" She falls back, staring at me in horror. "Is this a dream?"

"Dream of me often, do you?" I tease.

"Jai, is that really you?" Vale asks, staring at me in shock.

"You died. We saw you die. We held your body," Lucien whispers.

I nod. My eyes are only for my Quinn though, and I hope she will love me even though I'm human. I will never be able to run with her again, never be able to change to protect her, but if she lets me, I will stand at her side until our time is up. I will do anything for her.

"Quinn?" I murmur as she gapes.

"You're dead. I felt you die. I saw it."

"I did, and you did. The goddess offered me a deal," I admit.

"Goddess blessed," someone gasps, but I ignore them, my focus on her. I don't even know if her pack will let me stay, but if my girl has anything to do with it, they won't have a choice. She never was good at listening to others.

"I said yes so I could come back to you." She continues to stare at me, and I start to panic. "Quinn, say something, please."

She cries, flinging herself at me, and we tumble to the ground, her lips pressing to every inch of me she can reach. "You're real. You're alive! I felt you die. I felt you leave me, you bastard. Don't ever do that again." Her loving hands turn into punishing ones as she pounds me with her fists.

Groaning, I capture them, kissing her knuckles as she lifts up, kneeling over me. "Gentle, baby, I'm human."

"What do you mean?" she asks, staring down at me.

"She took my wolf, and I got you." Her eyes widen in horror. "It was a deal I made without hesitation, Quinn." I reach up, caressing her jaw. "I would have given much more to see you again, even for a moment, but I get you for a lifetime now. Wolf or not, that completes me. As long as I have you, it's okay."

"But your wolf . . ." She shudders.

"I'm still me." I press my hands to my chest. "If you'll have me."

"Have you?" She gapes, slapping me softer this time. "As if you'll get away from me again, you asshole."

My insecurities flee as she helps me up, and Vale and Lucien are there too, lifting my shoulders like I'm easily breakable and weak, something I have to get used to.

"Yeah, I mean, we accepted you as a psychopath, so why not as a human," Lucien jokes.

Vale groans but grins at me. "It's good to see you, brother." He leans in. "Don't do that shit again, okay?"

"Okay." I nod, looking around to see the pack still watching. "Erm, I'm naked."

"Shit," they all say at once, and I can't help but laugh.

I'm home.

Getting used to being a human again will take some time, but Marie and White usher the pack away, telling them to give me space. I know we will have to speak tomorrow, but tonight is for my mate, my brothers, and me.

They walk at my side, slowing their inhuman strides so I can keep up. Quinn grips my hand tightly, and I do not dare tell her she is breaking my fingers. She can break every single one as long as she never lets go again.

The moon shines above us, and I send a silent thank you to the goddess. Despite what she took, she gave me my family back.

I haven't been human since I was a teenager. I feel stumbly and wrong, but when Quinn looks at me, that all disappears. She stops and turns to face me, clearly sensing my distress.

"I love you no matter what you are, Jai. Have I not made that clear, hunter?" She drags her lips over mine. "Human. Wolf. Your heart belongs to me, your body too, whatever form it is. The goddess knew that, knew my love would not waver."

"I will never be strong enough to protect you—"

"I never needed protection." She grins. "I can protect myself. All I need for you to do is love me and never leave me again."

"I can promise that." Cupping her jaw, I kiss her softly, swallowing her moan of pleasure as her softness presses to me, so warm and alive.

So mine.

"Take me home," I murmur into her lips as she shivers against me. "Make me yours again."

Keeping my hand in hers, she speeds up, leading me through the forest. It's only when she turns to me, dragging me inside the house with a deep kiss, that I realise Vale and Lucien have disappeared—probably to give us our space. I send up a silent thanks. I don't mind sharing my girl, but right now, I need her. I need to feel like I'm enough like this, and it's clear she's determined to show me as she slides her hands down my body. The echoing, painful reminder of the soft way she touches me is so similar to that of us making love before this all happened.

We were trying to feel like forever then, but now we have it, and we don't have to rush. Still, our lips meet faster. Our pain, worry, and grief are conveyed in that kiss, bringing tears to my eyes.

She backs into the house, her hands never leaving me. I burn her taste into my human heart. I can't smell her desire as well anymore or memorise the tiny imperfections in her skin—all two hundred and seven of them—but she is alive. She's here, in my arms, and nothing else matters.

We fall into her bed, rolling as our hands explore each other as if it's the first time all over again. Our gasps are loud as our bare skin rubs together.

"I missed you. I missed you so much," she whispers, her hair creating a curtain around us, her bright eyes consuming me as desire burns through me.

"I missed you too," I admit. "Though it was no time for me. I am sorry I was gone for even a second, Quinn."

She swallows hard, her eyes searching mine. "Don't do it again, not for a minute."

"I promise," I murmur as I flip us, making her squeal as I grin and wiggle my eyebrows. "I might be human, baby, but I still have tricks." I drag my mouth down her neck, biting at the juncture between her neck and shoulder with human teeth. "Like how I know being bitten and licked here drives you wild."

"Jai," she gasps, gripping my hair as her chest arches up, her skin glowing with moon magic.

Smiling, I slide down her body, stopping to place a gentle kiss over her healing heart. The fact that she missed me this much kills me as well as heals that hole losing my family created. I am loved, and I am needed. I see it in every touch now, every look. It pieces me back together, leaving this once broken man whole.

She did that. She loved me at my worst, and now I'll make sure she gets to love me at my best.

I may be human once more, but I will love as deeply as any beast can. I will hand over my human heart and body to her and beg for it to be enough.

"It felt like I couldn't breathe without you, as if the air had been stolen from my lungs," she mumbles as I kiss her trembling belly.

She reaches down, grips my chin, and pulls me up until she can kiss me again.

"My soul was splintered, Jai, so don't you ever dare think I wouldn't want you, even as a human. I'll take you any way I can get you, just don't ever leave me again. I can't handle it. It destroyed me."

Cupping her face, I lean down and kiss her gently. "Never. I love you, Quinn. Now and forever."

"Then show me. I need you too much to wait. I lost you, Jai. I held your lifeless body, now remind me you're alive. Remind me you're mine." Her legs wrap around me, the strength in them almost painful, but I'd never tell her.

Let her hurt me.

Let her destroy me.

I crawled to her in death, and now I worship her in life.

Our lips meet again, like the moon and the stars joining forces. Something passionate and bright blooms between us as her hands slide down my back, gripping my ass, and with flowing movements, I slide deep into my girl.

I swallow her gasp as we come together, as we rejoice in life, and I'm reborn in her arms once more.

Our lips never once break apart. We do not need air; we just need each other.

Our bodies move with familiar, loving movements.

Pleasure spirals between us, our souls joined, mated, even if they can never fully be.

The hunter and the wolf.

We don't need words, just each other, and I show her that. I show her with my body that I'm here, that I'm hers, until the last star dies in the sky.

I come back to my home within her.

When the pleasure peaks, we fly over the edge together, safe in each other's arms as we fall with love so bright, it defied death.

CHAPTER SEVENTY-ONE

Quinn

I watch Jai sleep. The sun is up, and I know the pack will be waiting for answers, but he's human now. I don't know how much rest they need, but add dying to the equation and you bet I let him sleep in. If any wolf has a problem with that, they will have to go through me.

He's mine, and I will defend him as such.

One eye opens, then the other, the pair of mismatched orbs clashing with mine. It's a sight I never thought I would see again. I watched him all night, barely sleeping, as if worried he would disappear when I wasn't looking. My fingertip traces the familiar scar as he yawns and nips playfully at my finger when it reaches his lips.

"Have you been watching me?" He wiggles his eyebrows. "You kinky shit."

Laughing, I snuggle deeper into his side. "I had to make sure you were real."

"I know the feeling," he murmurs, wrapping me in his arms with a contented sigh and holding me tight—well, tight for his human strength. I want tighter, but I don't say anything. This is who Jai is now, and I meant what I said—I will love him like this. The pack won't like it, but they can fuck off.

He's mine, and he's staying.

"I suppose I should get up and speak to the pack—" My sentence cuts off into a giggle as he rolls us over and pins me, smirking as he leans above me.

"I have a better idea. Instead of going, how about coming?" He slides down my body as I groan.

"That was terrible." I gasp as his tongue drags along the length of my cunt. "Okay, it was great, really great. I'm all on board with that plan."

He rumbles out a laugh, those mismatched eyes meeting mine across my body. "I thought you might feel that way."

"You're so smart." I moan as his tongue lashes my clit. I throw my legs over his shoulders to get closer. My hands fist the sheets as my back arches, desire racing through me like fire. I gasp and writhe as he eats my cunt like it's his breakfast, and the edge of madness drives me crazy.

His fingers thrust into my cunt, stretching me as he tortures my clit. Those thick fingers fuck me hard and fast as he licks and sucks until my release slams through me so suddenly, I bow off the bed.

My scream rings out, pleasure coursing through me even as I hear someone knock at the door. I try to bite down on my lip, but Jai bites my clit, making me cry out louder.

A throat clears along with a knock. "Erm, Alpha, when you are, erm, finished—oh God, done. You know what? Meet us near the gym whenever," White says grumpily and stomps off, making us both laugh out loud.

By the time we are dressed and walking to the gym, it's an hour later. I got distracted by all his new scars, kissing each one better. What can I say? Human or not, Jai is hot.

When we reach the gym, Jai tenses, no doubt expecting reproach, but the looks of wonder the pack shoots him are surprising. It seems word of him being blessed by the goddess has gotten out, which causes me to relax. They won't reject her gift, which means I get to keep my man without fighting everyone for him.

Vale winks at me where he's leaning near White and Lucien. Con is off to the side, book in hand, and my mother bustles out, her eyes narrowed on me. "Young lady, what time do you call this?"

"Mother, I'm a grown woman—"

"It is way after sunup—"

"And alpha," I remind her.

"I don't care if you are the fucking moon. You do not skip breakfast," she retorts.

"I didn't skip mine," Jai says happily, even as I elbow him. He groans and stumbles to the side, and I wince, forgetting my strength.

"Shit, sorry." I reach for him, but he straightens with a wink. "Asshole."

"Talk now," she orders, pointing at us. "Do not make me angry."

Every single wolf instantly rushes inside. No one wants Marie's wrath. I'm not too proud to admit that I rush too.

Jai answers question after question while eating. I notice he doesn't eat nearly half of what we do, and I make a note to lessen his portion so he doesn't feel left out. I also need to remind the pack while he's not here so they don't accidentally hurt him. Maybe I can make him a running course so we can still run together.

Either way, when the meeting is over, we basically decide the goddess does what she wants, and we are glad he's back.

When we step outside, we decide to walk the pack lands. Everything is falling back into a normal routine.

The pack house is being rebuilt, and although we are grieving, life goes on. I don't know how the hunters will react to my message, but I don't care, not today.

"He's blessed." I hear a whisper and glance over my shoulder, grinning at the pups following us.

"Don't look now, but you have a fan club," I murmur to Jai.

He turns, grinning at the pups. They squeak and step back, lowering their eyes. "Alpha." They nod respectfully.

"No need to stand on formalities." I grin. "This is Jai." I push him forward.

They instantly descend on him, asking a million questions, to which he laughs, and I find myself watching him with a wide smile as he answers as many as he can before one of the pups steps back. "Jai, do you know how to play ball?"

"Of course I do. Don't you know us humans are famous for it?" He grabs the ball near their feet and grins as he jogs across the grass to an open patch. "How about you versus me? Come on, wolfies, show me what you've got."

I watch as the wolf pups amass on him. He plays with them, letting them score each time, laughing and tackling them playfully even as they crawl all over him. He seems happy, but I saw the sadness in his eyes last night. I cannot imagine the feeling of losing my wolf, and I make a promise there and then to ensure he never feels like he's not enough and to make him happy every day of his life so he never regrets the choice he made.

"He is something," White comments, joining me.

For a moment, guilt fills me. He lost his mate, while I got mine back. It doesn't seem fair. As if sensing my thoughts, he smiles down at me, draping an arm around my shoulders. "Don't fret, I'm not jealous. I'm just happy you get your mate. No one deserves happiness more than you, Alpha."

"Thank you, White, I mean it." I reach for him when a howl interrupts us. Spinning in shock, I see our betas chasing after a wolf barrelling straight towards Jai and the pups surrounding him.

A very familiar wolf.

Tetrim.

His fur is marked with slashes, he's bleeding profusely, and one of his legs is clearly broken, but he's still running, his eyes filled with hate as they lock on Jai. I know our betas won't be fast enough.

My heart sinks. "Jai!" I scream, my eyes wide as I rush over.

Time seems to slow down, echoing a heartbreaking hopelessness that I have been plunged into once more after watching my father be killed. Jai turns, spots the wolf heading towards him, and makes a split-second decision. He turns, giving the wolf his back as he crouches, his arms wide as he shelters the pups from the attack.

My heart breaks in that moment as my wolf breaks free and I sprint towards them. I run faster than I ever have before, my eyes locked on my human love who crouches, steady and strong, protecting the crying pups as shouts echo around us. My entire focus narrows to him as Tetrim slides to a stop behind him, bringing his paw down and slicing his back open. Jai doesn't even cry out. He grits his teeth, swallowing it to protect the kids.

I barrel into Tetrim, knocking him off course. He turns with a growl, his eyes filled with hate.

He's half mad. I see it in his gaze.

His head lowers, even as I growl. I want to spare Jai a look, but I can't. I cannot look away, but even with dominance pouring from my wolf, he chooses to ignore it or is too far gone.

I will have to kill him. More than that, I should have killed him a long time ago.

Had I not been so weak back then, my father might not be dead, our pack might not have lost so much, and my mate might not be behind me, maybe dying a second time in a week.

That fury bursts out of me in a roar that shakes the earth, and it's so strong, even I am surprised by it.

For a moment, he hesitates before readying himself. This time, I go for his throat. I leap at him—no warning, no sanctions, no second chances. He's had too many of those.

I make a calculated decision. I see his claws coming up for me as he rises, and I know he will impale me on them, but it will also get me close enough to get what I want. He's too mad to realise it, so I let them sink deep into my side, and then I open my muzzle and wrap it around his neck. He roars, vibrating under my teeth as I bite, digging in deeper. His other claws kick and slash at me as we roll, ripping me up.

I ignore the pain, tucking against his body as much as I can until he's under me, and then I yank my head back. I take his throat with me, but he's still not dead, so I slice at him, dissecting him and ripping him apart, my teeth tearing at his limbs and chest until I taste his heart, and then I bite down.

I shred it to pieces in my fury for what he has done and what he has made me become—someone who kills their own.

My head falls back with a howl, blood dripping down my muzzle, before I rip off his head and throw it. Turning, I see the wolves fall to their backs in submissive poses, but I ignore them.

Tetrim is dead.

It's over.

It's finally over.

I swallow the taste of his blood, knowing it will change me forever.

When I turn back, gore covering my fur, I find Vale and Lucien crouched over an unmoving Jai, and for a moment, my heart stills, breaking all over again, until he moans in pain, and I hurry over.

All the kids are gone, but I see pack members milling around worriedly. I quickly change back, barking orders. "Clear up the mess, no ceremony for him. Check the perimeter and see how he got through."

"Yes, Alpha."

"White, bring me the healer just in case," I call.

My entire focus is on my mate who lies on the grass, his own blood puddled beneath him. He was too brave to run and so fucking strong.

I rush to my mate as he gasps, lying on his front, his shirt torn open to expose furrows on his back cut to the bone. Oh god. I almost vomit at the sight, and my poor mate didn't even make a sound. I fall to my knees and then to my side, turning his head.

He winces, his eyes tight. "Sorry I wasn't fast enough to take the kids and run."

"Shh, you were amazing, my love," I tell him, leaning down to kiss his face. "Now let your mate fix you."

He reaches out with a groan, capturing my hand. "I'm sorry you had to kill one of your pack members. No matter what he did, I know you feel that loss greatly."

"Not as greatly as the regret I feel for not doing it sooner," I reply, leaning down to kiss him again before lifting my eyes to Vale and Lucien. "Hold him while I heal him."

"Do not waste your healing. I will be okay—"

I growl, cutting him off, and he tries to laugh, but it ends in a moan. "I am healing you," I state. "So hush."

Closing my eyes, I lay my hands on his back, feeling them slip in his warm blood, and for a moment, fury fills me again before I swallow it down, along with my guilt and grief. I push my magic through him, finding the wounds are so deep, they have punctured one lung and his spleen. He would have died. I heal them, taking extra time to make sure there is nothing else before healing the deep furrow. When I lift my head, he's breathing easily, his eyes closed in bliss.

Leaning down with a purr, I clean his back, swallowing his blood as I lap at it. He groans and buries his face in the grass. "Baby, you need to stop. It's super inconvenient for me to get hard right here."

I lick long lines along his back, exposing clear, pink skin. At his ear, I purr, "You will have scars, but I will kiss them all better later and ride you until you forget the taste of that agony."

"Fucking hell, just leave me here for a minute. I don't want to scare the children with what's in my pants right now," he mutters.

Grinning, I sit up as Marie rushes to my side, healer in tow. "Who dared to hurt my son-in-law?" she roars, casting her blazing eyes around the clearing. "He might be human, but he is one of us!" I shrink back under her wrath. "Who was it? Challenge me right now!"

"Mother." I reach for her, but she tugs away.

"I want names!"

"Jesus," Vale mutters.

"Marie," I snap, and she turns her head. "It was Tetrim. He's dead." I nod at the gore as a few wolves try to clear it away. I might have gone a little overboard, but hey, he touched my mate.

"Oh," she grumbles, deflating. "Well, someone could have told me." She sinks to her knees, brushing back Jai's shaggy hair. "Are you okay? Let's get you to bed. I'll make you my famous healing soup."

"I'm okay. Quinn healed me." He smiles, although it seems a little watery. "Sorry to be a bother."

"A bother?" She huffs, smacking his back. "You saved the pups. I heard that much. Human or not, you are one of us, boy, and we wolves don't talk about ourselves like that. Now, let's get you up."

Lucien grins. "He needs a minute."

"Why?" Marie frowns as I snigger.

"Oh, erm . . ." Jai blushes so hard, I think he might overheat.

"She was teasing him," Vale supplies happily. Marie glances from me to Jai, a wide smile curving her lips.

"Oh, well, you just lie there for a moment until it goes down. Quinny, stop winding the poor boy up." She huffs at me.

I hold my hands up but grin as we wait in silence.

"Is it down yet?" Marie asks.

"Dear God, let me sink into the earth," he mutters as I grin wider.

"It must be big. He's practically off the ground," Marie mutters.

Lucien falls backwards, roaring with laughter, as Jai buries his face in the grass.

"Mother," I admonish, and when he's not looking, I part my hands to show her. Her mouth opens in shock and she nods.

"Congratulations, both of you." She wiggles her eyebrows at me.

"I am just going to lie here and let the ground take me," he mutters.

"No, you're not. Mother, stop," I mumble. Grabbing him, I help him to his knees. His shirt falls off, and my eyes rove over his built chest, my tongue dragging across my lips.

"Stop looking at me like that," he says. "You aren't helping."

"Sorry." I grin, meeting his mismatched eyes as I lean in and kiss him. "Don't put yourself in danger like that again."

"No promises." He sighs. "We are extensions of you. Plus, we have a lot to make up for."

"Not to me," I tell him, but he smiles sadly.

"We do." He nods. "Human or not, I cannot sit idly by."

"But you could get hurt—"

"Then you will heal me." He kisses me softly. "Thank you."

I offer him my hand as I stand, and he goes to take it, but he falls back, gasping. "Jai—" I reach for him, but I stop as he begins to glow, my eyes widening.

A female voice echoes around the clearing. "Your sacrifice is to be rewarded. Anyone willing to risk their life for innocents should not be punished. Anyone willing to sacrifice half of themself just to be with their love deserves to be whole. Don't say we are not merciful. Enjoy, warrior, and stand with my chosen until the end."

"What?" I whisper. The voice was female.

The goddess, I realise, but how? Why?

Jai roars, his back arching so severely, I'm afraid it will break. I reach for him, but Vale holds me back as we watch fur sprout across his skin, and he suddenly explodes. Blood splatters us, and then in Jai's spot, is a wolf.

Jai's wolf.

Jai is a wolf.

He whines, nudging me, and then he shifts back to a very naked human Jai, his eyes wide. "She gave me my wolf," he whispers, astonished. "I'm a werewolf again." He tackles us all to the ground.

"Dude, you're naked," Vale complains, but we are all grinning.

Goddess blessed indeed.

Jai's head presses to mine as he smiles. "My Quinny."

"My wolf," I murmur, cupping his cheeks. "You're home."

CHAPTER SEVENTY-TWO

Quinn

With everything that has been going on, I haven't been keeping track of the days. The day after I spend all night running with my men through the woods, White comes to me.

"You know what tonight is, don't you?" he asks cagily.

"Erm . . . Saturday?"

"Mating hunt," he replies, and a slow grin curls his lips. "I think it's a good idea to go ahead with it. They need something positive to look forward to. Besides, I have a feeling you would like the ceremony to take place this time, no?"

I stare at him, unsure, and he sighs, crouching at my side. "If you aren't ready, do not force it, but I have known you all your life, Quinn, and I have never seen you this happy. Those men, despite what they were before, are here. They gave up their lives and humanity for you, and now they spend their days helping you lead. You love them. What's so scary about mating?"

"It makes it real," I admit. "It makes it binding, and then if I lose them—"

"What if you don't?" he retorts. "What if you lose them now? You were destroyed when you lost Jai, mating bond or not." He stands. "Think about it."

He walks to the door of the room I've claimed as an office until the pack house is built, and I stand. "Go ahead with the ceremony."

He turns, grinning at me. "Good choice, Alpha. I look forward to the outcome of the hunt."

"As do I," I reply shakily, nerves filling me.

I have been through this many times before, but never with someone I want to catch me. Usually, I'm outrunning them, lasting until sunrise.

Tonight, I want to be caught.

I want to be mated.

I want to be theirs.

Dom has kidnapped my men—not really, but as soon as news of the ceremony spread, they were gone. I don't even get to speak to them to see if it's what they want or to give them a way out, but I suppose it's too late now.

I feel a nervous, excited energy all day that won't go away, distracting me when I work, until Marie finally kicks me out of the kitchen, saying I'm hindering her and to go prepare. I don't miss the happy gleam in her eyes. She wants this for me. Despite the grief she feels every day, she wants me to mate with them.

Jang would, too, because I chose them. I need them, and, more than that, I let them in. I trust them, I turn to them, and moreover, I expect them at my side. I cannot go back to life without them. This ceremony is just proof of what we already know.

I am theirs, and they are mine.

Or at least I hope so.

They have to catch me first.

As the sun sets, I stand before the pack. There are five of us females running tonight, and they are all excited. Some already have their eyes on wolves, and some are just eager to see where this will lead.

I stand before them all, searching the crowd for my men, but I don't see them, and worry fills me. "They will be here," Dom promises from my side. "Just focus on running, Quinny, and make them work for it. You are the alpha, after all, and they are hunters. Let them hunt, wolf."

My grin is almost evil as I turn back to the crowd. Usually, Jang does this part, and I have never noticed his absence as much as I do now as I step forward. He should be here. He should witness my mating. He should preside over it, but I know he's here in spirit, so I swallow down my grief, knowing tonight is one of celebration and hope.

"Tonight, we will run," I call. "Unmated males are welcome to hunt us. If you catch us and we accept, we are yours, otherwise better luck next time. Jang had a whole speech, but I'm not my father, so I'll just say this. I have been running since I was eighteen, and tonight will be no different . . ." I search the crowd. "So catch me if you can." I turn and leap into the air, changing so I land on all four paws.

I look back, waiting, as the other females change and hurry past me into the forest just as the moon shines through the clearing, and then I see my mates, standing in the shadows. Three sets of eyes are on me, and they are already in wolf form as they slink out of the shadows and through the crowd.

I grin and run faster than I ever have because I won't make this easy on them.

If they want me, then they need to prove it.

Tonight, the hunters hunt their wolf, and if they catch me, then they can have me forever.

I veer from the other females, going deeper than most others as I hear howls go up, meaning the males are giving chase. Before, I would run as fast as I could, dodging and outlasting them all night, and I know my mates will have some competition—after all, no male wolf can give up on an unmated female, especially an alpha.

Their wolves will demand it unless they have already chosen one.

I hear crashing behind me, so I drop my head, moving faster, knowing they have caught my scent. Not too far off, there is a howl of agony, and I know someone got in the way of my men. They might be trying to fit in with my pack during the day as humans, but tonight, they are pure beasts, and whoever gets in their way will suffer.

The thrill that gives me has my wolf wanting to call out to them, to see them spill blood for her, but I swallow it back and splash through the creek, obscuring my scent, before I burst out of the other side.

Catch me if you can, hunters.

CHAPTER SEVENTY-THREE

My muzzle already drips with blood. A male wolf was too daring, trying to follow us as we pursued Quinn, so I simply showed him that was a bad idea. He limps back to the pack as I turn and run, following my mate's scent trail.

Dom took us aside this morning and gave us the rundown on tonight, telling us every law and taking us around pack land, so we knew exactly where we were going to hunt our woman.

Did she think we would not claim her?

She is ours, and tonight, we will show the world and her that.

Fuck history. Tonight, we solidify the future.

We track her to the stream—clever girl—and then over to the other side. We lose her scent there, but using our hunting skills, we notice little traces she cannot hide, like the partially bent leaves leading away.

I nod left at Lucien, then right at Jai. They branch out, and I head straight. We will corner her. I know she won't go down without a fight, but that doesn't matter. She is strong, but she's fighting not to be mated, and we are fighting to make her ours.

We will win.

Her trail picks up again, but we spot a smaller black wolf darting through the foliage, no doubt on her trail. My lips peel back in a snarl, aimed directly at the one who thinks he can hunt my mate. There is no rationality here, only feelings—possessiveness, lust, and anger.

Lucien is there.

The wolf lets out a sharp whine as Lucien bites his tail, and when he turns, Lucien bites his neck, taking him to the ground and pinning him until he whines in defeat. Standing, Lucien shakes out his fur and slinks back through the forest as I focus on my mate's trail.

I don't hear any other wolf in the vicinity, and I'm grateful for that because my patience is wearing thin, and if another one comes between my mate and me, I might just go too far. My brothers and I create a net she cannot slip past and then double back. Up here, the cliffs are to our left, so she cannot go that way, and we might have set some traps farther right. About ten minutes later, we hear her snarl as she almost triggers one.

That's our girl. She's figuring out we've been busy little hunters.

These big bad hunters want their wolf, and we are going to get her.

We are getting closer now, as she's forced to slow down to check for traps, and she can no doubt hear us making noise in the brush behind her, letting her know we are here. Anticipation fills me, my bloodlust turning to desire as my wolf bays for its mate.

There's a snap up ahead that tells me she triggered another trap, and I know exactly which one. Moments later, we are in the clearing, and she stands there, growling with her teeth bared, the wooden cage trapping her.

She changes back suddenly, standing as a human, and glares at us through the bars. "This is cheating," she hisses.

I change back too, walking towards her. I grip her chin through the slats, my other hand sliding down her body and forcing her thighs apart so I can grip her pussy. She's wet, and she pants, grinding into my hand as I grin at her.

"We're hunters, baby. We cheat," I murmur as I squeeze her. "So give up and let me have this."

"You want me?" She leans in, licking my chin as I groan. "Then you'll have to do much better than that." Suddenly, she is gone, and her wolf lunges through the bars. One of her fangs drags along my arm, making me chuckle. The shallow wound bleeds, but as I change back to my wolf, it heals.

The rope holding the bars together snaps as she throws herself at it, and then she's gone, darting off into the forest with us hot on her heels. She's so fucking fast that it makes me proud, but we are strong, and we are not losing her.

We will wear her down and hunt her over every inch of this land, and just before the sun comes up, I'll feel that sweet pussy gripping my cock as she screams my name for all of her pack to hear.

***

LUCIEN

She's pulling away, but little does our she-wolf know, she is running directly where we want her to. We knew she would get free. Quinn would never give up that easily, nor do we want her to.

She is an alpha, and she has survived this long on her wits and strength.

She is worth fighting for, and tonight, we are showing her that. We are showing her there is nowhere she can run where we won't follow.

She is ours.

She speeds up, which I didn't think was possible, and zigzags through the forest. She knows this land better than us, and I worry we missed something, even though we spent all day mapping it out and setting our traps. After our talk with Dom, we realised we needed to be both wolf and hunter tonight to catch our alpha.

She swerves back into our path, and I breathe easier as we chase her, my head down and legs pounding the earth. I feel a freedom I have never experienced before. Adrenaline and desire wars with my wolf's happiness to be running, to be hunting.

I'm just starting to tire when she swerves to avoid the dead end we are herding her towards, but when she finds the net hanging down, she backs away, snarling as she spins, eyeing the cliff edge as if debating climbing it before turning to us.

The mountains stand at her back, and she's trapped, but trapping an animal, especially Quinn, only makes them more dangerous. We know that all too well, so we spread out.

She lowers her head, ready to attack.

She will fight us until the bitter end.

Jesus, I love this woman.

I'm going to show her how much right up until sunrise.

CHAPTER SEVENTY-FOUR

Quinn

If they think backing me into their trap will work, then they should have known better. Silly hunters.

There are three of them, so I make a quick plan, and when Jai lunges at me like I knew he would, since he's still partly feral, I leap over him, landing on a red boulder. When Lucien heads my way, I hop over him, heading towards the forest, but Vale is there, hanging back, and he nips my side when I try to race past, spinning me back to the other two as they close in on me.

They have another thing coming if they think I'm not going down without a fight. Lucien lunges, and I swipe at his muzzle, drawing blood. He growls and smacks my ass with his paw as Jai nips my tail. I whirl and bite his side, making him yip as he falls back to avoid me taking a chunk of him with me.

Vale takes that moment to nip my ass, and I spin, trying to keep them all in sight, but it's no use. Lucien hits my side, nudging me towards the rock, and even when I snap at him, he's gone. Between them, they manage to back me into the rock.

Jai mounts me, and I kick him off. Lucien grips my muzzle in his mouth, stopping me from biting. I whine and swipe out, but then

Vale takes me to the ground, one paw on my chest. He's too strong, but I buck and twist, kicking and whining, cutting my muzzle on Lucien's teeth.

Jai is there again, mounting me, and I kick out, scratching him when his teeth dig into my neck, pinning me. He growls as he mounts me, ragging at my neck until I whine, but I still don't submit.

Jai's voice comes, and human teeth dig into my neck. "Submit so we can claim you, Quinny."

Snarling, I kick him, but he holds on even as a human, his teeth ripping at my fur until he groans at the taste of my blood. "Or keep fighting, it's making me hard."

Vale's paw digs in deeper as Lucien's muzzle tightens.

They are tired of playing.

With an angry whine, I finally submit. I have no other choice.

I slump into the dirt. Lucien's muzzle loosens, and Vale's paw lifts, and then I lunge, biting Lucien's leg. I hit him as Vale tackles me, and suddenly, I'm on my back with my belly in the air, his muzzle around my throat so firmly, I cannot move or I'll die.

It's a threat and a promise.

My mate has had enough of my fighting.

"Change, now," Jai commands. I look over to see him standing naked, blood on his lips and red dust covering him from the mountain. I roll back to look up at Vale, wanting to fight, but even as an alpha, I know I can't.

I'm caught. I'm theirs.

I shift back, and his mouth constricts, gently holding my human throat.

Jai is the only one in human form, and before I can even groan, his hands are on my thighs, shoving them apart, and then he slams into me. My scream echoes around the land and in Vale's mouth as he purrs.

I'm wet, but he's big, and the sudden intrusion hurts. The pain fades to a pleasurable ache, however, when he starts to move, slowly pulling from my pussy and sliding back in. All the while, Vale purrs, the sound heading straight to my clit where I feel someone's thick fingers begin to rub—Lucien. I would recognise the coarseness of his fingers anywhere.

He rubs and plays with my clit until I cry out, my back arching, bringing my throat closer to Vale's teeth, but I don't care as Jai's hands grip my thighs, forcing them wider as he hammers into me.

"Move," he hisses, more animal than man. "I need to bite her. I need her on all fours. I need to rut her and mate her like a beast." His voice is guttural.

It's his wolf.

Vale reluctantly releases my throat, and before I can fight them in any way, I'm flipped. My face is pushed into the dirt, my ass is dragged into the air, and then Jai is inside me again, hammering into my cunt. My breasts rub against the hard rock, the slight pain making me gasp as I push back, clawing at the ground as I beg wordlessly for more.

A hand grips my chin, dragging my head up until I meet Lucien's glowing wolf eyes. His fangs are huge, and his thumb digs into my jaw, prying it open to show my own. "Behave. Keep your fangs out of me," he growls, and then he fills my mouth with his length, thrusting all the way into my throat and forcing himself deeper until I gag and choke on him.

Their growls fill the air as they claim their mate, their muscles bulging from their wolves. Their cocks are inhumanly big and thicker at the end, ready to hook inside me and pump me full of their cum.

My claws rip up the red dirt as I am filled time and time again with Lucien's cock, and Jai hammers into my pussy so hard it hurts.

I glance to the side to see Vale prowling around in his wolf form, protecting us from any wolves who may come upon us or try to steal his mate.

My eyes jerk back to Lucien as he growls possessively and thrusts all the way down my throat, keeping me there until I gag. Jai snarls, his hips stuttering, and I know he's close.

I am too, and when he leans over me, his fangs pressing to my neck, I splinter apart for them as I clench around his beastly cock.

He roars, and then his fangs pierce my neck right to the bone, pinning me as he hammers into me, chasing his release as I cry out. He growls against my neck, his cock filling me once more, and his hot cum splashes inside me as he deepens the bite.

The scent of my blood fills the air, and I know it will scar.

It's the mating bite.

Lucien roars, and I watch as he punches Jai, sending him flying off me, ripping his teeth from my throat. Lucien moves behind me, slamming into my cunt and filling me with his swelling cock.

His hands tangle in my hair, yanking it to the side, and then his fangs sink into the other side of my throat. The agony mixes with my pleasure until I scream. He pins me in place, his fangs buried deep as he fucks me hard and fast.

His cock swells inside of me, and all I can do is moan. I feel too full, and he can't work it out of me. He just rocks inside me, hitting that spot over and over again until I scream into another release. He follows me over the edge, baying to the moon as he fills me with his cum. His cock is so swollen, we are locked together as wave after wave of pleasure washes over us.

Slumping forward, I feel my blood mixing with the dust covering my body, and my wolf whines in approval, but she still wants more. Heat floods my body, begging for my third and final mate to claim me. Lucien pants and then slowly pulls himself from my body. I feel their cum drip from me, and when that thick, swollen head leaves my cunt, it hurts so good, I almost come again.

Lifting my head with a pathetic whine, I call for my mate. Vale turns around, his bright eyes locked on me as he prowls over in wolf form. The sight has me shuddering despite the fact that I was just rutted by my other two mates and their cum is still dripping from me.

He tries to shift back, but his alpha wolf is riding him hard, and he only manages a partial shift. He's more human than wolf, but his cock hangs to his knee, purple and throbbing for me, and when he lunges at me, I cry out.

I don't flip, and he doesn't let me.

He pins me with brutal hands as he impales me on his cock, forcing a noise from my mouth I've never heard before. He ruts into me so hard I bleed, but my wolf loves it, loves him claiming me so brutally as the moon watches.

Dirt and dust cover us both, his claws piercing my skin as he fucks me. His massive cock almost splits me open. I feel my healing magic working overtime as he claims me, and I wouldn't want it any other way.

He grows even bigger inside me until I'm shoved forward, almost hitting the rock with each forceful thrust.

"Mine, ours, mine. Quinn." He repeats it as he fucks me, each word punctuated by a hard thrust until he can't take any more.

His teeth pierce the back of my neck, pinning me as he ruts me. His deep mating bite takes hold, leaving me weak and crying out below him.

As Vale claims me, I claim him. His arm comes around my front in offering, but I don't want his arm. I nip at it until he groans, his cock jerking inside me, and then I roll us and spin until I'm rocking on his cock, my hands on the dirt on either side of his head. I yank his head to the side and bite his neck, claiming him as mine, and that destroys him.

He roars, his hips coming off the earth as he slams into me, and his release floods my cunt. I gnaw at the bite, deepening it before sitting up and rocking on his hard cock, the taste of his blood in my mouth.

I cry out his name to the moon as I come, dripping down his huge cock.

I turn my head with a snarl, my eyes locking on my prey.

I am an alpha, after all.

Now it's my turn to claim them.

I lunge at Jai first, and he falls backwards as I clamber up his body and dig my teeth into his neck, forcing my fangs in so deep that the agony has him howling for me. I feel his cum splash across my trembling stomach as I swallow his blood, keeping him pinned until I release him. Panting, I stare down at my dazed mate.

"Mine," I snap, and then my head turns slowly to see Lucien.

He's watching me with hungry eyes, his cock hard once more, and he crooks his fingers in a come here gesture. I crawl to him on all fours, stopping to lick the tip of his cock before I slide up and slam down on his length, locking us together once more.

Lucien roars, his head thrown back below me, his fangs hanging over his bottom lip as I wind my hips, forcing his cock as deep as it can go, and then I strike. I bury my teeth in his chest right over his heart, and the sweet, coppery taste of his blood fills my mouth.

His cum fills me, overflowing from my pussy as I find my release.

I come so hard, I black out. When I come to, they are purring around me, their mating bites bleeding, and I can't help but grin.

I have been claimed, and so have they.

We are tied together for eternity now, and peace fills me for a moment.

When I curl up against my purring mates, I feel the first, sharp pain of my heat.

Oh fuck, I'm going into heat.

CHAPTER SEVENTY-FIVE

Quinn

My heat comes on hard and fast. Usually after a mating ceremony, we would go back and present to the pack, but they sense it as soon as I do, and their protective, possessive instincts roar to the forefront, and I know they won't let me be around any other male wolves. They would see it as a threat and they would kill them, but we can't spend the next however long it will take for my heat to subside out here in the dirt.

"The cabin," I rasp, my back bowing as I roll over as the first wave hits me. My pussy clenches, and my cream slides down my thighs. My skin starts to heat until I feel like I am on fire.

My wolf retreats with a whimper, leaving this to me as usual.

"What's happening?" Vale asks.

"My heat," I reply, my eyes squeezed shut as I lock my thighs together to fight back another wave. When it passes, I gasp and open my eyes. "It's fine. I usually ride it out alone. It's when I'm fertile, but luckily, I take pixie magic to stop me from being able to get pregnant, but I still get the fun side effects." My voice ends on a groan as a small wave of fire washes through me.

"What do we do?" Lucien asks.

"Just take me home." I pant.

"What does everyone else do?" Jai asks.

"They fuck like wolves until it abates," I mutter, gritting my teeth as agony tears through me, my cunt begging to be filled so badly it hurts. "It's fine. I can deal with it—"

"Not alone."

I'm in their arms, and before I know it, I'm rubbing against whoever holds me, their hard body making me purr as I scramble up their form.

"Shit." It's Lucien, and he holds me against him as he stumbles. "Okay, let's get you home, baby, and then we can help."

"Hurts." I whimper as he begins to run with me in his arms. "Luc, please." I lick and bite his neck, trying to get closer even as he keeps me away, his hips too low for me to reach. "Please, it hurts, please." I dig my claws into his shoulders, wrapping my legs around his waist. "I need you. I need you so badly." The words are just whines, the heat making me crazed.

"We will be there soon," he promises, his hand brushing comfortingly along my back, but I snarl.

Another wave hits me, and my back bows as I scream. It takes all logic with it, and I stab my claws into him and struggle against his hold until I can slam myself down on his hard length. They are my mates, so they will feel my heat, and it will drive them wild with want.

He roars and stumbles. We almost fall, but I don't care. I roll my hips, riding his cock, needing the relief he can offer.

"Fuck, fuck, fuck." He groans, grabbing my ass and squeezing, urging me on even as he keeps walking, trying to get me home. His wolf demands he gets me to our nest where we can fuck.

Biting his neck, I whimper as my release rolls through me, but it's not nearly enough, and the red-hot agony of my heat soon washes the stinging relief away until I'm dripping and winding my hips on his cock again.

"Fuck, I can't—" My back hits a tree, the bark cutting me up as his hand slaps above me and he hammers into my cunt.

He fucks me hard and fast, the bark tearing up my back until the agony overpowers the clenching of my heat, and when he roars, his cum filling me, it cools the red-hot pain in my core.

The relief makes me slump against him, but I know it won't be long until the burning heat comes back again. He clearly knows it, too, because he wraps his arms around me and starts to run.

We make it about halfway back before the stabbing, crippling pain hits me once more. I bow into his body with a scream. His cock is hardening, but not fast enough, and I rip myself from his arms and tackle the first body I find.

I can barely see, barely think, but my body knows theirs.

Their scent wraps around me.

Mate.

"I've got you. I've got you." The voice below me is tender, and his hands hold me as I grip his cock and sink down on it.

The searing agony is too much as I ride the cock, release after release rolling through me. It only dampens the wave of heat, so I rock harder, bouncing on his cock as claws slice at my side.

"Mine!" he roars as his cum splashes inside me, cooling that fiery agony until I slump once more. His arms wrap around me as he stumbles to his feet, and then I'm passed off.

"Run," he growls. "Get her to the cabin."

Jai.

I sigh as I cuddle into him, and then he is running. I bury my head into his neck as his big hand slides up and down my back, even as I jostle from how hard he's running. "Shh, we've got you. We'll make it all better."

"It burns," I whine.

"I know, baby, but we'll make it all better," he promises, and I hold on tight, trying to keep the next wave at bay.

The moment he enters the cabin, I pounce on him. Something

crashes as we fall, but I don't care. Moonlight shines in through my window, giving me enough light to see him beneath me.

His huge cock stands to attention, almost purple with need, the veins throbbing deliciously. I lean down and lick him, the drip of his precum soothing the burning hurt inside me.

"Baby." He groans. "You're going to make me come if you lick me like that. You smell too fucking good, feel too fucking good."

"No," I snarl, sliding up his body, rubbing my aching chest against his with a whine before offering him my nipples. "Suck them, make them better," I growl.

Groaning, he wraps his lips around my nipple and sucks out the sting. I moan, rubbing my dripping pussy along his washboard abs as his head turns and does the same to my other nipple. The tension in my back relaxes a little, and when he lifts me and drops me onto his cock, I cry out in ecstasy.

He bounces me there, his mismatched eyes watching me with so much hunger, it makes me cry out as I clench around him. My nipples ache, so I lean down and feed them to him, letting him soothe the pain as he powers into me, fucking me so hard I almost fall as the fire burns me alive. I sit up once more, chasing my release, needing the cooling ache only my mate can give me.

The door bursts open as Vale and Lucien enter, both panting. Their eyes glow with their wolves as they sniff the air, scenting my need, then they kick the door shut. Vale reaches me first, pushing me down onto Jai and pressing into my cunt alongside him.

The stretch is painful but oh so fucking good. They slide in and out of my cunt together, stretching me beyond pain and into bliss. I scream, coming all over their lengths, but I still need more.

Turning my head, I find what I need. Lucien stands there, presenting his dripping cock to me. I greedily suck him deep into my mouth, swallowing his precum and letting it soothe the burn as they force one orgasm after another from me.

I come continually, caught between their bodies as they fuck me so hard, they break my body apart, and I beg for more.

Lucien roars, shooting cum down my throat, and like a cooling wave, it allows me to breathe. Jai cries out below me, shooting my cunt full of his cum as Vale fights to hold on, but he gives in, bellowing my name as his cum fills me as well.

The ache retreats, and my eyes close as they pull from my sticky, unresponsive body. I'm covered in sweat and cum, but for a moment, all I feel is bliss.

I can't walk, but the guys make a nest around me with blankets and pillows. The fire burns low, and I lie in the middle of it all. They feed me before my stomach starts to cramp once more with the next heat wave, and when I roll onto my front, grinding my hips into the bedding, they are there, reaching for me and ready to relieve the ache.

My nipples are so engorged that Lucien accidentally cuts them with his teeth, and I press his head to my chest, holding him there as he sucks them while his brother rolls me over once more and lifts my hips, working his wet cock into my ass as Jai slides under me and works his inside my cunt.

It's sloppy and dirty and oh so good. My eyes cross as they claim me once more, working my body until their cum floods me, cooling the ache, and I know we are in for a long night.

The next few hours alternate between me trying to rest between waves and then waking them up by riding their cocks when I need more.

"I'm drained, baby," Vale says. His cock is trying to harden, but I've sucked him dry of his cum.

My guttural whine makes his eyes flash. "Shh, we've got you," he promises, cupping my jaw. "Jai, come serve our mate."

"Gladly." He reaches for me, tugging me onto him so my hands hit his thighs, and then he lifts me and sinks inside my cunt. Groaning, I close my eyes in bliss as I ride him, and when my eyes open, it's to see Vale and Lucien both watching me. Leaning back into the furs, Lucien holds his hard cock, ready to feed it to me.

Leaning forward, I hear Jai groan at the sight, and I beckon Lucien closer with a curl of my fingers. "Let me drink you dry," I purr. "I want to feel you pushing down my throat until it hurts."

"Fuck." He groans, lifting his hips as he circles his cock with his fist.

"Now," I growl.

"Needy mate," he teases as he gets to his knees and heads over, rubbing his cock over my parted lips. "Be a good girl and suck me down then. Swallow my cum, and let us make you feel better."

I do just that. I suck his cock desperately, hard and fast, until he cries out my name and his cum floods my throat. I continue to suck until he has to force my mouth open, and then he flops back.

Pushing back against Jai, I ride him harder, faster, until he cries out and his cum splashes deep inside me, washing away the burn.

I sigh happily and relax into the sweaty furs. Their hands stroke across my body as they murmur loving words, and my eyes flutter shut, the ache disappearing for now.

I let sleep claim me, hoping when I wake, the pain and heat might have gone away.

I should have known better. I wake up to a stabbing sensation in my cervix. My cunt pulses so tightly, it actually makes tears well in my eyes. My body is hot, my heart hammers, and my lungs ache.

I try not to wake them, I really do, but I can still feel the waves of my heat. I know they are exhausted and drained, so as quietly as I can, I slip my hands down my body, rubbing my slippery clit before thrusting my fingers into my messy cunt.

Biting my lip on a moan, I fuck myself hard and fast with my fingers, rocking into them, but it's not enough. "Quinn?" Vale murmurs, lifting his head, no doubt sensing my need. When he sees me, he blinks and frowns.

"It won't stop," I cry, tears sliding down my cheeks as I rock my hips, needing more. "I tried. I can't—"

"Shh." He crawls over to me, knocking my hands away, and then his mouth is on my pussy, licking it better. "I've got you. We always have you. We are your mates, Quinn. It is our duty to serve you." His glistening eyes meet mine over my heaving body. "And it's a fucking pleasure to have my mate needing us this badly."

I nod, still crying as I grind into his face, letting my cum and theirs drip into his mouth. He slips two fingers into me, then three before he works in four and then his whole fist. Keeping my cunt stretched, he licks me until I cry out with my release, and then he gets to his knees. His fist, covered in my cum, strokes his hard cock until his back bows, and then he shoots his cum into his fist and shoves it inside me, filling me with his release as I sigh happily.

The ache fades away to nothing but pleasurable bliss.

He slowly fucks my cunt with his cum-covered hand before pulling it out and placing a gentle kiss on my pussy. "Good girl, now sleep."

I nod, beyond exhausted. I cannot even feel my limbs anymore, but I can breathe easier.

My whole body is covered in drying sweat and cum.

When I slip into an exhausted sleep, no pain follows me.

CHAPTER SEVENTY-SIX

We've spent two whole days locked up in our nest, and it has been the best few days of my life—not just because my girl was ravenous and couldn't get enough of me, but because she let us help her. She handed over control and turned to us. She was weak, and I loved taking care of her.

She stopped whining in pain a few hours ago, and the sweet scent of her heat that drove us all wild has disappeared. I can smell it on our skin and the nest, making me hard, but the worst—or the best—of it is over for now.

Even though I'm exhausted even after sleeping for hours, I get up and start to make us all a huge breakfast, knowing we need it. My wolf growls in approval, my stomach grumbling. I've noticed I need to eat a lot more often, and after fucking my girl raw for two days with barely any time for eating, I'm starving, but when I glance over my shoulder and see her snuggling into my spot in the nest, her legs bent and her pussy peeking out, a whole different type of hunger emerges.

I guess that answers if I will ever get enough of her—no.

My hand drifts to her bite mark on my chest, and a proud smile curves my lips. I'll wear it proudly for everyone to see. Quinn chose us, chose me, and I'm almost beaming with happiness, but I try to keep quiet as I cook.

When I place it all on the table, her head lifts slowly, and she sniffs the air.

Fucking hell, I love that woman. I didn't think I could love her more, didn't think it was possible, but I do. I love her with everything in me. Before, there was only hate, and now I have happiness, a home, family, and friends. I have a love so deep, I know it will echo through the ages.

Our story started with nothing but pain and hatred, but it ends with love. I'll make sure of that.

I will spend the rest of my life making our girl happy and showing her each day how lucky we are to have her and how much we love her.

Vale groans. "I smell food."

"Are those eggs?" Jai asks with a yawn.

"Why don't you get up and see?" I nudge them as I head over and kiss my girl's lips. "Morning, beautiful. Come eat, your wolf needs it."

"We don't get that kind of sweetness," Jai grumbles as he tries to climb from the nest but falls over a mound of pillows. Groaning, he leaps back to his feet, naked and half asleep as he stumbles and falls into one of the chairs. He grabs a plate of bacon and stuffs some in his mouth.

"Save some for Quinn," I snarl, smacking the back of his head as I return to pour us all coffee. Something about taking care of my girl fills me with joy. I like being needed and useful for more than my weapons.

"It's fucking good," Jai mumbles around a bite, and when Quinn heads over, sliding into the chair next to him, he grabs a bunch and stuffs it into her mouth.

Her eyes widen, her cheeks puffing adorably with food as she chews and swallows. Her skin is marked all over by our teeth and hands, her hair is messy and falling across her shoulders, and the sun hits her, making her glow. She has never looked so beautiful.

Vale climbs out and walks our way, slumping into a chair and accepting a mug. Lifting my girl, I sit her on my knee, ignoring my hard cock since it never goes down when she's around, and then I make her a plate. She hums happily, eating everything, and when she's done, I make her another one, stealing some bits to munch on. I'll eat properly when she's done.

I need to make sure my mate is full first.

"No one came to check on us," Vale mumbles around a forkful.

"They would have smelled my heat and known better." Quinn grabs another stack of pancakes. "We'll need to go see them today and confirm the mating though."

Pride fills me as I move her hair aside and see the three bite marks on her neck. They are healed but scarred, and my fingers trace over them. She shudders with a gasp, wiggling on my lap.

"Are they sensitive?" I ask as I stroke them.

She nods, moaning as I continue to touch them. "Feels like you're petting my clit," she admits.

Chuckling, I lean in and kiss them. "Noted," I mumble as she moans. When she leans back, she stuffs more food into her mouth, making me smirk as I watch her eat. Knowing my mate is nourished and taken care of almost has me spilling, and I can't resist grabbing her hips. I lift her then slide her down my hard cock.

She groans, reaching to anchor herself on the table.

"Really? At breakfast?" Vale mutters. "Didn't you have her enough?"

"Never." I smirk, kissing over the bite marks to her ear. "Ignore me, baby, and go back to eating. I just need to be inside you."

Moaning, she nods and continues to eat as I lean back, happy to be inside her, watching her eat my food and moan around it. Vale just rolls his eyes, but I see his envy that he didn't think of it first, and I can't help but smile at him as she wiggles on my cock as she eats.

Jai is oblivious, stuffing his face with as much food as he can.

She leans back as she eats, sighing happily, the sounds making my cock jerk inside her.

I bite her ear. "Good girl, such a good girl. Just eat for me, baby. I need to fill you with my cum at the same time, so just keep eating, beautiful. That's it, my good girl." I groan, licking her bite marks as she eats for me.

I let her wiggle on my cock until I can't hold back my pleasure. I'm panting with it, my chest rising rapidly as I grip her hips and drive deeper into her as I spill. She moans, clenching on my cock as she comes for me.

"Good girl," I praise, kissing her bite mark. "You did so good. Keep eating now, fuel your body while I take care of the mess."

I grab a tea towel and clean up her cunt.

Once she's finished, I pick at the rest of the food until I'm full, then I lift her off my softening cock, reluctant to leave the heat of her body. I push my fingers through the mess on her thighs, shoving some back inside her before massaging the rest into her skin. "Don't shower. I want you to smell like me as we head back out there." I don't know where the thought comes from, but I can't escape it. The thought of Quinn in the middle of the pack, smelling like me?

Fuck, it's enough to make me hard again, and possessiveness roars through me.

She pouts. "Luc."

Vale grabs her hair, tilting her head back and kissing her until she moans. "He's right. Go out there smelling of us or we'll probably go a little crazy. My wolf still isn't one hundred percent calm, even with our bites on you."

"Fucking mates." She huffs as she pulls away and points at us. "This shit won't cut it all the time though, mark my words."

"What did I do?" Jai says around a mouthful of pancake.

"Nothing, you are perfect," she snaps and whirls, heading to her closet.

"Why did that feel like an insult?" he mutters and glances between us. "Also, what did I miss?"

JAI

After Quinn dresses in some tight denim shorts and a white crop top, we all stand at the door. She arches a brow at us as we glance at her outfit.

"Nope," Vale says. "Sorry, my wolf says nope."

"Well, your wolf can come out and I'll beat his ass. No man will tell me what I'm wearing," she warns, the look in her eyes telling us not to push this. My wolf is also feeling possessive. I blame the mating and then the heat, but I am not pissing off my mate.

"It's okay. We can fight." I nod as I lean in. "You wear what you want."

Gripping my chin, she tugs me closer for a deep kiss. "Baby," she purrs. "I can fight too. If anyone fucks with me, I'll just rip out their throat."

My cock jerks at the thought. "That's even better. I do love seeing you covered in blood and slightly crazy."

"Fucking hell," Vale mutters as he pulls the door open. "Let's go before they have to send out a search party and we spent the rest of our lives locked in here fucking."

On her way past him, she grabs his cock. "So mad, yet it's clear what you want."

"Quinn, I always want you," he admits without an inch of shame, slapping her ass as she walks by. "That's the problem. I'd never get anything fucking done. I'd live buried in your wet cunt and die there a happy man."

"I think we should—" I start to back into the cabin, but Lucien grabs my neck and hauls me out.

"No, because if someone comes looking and sees us fucking, you will likely kill them. Come on, we'll be social, and then before we know it, I'm sure she will have you on your back," he placates me.

"Fine," I mutter and catch up to her, taking her hand in mine as we walk. She smiles at me.

The birds chirp happily in the trees, the wind blowing our mixed scents to me, making my wolf purr in approval. It's a beautiful day. It's a beautiful land.

It's a beautiful fucking life.

All thanks to her.

I was living in the darkness until she came. I had my brothers, but I was so lost—to the madness, anger, and wilderness living inside me. She freed me, but more than that, she gave me a reason to live again.

Her.

Without her, there is no me. Where she goes, I will follow. To everyone else, she is their alpha, but to me, she is my everything. She is the reason my lungs draw in oxygen, the reason my heart pumps my blood around my body, and the reason I speak.

She is my entire reason for living.

Some might call it obsession, but I don't care. All I care about is that when she looks at me, I feel whole.

***

VALE

The knowing looks we get as we run into the wolves milling about is enough to have my cheeks heating, but I stand taller, proudly showing off my claimed bite mark. It is an honour to be mated to Quinn, and there are a few envious looks as they catch sight of it.

Marie spots us and hurries over. White is at her side, which is becoming normal. I think they have bonded over heartbreak, and it's sweet. "There you are." She grins. "I wondered how long it would last."

"Hi, Mum." She kisses her cheek, and Marie tilts her head, a happy grin covering her lips.

"Finally," her mum murmurs. "You have finally found your happiness, my girl. This calls for a celebration."

"No," Quinn starts.

"It is not every day our alpha mates," Marie snaps.

"Mother, I am only acting alpha." Quinn sighs.

Marie waves it away, a knowing look in her eyes—one we all have. No matter what Quinn thinks, she is alpha, and I have no doubt her pack will appoint her as such before long. It's where she belongs, where she has always belonged. Jang knew it, the goddess knew it, and so do we.

She was always destined to lead and protect others. It's where she thrives.

"Either way, I will make the announcement. Have you eaten?" She looks us over critically.

"Yes, ma'am." I nod. "My brother cooked."

"Good. You better take care of my girl," she warns us. "Now, go show your faces. The pack will be waiting anxiously."

Her and White bend their heads together as she waves us on. Taking Quinn's other hand, I lead her away as she groans. "My mother . . ." She shakes her head.

"Loves you," I tell her. "She loves you so much she stayed for you. Let her be happy while she can."

"You're right." She shoots me a frown. "I don't like it when you're right."

"Sorry, baby. I'll make sure to be wrong from now on." I grin.

"Stop fucking grinning," she mutters. There's my Quinn.

"Sorry, Quinn, no can do, not with you at my side." I wink.

"Fucking cheese ball. I liked you better as an asshole."

Leaning in, I lick my bite mark as she gasps. "Then I'll be an asshole for you later. I'll order this sweet ass to crawl for me until I fill it while you beg."

"I don't beg, ever," she snarls, her nostrils flaring.

"Sure, baby, we'll see," I murmur.

We get stopped by a few wolves, and I watch my girl as she

handles each issue they have. They flock to her, looking for guidance. She shines so brightly with life and strength, how could they not?

When we reach the pack house, she gasps, her hands covering her lips.

They are rebuilding it, and during the few days we have been gone, they have mapped out the structure and started. They have kept it nearly identical to the original pack house at our and Marie's urgings.

"I know Jang had his office in there. We all thought you might like to rebuild it and make it yours to feel close to him." She turns to me, her eyes watery, and I carry on. "We can have a room in there, though I'm betting we'll go home often, since there's more room to make noise." I lick my bottom lip at the reminder of how loud we get, and her eyes flare before turning back to the house.

"It won't be the same," she offers sadly.

"No, nothing will be," I agree, wrapping my arms around her from behind and resting my chin on her head. "But it will represent our past and future together. It will be a place of memories and healing—a new symbol of hope. I think we could all do with that."

"True," she whispers. "What if I can't live up to him?"

Turning her, I cup her cheeks and stare into her beautifully flecked eyes, memorising the amber there. "You are an incredible woman, Quinn, but moreover, you will be an incredible leader. I know because I have seen terrible ones, but you are not one of them. You are willing to sacrifice yourself for your people and do what it takes to keep them safe. They know that. That's why they look to you for guidance. You'll make mistakes, but we will be right here at your side to help you work through them. I wish I could bring your father back so he could help you through this, but I can't. We will, however, work to help you in the way he would. He would be so proud of you, Quinn."

"You think?" She blinks, and I catch the tear falling from her eye and kiss it away.

"I know," I reply and turn her to face the house again. "We will rebuild. This land will still be scarred from its passing, but it will be stronger for it, just like you, and when you are ready, the office will be waiting for you to carry on his legacy, the one he gladly left you, and when the time comes, you'll see him again, and you can tell him all about it."

She leans back into me, and we stand here for a while, watching as they build what will become her family's legacy—until a whistle cuts through the air.

CHAPTER SEVENTY-SEVEN

Quinn

I turn at the whistle, frowning as I escape Vale's arms. I spot Dom and Fiona—a female wolf who wants to become a beta one day—escorting a woman towards us.

From the smell that hits me, I know two things instantly.

One, she is a human.

Two, she is a hunter.

If her scent didn't give her away, the patch on her ankle-length leather coat would, but I see no weapons on her, and I know Dom would have searched her. She stands tall between them, easily six feet, her bobbed ginger hair swaying in the breeze. Her green eyes blaze vividly, darkened by mascara and impressive winged liner. She's beautiful, and the scar that dissects her lips and chin doesn't take away from that. If anything, it adds to her allure.

She walks with her hands casually held behind her head, not looking the least bit bothered. I don't even scent an ounce of fear on her as Dom pushes her to her knees before me.

I'm betting this is a message in response to the one I left them, and I eye her worriedly. She's a threat. I would be foolish not to think so. It's in the hard glint in her eyes. She's a killer, and the fact that she walked into a wolf pack without obvious weapons means she's either crazy or confident.

Or both.

"Who are you?" I ask.

"My friends call me Tate, but my enemies call me Angel."

"Shit." Vale groans.

I glance at him with a frown.

"I know that nickname." He leans in, lowering his voice. "She's a sector leader from up north. Last time I heard, she was rising through the ranks quickly. I think she might have even been with Black. She's brutal, but I also heard she's fair. Rumour is, Black didn't like her because she wouldn't listen to him and even let some monsters go. That's how she got the scar."

"Her own people?" I ask with a frown.

"My own people." She smiles. "I didn't agree with them killing a young vampyr. They didn't like that and tried to kill me."

"What happened to them?" I ask.

"I killed them," she answers without shame. "I don't hurt innocents, which is why I'm here."

"My message," I murmur.

"Message?" Vale frowns.

She cuts him a look and nods. "I've heard of all of you. It's nice to meet you, although I have to say I'm surprised, but in a good way." She looks back to me. "And you are Quinn, Alpha of the Red Mountain Pack."

"How do you know?" I cross my arms.

"I know a lot. Besides your message, I have friends in your world. I might be a hunter, but I'm a fair one, and they know that, so they come to me for help. There's a wolf not too far from here with a mate called Simon. We get together for game night sometimes, and he told me about you. He's the reason I'm here along with that message. He said he knew you and your father and that you are a force to be reckoned with. I think we could both use the other's help."

"How did you even find us?" I frown, my hands on my hips as I swallow that information.

The woman smirks at me, tugging at the scar on her lip. "Hunter, remember?"

"You have no weapons," I point out.

"I'm not here to hurt anyone."

"So you walk into a wolf pack unarmed?" I press.

"I figured you would either kill me or listen to me, so weapons wouldn't matter much either way. Besides, I still have my hands." She smirks.

A laugh bursts out of me. "Fine, why are you here, Angel?"

"Tate. I have a feeling we are going to be good friends. Can I get to my feet? I fucked up one of my knees last month chasing a dragon. It still hasn't healed right." I nod, and she stands, holding her hands out at her sides. "I saw your message. I like your handiwork, by the way. I went and checked it out. My new team is there now, cleaning up the mess and burning the bodies." I just stare. "Hard, I like that. Anyway, you're right. The hunters are an ancient group, and we were not always bad. My father was a good man, a good hunter, and he showed me his ways, helping not just humans but your kind too. I'd like to get back to that again, and I think you can help me. So, Quinn, let's work together. I'll clean up the hunters, and then we can stop evil in this world—both human and monsters alike—together. Sound good?" She holds out her hand, hope in her eyes.

For a moment, I watch her, and she lets me. I taste nothing but truth in her words, and the goddess brushes across me with the wind, letting me decide, but it's clear she supports this. Maybe Tate was sent here for a reason.

I lay my hand in hers and shake. "I'd like that, a truce, but only between you and me. I don't trust other hunters."

"You'd be stupid to, and you are not stupid, Alpha." She grins, shaking my hand. I don't squeeze, but she grins. "Strong grip. Yes, I think we will be friends, Quinn. I'll head back now and help with the cleanup. I don't mind getting my hands dirty. I'll send a message once my house is clear, and then I think we should get together, along with some other friends I have, and send out an accord."

"What other friends?" I ask.

"Oh, some vampyrs I met along the way. They are a good bunch, just slightly crazy, especially their queen. I met her on a hunt. She was hunting them too—sorry, judging them. We worked together at the end." She smirks, looking around, her eyes closing at the breeze. "Change is coming, and I'm thinking it starts with us women. Queens this time, not kings." She bows. "I'll be seeing you again, Quinn." She glances at my men. "Always room for more hunters with us."

"Our place is here," Vale murmurs.

"I had a feeling that was the case. Oh well, once a hunter, always a hunter, that doesn't change. Best of luck."

She turns and walks towards the trees, calm and whistling. "Escort her off our territory," I murmur, "but let her go." I smile. "I have a feeling Tate is about to become our best asset in this world."

Dom nods, and he and Fiona hurry after her as I turn to my men.

"I guess you're not the only hunters changing sides."

"I guess not." They smile as we turn to watch her go.

She is right. The world is changing.

I can feel it, and it starts with us.

"Con, what is it?" I frown, dropping my fork into my meal. The guys are helping rebuild, and I had been doing the rounds, healing and speaking to the pack and dealing with day-to-day issues. Word has spread not only about my mating, but the hunter as well, and everyone has questions, but they seemed happy, and every person congratulated me all while calling me Alpha.

I know I shouldn't get used to that title, but I am, and now Con stands here, which is strange enough as it is. He's started to come into the pack more, but he still prefers his solitude, and the fact that he has a shifty look in his eyes makes me narrow mine.

"Did you threaten to kill someone again?" I demand.

"No, I don't just come to you because I nearly killed someone." I raise my eyebrows, and he smirks. "Okay, not every time."

"Con," I warn.

"I need you to come with me."

Standing, I groan as I stretch. "I knew it. It's a dead body," I mutter as I follow him out. "I better be able to heal them—" I stop short.

I thought the gym was empty, and I figured everyone was busy. I released the new restrictions this morning. People are moving back home and returning to work, so I just assumed that's what was happening. Apparently, I was wrong because the entire pack is gathered in the clearing outside of the gym, and Marie, Dom, White, and my other betas are waiting for me. My mates grin at their sides.

"What's going on?" I ask as Con pushes me forward.

"We are gathered to vote in our alpha," Marie explains.

My heart aches as I skip a step, but I nod, stopping before the pack. I knew it would come sooner or later, and I clear my throat. "Of course. Thank you, everyone, for gathering. I appreciate you all listening to me and following me when we had no other leader. I will support whoever you vote in during this transition—"

"Pack"—I stop at the interruption, turning to Dom as he grins— "as beta, I am taking the right to do the honour for my friend. We are voting. Hands up if you want Quinn as alpha."

I blink, my head swinging around as almost every hand shoots up, and I gape.

"It was never to swear someone else in, but for you to get the title you deserve," White murmurs as he steps forward. "Dom is right. Although it's a bit more . . . informal than usual, I'm beginning to understand times change and so do we. Jang, may he rest in peace, put Quinn forward as his successor, and I know some of you worried she would not be able to handle the pressure as a youngster and as a woman." He lets that sink in. "I think she has proven every single one of you wrong. Not only did she lead us to safety and keep us alive, but she also healed this pack and kept us together. Quinn is an alpha through and through and deserving of the title. Jang trusted his daughter, and so did I. I selected her too." He looks back at me. "And I will stand at her side again. She is my alpha." He kneels.

"And mine," Dom states, kneeling.

Con lowers. "Mine."

The rest of the betas follow, nodding and bowing. "Our alpha."

I look back at the pack, barely able to speak as they all drop to their knees. "Our alpha, our alpha." The chant rings out across the land, and tears fill my eyes.

Marie steps forward, and everyone quiets down as she turns to me. In her hands is my father's chain—the one he never took off. It must have fallen when he did. It's a long, golden chain, and there's a howling wolf at the base—an alpha symbol. She heads my way. "You have always been an alpha, Quinn, but know this. The pack will follow you anywhere you go. We are yours, and you are ours. Our alpha. You fought for us, and now we'll fight for you. This might not be the ceremony we all wanted, but times change. Here, in the heart of our land, will you accept and lead?"

"I will," I whisper as I kneel, staring into my mother's proud eyes. I still worry I will lead them wrong, but with all their trust in me, I know I have to try for them, Jang, and myself. "I will live, I will die, and I will serve this pack until the goddess calls me home." The words come naturally.

She smiles, and I bow as she drapes the necklace over my head. It falls comfortingly between my breasts, and I cover it as I lift my head. "Then Quinn, as our mother and the matron of this pack, I deem you our new alpha. Stand and face your people."

She offers me her hand, and I stand, turning to face my pack as their heads tip back with joyous howls. The ground vibrates with their stamping hands and feet as they call to me, showing me their happiness. Marie smiles at me, tears in her eyes that reflect my own.

"I am so proud of you, my daughter, and your father would be as well, Quinn." She smiles brighter. "I mean Alpha."

I look back at the crowd, soaking it all in before I turn to my men. They howl and clap the loudest, and when I catch their eyes, they wink. It gives me an idea, and I glance at White.

"I want my men to be betas."

"It is your call, Alpha." He nods. "I would gladly share this title with them. They are worthy warriors."

I turn back and grin at them. "Then you are my betas, and I am your alpha."

"Our mate." Vale grins.

"Our love." Lucien nods.

"Our everything," Jai adds.

Standing before my pack, I feel my wounds finally begin to heal.

CHAPTER SEVENTY-EIGHT

Quinn

The pack is celebrating tonight—not just my mating, but my appointment as alpha. I escaped and found myself here, before the stone where we place our dead. I feel my men behind me, knowing they are never far behind, but they give me this moment of peace as the moon illuminates the area.

Kneeling on the hill, I glance down at the golden chain and hope I can make them proud. I will certainly spend my life trying. "I'll make you proud, Dad," I whisper. "I'll try my best every day to be the alpha you were, to be half as strong and sure . . . ," I trail off, licking my lips. "I wish I could see you one last time, just for a moment. It's selfish, but I want you to see me like this."

"I do, my Quinny."

The familiar rumble has my head jerking up, my eyes widening. Standing before me is my father, Jang. He's pale and slightly blue at the edges, as if he isn't quite here. Moon magic, I realise. He grins at me. "I never doubted you would be an incredible alpha. Look at you, my daughter. You are so strong, and I am so very proud of you."

"Daddy," I whisper, wanting to reach for him but knowing my

hands will go through him, so I curl them into fists. "I miss you so much."

"I know, my Quinn." He grins sadly. "But I'm right here, and I'll always be right here, even if you can't see me. I will be by your side until you join us again."

"Us?" I frown.

"Us." He grins.

Suddenly, the air near him parts, and I fall back. At his side, glowing just as he does, are my mother, father, and sister. They all smile at me.

"Look at you, Quinny." My mum grins widely, a familiar look that I haven't seen in so long. "You are so beautiful and strong."

"Mum." I cover my trembling lips, tears blinding me, and I blink them away, not wanting to miss a moment of this.

This is a gift from the goddess. Every alpha gets one, but Jang never told me what his was. It doesn't matter, though, because mine is the best gift I ever could have gotten.

"My Quinn," my father rumbles, smiling at Jang. "Our daughter, we are so very proud of you, never forget that. Lead with your heart, and you will never be wrong." He glances behind me. "Love so deeply it terrifies you. There is nothing more powerful in this world than love." He tugs my sister and mum closer. "Even when it is gone, it will remain."

"I miss you all so much." I sob.

"I know." My mum smiles. "We have always been right here, my daughter, and always will be, watching you. We are proud and so very happy to see you growing up."

"It's not fair. You should be here."

"No, my daughter," Jang murmurs. "This is how it should be. Everything happens for a reason, do not forget that. We are gone, but we are not lost. We live on in you and through your actions and stories, and when the end comes, we will be together."

"Please, please stay," I beg as they start to disappear.

"We will be in your heart until the end," my father calls. "Do not forget that."

"We will see you again, Quinny," my sister calls and waves happily as they fade, leaving Jang.

"Take care of her and my mate for me," he calls, and there's a rumble behind me.

"We will," my mates vow.

Jang looks at me. "My gift, all those years ago, was you." My eyes widen. "The goddess came on my appointment night and told me I would have a daughter, one destined for great things. She was so very right. It's your pack now, Quinn, and I cannot wait to see it blossom under your reign, my alpha." He kneels. "I love you, Quinny."

"I love you, Jang." I sob, placing my hand over my heart.

"It is goodbye, Quinn, but it isn't forever." He holds up his hand, and I echo the gesture. I swear I can feel him, and he smiles. "Look after your mum for me, if she will let you. I will see you once more in the moon." He disappears.

I sob, falling forward, and I feel the metal at my neck heat. I know it's them. They are here with me, comforting me, and then very real arms wrap around me, holding me as I cry.

"Shh, my love," Vale murmurs, kissing me. "Listen to the world. Feel it. They are here. They are in the blowing wind, in the creaking trees, in the animals around us. They are here, and they are with you."

"He's right." Lucien kisses my tears away. "And so are we. You will never be alone."

"Not ever again," Jai promises, holding me tighter. "It's us, Quinn, until the end."

"Who would have thought?" I choke out, wiping at my tears. "Hunters and a wolf."

That makes them grin, and the moon wraps around us lovingly.

I glance up at it. "Thank you."

There is no answer, but that is okay. I take my mates' hands, and

I stand there under its rays, knowing it's all going to be okay. I will grieve, and there will be days when I'll miss my family more than anything, but I have a family right here, and when the time comes, we will be together again.

They will wait for me until the end.

After all, we are all children of the moon.

EPILOGUE

"Now, little witch," the dark voice calls, the husky timbre making me shake.

For a god, he truly is a patient man, being held in my trap for so long. When I set it and cast a summoning spell, I didn't expect this, but I had nowhere else to turn. The magic in me called something dark, and I need help or it will be the downfall of my coven, my court, and this world as we know it.

"From the beginning once more," he urges, sitting cross-legged.

He disappeared a few days ago, and I panicked, but he returned, which begs the question—if he can leave, then why hasn't he?

"I told you," I say as I pace, "I don't know how I called it, and neither does the demon that feeds on our magic. When you left, I was trying to rid my coven of it. I thought if I could show them, I could banish the demon and we would be okay, but I called something much worse." I peer at him. "I called something wrong, something dark . . . something dead. Please, Phrixius, please help me."

I feel the demon I speak of pushing from the shadows as if the world takes a pause when such evil emerges. A cold chill goes over me as the demon's heat meets my back. The god stands then, anger furrowing his brow as he meets the demon's eyes—the eyes of the demon I've been haunted by my entire life, the demon I tried to rid myself of before I got all of us in this mess.

"He cannot, but I can. I told you, little witch, just make one pesky little deal and I'm yours," he purrs in my ear. His voice is smooth and relaxing, making me sway into him, wanting to give into the bargain he has been peddling since I turned eighteen.

One I can never agree to, but for a moment, I falter.

"No," Phrixius snaps, his fury breaking me from the spell the demon weaves around me, and with a furious look at the chuckling demon, Phrixius steps from the spell circle, righting his suit, and he doesn't stop until he stands before me.

Their powers surge through me, leaving me breathless.

"I will help you. You called and trapped me, after all," he counters.

"What could a god know of such dark, evil things?" the demon retorts.

"More than a lowly ground crawler," the god replies, leaving me swaying between them, my head aching from their power.

Something dark, evil, cold, and dead grasps my ankle and yanks me down, and with a scream, I reach for the demon and the god, but it's too late.

The thing I called forth rips me from my cave and into its grasp.

ABOUT K.A. KNIGHT

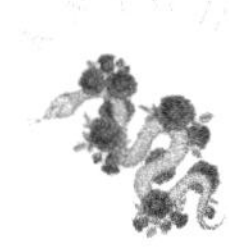

K.A Knight is an USA Today bestselling indie author trying to get all of the stories and characters out of her head, writing the monsters that you love to hate. She loves reading and devours every book she can get her hands on, and she also has a worrying caffeine addiction.

She leads her double life in a sleepy English town, where she spends her days writing like a crazy person.

Read more at K.A Knight's website or join her Facebook Reader Group.
Sign up for exclusive content and my newsletter here
http://eepurl.com/drLLoj

ALSO BY K.A. KNIGHT

THEIR CHAMPION SERIES *Dystopian RH*

The Wasteland

The Summit

The Cities

The Nations

Their Champion Coloring Book

Their Champion - the omnibus

The Forgotten

The Lost

The Damned

Their Champion Companion - the omnibus

DAWNBREAKER SERIES *SCI FI RH*

Voyage to Ayama

Dreaming of Ayama

THE LOST COVEN SERIES *PNR RH*

Aurora's Coven

Aurora's Betrayal

HER MONSTERS SERIES *PNR RH*

Rage

Hate

Book 3 *coming soon..*

THE FALLEN GODS SERIES *PNR*

Pretty Painful

Pretty Bloody

Pretty Stormy

Pretty Wild

Pretty Hot

Pretty Faces

Pretty Spelled

Fallen Gods - the omnibus 1

Fallen Gods - the omnibus 2

COURTS AND KINGS *PNR RH*

Court of Nightmares

Court of Death

Court of Beasts

Court of Heathens (Coming soon!)

FORBIDDEN READS (STANDALONES)

Daddy's Angel *CONTEMPORARY*

Stepbrothers' Darling *CONTEMPORARY RH*

LEGENDS AND LOVE *CONTEMPORARY*

Revolt

Rebel *coming soon..*

PRETTY LIARS *CONTEMPORARY RH*

Unstoppable

Unbreakable

FORGOTTEN CITY *PNR*

Monstrous Lies

Monstrous Truths

Monstrous Ends

DEN OF VIPERS UNIVERSE STANDALONES

Scarlett Limerence *CONTEMPORARY*

Nadia's Salvation *CONTEMPORARY*

Alena's Revenge *CONTEMPORARY*

Den of Vipers *CONTEMPORARY RH*

Gangsters and Guns (Co-Write with Loxley Savage) *CONTEMPORARY RH*

STANDALONES

The Standby *CONTEMPORARY*

Diver's Heart *CONTEMPORARY RH*

Crown of Stars *SCI FI RH*

AUDIOBOOKS

The Wasteland

The Summit

Rage

Hate

Den of Vipers *(From Podium Audio)*

Gangsters and Guns *(From Podium Audio)*

Daddy's Angel *(From Podium Audio)*

Stepbrothers' Darling *(From Podium Audio)*

Blade of Iris *(From Podium Audio)*

Deadly Affair *(From Podium Audio)*

Deadly Match *(From Podium Audio)*

Deadly Encounter *(From Podium Audio)*

Stolen Trophy *(From Podium Audio)*

Crown of Stars *(From Podium Audio)*

Monstrous Lies *(From Podium Audio)*

Monstrous Truth *(From Podium Audio)*

Monstrous Ends *(From Podium Audio)*

Court of Nightmares *(From Podium Audio)*

Unstoppable *(From Podium Audio)*

Unbreakable *(From Podium Audio)*

Fractured Shadows *(From Podium Audio)*

SHARED WORLD PROJECTS

Blade of Iris - Mafia Wars *CONTEMPORARY RH*

CO-AUTHOR PROJECTS - *Erin O'Kane*

HER FREAKS SERIES *PNR Dystopian RH*

Circus Save Me

Taming The Ringmaster

Walking the Tightrope

Her Freaks Series - the omnibus

STANDALONES

The Hero Complex *PNR RH*

Dark Temptations *Collection of Short Stories, ft. One Night Only & Circus Saves Christmas*

THE WILD BOYS SERIES *CONTEMPORARY RH*

The Wild Interview

The Wild Tour

The Wild Finale

The Wild Boys - the omnibus

CO-AUTHOR PROJECTS - *Ivy Fox*

Deadly Love Series *CONTEMPORARY*

Deadly Affair

Deadly Match

Deadly Encounter

CO-AUTHOR PROJECTS - *Kendra Moreno*

STANDALONES

Stolen Trophy *CONTEMPORARY RH*

Fractured Shadows *PNR RH*

Burn Me *PNR*

CO-AUTHOR PROJECTS - *Loxley Savage*

THE FORSAKEN SERIES *SCI FI RH*

Capturing Carmen

Stealing Shiloh

Harboring Harlow

STANDALONES

Gangsters and Guns *CONTEMPORARY*, IN DEN OF VIPERS' UNIVERSE

OTHER CO-WRITES

Shipwreck Souls *(with Kendra Moreno & Poppy Woods)*

The Horror Emporium *(with Kendra Moreno & Poppy Woods)*

FIND AN ERROR?

Please email this information to thenuttyformatter1@gmail.com:

- *the author name*
- *title of the book*
- *screenshot of the error*
- *suggested correction*

www.ingramcontent.com/pod-product-compliance
Lightning Source LLC
Chambersburg PA
CBHW051125300726
48981CB00023B/552/J

9 781399 977258